THE PRINCE

TIFFANY REISZ

First published in Great Britain 2012
Mills & Boon Spice, an imprint of Harlequin (UK) Limited,
Eton House, 18-24 Paradise Road, Richmond, Surrey TW9 1SR

© Tiffany Reisz 2012

ISBN: 978 0 263 90582 3

84-1212

Harlequin (UK) policy is to use papers that are natural, renewable and recyclable products and made from wood grown in sustainable forests. The logging and manufacturing processes conform to the legal environmental regulations of the country of origin.

Printed and bound
by CPI Group (UK) Ltd, Croydon, CR0 4YY

Tiffany Reisz lives in Lexington, Kentucky. She graduated with a BA in English from Centre College and is making her parents and her professors proud by writing erotica under her real name. She has five piercings, one tattoo and has been arrested twice. When not under arrest, Tiffany enjoys Latin dance, Latin men and Latin verbs. She dropped out of a conservative seminary in order to pursue her dream of becoming a smut peddler. If she couldn't write, she would die.

Also by Tiffany Reisz:

SEVEN-DAY LOAN
(part of *12 Shades of Surrender: Bound*)

THE SIREN
(The Original Sinners 1)

THE ANGEL
(The Original Sinners 2)

Watch out for the fourth book in
The Original Sinners series

THE MISTRESS

Coming Soon

To Miranda Baker, who always makes me ask,
'What would Nora do?' when I really want to ask,
'What would Miranda Baker do?'

Four things greater than all things are
women
and horses
and power and war.

—Rudyard Kipling

PROLOGUE

File #1312—From the archives
SUTHERLIN, NORA
Née Eleanor Louise Schreiber

Born on March 15, 1977 (beware the Ides of March)

Father: William Gregory Schreiber, deceased (you're welcome, ma cherie), formerly incarcerated in Attica on multiple counts of grand theft auto, and possession of stolen property. Had connections with organized crime—see file #1382.

Mother: Margaret Delores Schreiber, née Kohl, age fifty-six, currently residing near Guildford, New York, at the Sisters of Saint Monica convent (cloistered), known now as Sister Mary John.

Daughter and mother—estranged but currently in détente.

Age 15, Eleanor met Father Marcus Lennox Stearns (Søren, born to Gisela Magnussen). After her arrest for stealing five luxury vehicles in one night to aid her father in paying off a debt, Sutherlin was sentenced to probation and twelve hundred hours of community service supervised by Father Stearns. It was during these years that Sutherlin learned to submit. At age eigh-

teen she became his collared submissive. At age twenty-eight she left him after terminating a pregnancy (father—me). For a year she lived with her mother at the convent upstate, before returning to the city and becoming a dominatrix in the employ of the devastatingly handsome Kingsley Edge, Edge Enterprises. At the time of this filing she has had five books published, four of which have been bestsellers. (See attached for financials. Her editor is Zachary Easton, publisher Royal House. See file #2112, drawer seven for Easton's file.) At age thirty-three, after spending five years apart, she returned to her owner and has been with him ever since.

Sexual preferences—Sutherlin is bisexual although she generally shows a preference for men. A true switch, she tends to top with anyone but her owner (because, as we all know, he would break her if she tried).

Weaknesses—Blondes—men and women, younger men, tiramisu.

Ultimate weakness—Unknown. Possibly John Wesley Railey, born September 19, Versailles, Kentucky. Heir to the Railey Fortune (estimated at $930 million as of 2010) and The Rails Farm (Thoroughbreds, saddlebreds), Railey, known to friends and family as Wes or Wesley, lived with Sutherlin from January 2008 until April 2009. As the sole heir to the largest horse farm in the world, Wesley is known colloquially as the Prince of Kentucky. Six feet tall, a type 1 diabetic, boyishly handsome, not sexually active at the time of his filing (Railey file #561, drawer 4). Sutherlin has displayed intense emotion, affection and loyalty (and possibly even love) where Railey is concerned.

Strengths—Extremely intelligent, IQ 167, physically strong, cunning, highly manipulative when necessary, extremely beautiful (see attached photographs), Sutherlin is far more dangerous than she appears.

The final line in the file the thief read over and over again.

In all things involving Nora Sutherlin, proceed with caution.

Three months…for three long and sleepless months, the thief toiled over the file, which had been encrypted in layer upon layer of cipher. The thief knew French and Haitian Creole, but merely knowing the languages wouldn't crack the code. One had to know Kingsley Edge, and luckily, the thief did—intimately.

The file thief read through all four pages of notes on Nora Sutherlin a thousand times until the words were as familiar as the thief's own name. And as the thief read the pages until they grew tattered from wear, an idea began to form and grow until it gave birth to a plan.

The thief closed the file for the final time, and then and there decided the best course of action.

The thief would proceed…cautiously.

NORTH
The Past

They'd sent him here to save his life.

At least that was the line his grandparents laid on him to explain why they'd decided to take him out of public school and send him instead to an all-boys Jesuit boarding school nestled in some of the most godforsaken terrain on the Maine-Canadian border.

They should have let him die.

Hoisting his duffel bag onto his shoulder, he picked up his battered brown leather suitcase and headed toward what appeared to be the main building on the isolated campus. Everywhere he looked he saw churches, or at least buildings with pretensions of being one. A cross adorned every roof. Gothic iron bars grated every window. He'd been wrenched from civilization and dropped without apology in the middle of a medieval monk's wet dream.

He entered the building through a set of iron-and-wood doors, the ancient hinges of which screamed as if being tortured. He could sympathize. He rather felt like screaming himself. A fireplace piled high with logs cast light and warmth into the dismal gray foyer. Huddling close to it, he wrapped his arms about himself, wincing as he did so. His left wrist still ached from the beating he'd taken three weeks ago, the beating that had convinced his grandparents that he'd be safe only at an all-boys school.

"So this is our Frenchman?" The jovial voice came from behind him. He turned and saw a squat man all in black beaming from ear to ear. Not all black, he noted. Not quite. The man wore a white collar around his neck. The priest held out his hand to him, but he paused before shaking it. Celibacy seemed like a disease to him—one that might be catching. "Welcome to Saint Ignatius. Come inside my office. This way."

He gave the priest a blank look, but followed nonetheless.

Inside the office, he took the chair closest to the fireplace, while the priest sat behind a wide oak desk.

"I'm Father Henry, by the way," the priest began. "Monsignor here. I hear you've had some trouble at your old school. Something about a fight…some boys taking exception to your behavior with their girlfriends?"

Saying nothing, he merely blinked and shrugged.

"Good Lord. They told me you could speak some English." Father Henry sighed. "I suppose by 'some' they meant 'none.' *Anglais?*"

He shook his head. *"Je ne parle pas l'anglais."*

Father Henry sighed again.

"French. Of course. You would have to be French, wouldn't you? Not Italian. Not German. I could even handle a little ancient Greek. And poor Father Pierre dead for six months. Ah, *c'est la vie*," he said, and then laughed at his own joke. "Nothing for it. We'll make do." Father Henry rested both his chins on his hand and stared into the fireplace, clearly deep in deliberation.

He joined the priest in his staring. The heat from the fireplace seeped through his clothes, through his chilled skin and into the core of him. He wanted to sleep for days, for years even. Maybe when he woke up he would be a grown man and no one could send him away again. The day would come when he would take orders from no one, and that would be the best day of his life.

A soft knock on the door jarred him from his musings.

A boy about twelve years old, with dark red hair, entered, wearing the school uniform of black trousers, black vest, black jacket and tie, with a crisp white shirt underneath.

All his life he had taken great pride in his clothes, every detail of them, down to the shoes he wore. Now he, too, would be forced into the same dull attire as every other boy in this miserable place. He'd read a little Dante his last year at his lycée in Paris. If he remembered correctly, the centermost circle of hell was all ice. He glanced out the window in Father Henry's office. New snow had started to fall on the ice-packed ground. Perhaps his grandfather had been right about him. Perhaps he was a sinner. That would explain why, still alive and only sixteen years old, he'd been sent to hell on earth.

"Matthew, thank you. Come in, please." Father Henry motioned the boy into the office. The boy, Matthew, cast curious glances at him while standing at near attention in front of the priest's desk. "How much French did you have with Father Pierre before he passed?"

Matthew shifted his weight nervously from foot to foot. *"Un année?"*

Father Henry smiled kindly. "It's not a quiz, Matthew. Just a question. You can speak English."

The boy sighed audibly with relief.

"One year, Father. And I wasn't very good at it."

"Matthew, this is Kingsley..." Father Henry paused and glanced down at a file in front of him "...Boissonneault?"

Kingsley repeated his last name, trying not to grimace at how horribly Father Henry had butchered it. Stupid Americans.

"Yes, Kingsley Boissonneault. He's our new student. From Portland."

It took all of Kingsley's self-control not to correct Father Henry and remind him that he'd been living in Portland for only six months. Paris. Not Portland. He was from Paris. But to say that would be to reveal he not only understood English, but that he spoke it perfectly; he had no intention of gracing this horrible hellhole with a single word of his English.

Matthew gave him an apprehensive smile. Kingsley didn't smile back.

"Well, Matthew, if your French is twice as good as mine, we're out of options." Father Henry lost his grin for the first time in their whole conversation. Suddenly he seemed tense, concerned, as nervous as young Matthew. "You'll just have to go to Mr. Stearns and ask him to come here."

At the mention of Mr. Stearns, Matthew's eyes widened so hugely they nearly eclipsed his face. Kingsley almost laughed at the sight. But when Father Henry didn't seem to find the boy's look of fear equally funny, Kingsley started to grow concerned himself.

"Do I have to?"

Father Henry exhaled heavily. "He's not going to bite you," the priest said, but didn't sound quite convinced of that.

"But…" Matthew began "…it's 4:27."

Father Henry winced.

"It is, isn't it? Well, we can't interrupt the music of the spheres, can we? Then I suppose you'll just have to make do. Perhaps we can persuade Mr. Stearns into talking to our new student later. Show Kingsley around. Do your best."

Matthew nodded and motioned for him to follow. In the

foyer they paused as the boy wrapped a scarf around his neck and shoved his hands into gloves. Then, glancing around, he curled up his nose in concentration.

"I don't know the French word for *foyer.*"

Kingsley repressed a smile. The French for "foyer" was foyer.

Outside in the snow, Matthew turned and faced the building they'd just left. "This is where all the Fathers have their offices. *Le pères...bureau?*"

"Bureaux, oui," Kingsley repeated, and Matthew beamed, clearly pleased to have elicited any kind of encouragement or understanding from him.

Kingsley followed the younger boy into the library, where Matthew desperately sought out the French word for the place, apparently not realizing that the rows upon rows of bookcases spoke for themselves.

"Library..." Matthew said. *"Trois..."* Clearly, he wanted to explain that the building stood three stories high. He didn't know the word for *stories* any more than he knew *library,* so instead he stacked his hands on top of each other. Kingsley nodded as if he understood, although it actually appeared as if Matthew was describing a particularly large sandwich.

A few students in armchairs studied Kingsley with unconcealed interest. His grandfather had said only forty or fifty students resided at Saint Ignatius. Some were the sons of wealthy Catholic families who wanted a traditional Jesuit education, while the rest were troubled young men the court ordered here to undergo reformation. In their school uniforms, with their similar shaggy haircuts, Kingsley couldn't tell the fortunate sons from the wards of the court.

Matthew led him from the library. The next building over was the church, and the boy paused on the threshold before reaching out for the door handle. Raising his fingers to his lips, he mimed the universal sign for silence. Then, as carefully as if it were made of glass, he opened the door and slipped inside. Kingsley's ears perked up immediately as he heard the sound of a piano being played with unmistakable virtuosity.

He watched as Matthew tiptoed into the church and crept up to the sanctuary door. Much less circumspectly, Kingsley followed him and peered inside.

At the piano sat a young man…lean, angular, with pale blond hair cut in a style far more conservative than Kingsley's own shoulder-length mane.

Kingsley watched as the blond pianist's hands danced across the keys, evoking the most magnificent sounds he'd ever heard.

"Ravel…" he whispered to himself. Ravel, the greatest of all French composers.

Matthew looked up with panic in his eyes and shushed him again. Kingsley shook his head in contempt. Such a little coward. No one should be cowardly in the presence of Ravel.

Ravel had been his father's favorite composer and had become Kingsley's, too. Even through the scratches on his father's vinyl records, he had heard the passion and the need that throbbed in every note. Part of Kingsley wanted to close his eyes and let the music wash over him.

But another part of him couldn't bring himself to look away from the young man at the piano who played the piece—the Piano Concerto in G Major. He recognized it instantly. In concert, the piece began with the sound of a whip crack.

But he'd never heard it played like this…so close to him Kingsley felt he could reach up and snatch notes out of the air, pop them in his mouth and swallow them whole. So beautiful…the music and the young man who played it. Kingsley listened to the piece, studied the pianist. He couldn't decide which moved him more.

The pianist was easily the most handsome young man

Kingsley had ever seen in all his sixteen years. Vain as he was, Kingsley couldn't deny he'd for once met his match there. But more than handsome, the pianist was also, in a way, as beautiful as the music he played. He wore the school uniform, but had abandoned the jacket, no doubt needing the freedom of unencumbered arm movement. And although he was dressed like all the other boys, he looked nothing like them. To Kingsley he appeared like a sculpture some magician had turned to life. His pale skin was smooth and flawless, his nose aquiline and elegant, his face perfectly composed even as he wrung glorious noise out of the black box in front of him.

If only...if only Kingsley's father could be with him now to hear this music. If only his sister, Marie-Laure, were here to dance to it. For a moment, Kingsley allowed himself to mourn his father and miss his sister. The music smoothed the rough edges of his grief, however, and Kingsley caught himself smiling.

He had to thank the young man, the beautiful blond pianist, for giving him this music and the chance to remember his father for once without pain. Kingsley started to step into the sanctuary, but Matthew grabbed his arm and shook his head in a warning to go no farther.

The music ceased. The blond pianist lowered his arms and stared at the keys as if in prayer before shutting the fallboard and standing up. For the first time Kingsley noted his height—he was six feet tall if he was an inch. Maybe even more.

Kingsley glanced at Matthew, who seemed to be paralyzed with fear. The blond young man pulled on his black suit jacket and strode down the center of the sanctuary toward them. Up close, he appeared not only more handsome than before, but strangely inscrutable. He seemed like a book, shut tight and locked in a glass box, and Kingsley would have done anything for the key. He met the young man's eyes and saw no kindness in those steely gray depths. No kindness, but no cruelty, either. He inhaled in nervousness as the pianist passed him, and smelled the unmistakable scent of winter.

Without a word to either him or Matthew, the young man left the church without looking back.

"Stearns," Matthew breathed, once the pianist had gone.

So that was the mysterious Mr. Stearns who inspired both fear and respect from the students and Father Henry. Fascinating... Kingsley had never been in the presence of someone that immediately intimidating. No teacher, no parent, no grandparent, no policeman, no priest had even made him feel what standing in the same room with the piano player, with Mr. Stearns, had made him feel.

Kingsley looked down and saw his hand had developed a subtle tremor. Matthew saw it, too.

"Don't feel bad." The boy nodded with the wisdom of a sage. "He does that to everybody."

NORTH
The Present

The fear had been his favorite part. The fear that followed him like the footsteps through the woods where he'd fled for sanctuary and found something better than safety. The footsteps…how his heart had raced as they grew louder, drew nearer. He'd been too afraid to run anymore, afraid that if he ran he would get away. He ran to be caught. That was the only reason.

Kingsley remembered his sudden intake of air as a viciously strong hand clamped down onto his neck…the bark of the tree trunk burning his back…the smell of the evergreens around him, so potent that even thirty years later he still grew aroused whenever he inhaled the scent of pine. And after, when he woke up on the forest floor, a new scent graced his skin— blood, his own…and winter.

Three decades later he could never uncouple sex from fear. The two were linked inextricably, eternally and unrepentantly in his heart. He'd learned the potency of fear that day, the power of it, even the pleasure, and now thirty years later, fear had become Kingsley's forte.

Unfortunately, at this moment his Juliette was not afraid. He could change that.

Kingsley watched her out of the corner of his eye while he sipped his wine. Standing next to Griffin and young Michael, she smiled in turns at each of them while they bent her exquisite ears with the tale of how Nora Sutherlin had brought them together. For one single solitary day without hearing about the amazing Nora Sutherlin, he would cash out half his fortune, lay it on a pyre in the middle of Fifth Avenue, set it afire and watch it turn to ashes. If only it were that easy to kill the monster he'd created.

No, he corrected himself. *The monster they had created.*

Juliette glanced his way and gave him a secret smile, a smile that needed no translation. But he would wait, bide his time, let her think he wasn't in the mood tonight. He'd let her anticipation build first before replacing it with fear. How beautifully Juliette wore fear, how it shimmered in her bistre eyes, how it shivered across her ebony skin, how it caught in her throat like the scream he'd hold inside her mouth with his hand....

Kingsley's groin tightened; his heart began to race. Setting his wineglass down, he strode from the bar through the back room and into the hallways of The 8th Circle. Right outside the door to the bar, his foot connected with something lying on the floor. Curious, he bent down. Shoes. A pair of shoes. He picked them up. White patent-leather stilettos...size six.

Shoes last seen on the feet of Nora Sutherlin.

Staring at the shoes, Kingsley pondered how and why they'd ended up in the hallway outside the bar. Nora could do almost anything in her high heels. He'd seen her top some of the most hardened masochists in them. She'd beaten them, whipped them, flogged them, kicked them.... She could stand on a man's neck in high heels, walk on his bruised back, balance on one leg while her other foot was being worshipped.

He knew of only one activity she couldn't do in her towering high heels—run.

He carried the shoes down to the bottommost floor, where he and a few of the other VIPs kept their own private dungeons. At the last door on the left, he paused, but didn't knock, before entering.

A man, blond and tall and deep in thought, stood by the bed, his arms crossed, his brow furrowed.

"Have you ever heard of knocking?" Søren uncrossed his arms and leaned his shoulder against the bedpost. Kingsley clenched his jaw.

"I've heard rumors of knocking. I never believed them." Kingsley stepped into the room. No one's dungeon at the Circle exemplified the concept of minimalism better than Søren's. It held nothing more than a four-poster wrought-iron bed tucked into an alcove, a Saint Andrew's cross front and center, and a single trunk filled with various implements of torture. Søren's sadistic side was the stuff of legend at The 8th Circle and throughout the Underground. He didn't need a thousand types of floggers and single-tails and dozens of canes and tawse and toys. Such a piece of work was Søren—he could break a submissive with a word, a look, with his penetrating insight, his calm, cold dominance that left even the strongest quaking at his feet. He cowed them with the beauty of his exterior first, and second, with the beast that was his heart.

"I brought you a gift."

Kingsley held out the shoes by the straps. Søren raised an eyebrow.

"Not really my size, are they?"

"Your pet's." Kingsley dropped them on the bed. "As you know. You must have walked past them as you left the bar."

"I left them there so she would find them when she came back for them."

Kingsley gave a small, mirthless laugh.

"Didn't I overhear you telling her that if she had any mercy in that dark heart of hers, she wouldn't run from you to her Wesley?"

Søren didn't answer. He merely stared at Kingsley with his eyes of steel. Kingsley resisted the urge to grin. *Schadenfreude*... such an unbecoming emotion. He kept it to himself for as long as he could. Then, turning on his heel, he swept out of the room, quoting an old poem as he left Søren in his dungeon, with only Nora's shoes on the bed for company.

"I saw pale kings and princes, too,
pale warriors, death-pale were they all;
they cried—'La Belle Dame sans Merci
Hath thee in thy thrall.'"

Kingsley returned to his own dungeon and paced as he waited. His bed sat in the very center of the room, unlike the priest's at the end of the hall. For Søren, pain was sex. He could possibly be what the church demanded him to be—a celibate priest—if it weren't for Nora, for his Eleanor, who needed the flesh as much as Kingsley needed the fear. He could only imagine the tantrum she would throw if her owner decided to cut her off sexually. But Søren would never do that. He inflicted pain for his release, and the sex that followed was mere afterglow. And who didn't enjoy the afterglow?

Kingsley paused midstep as he heard the floor creak in the hallway outside his chamber. Silently, he moved to stand by the door and waited. He'd spent two years in the French Foreign Legion after leaving school, and five years pretending to still be in the French Foreign Legion while he served his country in other quieter ways. He'd learned the lessons of a spy well. *See everything but never be seen. Hear everything but never be heard.* When Juliette slipped through his door, he knew she expected to find him in bed, waiting for her. When his hand shot out and captured her by the arm, she gasped in fear.

Parfait.

His hand over her mouth killed her scream as Kingsley shoved her into the wall. He kicked the door closed even as Juliette attempted to wrest herself from his grasp. And although at five-ten, his willowy Juliette could not match his strength—no woman could—that didn't stop her from trying, from digging her heels into the hardwood floor as he dragged her toward the bed. Twisting in his arms, she cried out against his hand. My God, she was as good at this game as he was. Even racked with desire as potent as his, she could still put up the most impressive fight, even when he knew she wanted him as much or more than he needed her.

He loosened his grip on her wrists long enough to turn her. He wanted her facedown tonight, bent over the bed, impotent in her struggles. The spreader bars, cuffs, shackles and ropes hung unwanted, unneeded on the walls all about them. He'd rather hold her down with his own body than employ any tools.

"Monsieur…" she panted, her eyes wide with fear as he shoved her forward and she fell across the bed. The scent of fear and sweat graced her skin like the most drugging of perfumes. *"Non…s'il vous plaît…"*

Her voice broke at the end of her plea and Kingsley almost laughed. Anyone who'd ever chanted "no means no" had never met his Juliette. This wasn't only his favorite of their games. It was hers.

Kingsley gripped her by the back of the neck and pressed her face into the sheets to silence her. With his free hand, he wrenched the back of her dress up, tearing it in the process. She did look so lovely in white. How it glowed against her dark skin. He'd found her on a beach in Haiti years ago…when she'd been eighteen, barely more than a child. But she'd suffered the miseries of a thousand lifetimes in those years. He'd brought her back with him, made her his property. And in the unlikely event she ever forgot who owned her now, this was how he refreshed her memory.

With his knees he pried her thighs apart as he opened his pants. When he shoved himself inside her, she let out a scream that anyone in the hall would have heard. But it didn't matter. No one would come to her aid.

He rode her hard with brutal thrusts. Breathing deeply, Kingsley willed his pounding heart to slow. He wished to savor this moment, savor her fear. He never imbibed her fear right away. He'd always let it breathe first, decanted it, before pouring it out and drinking it deep.

At times Juliette forgot it was him, her Kingsley, and got lost in the memory of the man who'd done this to her out of hatred and not love. Kingsley knew when her body went stiff underneath him, when she stopped struggling, that her fear had reached its peak.

He lived for those moments.

Her grunts and cries of pain and fear were the sweetest sounds he could imagine. Only they could silence the music in his ears that he heard from the time he woke until he fell asleep and into blissful oblivion again. One piano concerto thirty years ago…and still he couldn't unhear it.

Juliette's breathing quickened. She made a last valiant attempt at escape, but Kingsley merely dragged her arms behind her back and held her immobile. He thrust again, thrust hard, and with a shudder he came inside her, as her inner muscles clenched around him with the orgasm she'd fought against until finally surrendering to him.

He lingered inside her and simply enjoyed the bliss of the moment, the emptiness of it. His people were so right to call orgasm *le petite morte*…the little death. He died while inside her and he cherished that death, that freedom, those few seconds when he was released from the spell of the only man in the Underground who wore a collar but belonged to no one.

Juliette's laughter jarred him from his musings. He couldn't help but join her in her postcoital amusement. Releasing her hands, he pulled out of her, and relaxed onto the bed as she straightened her clothes before draping herself over his chest.

"You scared me, monsieur. I thought you were still with *le père.*"

"I meant to scare you. And no, he's praying, *je pense.*"

"Praying for what?" Juliette turned her eyes up to Kingsley and he stroked her cheek. His beautiful Juliette, his Jules, his jewel. He treasured her above all others. Only one person had he ever loved more. But the one he loved more, he hated with equal passion. He wished that the mathematics of the world were like the mathematics of the heart—then his equal love and hate would mean he felt nothing instead of double.

"For his lost pet to come back to him someday, I'm sure."

Juliette sighed and relaxed against him.

"But she is not lost." Juliette kissed his chest. "She's just off her leash."

Kingsley laughed.

"It's much worse than that, *mon amour.* His pet's run off, and this time, she hasn't got her collar."

SOUTH

As long as Wesley's parents hadn't heard of her, every-thing would be okay. And surely they hadn't heard of her. Why would they have heard of her, a BDSM erotica writer from New York? Did they even sell her books in Kentucky? Ludicrous thought. Of course they hadn't heard of her. And everything would be a-fucking-okay.

Nora sighed as they crossed the Mason-Dixon Line at Hagerstown, Maryland, and entered the South. Her stom-ach clenched hours later when they crossed the state line into Kentucky.

What the holy hell was she doing in Kentucky?

After she'd gotten over the shock of seeing Wesley again, she'd tried talking him into staying with her in her house in Connecticut. But he'd been unusually insistent.

"Kentucky," he'd said.

"Please," he'd said.

"I lived in your world. Come live in mine for a while," he'd said.

She'd finally acquiesced, unable and unwilling to ever again see sadness in those big brown eyes of Wesley's. But at her insistence they'd driven in separate cars—he in his Mustang, she in the Aston Martin Griffin had delivered to her. After all, Nora never went into any situation without an escape plan. She'd learned that lesson well back in her days as a professional Dominatrix. She hadn't commanded her exorbitant fees by simply being more beautiful or more vicious than other pros. She did what few others of her kind did. Instead of working from a guarded, well-staffed dungeon, she went to her clients' houses, their hotel rooms, wherever they paid her to go. Back then she'd joked her motto was Have Riding Crop, Will Travel. And travel she had. From New York to New Orleans, from Midtown to the Middle East, she went wherever Kingsley sent her. And for her own safety she relied on two things—her notoriety as the most dangerous Domme in the world, and Kingsley's reputation as the last man in America anyone wanted to cross. She had only to say her name or his and the Underworld toed the line.

Now Nora prayed that where she went no one would have heard of her. Especially Wesley's parents. Surely, as conservative as Wesley painted them, they'd never even been in the erotica section of a bookstore, much less heard the name Nora Sutherlin.

But it didn't hurt to ask. She fished her cell phone out of her bag and called Wesley.

"Yes, we're almost there," he answered before she even said hello. Every hour on the hour she'd called to him to ask, "Are we there yet?"

"That's not why I'm phoning this time."

"Sure about that?"

"Nope. So you never told me what your parents think about me coming to visit." Nora turned on her blinker as they veered onto exit 81.

"They're fine with me having visitors. A lot of my college friends came by over the summer."

Nora pursed her lips. She would have stared Wesley down had he not been in the yellow Shelby Mustang two cars ahead of her.

"Nice nonanswer there, kid."

"It's fine." He laughed and Nora couldn't help but smile. God, she'd missed that boy's laugh in the fifteen months they hadn't seen each other, hadn't spoken. Wesley's absence from her life had been a void no amount of sex or money or kink or fame had been able to fill.

"Seriously, Nor. My parents are nice people. They like all my friends."

"Friends. Good. Let's go with friends for introductions. Let's practice. You'll say, 'Ma, Paw—'"

"You're getting my family confused with the Waltons again."

"Hush, John-Boy, we're practicing. You say to them, 'Mother, Father—this is my friend Nora. I used to work for her back at Yorke. She's come to visit and not cause any trouble.'"

"Not going to be able to say that with a straight face."

"Which is why we're practicing, Your Highness."

Wesley groaned, and now it was Nora's turn to laugh at him.

"You're never going to drop that, are you?"

Nora could easily envision him rubbing his forehead in amused frustration.

"I kind of like it—the Prince of Kentucky. Very sexy title."

"One stupid reporter called me that three years ago in one article—"

"Yeah, in an article about you hanging out with Prince Harry at the Kentucky Derby. Crazy that he's turned into the sexy one now. Can you get me his number?"

"We didn't stay in touch."

"So, if you're the Prince of Kentucky," Nora continued, unwilling to drop a thread of conversation that made Wesley so delightfully uncomfortable, "who's the Princess? Are you supposed to marry the governor's daughter or something?"

"God, I hope not."

"What? She a dog?"

"She's a very cute nine-year-old girl," Wesley said as the first of the stars showed themselves at the edge of the southern sky. At the pace they were going, they'd be at Wesley's house within the hour. "She also happens to be my cousin."

Now Nora had to groan. Of course Wesley couldn't just be the son of rich horse farmers. He had to be related to the governor, as well. Her poor little intern… She'd once thought had no money, no connections, no nothing… What else didn't she know about him?

"Well, hey. You know what they say about Kentucky…"

"You're disgusting."

"True. But I'm also winning." Nora hit the gas and passed Wesley's Mustang. He apparently didn't take kindly to her doing so on his home territory. Nora glanced in her rearview mirror and saw his car speed up. "Don't worry, kid. I have no idea where I'm going. You're gonna win this…oh, holy shit. Was that a castle?"

Nora craned her neck to look at the turreted building they passed.

"No. Sort of. It's a hotel now. But it is a castle. Some lunatic built it for his wife years ago. Was her dream to live in a castle. She never got to do so."

Nora frowned. "That's sad. She died before they finished it?"

"Nope. Divorced."

Laughing, Nora glanced back one more time at the strange sight of a castle situated in the middle of Kentucky bluegrass.

"Women. Just can't please them sometimes. I think I'd stay married to a guy who built me a castle. Especially one that pretty."

Nora heard Wesley laughing softly on the other end of the line. She wasn't sure she'd ever heard him laugh like that before—sort of throaty, kind of arrogant and undeniably sexy.

"Wait until you see *my* castle."

"Are we there yet?" she asked as they hung up their cell phones.

Nora followed Wesley's taillights all the way to a town called Versailles, which he mispronounced as "Ver-sales." They turned onto a dark winding road and had to slow down considerably. The entire way there Nora tried to will herself to be calm. It would be fine. Everything would be fine. She had Wesley back again.

Over the summer, she'd come to accept that she'd have to live without Wesley, that she couldn't be Søren's property and Wesley's...*whatever* at the same time. Life with Søren seemed like a beautiful prison most days, a prison she chose, a prison she would never leave. Only Wesley's absence had made it feel like a punishment and not a palace....

"Oh, holy shit," Nora breathed. "That's a fucking palace."

Ahead of her, lit up like the Rockefeller Center Christmas tree, was the biggest goddamn house she'd ever seen in her life. Kingsley's three-story town house, Griffin's estate, even Søren's father's New Hampshire mansion...all of them looked like suburban ranch homes in comparison to the stately sprawling ivory box before her. She counted no less than twenty-eight windows on the front of the house alone. Windows, doors, balconies...she'd seen smaller palaces nestled in the

Rhine Valley of Europe, palaces that housed real European aristocracy and not just old American money.

Wesley pulled into the circular cobblestone drive and turned off his engine. Nora followed suit. She hoped it was late enough no one would be out and about to witness her wide-eyed, jaw-on-the-ground reaction to Wesley's house.

Stepping out of her car, she nearly tripped on a crack in the cobblestone. Wesley caught her and pulled her close.

"I only tripped so you'd catch me," she lied, wrapping her arms around him.

"I only put that crack there so you'd trip." He smiled down at her and her breath caught in her throat.

Wesley raised a hand and mussed her hair with such easy familiarity that the past year and a half they'd spent apart vanished, as if all the longing and loneliness were merely the residue of a nightmare from which she'd just awoken. In the dream, she'd lost her best friend in a labyrinth and no path she took could bring her any closer to him. But now she'd screamed herself awake and found him right next to her in bed. And when she looked up at him, at those big brown eyes and that too-sweet smile, and asked him, "So what now?" she couldn't even begin to care what the answer was. She had her Wesley back. Maybe for only a day or a week or a month… but they were together now and she'd go anywhere as long as he went with her.

"What now? We go in the house and grab some food—"

"Grand idea. Totally starving."

"Then we'll go to my house—"

"Wait. What? Whoa, you have your own house? Is there a house inside this house that's your house?"

"Guesthouse. In the back. No food in it, though, right now. We can fix that tomorrow." Wesley took her by the hand and led her toward the front door of his palace.

"And then?" Nora prompted, eager to figure out exactly what he expected of her. Would it be like old times? Them living under the same roof and trying not to fall into bed together? Or did he want more from her?

Wesley grinned down at her and her heart knotted up in her chest. God damn, she had missed this kid—so fucking much that being back with him hurt almost as much as letting him go had.

"Then…" Wesley said as he ran his hands up her arms, and Nora shivered with a need she thought she'd long buried, a need for hands on her that were always gentle. She shook off the thought and the need. Surely after they'd been a year and a half apart, Wesley's feelings for her had changed. She couldn't quite believe how much *he* had changed. He seemed taller now. His Southern accent had gotten a little thicker. His longer hair made him look older. Now he looked like a man, not the boy she'd known and loved and teased and tortured.

The suspense was more than Nora could handle. Fuck it. She'd kiss the kid and see what happened. Rising up on her toes, she gripped Wesley by the back of the neck and brought his mouth to hers. He didn't protest.

The front door of Wesley's castle opened and a man's voice called out to them. "John Wesley! You know you're allowed to kiss Bridget in the house."

Wesley took a step back and turned toward the voice. Nora saw a man standing in the front doorway who looked like every handsome rich white Southerner she'd ever seen on television or movies. Salt-and-pepper hair, broad shoulders, a broader smile…or it had been a broad smile until he got a good look at Nora and saw she wasn't Bridget.

Nora smiled in a manner she hoped appeared friendly and nonthreatening, as opposed to her usual smiles, which tended to be described as "seductive" and "dangerous."

"Hey, Dad." Wesley grabbed Nora's hand and half escorted, half dragged her forward.

Wesley's father narrowed his eyes at her. "Who's your friend, J.W.?"

Nora looked at Wesley and mouthed *"J.W.?"*

Wesley mouthed back *"Eleanor."*

"Dad, this is my girlfriend, Nora Sutherlin."

Nora's eyes went even wider than they had at the first sight of the house. Girlfriend? Who? Her?

Wiping the look of shock off her face, she purposefully widened her smile at Wesley's handsome father.

At that smile, Wesley's handsome father gave her a look of deep, abiding, profound and unremitting disgust.

"Oh, yeah." She sighed, as her one and only prayer about this trip went unanswered. "He's heard of me."

NORTH
The Past

Kingsley ate dinner with the other boys in silence, keeping his mouth occupied with food so as not to let any smirks and smiles betray his knowledge of English. He wasn't entirely sure how long he could keep up the ruse, wasn't entirely sure why he even tried. But as he sat in the dining room at a carved, black oak table, the boys on the left, the priests on the right, Kingsley tried to decide what sin he'd committed that had earned him this ice-cold hell on earth.

He wanted to blame Carol, head cheerleader at his old school. Blonde girls were a weakness of his. Or Janice, who sang the National Anthem at every home game. Sopranos with red hair could do no wrong in his book. Susan…Alice…and his blue-eyed Mandolin, the long-haired daughter of unrepentant hippies… He'd started in August and had fucked three dozen girls at his small Portland high school by Thanksgiving break. But he couldn't blame a single one of them for sending him to this prison.

He blamed the boyfriends.

Naturally strong and quick, Kingsley knew he could take

on any boy in the school who came at him. But seven boys all at once? No one could have walked away from that. And he hadn't walked away.

He'd crawled.

He'd crawled a few feet before passing out in a puddle of blood that had come from a cut over his heart. The cut had likely saved his life. He remembered little from the beating he'd taken behind the stadium, but he did remember the knife. When the knife came out even the other boys who'd been kicking him, punching him, spitting on him as he fought to get back to his feet, took a step back. The boy with the knife—Troy—hadn't been a boyfriend. Worse, he'd been a brother—Theresa's older brother—and he took the protection of his sister very seriously. The knife came out and slashed at Kingsley's heart. And that's when the other boys had dragged Troy off and left Kingsley bleeding on the ground, broken and bruised but alive.

And as he looked around the dining hall and saw nothing but other boys—boys aged ten to eighteen, tall and short, fat and thin, handsome and unfortunately not so—he wanted to go back to that moment behind the stadium and step into the knife instead of away from it.

He sighed heavily as he took a sip of his tea, dreadful stuff, really. He missed the days when his parents had given him wine with his dinner.

"I know. Tastes like piss, doesn't it?" Father Henry's voice came from over his shoulder.

Kingsley almost nodded in agreement, but remembered that he didn't understand English. Turning toward the voice, he composed his face into a mask of confusion.

Father Henry pointed at Kingsley's tea and mimed a vicious grimace and a gag. Kingsley allowed himself a laugh then. Everyone spoke the universal language of disgust.

"Come with me, Mr. Boissonneault," Father Henry said, pulling out Kingsley's chair and motioning for him to follow. "Let's see if we can't find you a translator."

Translator? As Kingsley stood up his heart started to race. Father Henry had said no one at the school spoke French but Mr. Stearns. And every student in the school seemed to be in the dining room, huddled over steaming bowls of tomato basil soup. Every student but Stearns. Not that Kingsley had been looking for him, watching the door, scanning the room between every sip of piss tea.

Father Henry led him to the kitchen and through a wall of steam. By a hulking black oven a young priest waved a spatula as he repeated a sentence over and over. He seemed to be conducting himself—the words his music, the spatula his baton.

"And now you, repeat this…*Você não terá nenhum outro deus antes de mim.*"

"*Si,* Father Aldo." The words came from a table a few feet away from the stove. "*Você não terá nenhum outro deus antes de mim.*"

Kingsley almost shivered at the sound of the voice—an elegant tenor, rich and educated, but also cold, aloof and distant. The voice belonged to Stearns, the blond pianist, he saw, when he took two steps forward and peered around a refrigerator. At Stearns's feet lay a black cat curled up in a tight ball, glaring at Kingsley with bright and malevolent green eyes. He watched as Stearns rubbed the cat's head gently with the tip of his shoe as he recited the words in a language Kingsley didn't recognize.

"*Muito bom,*" said the priest, crossing the spatula over his chest and bowing. "Father Henry, what are you doing in my kitchen? We've had this talk."

"I'm sorry to interrupt, Father Aldo, Mr. Stearns."

"No. You are not sorry. You always love to interrupt. It

is what you are best at," Father Aldo scolded with a broad smile on his face. Kingsley tried to place the accent. Brazilian, maybe? If so, it would mean the language he was teaching Stearns was Portuguese. But why would anyone in Nowhere, Maine, want to learn Portuguese?

"Father Aldo, I only interrupt you because you talk so much. I have to interrupt if I'm going to say my piece before sundown."

"The sun is down, and yet you are still interrupting."

"You're interrupting my interrupting, Aldo. And I am very sorry to interrupt Mr. Stearns's lesson. But it's his language faculties we need. This is Kingsley Boissonneault, our new student. He doesn't speak any English, I'm afraid. We're hoping Mr. Stearns could be of some assistance. If he would oblige…"

"Of course, Father." Stearns closed the book in front of him and stood up. Once more Kingsley was stuck by the blond pianist's height, his face so unbearably handsome. "I will be happy to help in any way I can. Of course, Monsieur Boissonneault doesn't need my help. After all, he speaks English perfectly. Don't you?"

Kingsley froze when Stearns directed the last two words at him.

Father Aldo and Father Henry both looked at him with raised eyebrows.

"Mr. Boissonneault?" Father Aldo said in his accented English. "Is this true?"

"Of course it is." Stearns stepped over the black cat and stood before Kingsley.

Kingsley should have been afraid, should have been embarrassed. But that one step toward him, that look of penetrating insight, inspired other feelings in him, feelings he immediately shoved down deep into himself.

"He laughed while you two were arguing. He knew exactly what you both were saying. If he's a French speaker in Maine he's either from France, where he would start learning English at age seven or eight, or he's Quebecois and therefore at least passably bilingual."

Father Aldo and Father Henry continued to stare at him. Stearns studied him with penetrating, steel-gray eyes.

"I am most certainly not Quebecois," Kingsley finally said, the pride in his Parisian blood trumping any desire to remain silent and anonymous. "I'm from Paris."

Stearns smiled and Kingsley felt that smile in his blood like a shard of ice.

"A liar and a snob. Welcome to Saint Ignatius, Monsieur Boissonneault," Stearns said. "So pleased to have you here."

For the second time that day, Kingsley fantasized about stepping into Troy's knife and letting the blade sink into his heart. Surely a blade of real steel would hurt less than the steely judgment in Stearns's eyes.

"I didn't want to come," Kingsley protested. "I'm here against my will. I shouldn't have to talk if I don't want to."

"You have a bright future with the Cistercians," Stearns said, crossing his arms over his chest. "They take vows of silence, too. Although for reasons of piety and not obnoxious attention seeking."

"Mr. Stearns," Father Aldo gently chided. "We may be Jesuits, but we do practice the rule of Benedict here."

Stearns exhaled heavily. "Of course, Father. Forgive me." He didn't sound particularly contrite to Kingsley, but neither Father Aldo nor Father Henry raised any further objections. They seemed as cowed as Matthew had earlier. Who was this Stearns person?

"Perhaps you would show Mr. Boissonneault the dormitories. Give him more of an introduction to the school than young Matthew did," Father Henry said. "If you have the time."

Stearns nodded, took one more step toward Kingsley and looked down into his eyes. Down? Kingsley had been measured in the hospital and stood at exactly six feet. Stearns had to be six-two at the least.

"I have the time." Stearns gave him another smile. "Shall we?"

Kingsley thought about saying no, demurring, protesting that Matthew had given him a thorough introduction to the school and he needed no other, but *merci beaucoup* for offering. And yet, although Stearns already seemed to dislike him, loathe him even, Kingsley couldn't deny that everything in him wanted a moment alone with this mysterious young man who even the priests deferred to.

"Oui," Kingsley whispered, and Stearns's sculpted lips formed a tight line.

Kingsley followed him from the kitchen. As soon as they were out of the door and alone in the hallway, Stearns turned and faced him.

"Père Henry est un héro," Stearns began in flawless French. *Father Henry is a hero.* "You'll have to forgive him for knowing very little about France. During World War II, he was in Poland smuggling Jews to safety and hiding women and girls from the Russian soldiers. I only know this because another priest here told me. Father Henry does not talk about the hundreds of lives he helped save. He talks about Italian food and mystery novels. Father Aldo is Brazilian. He and twelve others were held captive by guerrillas in 1969. Father Aldo was twenty-nine years old and, despite being from a wealthy and politically connected family, was the last captive to be released—by choice. He would not leave until the others were

safely freed. He forgave his captors and publicly asked the court to show them leniency. Now he cooks for us."

"Why are you telling me all this?" Kingsley asked in English, feeling for the first time since his parents' death that he could easily start crying.

"Father Henry asked me to introduce you to Saint Ignatius. That is what I'm doing. Coming?" he asked, still speaking French.

Kingsley said nothing, but followed him down the hall.

Stearns paused in the doorway to the dining room. Only two boys remained at the table, eating and talking.

"*Ton ami* Matthew," Stearns said, inclining his head toward the small redheaded boy who had first given him a tour of the school, sitting next to a slightly taller boy with black hair and glasses. "He came here a year and a half ago. Although eleven years old when we saw him first, he looked hardly older than eight. His parents had neglected him to the point of starvation. A wealthy Catholic family in the neighborhood where Matthew was found digging through garbage cans is paying his tuition here. The boy he's sitting with is the son of the people paying Matthew's tuition. Neither of them knows that. They became friends on their own."

Kingsley swallowed, said nothing and followed Stearns from the dining room.

"I think Father Henry meant for you to tell me what time classes start, that sort of thing."

"Breakfast is at seven. Chapel is at eight. Classes start at nine. Tomorrow you'll meet with Father Martin, who will set your class schedule."

"I suppose Father Martin is a hero, too."

"Father Martin is an astronomer. He discovered three comets and invented a formula for calculating the expansion of the universe. Retired now. His eyes aren't strong enough to keep searching the heavens. So now he teaches math and science to us."

Stearns led them from the dining hall, outside and to the library. The main room was empty but for three boys about Kingsley's age huddling by the fireplace on the west wall. Stearns picked up an abandoned book off a table, glanced at the spine and headed to a bookcase not far from where the boys sat and talked.

"Stanley Horngren—he's the one wearing the jacket," Stearns said, inclining his regal blond head toward one of the boys. "He has twelve brothers and sisters. He works two jobs every summer in order to pay his own tuition here and not burden his family with the extra expense. James Mitchell, sitting next to him, is here on a full academic scholarship. Rather impressive considering he is completely deaf and never had access to a school for the deaf. When you speak to him, speak clearly and make sure he can see your lips. And speak only in English," Stearns said, giving Kingsley a dark look. He slipped the book onto a shelf in what was no doubt the correct spot. "The boy on the sofa is Kenneth Stowe. He spent two years in an institution because his teachers thought he was mentally deficient. In reality he has a minor learning disability and a genius IQ. He is now a straight-A student. The library closes at nine. If you need to stay later, you can ask Father Martin for a pass."

Stearns turned on his heel and headed back outside. He paused outside the door to the church.

"Weekend Mass is at 5:00 p.m. on Saturdays and 10:00 a.m. on Sundays. It's a traditional Catholic mass. Are you Catholic?"

Kingsley shook his head. "We're descended from the Huguenots."

Stearns exhaled through his nose. "Calvinists." He said the word like a curse before continuing on. "You are encouraged but not required to attend chapel. You will not be asked to cut your long hair. You will be asked to wear the school uniform, but for no reason other than it helps foster an environment of equality. None of us here is better than any of the others. You do understand that, yes?"

Kingsley stared at the floor. "Yes."

Stearns took them to the dormitory building, stopping outside long enough to gather an armful of logs. Kingsley picked up some firewood as well, thinking they would be carrying it up to their dormitory room on the second floor, but instead Stearns went into the room where the youngest boys slept and piled the wood neatly next to the hearth.

He took the wood out of Kingsley's arms and added it to the pile.

Several young boys sat on their beds reading. Only one managed to mumble a muted "thank you" as the two of them walked out. Stearns said nothing, only tapped the boy lightly on the forehead in a gesture almost brotherly. All the boys in the room followed Stearns with wide, awe-filled eyes.

Kingsley trailed after Stearns to the top floor of the dormitory, where the oldest boys slept.

"Lights-out is at nine," his guide continued in his shockingly fluent French. Had Kingsley not known otherwise, he would have assumed Stearns was a native. "If you have homework that keeps you up later, you can work in the common room downstairs. As Father Henry says, 'Firewood does not grow on trees.' Please replace any of the wood you use."

"*Bien sûr,*" Kingsley said, but knew he wouldn't have thought to replace the firewood without someone telling him.

"Eighteen of us sleep in this room. Nineteen now that you're here. Nathan Weitz has night terrors for reasons he hasn't chosen to share with anyone yet. At least once a week he wakes up screaming. Ignore it. He will go back to sleep in a few minutes. If you see him sleepwalking, follow him. Last winter he wandered outside and nearly developed hypothermia. Joseph Marksbury is in charge of the chore list. I suggest you talk to him before he comes to you, unless you want nothing but bathroom duty for the entire semester. Now if you'll excuse me, I need to get back to my Portuguese."

"You're learning Portuguese, too?" Kingsley asked. "How many languages do you speak?"

"Eight."

"I'm bilingual. What do they call someone like you?"

Stearns arched an eyebrow at him. "Intelligent."

Kingsley started to laugh, but then realized Stearns hadn't been joking.

"Eight," Kingsley repeated. "I would go crazy with so many words in my head. I have enough trouble keeping my French and English separate."

"A few students here speak a little French, but since Father Pierre died, I'm the only one fluent at the school. If you need to speak French, speak it to me. And as you've seen, this place is full of kind and courageous priests and intelligent and hardworking young men, many of whom have had to overcome great obstacles to be here. If you ever feel the need to lie again, tell your lies to me."

Kingsley blushed and crossed his arms. "I'll apologize to Matthew."

"A very good idea, Mr. Boissonneault," Stearns said.

"You can call me Kingsley. That's my name."

Stearns seemed to mull the invitation over.

"Kingsley..." He nodded, and Kingsley tensed at the sound of his name spoken by the blond pianist who seemed to own the school. "This school has been my salvation. I would appreciate if you at least pretended to show it some respect."

Stearns turned and started to walk from the dormitory room.

"Merci," Kingsley said, before he was gone. "Thank you."

"For what?" Stearns asked from the doorway.

"The Ravel today. *Mon père aimait Ravel.*"

For a moment Stearns only stared at him. Kingsley wanted to shrink from his penetrating gaze, but held his ground and didn't blink, didn't look away.

"*Aimait?* Your father is dead?"

Kingsley nodded. "*Et maman.* A train crash last May. You play piano beautifully. I've never heard Ravel like that before."

Stearns came back into the room and stood before him. Kingsley felt his eyes on his face again and found himself suddenly shy. Shy? At age sixteen Kingsley had slept with nearly fifty girls already. No, not just girls—women, too. Even the wife of his late father's business partner.

"I was named Marcus Stearns," Stearns finally said. "No one ever calls me Marcus."

"Why not?"

"Because Marcus is my father's name, and I am not my father's son." He spoke the words slowly, deliberately, as if imparting a threat instead of just information.

"Can I call you something other than Stearns? It seems very formal."

Stearns seemed to ponder the question.

"Perhaps someday."

"Anything else I need to know?" Kingsley asked, intimidated by him, but for some reason not wanting to let him go yet.

Stearns fell silent and looked at Kingsley's suitcase sitting at the foot of a bed. "Your bed is the one next to mine," he finally said.

Kingsley's hands tingled at the mention of the proximity of their two beds. He didn't know why he was reacting to this young man the way he only ever reacted to a beautiful girl. He couldn't stop staring at him, couldn't stop wondering what secrets he kept, and what it would be like to hear those secrets whispered across a pillow at night.

"How did you get stuck sleeping so far from the fireplace?"

"I volunteered. I stay warm enough. A word of advice," Stearns said, turning to stare Kingsley in the eyes, "do not wake me up at night."

Kingsley barked a laugh. "What? Will you kill me?"

Stearns turned and headed toward the door again.

"Or worse."

NORTH
The Present

Kingsley took a length of rope and twisted it into a slipknot. With wary eyes the girl watched him as he brought the rope down over her head and let the knot rest at her throat.

"It's a simple game, *chèrie*." He made a circuit of her body and nodded his approval. Lovely girl. Twenty-nine years old. Blue eyes. A yoga instructor or something equally silly. He'd bend her in half tonight, and she'd thank him for it after. "One end of the rope is around your neck. The other end…" He tapped the back of her knee until she raised her leg like a well-trained show pony. Grasping her calf, he raised it, and looped the other end of the rope around it. "Goes *là,* on your lovely, well-turned ankle. You say you can hold your yoga poses for hours. Let's see how long you can keep your back leg up and bent while I fuck your ass. The leg starts to drop…you start to choke. Simple. *Oui?*"

Her pupils widened. She swallowed audibly.

"*Oui,* monsieur," she whispered.

"*Bon.* Now allow me to simply tighten this a bit."

Kingsley bound her wrists to the bedpost in front of her and shortened the rope that connected her neck to her ankle by a few inches. So far he could tell her boasts had been honest. Her leg stayed up, high and bent, and her breathing remained unconstricted. Of course, once he started fucking her, she might lose her concentration.

He did love this game.

From the bedside table, he pulled out his lubricant and a condom. Her fear and her arousal mingled so powerfully he could smell it from three feet away. Standing behind her, he started to open his pants.

The door to Kingsley's bedroom opened and Søren strode inside, glanced at them with only the merest arch of an eyebrow before sitting down in the armchair by Kingsley's bed and throwing his long legs up onto the covers, shoes and all.

"We need to talk."

Kingsley leveled a stare at Søren that would have sent any submissive at The 8th Circle into paroxysms of panic. Søren only stared back without blinking.

With a sigh of frustration, Kingsley unknotted the ropes, slapped the girl on her bottom and uttered a quick, angry, "Out."

"But…" She looked first at him, then at Søren, who, thankfully, had come to the town house incognito tonight. No collar. He wore only a black T-shirt, black pants and he carried his black motorcycle helmet in his hand.

"Out," Søren repeated, and this time she listened. Quickly, she gathered her clothes off the floor and raced from the room. Kingsley started to shut the door behind her, but his second favorite girl, Sadie, slipped inside and sat at his feet.

"You've never heard of knocking, have you?" Kingsley asked, dropping into French. He grabbed Sadie, his lone female rottweiler, by the collar and shepherded her to the bed.

She hopped up nimbly and onto his covers, making herself at home.

Søren smiled and answered in English. "I've heard rumors of knocking. I never believed them."

"I had a lovely evening planned."

"Now you have a new plan. I called. Irena answered, not Juliette."

"Juliette is gone." Kingsley sat on the bed next to Sadie and scratched her ears.

"Gone. Where has she gone?"

"Haiti. She left today." He kept scratching Sadie, refusing to meet Søren's gaze.

"You never let Juliette go to Haiti alone."

Kingsley raised his chin. "Special circumstances."

"How special?" Søren pulled his legs off the bed and set his feet on the floor. With one movement Søren signaled their conversation had ceased to be of the casual variety.

"I saw a ghost."

Søren raised his hand and mindlessly rubbed his bottom lip with the tip of his thumb. Kingsley bit his own bottom lip in a sympathetic response. Those lips…both cruel and sensual…the damage they'd done to him he couldn't even begin to calculate. And yet he craved them as much now as he had a lifetime ago.

"I don't believe in ghosts and neither should you, Kingsley."

"Why not? I've been in love with a ghost for thirty years." Kingsley strolled over to the armchair and sat on the ottoman between the other man's knees.

Søren narrowed his eyes at him. "The body's not even cold yet. Eleanor's been gone one day and you're already trying to get me into bed again?"

"Again?" Kingsley laughed and rolled his eyes. "Always. Are you surprised?"

Søren shrugged. "Not really. Tell me about your ghost."

On the nightstand lay a folder. Almost reluctantly, he picked it up and carried it over.

Søren eyed him for a moment before taking the black file folder from him and opening it. He studied the contents before closing the file again and looking back at Kingsley.

"It's us at Saint Ignatius. Eleanor has a copy of this photograph. What of it?"

Kingsley took the file and opened it. Thirty years disappeared in that foot of space between his eyes and the photograph he gazed at. Thirty years gone in a heartbeat.

Kingsley still remembered the day it was taken. His closest friend at St. Ignatius, a native Mainer named Christian, had gotten a camera for Christmas and decided some day he would work for *National Geographic*. The first animals he'd stalked with his lens were his fellow students. That day, the day the photo had been taken, Kingsley and Søren had disappeared into the woods by the school and had argued. Underneath his school uniform Kingsley's body had sported bruises and welts over nearly every inch of his back and thighs. The only marks visible were two small fingertip-shaped bruises that remained on his neck from the act that had ended the fight.

"I have a copy of the photograph, too," Kingsley confessed. "I've kept it all my life."

"And?" Søren crossed his ankle over his knee and waited.

"And…" Kingsley slid the photo out of the file and turned it over. On the back someone had inked their initials. The white of the celluloid had faded and yellowed. "This isn't my copy. This is the original."

Søren narrowed his eyes at Kingsley. "The original?"

Kingsley nodded. "I received this in the mail yesterday. No note. No letter. No return address on the envelope. The photograph in the folder and nothing else."

Søren said nothing for a moment. Kingsley waited.

"Postmark?"

"New Hampshire—your home sweet home."

Søren came slowly to his feet and walked to the window. Pushing back the curtains, he gazed out onto the Manhattan skyline. Kingsley would have written the man a check for a million dollars then and there to know what he was thinking. But he knew Søren too well. Money meant nothing to him. Secrets were a far dearer currency.

"It isn't Elizabeth," Søren said. Kingsley stood next to him and watched his gray eyes watch the city.

"Are you certain of that?"

"What possible motive would she have for this? For stealing Eleanor's file from your office? For sending you that photograph?"

"You know Elizabeth better than I. She's devoted her whole life to helping abused children."

"And?"

"You and your Little One? How would she feel if she learned about you two?"

"Eleanor is thirty-four."

"She wasn't thirty-four when you fell in love with her. I know you did nothing wrong with her. I know you kept her safe and protected her even from yourself, even when your own pet begged you not to. But would Elizabeth see it that way?"

Søren exhaled and furrowed his brow.

"No. No, Elizabeth would not. She'd assume the worst, assume I was like our father."

"Your sister is even more damaged than you are, Père Stearns. She would destroy you first and not even bother to ask questions later."

"Possibly. But she certainly wouldn't go to these lengths to do it, not when a phone call would suffice."

"Elizabeth would do everything in her power to destroy you if she knew about you and your pet. But yes, this doesn't seem to be her style. Or your pet's." When he said "pet" Sadie lifted her massive head and stared at him with worshipful devotion. If only all the women in his world were so easy to control...

Kingsley glanced at the photograph one more time. Elizabeth, Søren's sister...a beautiful woman even at age forty-eight. Beautiful but broken. No, far more than broken—shattered. Kingsley had been in her presence only a few times, and he'd met French soldiers—war veterans, men who'd liberated death camps and watched the Nazis put Paris under their heels—with fewer ghosts in their eyes than Søren's sister. If she'd merely been raped by her father as a child, she might have survived without the damage she carried inside her. But she'd turned her darkness onto her own brother. When she'd ceased to be a victim and become a perpetrator herself...there was no telling what such a broken soul was capable of. Kingsley knew broken souls—he possessed one of his own, after all.

"Who else then?" he asked, sliding between the window and Søren. Søren glared down at him. Kingsley only grinned and waited for him to move. He didn't.

Søren stood in silence. Kingsley knew not to speak, knew not to rush the answer. It would come in time. Patience. Søren always rewarded patience. Eleanor had learned that as a girl. Had she tried to force his hand, Søren would have walked away from his obsession with her. She seduced and teased, challenged and defied, but all the while she waited, wanting answers but never demanding them. Until the day Søren told her everything and gave her everything. And then she'd had the audacity to walk away from it all. Søren laid out feasts for her that she merely picked at, while Kingsley lapped up the crumbs that fell to the floor.

"It's not Elizabeth," Søren said again. "But she might know something. After all, Lennox is entirely populated by Elizabeth and her two children. If it was postmarked from there, then…"

"Then what, *mon père?*"

Kingsley waited, hoping Søren would say exactly what he wanted him to say. Eleanor gone. Juliette gone. Just the two of them once more. It could be perfect again, like it was when they were boys in school together. If only Søren would say what he needed him to say.

"Then we should go talk to her—you and I."

Kingsley nodded. *"Oui."*

Perfect.

SOUTH

At moments like these Wesley wished he was as fluent in profanity as Nora. A good "fuck" would have summed up his feelings pretty well right now. From the look on his father's face Wesley could tell that this wasn't the first time he'd heard the name Nora Sutherlin. But how did his dad know who she was? Two types of people knew that—erotica readers and kinky people. Wes didn't like to think his father fell into either of those camps.

"Um…Dad?"

"J.W.… Where's Bridget?"

Wesley glanced down at Nora. He hadn't quite told her about Bridget yet.

"I don't know. At her house, I guess. We broke up."

Wesley's father gave him that look—that skeptical, eyebrow-half-cocked look that never boded well for anybody on the receiving end.

"When? You two were out here on the porch a week ago, laughing so loud I thought I'd have to turn the garden hose on you both to cool you down."

Wincing, Wesley immediately stopped looking at Nora. Last thing he wanted was to see the expression on her face at that piece of news. But she must have taken it well, for Wesley felt her palm on his lower back. She gave him a quick pat before sliding her hand into the rear pocket of his jeans. As much as he liked having her hand on his Levi's, her groping his ass might not be the best way to say hi to Dad tonight, given the mood he was in.

"We broke up after that. It wasn't working. It—"

"Mr. Railey, I'm sure this is kind of a shock to you, me showing up out of nowhere," Nora said, pulling her hand away from Wesley and taking a step forward. "The whole thing's something of a shock to me, too. But Wes and I have known each other a long time. And—"

"My son is twenty years old, Miss Sutherlin. He hasn't known anybody for a long time."

Wesley watched Nora plaster a smile on her face. He'd seen that smile before. She usually used it on men she was trying to con into performing for her. That smile had gotten her out of more speeding tickets than Wesley could count—two on this trip alone. He wished he could communicate telepathically with Nora. The first thing he'd tell her would be *stop smiling. Trust me on this.*

"I feel like we've gotten off to a bad start, Mr. Railey," Nora continued. "Can we talk inside for a few minutes? Wesley used to work for me back in Connecticut. He—"

Wesley's father started forward at a leisurely place. Nothing new with that. Jackson Railey was well-known for doing everything at a leisurely pace. Back when he was a kid, Wesley had thought it meant his father was the laid-back sort, never in a hurry, never rushing himself or anybody else. As he got older, got smarter, he realized his father moved slowly because he liked making people wait for him. He'd make his mind up in a second, but make you wait a minute for the answer. He'd spend hours on something that should take only minutes, to prove he had the time and money to waste…even if nobody else did.

"I know who you are, Miss Sutherlin."

Wesley's heart raced harder with every step his father took closer to Nora. Things had started out ugly and were getting uglier by the second.

"A fan? How nice." She kept smiling.

"Not quite, madam."

"Dad. Let's go in the house and talk." Wesley took a step to the side, trying desperately to put himself between his father and Nora. His dad wasn't the violent type, but he didn't need to be. Words were weapon enough for his father, especially when he was angry like this.

"That woman is not allowed to cross the threshold of my home, J.W. And quite frankly, I'm shocked that you'd even suggest it."

"That woman?" Wesley stood up straighter and stared into his father's blue eyes. He'd gotten his brown eyes from his mother, his temperament from her. Most days it was only the similar set of their jaws that betrayed Wesley and his father were even related. "'That woman' is my best friend, Dad. She's also a four-time *New York Times* bestselling author."

"Five, actually," Nora interjected with a sly wink at him.

That wink gave Wesley the courage to keep going. No matter what his dad said to her, Nora could take it. In their fifteen months apart, he'd almost forgotten how much fun she had getting yelled at.

"Sorry, Nor. Forgot about the new book. Multi-*New York Times* bestselling writer. She's also—"

"A whore."

The word came out of his father's mouth and hung in the air between them. Wesley's right hand balled up into a fist. His dad might not be violent, but he was coming damn close to getting Wesley to that point.

"Ohh…" Nora said with that wicked smile of hers, that smile that made men either fall at her feet or run for their lives "…he totally went there. I can respect that."

"Take that back, Dad." Wesley leveled his coldest stare at his father. "You don't know what you're talking about."

"I know exactly what I'm talking about, J.W. Did you think your mother and I believed it when you said you just wanted to come back home to Kentucky because you were homesick? You spent two years telling us how much you loved it at Yorke, how much you wanted to spend your whole life in Connecticut, how happy you were, and then one day it's 'I'm ready to come home.' You think we bought that? Your mother did, because that's what she wanted to believe. I knew better. Did a little digging—"

"Jesus, Dad, you investigated me?"

"Had to be done. And I did it for your own sake."

Nora laughed softly. "Can I take a moment here to tell you both how cute your accents are when you're angry?"

Wesley and his father both looked at her, Wesley in shock, his father in disgust.

"Okay, that's a 'no' then. Carry on." She took a step back and waved her hand at them to continue.

"You think this funny, don't you, miss? Well, it's not funny to me. Or to my wife. Our son was a wreck when he dragged his tail back down here. I had an uncle come home from Vietnam looking less shell-shocked than my boy did that day he turned up here."

The smile fell from Nora's face. Nodding, she stepped forward again and took Wesley's hand. He squeezed her fingers and found them surprisingly cold, as if she was nervous or something. His Nora? Nervous?

"I'm sorry, Mr. Railey. I know I hurt your son. And I'll regret it until the day I die. But I—"

"Hurt my son?" Wesley's father shook his head and gave a horrible, cold laugh. "You didn't hurt my son. He falls off a horse and gets hurt. You broke that boy's spirit. Crushed him. I know about the smut you write. The wife's got a whole case of trash like that in the library. From what I can tell, only thing different about your books and the ones she reads is that in yours they get a little more creative. Your books don't bother me a bit. That you sell your body doesn't even bother me. What does bother me is that you pulled your tricks on my son. You used him, chewed him up and spit him out."

Wesley opened his mouth to protest, but Nora spoke up first.

"You say you know me, Mr. Railey, but obviously, you don't. If you did, you'd know I don't spit out."

"Nora, please," Wesley said, ready to drop on his hands and knees to beg her to let him handle this. Not that it would work. For a single second Wesley felt a pang of sympathy for Søren. Nora was lawless, unmanageable, uncontrollable. You told her one thing, she did everything but that. She laughed when others cried. Danced when others sat. She clawed her way to the top and didn't even chip a nail on the way up. No one could break her. No one could handle her. No one could shut her up.

God, he had missed this woman.

Wesley turned to his father, stepped directly in front of Nora and raised his chin.

"Dad, my private life with Nora…what happened between the two of us isn't any of your business. We worked it out. And she's not a whore. I can't believe you'd say that."

"I said it, and I'll say it again. What else do you call sell-ing your body?"

"A good career move." Nora peeked around Wesley's arm. "Although technically, I was a Dom—"

"Nora, can you give me a minute here?" Wesley tried to ask as politely as his raw nerves would let him.

"Take your time, Wes." She patted him on the back again.

"Dad, I love you. But you're kind of pissing me off right now. Nora's my best friend. She's my girlfriend. She's staying here with me while I figure out what I'm going to do next. If you've got a problem with that—"

"I certainly do have a problem with that—"

"Then we'll go to a hotel."

"Hotel's a good idea," Nora said from behind him. "I liked that castle we passed. Can we rent a turret? I'll call about the weekly rates."

"I'll stay in a Motel 6 before I'll let anybody treat you like this, Nora."

"They do leave the lights on for you, I hear. Nice of them." Nora already had her phone out, clearly ready to get the hell out of Kentucky. Or at least off his front lawn. He couldn't quite blame her.

"Motel 6? What on earth?" Wesley's mother called out from the front porch. "Wesley? Did you make it home?"

"Hey, Momma." He grabbed Nora's hand and pulled her across the lawn to where his mother stood under the archway. "I want you to meet my girlfriend, Nora. She came down from Connecticut to visit me."

Wesley wanted to pull his mother into a bear hug, but de-cided against it. His dad had accused him in the past of using his mother to get away with murder. He wanted his father to accept Nora, not merely tolerate her because his mother liked her.

"Hello, Mrs. Railey." Nora had a smile on again, but not the smile that made Wesley nervous. A simple smile he had only seen her wear it in private with him, or when she met a child. He'd never met anybody as good with kids as Nora. Broke his heart that she claimed to not want any. "It's very nice to meet you."

"Nora, you say?" his mother repeated, and returned Nora's smile. His mom looked tired tonight. The business side of the farm wore her out, enough that Wesley feared guilt alone would keep him on the farm forever. "So nice to meet you, too. But, Wesley, I thought…"

Wesley laughed. "Mom, Bridget and I broke up a while ago. Nora and I were together when I was at Yorke. We're back together again."

"I'm much younger than I look, I promise." Nora's smile broadened. "I'm aging horribly."

His mom laughed. "I had a feeling my Wesley would fall for an older woman. Girls his age just aren't smart enough for him." She reached up and ruffled Wesley's hair. Nora stuck her tongue out at him and gave him that *Karma's a bitch, ain't it?* look.

"I'm definitely not smart enough for him. Must not be if I let him get away once. I'll be more careful this time."

"Smart girl."

Wesley grinned as his mother reached out and patted Nora on the arm.

"It's getting late, Mom. Shouldn't you be in bed?" he asked, worried that his argument with his father had woken her up.

"Yes, Caroline. I think that's a good idea," said Wesley's father in a tone that brooked no argument.

"Yes, sir," she said, and reached for her husband's hand. "Put me to bed. Make sure you tuck me in nice and tight."

"I always do. Gotta tuck you in or you might run away on me."

Wesley's mother smiled broadly and her pale face instantly lit up with love.

Wesley couldn't help but smile, too. He and his father had their differences, but they both worshipped the ground Caroline Railey walked on. That alone kept them from launching the New Civil War on Kentucky soil most days.

"It was nice to meet you, Nora," she said, glancing over her shoulder as Jackson led her into the house. "Wesley, you make sure she's got enough blankets. Might get even colder tonight."

"I will, Mom. She's out in the guesthouse with me."

"I did not hear that, young man," she said, laughing. Wesley glanced at Nora, who grinned at him.

Alone with her once again, Wesley slumped against one of the pillars on the front porch.

"Okay, that went worse than I thought it would," he confessed. "Nora, I'm so sorry. I can't believe my dad investigated you and me and—"

She closed the distance between them in two big steps and threw her arms around him.

"Whoa, where did that come from?" He wrapped her tight in his arms.

"Wes, you're my hero. I can't believe you talked back to your dad like that. He's a little on the…" Nora pulled away and mimed the *Psycho* shower-stabbing scene. Wesley could only nod in agreement.

"Yeah, can't argue with that. He's a good guy. He is. Just overprotective of me and Mom."

"Family man. I respect that. My father would have sold me down the damn river to pay off a ten-dollar debt if he thought he'd get a Hamilton for me."

"Dad only dislikes you—"

"Hates…he hates me," she corrected.

"Fine, he only hates you because he thinks you hurt me."

Nora reached up and caressed Wesley's cheek. He turned his face into her hand and kissed her palm.

"Wesley…I did hurt you."

He nodded and said nothing else. Nora hugged him again. She held him for a long time, so long he forgot what she was hugging him for. He kissed her hair, inhaled the scent of her— orchids. Nora always smelled like orchids…. Someday he'd remember to ask her why.

"I should go." She pulled away.

"What?"

"I can stay in town somewhere. I don't want to cause you more trouble than I already have. Nora Sutherlin in the house equals trouble. It's basic math."

Wesley shook his head and took her hand. "When did you start doing math? Don't answer. Listen…you're not going to cause trouble. We're going to hang out and relax and spend time together and figure stuff out. No trouble, right?"

Nora sighed heavily. She crossed her arms and leaned back against the pillar behind her.

"Stay a week. Promise me a week," Wesley said. "If it's still this bad with my father in a week, then we'll go back to Connecticut. Okay?"

Wesley watched Nora. She closed her eyes and exhaled through her nose. Was there a more beautiful woman in the world than Nora Sutherlin? Even after driving all day, and wearing nothing fancier than jeans and a tight white T-shirt over those amazing breasts of hers that haunted his waking dreams, and her thick black hair back in a ponytail and with her eyeliner smudged and her lipstick fading… Behind that outer layer that drove him wild with one look was her mind, her sense of humor, her spirit no one could crush—not even Søren.

Damn. No other word for Nora Sutherlin. Just *damn*.

"Okay. One week," she promised, opening her eyes.

"Good. Think you can behave yourself for one week?"

"Probably not. But I'll try. For your sake."

"Thank you."

"No problem," Nora said, heading toward her car. "I mean, really…not even I could cause any trouble in a week, right?"

NORTH
The Past

For two weeks, Kingsley did nothing but watch Stearns. He went to class, he ate his meals, he pretended to befriend the other boys...but everything he did was a mere ruse, a mask, misdirection. To make up for his behavior on his first day at Saint Ignatius, Kingsley played the saint of the school in the eyes of everyone around him. But he existed solely for Stearns, solely for sin.

But Stearns wasn't playing along.

"Aristotle," Father Robert intoned as his broken piece of chalk squeaked on the blackboard, "had a rather unusual idea about the mind, about consciousness. He thought that the seat of consciousness was the heart. The brain was a mere cooling factory—ventilation. Interestingly, the ancient Egyptians also thought the brain was a pointless organ while the heart itself was the seat of soul and thought. Modern science tells us this is wrong. But what does Jesus have to say?"

In the back of his mind, Kingsley knew the answer to this question. He'd never gone to church consistently as a child. But sometimes his mother would take him. A nearby Catholic church had one service in English for all the American expats like her. She'd go not to worship God so much as to bask in her first language for an hour. Kingsley enjoyed those times alone with his mother. His sister, Marie-Laure, never could get out of bed before noon on the weekend. His father, a proud Huguenot, refused to step foot in a Catholic church. So Kingsley had her all to himself. Nothing made him happier even as a small child than having a woman's complete attention. Although sometimes he had paid attention to the priest and the readings. And something in one of those readings had stuck with him even so many years later. Something about the mind...

The classroom remained silent. Kingsley picked up his Bible and started to flip through it. Maybe if God was on his side, he'd find the page, the verse. Stearns was also in this theology class, sitting off to the side by the window—the coldest seat in the class. He'd been the first to arrive. He could have sat by the fireplace, but he never did.

"No one?" Father Robert turned around and faced the classroom. "Anyone?"

Kingsley saw Father Robert glance at Stearns, who appeared to suppress a sigh.

"Matthew twenty-two, verses twenty-seven through twenty-eight," Stearns said, when it became clear no one else would speak.

"Very good, Mr. Stearns. Can you recite those verses for us?"

Recite? Kingsley stared at Stearns, who seemed the very picture of scholarly perfection. His school uniform was spotless and not a single hair on his blond head was out of place. No matter how hard Kingsley tried, he couldn't help but appear tousled and rumpled. Father Henry teased him about always looking as if he had just crawled out of bed—if only.

Without opening his Bible, Stearns opened his mouth.

"Jesus said to him, 'You must love the Lord your God with all your heart, with all your soul and with all your mind.' This is the greatest and the first commandment."

"Very good, Mr. Stearns. And what does this verse have to do with our discussion of the mind and the heart?"

"Jesus makes a distinction between the mind and the heart and the soul. They are separate entities."

Separate entities? Kingsley's eyes widened at Stearns's words. Who was teaching the class?

"Is this proof that the mind and heart and soul are completely separate and have nothing to do with each other?" Father Robert continued. He waved his hand at the ten students in the class, as if trying sweep answers out of their mouths. None were forthcoming.

"Mr. Stearns?"

Stearns sat up an inch straighter. "Not necessarily. The baptismal formula that decrees to baptize 'in the name of the Father, the Son and the Holy Spirit' was used as proof by the First Council of Constantinople that while the Trinity contained three distinct persons, they were one as well as three. When Jesus tells us to love God with our heart, soul and mind, He is telling us that they are three and one, just as the Godhead."

"Very good, Mr. Stearns. Now, if you'll turn in your catechisms…"

As the class opened their books, Kingsley could only continue to stare at Stearns. The clouds outside the window parted a moment and a ray of sunshine—not seen for days—filled the classroom with white light. Kingsley could count every single eyelash that rimmed Stearns's eyes. And until the sun hid itself behind a cloud again, Kingsley ceased to breathe.

The sun disappeared. He exhaled. Stearns turned his head and met Kingsley's unapologetic stare.

Kingsley knew he should look away. Politeness demanded it of him. Discretion demanded it of him. If he didn't stop staring, he had a feeling Father Robert and Stearns himself would demand it of him.

But he couldn't look away, any more than he could have looked away had he come face-to-face with God Himself.

As Peter read from the catechism, Stearns stood up and, without asking permission, left the classroom. Father Robert didn't say a word to stop him, merely continued the conversation with the other students. Kingsley's heart pounded, his hands clenched. Had he been sitting in a Judas chair he couldn't have been any more uncomfortable.

After ten seconds of trying to hold still, he got up and followed Stearns.

Once in the hall, Kingsley looked around wildly. No Stearns to be seen. Which way had he gone? Out the front? The back? Upstairs?

Kingsley had no idea why he'd been seized with this mania, this absolute need to follow Stearns. But he'd done it now, left class without permission. No going back.

He heard the ringing of footsteps on the tile floor echoing off the concrete walls. Racing toward the sound, Kingsley found Stearns pacing the foyer between the third and fourth stories, a small Bible in his hand.

Stearns stopped in his pacing and faced Kingsley. He didn't speak. Kingsley opened his mouth. Nothing came out.

"You left," he finally said, reverting to French. *Vous avez quitté.*

Vous? They were the same, students in the same school. Why did Kingsley automatically use *vous* instead of the more familiar *tu?*

"*Tu as quitté aussi.*" You also left.

Tu. Not *vous.*

"I followed you." Kingsley felt beyond foolish, stating the obvious. But he had no other words, no other reason. What could he explain? He was here because he was here. "Why did you leave?"

Stearns glared at him before turning back to his pacing.

"I'm allowed to leave."

"I know that. You're allowed to do anything you want. But that doesn't answer the question." Kingsley stared at him, dropped the English and asked again in French. *"Pourquoi?"*

"You were staring at me."

Once, Kingsley had heard some phrase about discretion and valor, something his mother had said in English. He had forgotten how it went, however. Didn't matter. He was beyond discretion now and couldn't care less about valor.

"Oui. I was."

"Why do you stare at me all the time?"

"Why do you care?"

Stearns didn't answer for a moment. Finally, he met Kingsley's eyes. "I don't know. But I do."

Had he been offered a million dollars at that moment in exchange for un-hearing those words, Kingsley would have said "Keep the money."

"You should go back to class," Stearns said, turning his attention back to his Bible.

Kingsley rolled his eyes. "Does it bother you that Father Robert treats you like that?" He crossed his arms over his chest and leaned against the wall.

Stearns turned around again.

"Like what?"

Kingsley shrugged. "I don't know. You do all the work in class. No one else answers any questions but you. He made you recite Bible verses. Recite them. Not read them. You perform for him."

After looking at Kingsley a moment, Stearns resumed his pacing and reopened his Bible.

"He's not making me perform. Father Robert loathes silence. No one here makes me do anything."

"I've noticed."

"And what is that supposed to mean?" Stearns leveled his steely gaze at him again. Something in that stare caused Kingsley's courage to falter. He took a quick breath and pushed ahead. This was the longest conversation he'd managed to have with Stearns since that first terrible day here. Even if he infuriated him, at least it would keep him talking.

"It's only…you can come and go as you please in the classes. No one else can do that. You never eat in the dining room with us, although Father Henry said it was required for us all. Curfew doesn't seem to apply to you. Why?"

"The rules are designed to keep students in line and safe. The Fathers know that if I stay up after curfew it's because I'm reading. If I leave class it's because I have other work to occupy myself. I eat with Father Aldo in the kitchen as it's the only time we have for my Portuguese lessons."

Kingsley shook his head. "No. It's different. There's more. You get special treatment here, and I want to know why."

"It isn't special treatment. I'm treated like an adult. And I've earned that. Behave like one, Kingsley, and you might earn it, as well."

Stearns gave him one last glare before brushing past him and taking the steps down.

Kingsley knew he should go back to class. He wanted to follow Stearns but something told him Stearns had met his quota of words and wouldn't be giving up any more to Kingsley today. Maybe tomorrow. Or the day after. He'd keep waiting, keep watching…. Kingsley could tell he annoyed Stearns. Not the reaction he was going for, but better than nothing.

Stearns usually walked around as if no one else in the world existed but him. To get under his skin was step one. Into his bed, that would be step two.

"King? What are you doing out here?"

Kingsley glanced over his shoulder and saw Christian coming down the hall. He and Christian had become fast friends almost by default the past two weeks. They were two of only five of the boys at Saint Ignatius who apparently had any experience with girls whatsoever. Christian also had a dirty sense of humor and the foulest mouth in school, when the priests weren't around, that is. The virgins at the school gave them looks of awe mingled with jealousy when he and Christian and a couple of the others swapped stories of girlfriends and blow jobs and brushes with furious brothers and jealous boyfriends.

"Stearns," Kingsley said, not looking Christian in the eyes. He couldn't stop staring at the steps that Stearns had disappeared down.

"Yeah, he pisses me the hell off, too. But what are you going to do about it?"

"You don't like him?" Kingsley asked, finally wrenching his attention away from the staircase.

"'Course not. What's there to like? He's smarter than all the priests put together. The kids shit bricks the second he walks in the room. He won't talk to any of us. I've gotten maybe five words out of him in four years."

Kingsley suppressed a smile. Five words? He'd just had a full five-minute conversation with Stearns. That must be some kind of school record.

"Everyone acts like they're scared of him," Kingsley offered. "Maybe that's why he doesn't talk more."

Christian half laughed and clapped Kingsley on the shoulder. "It's not an act. We *are* scared of him."

"Why? He seems…" Kingsley searched for the right word.

Safe wasn't right. Stearns seemed anything but safe. "Rational?"

"Kingsley…" Christian began, and took a breath. "I keep forgetting you're new here. Something you should know about your friend Mr. Asshole Stearns."

"Quoi?" Kingsley asked. "What?"

"Rumor has it that at his last school…he killed somebody."

NORTH
The Present

The drive from the city to Søren's sister's house in New Hampshire took approximately four hours. Søren usually grabbed every opportunity to take his Ducati out on the open roads, but Kingsley managed to talk him into riding in the Rolls-Royce with him. They needed to talk, Kingsley insisted. They needed to plan. With a skeptical tilt to his smile, Søren finally agreed. Kingsley knew full well that Søren wasn't fooled. They had nothing to talk about yet. They knew nothing yet. Kingsley simply wanted to be alone with Søren in the back of his Rolls-Royce.

"What will we tell her?" Kingsley asked as they neared Elizabeth's house. "She'll want to know why we're here."

"We will tell her the truth. You received a threatening package postmarked from Lennox. I'll watch her eyes, her face. We'll see what it betrays."

Søren sat on the opposite bench seat, staring out the window. He'd made little eye contact for the entire drive. Unusual for him. Søren seemed to delight in intense eye contact. He could read someone with a single glance—know their

motives, their plans, what they wanted, who they trusted....
As teenagers, Kingsley had thought it a great parlor trick. It
wasn't until years later, working as a jack-of-all-trades for the
French government, that he understood the root of Søren's
talent. Abused children often grew up with extraordinarily
astute abilities to judge character. It wasn't a gift. It wasn't a
parlor trick. It was life or death, a survival skill. But Søren
wouldn't look at him today. Kingsley decided to take it as a
compliment.

The Rolls pulled into the long and winding drive that led
to Elizabeth's house. Although Søren wouldn't look at Kingsley, that didn't stop Kingsley from looking at him.

"I'm fine, Kingsley," he said, giving him the barest of
glances before turning his eyes outside the window again.

Kingsley nodded toward the house. "Your mother was raped
in that house. Raped by your father."

"This is not news to me," Søren said, his voice even. "That
is, in fact, the reason I exist."

"*You* were raped in that house. By Elizabeth, with whom
we are about to have a polite chat."

"Kingsley, I said I was fine."

"I know you're fine. I know you aren't simply saying you're
fine. And that's why you alone of all the men and monsters in
this world terrify me."

"That is a lie and you know it. You and Eleanor are the only
two people in the world who aren't afraid of me."

"Tell yourself that if it helps you sleep at night."

Søren finally looked at him, looked him straight in the eyes.

"Boo," Søren said, and Kingsley could only laugh.

"No ghosts, please." Kingsley held up his hands. "There's
more than enough ghosts in that house."

"I'm not one of them." Søren sat back against the leather seat.

"Elizabeth is. She haunts that house still...or perhaps it haunts her."

"I've asked her to move. She'll have none of it." Søren shrugged elegantly. He touched his neck where his Roman collar rested against his throat—a gesture that Kingsley rarely witnessed. He knew most priests seldom wore their clericals when visiting family. With his other sister, Claire, and his niece Laila, Søren always wore lay attire. But with Elizabeth he wore his clericals and his collar. Always. Simply another part of his armor.

"Masochist, you think?" Kingsley asked, smiling. "Fitting, since her brother's a sadist."

"Possibly. Or perhaps she has something to prove to herself. That our father didn't win."

Kingsley raised an eyebrow, stretched out his legs and rested them, ankles crossed, on the seat next to Søren's knees.

"Or..."

Søren glared at him. "Or what?"

One deep winter's night thirty years ago, after Søren had bared his body to Kingsley, he'd allowed himself to bare a sliver of his soul. He'd told Kingsley of his sister Elizabeth, what she'd done to him that night when he was a boy of eleven and she only twelve. And then, after a long pause, Søren had told Kingsley what they'd done together the next night and every night after until their father had caught them in the act.

"Perhaps it's nostalgia."

Søren didn't deign to answer that with anything other than an even colder glare.

"You can't deny jealousy would make sense as a motive for this," Kingsley continued, taking his legs off the seat and sitting forward to return Søren's glare.

"Jealousy? Really?"

"Don't act so skeptical. I sent that reporter to Elizabeth to ask her questions about you. A strange woman she'd never seen before investigating her brother and what did Elizabeth do? Told her every last thing about you two."

"Elizabeth was trying to protect me."

"Or she was bragging."

"I pray for you, Kingsley."

Kingsley grinned. "Pray harder."

"It's not Elizabeth. She hates what happened between us as children even more than I do."

"Hate? Really? You know you enjoyed yourself. What did you call it, that summer you two played together? Like Adam and Eve?"

Søren fell silent for a terrible moment before answering. "I said we were like Adam and Eve...in hell."

The chauffeur opened the door and Søren got out without another word. In silence, they walked to the front door.

Before Kingsley could knock or ring the bell, the door flew open, to reveal Elizabeth standing in the vaulted foyer. Last time Kingsley had seen her, she'd looked ten years younger than her actual age. Auburn hair, violet eyes...a true New England beauty. But today she looked panicked, frantic and aged by fear.

"Thank God," she breathed. Rushing forward, she threw her arms around Søren's neck. Kingsley tensed, but Søren embraced her with the affection of a brother and nothing else. "Andrew called you?"

Søren pulled back. "No. No one called us. What is it?"

She ran a hand through her curly hair. "I even thought about calling the police," she said and Kingsley's eyes widened in surprise. Elizabeth had as good a relationship with the police as he did with reporters. Although he did recently fuck a reporter into near unconsciousness in the back of his Rolls. But that was business, not pleasure. Well...business *and* pleasure.

Elizabeth glanced back and forth between Søren and Kingsley.

"Tell me what happened." Søren spoke the words in his comforting pastor's voice, although Kingsley could detect the faintest trace of fear under that calm.

Fear? Søren? Kingsley never thought he'd live to see this day.

"I'll show you. Come with me." Elizabeth finally noticed Kingsley. "You, too, Kingsley. I don't know why you're here, but I'll take all the help I can get."

"Always happy to be of service. We are family, after all...in a way." He glanced at Søren, who said nothing to that. Elizabeth knew of her brother's brief, tragic marriage to Marie-Laure, Kingsley's sister. What she thought of it, he neither knew nor cared, but the marriage, ill-fated as it was, at least gave Søren a safe excuse to consort with the likes of him.

"I don't know if this is a family you'd want to lay claim to," Elizabeth said as she led them deep into the house toward the center staircase. At the top of the steps she turned left and guided them toward the east wing, the nursery wing.

Surreptitiously, Kingsley watched Søren's face. Every room in this house held memories of the horrors of his childhood. His mother had given birth to him in her tiny room at the end of the east wing. Out of sheer willpower, she'd labored completely in silence, not willing to let Søren's sadist of a father have the satisfaction of hearing her scream. In the library, Søren had nearly lost his life when his father had found him coupling with his sister on the floor by the fireplace.

Elizabeth led them to the last room on the left.

Søren's childhood bedroom.

She opened the door and let the state of the room speak for itself.

"Mon Dieu..." Kingsley breathed, and covered his mouth.

In this room, an eleven-year-old Marcus Stearns had fallen asleep one night and woken up inside his own sister.

In that bed, he'd lost his virginity in an act of rape and incest.

And now someone had set that bed on fire and burned it to the floor.

On the wall, written in ashes, were the words *Love Thy Sister.*

"Should Kingsley...?" Elizabeth whispered.

"Kingsley knows. He's one of two people I've told."

Wincing internally, Kingsley glanced at Elizabeth's face. Did Søren just let it slip that he had another confidant? Like her brother, Elizabeth was dangerously intelligent. Kingsley prayed she'd assumed Søren meant his own confessor. If she learned her priest-brother had seduced a girl in his congregation...the whole world would burn for it.

Elizabeth nodded. Søren only stared at the words on the wall.

"I didn't call the police," she continued. "I didn't want to explain to them about us, what that meant. But I have alarms on the doors. I always arm them at night. I even have cameras on the front of the house, the driveway. No one came up. Should I call the police? I will if you say so."

Søren slowly shook his head. "No. You shouldn't. This is beyond them."

"Then what—"

"Get out." Søren faced her and placed a hand on her shoulder. "Get out and take the boys with you, far away. Europe. Asia. Australia. Go abroad and stay on the move. Leave now."

"What's going on? Why did you come today? I found the bed like this just this morning. I sent the boys to a friend's. Been trying to decide what to do all day."

Søren looked back at that pile of ash where his bed had once stood, and didn't speak.

Kingsley answered for him. "I received a photograph in the mail, taken of the two of us in our school days. It was postmarked from here. No other identifying marks. Merely a school photo, but threatening nonetheless."

Elizabeth pulled away from the door and walked down the hallway a few steps before turning back around.

"Marcus, what's happening?" she asked, her voice low and cold.

Kingsley stiffened. No one called Søren by his birth name of Marcus...ever. He didn't allow it. And surely Elizabeth knew better, knew how much he hated being called by the name his father also bore. Either she was so distraught she'd forgotten, or so angry she didn't care.

Søren looked at her and exhaled. "I don't know, Elizabeth."

"You're lying to me. You know more than you're telling me."

"I do know more than I'm telling you. But I am not lying. I truly do not know who is behind this. Tell us everything *you* know."

Shaking her head, she turned her back to them. "I have. I woke up this morning. I got out of bed. I noticed a strange smell in the house. I followed it. I checked every room. I came to this one last. I try to never go in here. You know that."

Her brother nodded. Kingsley didn't want to imagine what Søren felt, standing in the doorway to this room. He'd paused on the threshold like a film vampire, unable to cross without an invitation. No invitation came.

"I opened the door. I saw the bed, the words on the wall. I nearly vomited. Someone knows about us, about what happened. I racked my brain for anyone who could know. My mother is dead. Our father. Who does that leave? I told that reporter about us. But surely—"

"I know Suzanne," Søren said. "Not only wouldn't she do this, she couldn't. She's in Iraq right now."

"That's it. And you say Kingsley knows." Elizabeth pointed his way. "Who else? You said he was one of two people you'd told. Who was the other?"

Søren's jaw clenched almost imperceptibly. But Kingsley noticed.

"No one who would tell."

"Are you sure about that?" she demanded.

"I'd stake my life on it."

"Then that's it." She lifted her hands into the air before laying them on her face. "I just can't imagine who or why... Kingsley."

"Oui?"

"You know. Have you told anyone?"

It took all of Kingsley's self-restraint not to level a look of utter disgust at her. He'd been a spy for the French government. A spy and so much more. Idle gossip could have gotten him killed in those days. He knew to use his mouth for activities other than gossiping.

"I have a reputation for having a tongue that gets around, *ma chèrie*. But not for talk. Your secret is safe with me. The only person I have told has been dead for thirty years."

Elizabeth shook her head and exhaled. "Of course. I'm so sorry. This is the panic talking."

"Pack, Elizabeth," Søren ordered. "You're wasting time. We'll learn nothing staring at each other. Kingsley and I will find out what's going on. Call me in a month. I'll let you know if it's safe to come back. Tell no one where you're going. Not even me."

She stared at them both a moment longer before turning and nearly running to the other wing of the house.

Kingsley opened the bedroom door again and studied the carnage. Nothing at all remained of the bed. He couldn't even grasp how the perpetrator had managed to burn only the bed and leave nothing else damaged. Such a conflagration should have burned the house down. Ashes on the floor. Ashes on the wall. Nothing else out of place.

Love thy sister.

It sounded almost biblical. Love thy neighbor. Love the Lord thy God. What did it mean? Was it an order? Or a signature?

Love, Thy Sister.

The rest of the room remained untouched. As a child Søren had sat at that small ornate desk and practiced his English. As a quiet form of revenge, his mother had taught him Danish but not English. When his absentee father discovered his five-year-old bastard son didn't understand a word of English, Søren's mother had been sent back to Denmark. And every language but English had been banished from the house. Kingsley sometimes wondered if that act had been the root of Søren's obsession with learning languages.

Next to the desk sat a bookshelf. On it were many classics of children's literature in beautiful leather-bound editions, very likely worth a small fortune in their mint condition. Mint condition because young Marcus Stearns had never touched the books, never cracked the covers. He'd read the Bible as a child. Shakespeare, Milton. No George MacDonald or C. S. Lewis. Only Lewis Carroll's books had gotten Søren's attention at all. Considering Carroll's obsession with young Alice Liddell, and a young Eleanor Schreiber's obsession with the books, it seemed rather fitting.

Next to the bookshelf was the window that looked out on

the rolling manicured lawns. A small wooded area bordered the back of the house. Søren had confided to Kingsley years ago that he and Elizabeth would often take their activities into the woods, far from the prying eyes of the household staff. There they were, just two children playing in the forest. So innocent. So bucolic and pastoral. If only the maids had known what passed between them behind the veil of those trees.

"The trees…" Kingsley said, gazing out the window onto the lawn.

"What of them?" Søren asked, still steadfastly refusing to cross the threshold and enter his old room.

"Whoever got into your room came from the trees." Kingsley stood at the window and pointed. "He couldn't have come through the doors. Elizabeth keeps them locked and alarmed. Had to come in the window. To avoid the cameras, he must have come through the woods. No other logical possibility." Kingsley looked back at Søren. "Shall we?"

Søren didn't answer. He stepped from the threshold back into the hall. Kingsley followed him down the stairs and out the rear door. They strode across the lawn in silence.

"I can go look alone if you prefer," Kingsley offered. "I know this isn't your favorite place."

"It's in the past, Kingsley. All in the past. If Elizabeth can stomach living here, I can certainly survive a day on the premises."

"When did you come here last?"

"My father's funeral…years ago."

"Did you go into your room then?"

"Yes. My father was dead. It seemed a fitting celebration."

They stopped speaking when they entered the copse of trees adjacent to Søren's old bedroom window. The forest ground did seem recently disturbed, but with Elizabeth's two sons living in the house, there was no telling if it had been done by them or the perpetrator.

The two men wandered a few minutes through the woods until they came to a clearing. Kingsley saw footprints in the dirt, small ones. Most likely Andrew's—Elizabeth's eleven-year-old son. They could belong only to a boy or a very petite woman.

Kingsley gazed up at the trees and breathed in the scents of the forest.

"Pine..." he murmured. With a deep inhalation, he took in another lungful of the clean, sweet air. Closing his eyes, he became sixteen years old again. He'd been scared that day in the forest, more scared even than today. And out of fear he'd run deep into the woods. He'd run then not to get away, but only to build the anticipation, to delay the inevitable. And to save a little face. He'd wanted it to happen, but there was no reason for Søren to know quite how much. But then...he'd been caught. He could still feel that iron grip on his neck, those fingers against his throat. The hard forest floor biting into his back and the mouth at his ear.

"Kingsley, really."

Laughing, Kingsley looked at Søren. "I can't help myself. The memories are too potent."

"Try," Søren said, although Kingsley could see the hint of a smile on his lips.

"Do you never think of it?" Kingsley asked, leaving large bootprints in the marshy soil as he strode toward him. "That night in the woods at school? That day changed us both, changed everything."

"No good will come of us discussing this, as you know. The past must stay in the past."

Kingsley shook his head. "*Non*. The past will stay in the

past unless it doesn't want to. Something in your past doesn't want to stay there."

"What do you mean?"

"It was Eleanor's file that was stolen, out of the thousands of files I have. It was a photograph of you and me that I received in the mail. And it was Elizabeth's house that was broken into and defiled. Eleanor, Elizabeth and me... What do we all have in common?"

Søren glanced down at the prints on the ground. Right next to Kingsley's large bootprint was a much smaller bare footprint, lined up side by side.

From there Søren looked up to the heavens and closed his eyes. Kingsley said nothing and let him pray.

Slowly, Søren exhaled and opened his eyes.

"Me."

SOUTH

For the second time that night, Nora's jaw hit the ground and stayed there.

"Wes."

"Nora?"

"Seriously?"

"What?"

"You said you stayed in the guesthouse."

"This is the guesthouse."

"It's bigger than my house in Connecticut."

"We have a lot of guests."

Nora dropped her bag in the foyer and gazed around. The guesthouse looked nothing like the main house, but was no less grand in its own smaller way. The rough stone exterior masked an exquisite interior replete with plush tan and black furniture, well-matched and comfortable. Nora counted two stories, although she sensed a basement lurking underneath them. One entire wall in the living room consisted of a massive stone fireplace that climbed all the way to the ceiling.

"Wesley, this is a little ridiculous. What is this place?"

"You wouldn't believe me if I told you."

"Tell me anyway."

"These are the old slave quarters. Refurbished, obviously."

Nora's eyes went wide. "Are you serious?"

He nodded. "Kentucky was a slave-holding state. We didn't secede during the Civil War so the Emancipation Proclamation actually didn't apply to us."

"You're telling me that you live in actual slave quarters? Actual slaves lived in this house?"

Wesley grimaced. "Well…if you can calling it living."

Nora gazed around and nodded in approval. "Kinky."

"Come on. I'll show you your room."

"Is it a slave room?"

"Probably."

"Are you going to beat me and make me change my name to Toby?"

"How racist are you, Nora?"

"My lone female friend is Haitian, Wes. We like to watch *Roots* together and chug our vodka every time someone says Toby."

"That's it. Motel 6 time."

Laughing, Nora threw her arms around Wesley again and pulled him into a hug. She couldn't seem to stop doing that. The reality of him still shocked her. Fifteen months apart and suddenly…here he was right in front of her. In her arms. All six feet of his beautiful, twenty-year-old body. Nora sighed against his shoulder and basked in the warmth of him, the scent of him.

"Summer…" she whispered as she inhaled deeply. "You always smell like summer. Did I ever tell you that?"

Wesley chuckled and Nora smiled when his chest vibrated with the sound.

"You have. You told me that the first night I stayed at your house. You were out on the back porch sniffing the air. You said it smelled like…"

Nora looked up at him. "Søren."

Wesley nodded. "Yeah. That guy."

"You met him. Finally. What did you think?" Nora pulled away and sat on the back of the couch.

"I think he's too tall."

She crossed her legs at the ankles and smiled. "You can tell me the truth. There is no horrible thing you can say about him that I haven't already heard or already thought and probably already said to his face."

"Fine, then. I think he's an asshole. He's arrogant and cold, and he really truly believes you are his property. You get that, right? I know you kinky types like to play the property game. 'He's my slave.' 'She's my pet.' It isn't that. He thinks he owns you. A hundred and fifty years ago, you'd be staying in this house when it was real slave quarters, and he would rape you and whip you whenever he felt like it."

"Probably." She didn't argue, couldn't argue. "Good thing it's the twentieth century, right?"

"Twenty-first."

"He's not a bad person. He isn't. He is, in fact, the best man on earth, not that anyone ever believes me when I tell them that."

Wesley exhaled slowly. Nora cocked her head and smiled at him. She wasn't sure if he saw the smile and she didn't care. She just couldn't look at him without smiling. That face of his, so sweet and handsome. Those sweet eyes. That goddamn too-long hair she was going to cut the second he let his guard down.

"I'll say one nice thing about him," Wesley finally said. "He did let you come with me."

Nora swallowed. "There was no letting me. Wes, just the

thought you were within a hundred yards of me...no army in this world or the next could have stopped me from getting to you."

She met his eyes and saw the surprise in them. The surprise quickly changed to something else.

Wesley took a step forward. Then another. Nora didn't make him take the third step. She stood and reached out for him and was in his arms once again. But this time no one stopped them when his lips crashed down onto hers. He tasted like summer and his touch burned her body like the sun.

His tongue sought hers with such tentativeness she nearly giggled. Poor kid. He had no idea how much he could give her, how much she would take from him. Digging her hands into his too-long hair, she pulled them even closer together, sighed into his mouth and rejoiced silently when Wesley took the hint. His hands slid down her back and cupped her bottom gently. The intimacy of his touch resonated deep within her. Some part of her had missed this...whatever it was, this tenuousness in him, this respect she felt in his hands, on his lips. He was careful with her. That was it. He touched her as if he worried he'd break her.

She'd never been with a man who hadn't wanted to break or be broken by her.

This would take some getting used to.

"You're so beautiful," Wesley whispered in her ear. "I haven't stopped thinking about you since the second we broke up."

He wove his hands into her hair and held her to his chest.

Okay, she was already used to this.

"I missed you, too. I know you might not believe that, but I missed you every damn day. I..." Nora held on to Wesley as if her life depended on it, and in that moment she thought it might. "I love Søren. I won't lie to you. You don't get what we have, and that's fine. Very few people do. But when I was with you… Wesley, I liked who I was when I was with you. You make me a different person, a better person. And then you were gone and that Nora was gone, too. I missed you, yes. So fucking much. But I missed who I was with you just as much."

Wesley kissed the top of her head. Taking her by the shoulders, he stared down at her.

"There's only one Nora Sutherlin—the smart, funny, sweet, silly running-around-in-penguin-pajamas Nora Sutherlin who cares about writing and me and getting in two naps a day. The Nora you were with me was the real Nora, is the real Nora. Not the sadist Nora. Not the infamous Nora. Just… my Nora. If I don't do anything else this week, I will convince you of that."

"Good luck." She smiled at him through tears. "That's going to take a lot of convincing."

"Then I better start right now."

"It's kind of late. Bedtime, kiddo."

Wesley cupped the side of her face and brushed a tear off her cheek with his thumb.

"You're right. It is late." His hand moved from her face to her neck and down to her waist. His fingers hesitated only a moment before digging into the fabric of her T-shirt and starting to pull it up. "Let's go to bed."

Nora inhaled in shock and almost coughed. "Really?"

Wesley nodded and grinned.

"Really. Seriously. And I need you to believe that, 'cause I'm not going to be able to get this off of you without a little cooperation on your part."

"Oh, yeah. Sorry." Nora lifted her arms and let Wesley pull her shirt off. She stood in front of him in the living room in her jeans and a black bra. She felt grimy from driving, exhausted, sore…and so turned on she could scarcely see straight. Reaching up, she unbuttoned the top button on Wesley's wrinkled French-blue oxford shirt. "You know, I've always loved this color on you. Don't know if I ever told you that."

"You did once," he said, running his hands up and down her arms. His fingertips on her suddenly bare skin sent shivers through her entire body. "Two years ago. That's why I wore it."

"You bought a French-blue shirt just to wear for me? Not even knowing if you'd see me again?"

"No." Wesley dipped his head and kissed her quickly on the lips. "I bought five of them."

Nora didn't speak. She'd lost all power to. All she could do was keep unbuttoning. With each open button she pushed a little more of his shirt off his shoulders, until it came down his arms and hit the floor.

"Looks even better there than on you," she said.

"I think all your clothes will looking amazing on the floor."

Nora kissed his bare shoulder. "Let's go find out."

She reached for his hand and started to drag him toward the stairs. But he yanked her to him instead and lifted her in his arms.

"You've got to be kidding, Wes. I weigh a lot more than I look."

"Yeah, you do. What's up with that?" he asked as he carried her to the steps.

"Muscle. Pure muscle. And a pretty big ass."

"Perfect ass." He slapped it awkwardly and Nora giggled with luxurious, decadent happiness.

"You're really going to carry me up the stairs? That's so *Gone with the Wind*."

"Never saw it." Wesley mounted the wide, carpeted stairs.

"It's a classic," she chided. "Civil War stuff. Big dresses. Overacting. Hot nonconsensual sex."

"It's also four hours long. I got stuff to do."

They arrived at the top of the stairs without incident.

"What stuff do you have to do that's more important than watching the most legendary movie about the South ever filmed?" Nora asked as Wesley used his foot to push open the door to his bedroom.

He half laid, half threw her onto the bed, which was dressed in red-and-white sheets, and Nora sank deep into the covers.

Wesley met her eyes and slipped a hand into her hair. "Well, tonight I need to make love to you."

Nora's hands went momentarily numb at his words. The sweetness of them coupled with the look in his eyes crashed over her like a wave.

"Good excuse." She ran her palms over his bare shoulders. He had such beautiful arms, such young, supple skin. For a moment she actually felt self-conscious of her thirty-four-year-old body.

"What?" he asked as she swept her fingers through his long, dark blond hair. "What's wrong?"

"Your hair."

Grinning, Wesley shook his head. "I'll get it cut tomorrow. I swear."

"Good. But that's not it. You don't have a single gray hair."

Wesley rolled his eyes. "Neither do you, Nora."

"Yeah, and I pay three hundred dollars every six weeks to keep it that way."

For a moment his smile faltered. "I didn't know you colored your hair."

She shrugged. "Have to. Trademark black hair. Not trademark black-with-more-gray-than-I'd-care-to-admit-to hair. I'm thirty-four. You know that, right?"

"Of course I know. I don't care about our age difference. I was just… I didn't know you colored your hair, is all. Can you go red next time? I have a thing for red."

Nora grinned. "How about we trade? I'll get blond hair and you can go black."

"Would it bring out the brown in my eyes?" he asked, and playfully batted his eyelashes.

"Don't do that," she teased. "You look like you're having a seizure."

"Oh, sorry." Wesley's eyelashes started behaving themselves again. "Where were we? I think we missed talking to each other so much, it's getting in the way of the…you know. Not talking."

"We don't have to do this tonight. If you're tired or if you want to talk… I'm not leaving you. I'm here. I'm with you. I don't care if your dad already hates me. I've been hated by the best. I can take it."

"No. I want to do this. I've wanted to do this since the day I saw you at Yorke."

Nora pressed her lips to the hollow of his throat.

"Okay. We can do this. If you've been waiting for two years now…"

"Two years? I've been waiting twenty." Wesley grinned sheepishly at her.

For the third time that night Nora's eyes went wide with shock and her mouth dropped open in surprise.

She pushed back against the bed and scrambled into a sitting position.

"Nora…what?"

"Wesley? You're *still* a virgin?"

NORTH
The Past

Maine. Kingsley hated Maine. The weather, the people, the absolute lack of…anything. Anything at all worth living for. Hated it. Loathed it. Could find nothing redeeming about the place at all.

So why could he not stop smiling lately?

Spring came early that year. The snow began to melt and the browns and greens of the forest floor proved their resilience again. After one week of not winter, spring fever hit the school and the entire student body—all forty-seven of them—poured onto the one flat patch of ground, bringing with them baseballs and footballs.

Footballs? Kingsley rolled his eyes. He would show these stupid American boys real football. From under his dorm bed, he pulled out his soccer ball and took it to the lawn. With the other boys tossing Frisbees and American footballs back and forth to each other, Kingsley stood alone off to the side and started juggling the ball with his knees. For fun he'd switch legs, switch from knee to ankle, left to right, and then back again. When a few minutes passed and the ball hadn't stopped, hadn't fallen to the ground, he began to acquire an audience. The audience of fellow students started to tease him, chide him, as they tried to break his concentration. But Kingsley could do this, had done this trick for over an hour once. For some reason he thought better when juggling the soccer ball. His mind cleared and everything he worried about disappeared—his parents now gone, his grandparents elderly and worried about him, his sister, Marie-Laure, a struggling ballerina in Paris. She wrote him letters constantly, tearstained letters he could hardly bear to read. Her grief, her desperation...she swore she'd go mad if she couldn't see him again soon. He almost believed her.

But when alone with the soccer ball, she and everyone else disappeared.

Almost everyone else.

One face refused to dissipate from Kingsley's mind. One infuriatingly handsome face that he noticed out of the corner of his eye, watching him along with every other boy at the school. Unlike the others, Stearns didn't catcall him or do anything to break his focus. But the eyes alone, that simple stare of his, nearly caused Kingsley to drop the ball.

Left knee. Right knee. Right knee. Left knee.

Kingsley kept bouncing, kept breathing.

Just to elicit an "ohhh" from the audience and maybe to impress Stearns a little, Kingsley popped the ball into the air and bounced it off the top of his head and back to his knee. He popped it up again and let it rest a second on the back of his neck before sending it up again and back to his knee.

Right knee. Right knee. Left knee. Left ankle. Right knee.

"So can you actually play soccer, King?" Christian asked. "Or do you just play with your balls all day."

"I can play," Kingsley said without elaborating. He could do more than play. Back in Paris, he'd been the best in the school. He'd already been scouted by the Paris Saint-Germain Football Club and had every intention of joining them as soon as he came of age. But that was before the accident, before Maine. "The problem is, no one else here can play against me."

"Sorry. We're all Americans," Christian teased. "We play real football."

Kingsley laughed. Left ankle. Right ankle. "You should be sorry. I had an entire team on me once trying to keep me from the goal. Still made it."

"Really?" Derek demanded. "A whole team?"

"Felt like it," Kingsley said, grinning. "But what does it matter? None of you know how to play. So I'll just play with myself." He winked at Christian and for a few minutes the conversation was peppered with nothing but masturbation jokes.

Right knee. Right knee. Right knee. Left.

Oohs. Ahhs. Teasing. Laughter.

"I know how to play."

In the shock of the silence that followed, Kingsley dropped the ball.

The twenty assembled students collectively turned their heads toward Stearns.

"You can play soccer?" Kingsley picked the soccer ball up off the ground. Stearns's words had stunned everyone so thoroughly that not a single person teased Kingsley about dropping the ball after nearly ten minutes of juggling.

"I went to school in England." Stearns slipped off his jacket and started to roll up his sleeves.

Kingsley could only stare at him, at his forearms he slowly unveiled with each turn of his cuff.

"But…you play piano." Kingsley had no idea what that meant, only that he'd assumed a musician could not also be an athlete.

Stearns didn't answer. He crossed his arms over his chest and waited. Everyone remained silent. Kingsley could feel the tension, the waiting expectation in the air. He didn't know what to say, what to do. Stearns raised an eyebrow, and in his steel-gray eyes, Kingsley noted something he hadn't seen before—amusement. Not only did Stearns clearly know how uncomfortable he made Kingsley, but he enjoyed it, too. The amusement annoyed Kingsley. Beyond annoyed him, it pissed him the hell off. Who was this guy who delighted in making people uncomfortable? What kind of sadist was he?

Stearns raised his blond eyebrow a millimeter higher. A smile played upon the corner of his perfect lips.

"School in England, *oui?*" Kingsley asked.

"Oui," Stearns said. The eyebrow inched even higher. The smile spread over his entire mouth.

"That would explain your pretentious accent."

A gasp rippled through the crowd. Kingsley realized he must have been the very first student to ever talk back to Stearns. If only, perhaps, because Stearns never seemed to talk to anyone.

"And who are we to talk pretentious accents?" Stearns asked, employing an exaggerated faux French accent. The accent sounded just like Kingsley's natural way of speaking. He could speak English without his French accent, but it exhausted him so he seldom bothered trying. Especially since girls swooned over his French accent. Too bad Stearns seemed immune to its charms.

"Très bien," Kingsley said. "Can you play as well as you talk?"

"We can find out. Drop the ball." Stearns took a step forward.

"We don't have a field."

"Make one up."

Kingsley glanced around. They really didn't need a field, as they didn't even have teams. With two players all they really needed was a goal.

"The trees…" Kingsley nodded toward two trees at the end of the field. "That's our goal. I'll try to score. You try to stop me."

"You said you scored with an entire team on you. Surely you can score against only me."

"Bien sûr." Of course he could. Offense had been his forte.

"Then drop the ball." Stearns took another step forward. The assembled students took a step back.

Kingsley couldn't believe quite believe this was happening. The entire school watched in awed silence.

He dropped the ball.

At first Kingsley was afraid he'd been conned. Stearns didn't move a muscle, only stared at him. Kingsley lifted his left foot in readiness to kick the ball.

Stearns beat him to it.

The ball sailed across the field, and out of instinct and training, Kingsley went after it. Stearns stayed right next to him, right next to the ball. Kingsley thought this game would be a lock. No pianist, no matter how tall or intimidating, should be able to give him any competition. But Stearns had the longer legs, the concentration and some incredible athletic ability of his own. Shoulder to shoulder they ran down the field. Just when Kingsley thought he had control of the ball, Stearns would kick out his foot and take possession again. Kingsley had never played with someone so aggressive before—aggressive and calm. A terrifying combination. Terrifying but also exhilarating. He'd never been this close to Stearns before. He could hear his breathing—loud but slow. He could smell the scent of his skin—winter tinged with heat. In the middle of such a vicious volley for the ball, there was no reason Kings-

ley should notice that Stearns had unusually dark eyelashes
for having such pale blond hair. But he noticed. He noticed
everything.

They neared the two trees they'd declared their goal. Kingsley swept his foot out, got the ball back and with one elegant kick let it soar toward the trees. No stopping it now. He
started to smile.

But Stearns went into high gear. His long legs outpaced the
ball's high, arching flight, and with his hands outstretched, he
caught it before it could pass between the trees.

The assembled crowd exploded into impressed laughter and
cheers. Kingsley could only stare at Stearns, who held the ball
in one hand, quietly smiling.

"You can't be goalie and defender, too." Kingsley glared
at him.

"Why not? You didn't set any rules. You simply named
the goal and told me to stop you from getting the ball there.
Done."

"It's not fair."

"Then we'll do it again."

Stearns dropped the ball and bounced it on his ankle and
then to his knee.

Right foot. Right foot. Right ankle. Right foot.

Kingsley said nothing, only watched. Stearns wasn't just
good at handling the soccer ball, he was as good as Kingsley himself.

"No," he said. "I don't want to play anymore."

"Because you lost the point?" Stearns asked, kicking the ball
back into the air and catching it with one hand. Every move
he made seemed designed to dazzle with the sheer effortless-
ness of it. Kingsley could make magic on a soccer field, but
he had to work his ass off for every point. Stearns had barely
broken a sweat.

"Because there is no point. You'll play however you like and win no matter what I do."

"Possibly. But if you set the rules, I'll follow them."

Kingsley shook his head, snatched the ball out of midair and started for the dorm.

"New rule—find someone else to beat."

Kingsley left the field with all eyes on him as he departed. But he didn't care about them. He only cared that Stearns watched him. Kingsley didn't even know where his burst of anger had come from. Stearns was right—Kingsley hadn't set any rules. But still, Stearns infuriated him. He was perfect. Kingsley had never met anyone smarter, more handsome, more talented.... He seemed unreal, like an angel or some sort of mythical creature. Kingsley loathed Stearns for it, for his beauty, his perfection...loathed him, desired him, ached for him all at once. The anger on the field—it hadn't been anger at all, Kingsley realized, as he reached the dorm room and collapsed onto his bed. It was frustration.

The frustration worsened as the minutes passed and Kingsley replayed the entire scenario in his mind, while he gazed up at the ceiling of the dorm room and counted the cracks in the plaster. It could have been his chance to finally get close to Stearns. After all, Stearns never spoke to anyone but the priests, never consorted with any of the other students. Rarely if ever did he speak to a classmate unless the brave soul spoke to him first. And here Stearns had voluntarily joined him for some soccer. And Kingsley had ruined it.

"You're good."

Kingsley turned his head toward the source of the voice. Stearns stood in the doorway of the room.

Shrugging, Kingsley looked back up at the ceiling. His heart pounded in his chest, his breath quickened. He forced himself not to think about the reasons why.

"So are you. You played a lot in England?"

Stearns stepped into the room and came toward Kingsley's bed.

"I did. But I haven't played in a long time. I was ten when I left that school."

Groaning, Kingsley sat up and crossed his legs. "This is why everyone hates you, you know. Because you're so damn perfect. You haven't played soccer in seven years and you're better than me. I was scouted by the Paris Saint-Germain. That's a professional team."

Stearns didn't say anything at first. Kingsley waited and stared.

"Everyone hates me?"

He didn't sound hurt when he asked the question, but Kingsley immediately wanted to go back in time and take it back. He wanted to take everything back—the display of temper on the field, the angry words, the frustration that drove him closer and closer to the breaking point every day.

"Non, pas du tout," Kingsley said, exploding into a flurry of French. For some reason, he felt only in French could he apologize effusively enough. "No one hates you. I just said that out of...well, I don't hate you. I just *wish* I hated you."

Stearns came even closer. He sat on the bed opposite Kingsley.

"Why do you wish you hated me?" Stearns leveled a stare at him and Kingsley once again noted the dark lushness of his eyelashes and how they made his gray eyes seem even more impenetrable.

Kingsley sighed. He dropped the soccer ball on the floor between them. Gently, he toed the ball and let it roll toward Stearns. Stearns set his foot on top of it to hold it stationary.

"What are you?" Kingsley asked, not knowing what he meant by the question, but needing the answer.

Stearns seemed to understand the question even if Kingsley didn't. He sighed and tapped the ball so it gently rolled toward Kingsley.

"Father Pierre, the priest who taught me French, he had a theory about me."

"Was it that you're the Second Coming of Christ? If so, I've already heard that one."

Stearns said nothing, only glared at Kingsley with his lips a thin, disapproving line.

"I'm sorry. Seriously, tell me his theory. I want to know."

"Father Pierre had a photographic memory. He had the Bible committed entirely to memory—French and English. He could recall nearly everything he'd ever read decades after one glance. Amazing."

"So you have a photographic memory?"

Stearns shook his head. "No, not at all. It's different for me. If I do something once, do it well, I know how to do it…completely, almost intuitively. If I kick a soccer ball, my body understands the game. I learned the scales on the piano and somehow knew how to play. Father Pierre believed I have photographic muscle memory."

"Football involves your feet. The piano your hands. Father Pierre's theory doesn't explain how you're so good at languages." Kingsley tapped the ball and sent it back to Stearns.

"But it does. The tongue is a muscle."

Stearns said the words simply. Of course. Of course the tongue was a muscle. But the implications of the words… That Stearns could use his tongue once for something—a kiss, perhaps—and would forever know the perfect way to kiss…

"I lied," Kingsley said softly. "I do hate you."

Stearns only smiled again. "Why?"

"You…" Kingsley stopped. "I think about you too much."

"That is a problem." Stearns rolled the ball to him once more.

"*Oui. Une grande probleme.* I should be thinking about so many things…school, my sister in Paris, my parents, Theresa, Carol, Susan, Jeannine…"

"Who are they?"

Kingsley smiled. "Girlfriends."

Stearns eyes widened slightly. "All of them?"

Nodding, Kingsley answered, "*Oui.* Or were. Before I came here. They write me letters, though. Wonderful terrible letters. I could sell those letters at this school and make enough money to pay my own tuition here." Kingsley wagged his eyebrow at Stearns. "These girls…they want me. I wanted them."

"Wanted? Past tense?"

"Past tense. *Oui.* I can barely remember what they look like now. I want to believe it's because of what happened that I forgot them. But it isn't." Kingsley glanced at Stearns and then back at the floor. He barely touched the ball with his toe and the ball rolled between Stearns's feet.

"What happened to you?"

"The football team. American football, not real football," Kingsley clarified. "I had this girl—beautiful girl. And she had a brother. A very large brother. He found out we were together, that I'd taken his sweet sister's innocence…." Kingsley almost laughed out loud just saying the words. Theresa? Innocent? The girl had spread her legs for half the school before he'd gotten to her. But Theresa hadn't just spread for Kingsley, she'd fallen in love with him. And when he'd slept with another girl the next night…then she went crying to her brother.

Kingsley told Stearns the entire story…the hand on the back of his neck in the parking lot behind the stadium. The seven football players who'd surrounded him…the knife that Troy had drawn on him…the deep slash to his chest that had ultimately saved his life.

"A knife? You were cut?" Stearns cocked his head to the side and gave Kingsley a long, enigmatic look.

"Oh, *oui*. You haven't seen the scar?" Kingsley yanked his T-shirt off over his head. He moved to the other bed and sat next to Stearns. "Lovely, no?"

Angling himself toward Stearns, Kingsley displayed the wound on his chest. The gash had mostly healed, after careful stitching and treatment, but a two-inch-long white line of scar tissue still decorated the skin over his heart.

Stearns said nothing, only studied the scar. Slowly, he raised his hand and with a fingertip caressed it from tip to tip. Kingsey held perfectly still and didn't let himself move or breathe. How could he? Stearns was touching him. The words echoed in his mind: *Stearns was touching him… Stearns was…*

Kingsley leaned forward and pressed his lips to Stearns's mouth.

And for one perfect second, Stearns let him leave them there.

Once that perfect second passed, Kingsley found himself flat on his back, his hands by his head, his wrists pinned hard and fast into the mattress. Stearns gripped his wrists so tightly that Kingsley thought he heard something crack inside his hand.

"I'm sorry," he breathed. "I don't know what…"

He struggled against Stearns's viselike grip, but no amount of pushing back could free him. Stearns held himself steady overtop of Kingsley, one knee on the bed, one foot on the floor, and pushed him deeper and deeper into the mattress.

Stearns's face hovered only six inches from his own. The pain in his wrists, the fear in his heart, all threatened to send Kingsley into a panic. But underneath the panic he felt something else—a strange calm, a sense of surrender. As much as Kingsley wanted Stearns, he would be content letting him do anything to him, even kill him.

"I'm sorry," Kingsley repeated. "I—"

"Stop talking." Stearns spoke the words coldly, calmly, and Kingsley obeyed immediately. He pushed up again and Stearns pushed back down with even greater force.

"Stop moving."

Kingsley froze.

Waited.

Realized he'd never been so aroused in his entire life.

Looking up into Stearns's eyes, Kingsley noticed the pupils had dilated hugely. And Stearns's perfectly pale skin had flushed slightly. The exertions on the soccer field hadn't caused half the reaction that simply holding him down on the bed clearly did.

"You are playing a very dangerous game, Kingsley." Stearns lowered his voice as he spoke the threat, and every nerve in Kingsley's body tightened.

He remained silent as ordered. Stearns's thumb moved to press into the pulse point on Kingsley's right wrist. The touch was so surprising, so suddenly gentle, that Kingsley moaned with the pleasure of it. A soft moan, barely audible. But Stearns clearly heard it, for his hooded eyes widened once more.

"You aren't afraid of me right now." A statement, not a question, and yet Kingsley heard the question underneath the words. *Why?*

"There's nothing you could do to me now that I wouldn't want."

Stearns looked Kingsley up and down, as if he realized an alien lay beneath him instead of a person.

"What are you?"

Stearns asked him the same question Kingsley had asked him, but Kingsley had a much simpler answer.

"I'm French."

Stearns took a deep and ragged breath. Closing his eyes, he

pushed Kingsley one millimeter deeper into the bed before finally letting his wrists go.

Kingsley forced himself to sit up as Stearns strode toward the door.

"Did you really kill a boy at your last school?" he called out after him, desperate to do anything, say anything to get him to stay.

"Yes." Stearns paused in the doorway.

"What did he do?" Kingsley started to walk to the door. The look Stearns gave him stopped him in midstep.

"He kissed me."

NORTH
The Present

K ingsley couldn't take his eyes off Søren the entire drive to the airport. After what they'd witnessed at Elizabeth's house, after what they'd talked about, after what Kingsley had seen in Søren's eyes, he couldn't bring himself to look anywhere else but at his closest friend, his dearest foe. What was this madness happening to them? In thirty years, Kingsley had seen rage in Søren's eyes, lust, need, hunger, piety, even the occasional flashes of love. But never had he seen fear before, real fear. Not like he'd seen at Elizabeth's house, in the doorway of his old classmate's childhood bedroom.

"Stop staring at me, Kingsley," Søren said as he turned his eyes from the road outside the window to Kingsley's face.

"I've been staring at you for thirty years. You should be used to it by now, *mon ami.*"

Søren gave a slight laugh, which helped. He scared Kingsley.

"I suppose I should be. You don't have to come with me. This may very well prove to be a pointless trek. And I know you don't hold the fondest of memories of Saint Ignatius."

Kingsley exhaled slowly. The words were both true and a lie.

"Before Marie-Laure…" he began, and paused to steady himself. Talk of his sister troubled him like no other subject. "Before she came, everything was perfect. My fondest memories are of Saint Ignatius. I wish you believed that."

"I do believe it." Søren sighed. "I only wish you didn't."

Kingsley tilted his head. Only fearless audacity had ever gotten Søren's attention in the past. It's what had worked that day in their dorm room, when Kingsley had kissed him. Maybe it would work now.

"Does it bother you that I'm still in love with you?"

"Kingsley, really." Søren crossed his ankle over his knee.

"I am. I am that I am."

"Blasphemy will get you nowhere."

"I have given up trying to get anywhere with you. *Mais… c'est vrai.*"

"Thirty years, Kingsley. We were lovers thirty years ago."

"*Non.*" Kingsley leaned forward in his seat. He glanced to make sure the window between them and the chauffeur was completely closed. The last thing he needed was for his past with Søren to get out. The BDSM community gave great lip service to respecting the kinks of others, but he knew male submissives were often looked down upon by male Dominants. And female Dominants. And female submissives…

"No?"

"It wasn't thirty years ago. It was fourteen years ago. That was the night—"

"I remember the night." Søren cut him off coldly and Kingsley leaned back in the seat once more.

"*Bon.* I'm glad you remember. I've never forgotten that night even if you want to."

Søren looked away once more and gazed out the car window. "I did not forget. And I did not want to forget that night."

Kingsley's heart rose a notch at Søren's words. *I did not want to forget that night.*

That night…

Still a few minutes from the airport, Kingsley closed his eyes and let his thoughts fall away, fall into the past. That night… he would remember that night on his death bed.

He still recalled the icy chill that had passed through his body the day Søren confessed he'd fallen in love with a girl at his church. Kingsley had known things would be different between them once they'd reunited as adults, after ten years apart. Søren had come back from his exile with a white collar around his neck. Kingsley had returned from hell with healed bullet wounds on his body and unhealed holes in his heart. They'd been polite to each other after they'd reunited. At times even affectionate. But Kingsley's dreams that he and Søren would take up where they'd left off at Saint Ignatius's were dashed as night after night passed and Søren left him alone in his bed.

And then those words…those terrible words.

"Kingsley…I found her."

Søren had seen Kingsley's distress and reassured him that nothing would change. They had dreamed of such a girl as this, dreamed but never dared to hope she actually existed. The one girl wilder and more dangerous than the two of them put together…Søren had found her. And he would share her.

But the years passed and Søren left his Eleanor a virgin. Kingsley was driven nearly mad with longing, with hunger to be with this perfect wild creature Søren had found for them. His desire wasn't really for Eleanor, although he'd never met a woman more exciting, more intoxicating. To share her meant he and Søren would be in the same bed once again. Even if

Eleanor lay between them, Kingsley would have a chance to at least see him once again naked and beautiful and aroused.

Perhaps even touch him.

And touch him he had.

For a few months, Søren had kept Eleanor to himself. That didn't surprise Kingsley. The girl needed training, needed taming. And for all Søren's promises that she would belong to them, Kingsley knew that Eleanor would belong to the priest alone. Søren had wanted to own this girl.

He'd fallen in love with her instead. And whether she realized it or not, because of his love for her, she owned him as much as he owned her.

But then the night came that Søren brought Eleanor to the town house, to Kingsley's bed. He'd had to talk to her first. She'd been so scared to let any man but her owner touch her that the heels of her shoes had vibrated audibly against the tile floors.

Alone in the music room of his town house, Kingsley had talked to her, teased her, promised her he wouldn't harm her. And she'd finally relaxed, finally smiled. And the minute they'd entered his bedroom, she'd become the siren Søren had described to him.

"Which one of us first?" Søren had asked over Eleanor's shoulder.

And Kingsley seized the opportunity to torture her as Søren had tortured him so many times.

"Lady's choice, of course."

The glare Eleanor gave him nearly burned a hole into Kingsley. And made him want her even more.

Still angry that her owner had decided to share her with another man, Eleanor had answered, "Kingsley."

And the fun had begun.

Eleanor dropped to her knees in front of him and opened

his pants. Once she took his cock in her mouth, he immediately realized why Søren had fallen so hard for this girl. She would submit to anything. And although she protested, complained, fought back, in her soul she wanted to submit, loved to submit, needed to submit.

So Kingsley made her submit. First to his cock and then to his crop.

After the beating, Søren had taken Eleanor to the bed and tied her hands over her head. Sitting in front of her, Kingsley slid a single finger inside her and pulled forward, opening her up. And when Søren began to push into her, Kingsley left his finger inside. She'd been so wet from the shared penetration of his finger and Søren's that the fluid had dripped over his hand and stained the cuff of his shirt. He'd kept the shirt hanging in his closet...never worn again, never washed.

Then the time came. Søren lay on his back, propped up against a mountain of pillows. He pulled Eleanor—naked but for a pair of white high heels—back against his chest.

And as Søren held her in his arms, Kingsley had fucked her. Never before or since had he fucked a woman so hard or so thoroughly. She'd moaned in her pleasure, winced in her pain and closed her eyes in her ecstasy. And when her eyes shut, Kingsley looked at Søren, who looked back at him. And Kingsley knew it would happen that night.

They exhausted Eleanor after an hour and let her rest.

Wine...Søren had said he wanted wine.

No...Kingsley furrowed his brow. The fog of memory cleared. Kingsley had suggested the wine. Søren had agreed to it readily. He'd kissed his Eleanor and tucked her into bed. Side by side they'd left the bedroom.

They never got the wine.

Once out in the hallway, Kingsley felt a hand on the back

of his neck, fingers pressing into his skin. He remembered that hand, those fingers....

Søren brought his mouth to Kingsley's ear. "Stop me right now," he'd ordered, and Kingsley had suppressed his smile.

"Stop what...sir?"

"This."

And Kingsley suddenly found himself pushed against the door of one of the many guest rooms, Søren's chest pressed to his back.

"I'll hurt you if you don't stop me." Søren dug his hand into Kingsley's long hair, twisted it and bared the side of Kingsley's neck. When Søren's lips touched the throbbing vein under his ear, Kingsley knew nothing he said or did would stop either of them now.

Kingsley opened the door to the guest bedroom.

Søren closed it behind them.

"Bed," Søren had ordered, and Kingsley obeyed without question. He'd always obeyed Søren without question, and always would—in the bedroom if nowhere else.

Kingsley had learned early on about Søren's...tastes. It didn't take long to learn that the young man he'd fallen in love with at school had been broken. But broken in such a way that when he'd healed, he'd become stronger than before the break. Because of that brokenness, only inflicting pain could arouse him. Physical pain preferably, but brutal humiliation would also do. So when Søren wrenched Kingsley's arm behind his back, Kingsley knew not to suppress his gasp of pain. Those sounds—the gasps and whimpers, the sobs and tears—they were what Søren lived for. Kingsley had accepted it as a young man, understood it instinctively. It wasn't until he began to play the game himself that he understood the erotic power of inflicting pain on a lover and watching him or her accept it, revel in it, even love it.

A part of him had wanted the old affection, at least for this act. And if not affection, then at least some measure of mercy. But Søren was in no mood for mercy that night, and Kingsley hadn't had to fake his initial cry of agony at the first penetration. He'd had to bite down on the sheets to stifle his own scream. Søren had nearly wrenched Kingsley's shoulder from its socket from the sheer force of his thrusts. And after, there'd been blood, and Kingsley had savored the sight of it.

Proof. He held out his fingers toward Søren.

"You can't deny this, *mon ami*. Can you?" He brandished his bloodstained hand. "You still want me."

Søren had been standing by the door then, waiting for Kingsley to finish dressing, to pull himself back together.

"I never denied that I wanted you. I only denied taking you."

"Pourquoi?" Kingsley demanded. "Why? You take *her* every way you can, every chance you have. Why her and not me?"

Søren hadn't replied, and for that Kingsley had been forever grateful. He knew the answer, but to hear it would have broken the one last unbroken part of his spirit.

They'd returned to Kingsley's bedroom, and Søren hadn't turned on the lights. If he had, Eleanor would have seen the bleeding bite marks on Kingsley's chest, the bruises on his hips, the welt on his lower back. Kingsley had sunk into Eleanor's body and relished the ease of it, of fucking a woman so supple and so willing. But not submissive. Kingsley had seen something in Eleanor that night—a spark of violence in her eyes, a flash of rebellion and defiance. Søren thought he'd found the perfect match in her, the perfect submissive. Perhaps she was as perfect as he; surely she was as beautiful. But no submissive. Not at all. Kingsley knew a switch when he saw one. After all, he looked at one every day in the mirror.

Again and again, that night they'd taken Eleanor, until

she could barely stay awake. And even then it didn't matter. Kingsley had slid onto her unconscious body, pushed inside her and slowly thrust. She'd woken up for a moment, softly laughed and lapsed back into sleep. And Kingsley still fucked her. Anything to prove to Søren that while he'd been hurt by their interlude, he hadn't been harmed.

And in the hour before dawn, while Eleanor slept, Kingsley knelt on his hands and knees at the side of the bed. With his mouth, Kingsley showed Søren his gratitude that the priest had shared his most precious possession with him that night. Kingsley swallowed and relished the semen in his stomach. What he'd had with Søren had died once, and for one night been resurrected. The evening would not have been complete without a final communion.

Eight years later he discovered that Nora had seen it all. And eight years later it had been her he'd knelt in front of. If he couldn't have the master he wanted, he could at least serve the master's slave.

"Kingsley?"

"Oui, mon ami?" Kingsley opened his eyes.

"I don't want to know what you're thinking about, do I?" Søren asked.

"You already know." Kingsley tried and failed to mask the bitterness in his voice.

"Don't hate her," Søren ordered. "It's me who hurt you. Hate me."

The Rolls-Royce arrived at their destination—the airport, where a private plane awaited them both. The photograph of them that Kingsley had been sent…the original had been stored at Saint Ignatius, their old school. Not knowing where else to go, what else to do, Søren had decided to travel there and make discreet inquiries. Kingsley refused to let him go alone.

The chauffeur brought the car to a stop at the gate, got out and opened the door for them.

"Don't worry, *mon ami*," Kingsley said to Søren. "I do."

SOUTH

Nora made a mental note that the next time she asked someone, "Have you seen Wesley Railey?" and they answered, "He's in the stables," she would follow up with, "Which of the seventeen goddamn stables are you referring to?" For two hours she wandered from barn to barn—all of them white with elegant red trim—seeking out Wesley and not finding him. The kid knew how to hide better than she did.

Kid… Nora made a second mental note, to stop thinking of Wesley as a kid or the kid or any kind of kid. She wouldn't be hunting him through seven thousand identical stables if she could wrap her mind around the idea that Wesley was an adult now. Last night in his bed…she should have gone through with it. It's what he'd wanted, what he deserved. But she'd been so shocked by the fact of his virginity that she'd freaked out last night, like she'd freaked out a year and a half ago, the last time they'd tried having sex. Supposedly, she was the one with all the sexual experience. So why was she the one who kept getting scared?

Finally, in barn number two million and thirty-five, she found Wesley in a stall, brushing the mane of the fattest horse she'd ever seen.

"Good Lord, what are you feeding that thing?" Nora gaped at the huge stomach on the red beast.

"Other horses." Wesley didn't even look at her.

"Please tell me you're kidding." She'd heard of cows being fed other cows, but she prayed horses didn't eat other horses.

"I'm kidding. She's only got one other horse in her."

Nora sighed with relief. "Knocked up, huh?"

"Very. She's due this week. Any minute now."

Wesley ran the thick bristle brush over the mare's back and the animal shivered in obvious pleasure.

"What's her name?" Nora opened the stall door and stepped gently inside. Last thing she wanted to do was spook a pregnant horse.

"Track Beauty. Mom named her. She's our top broodmare."

Nora reached out and touched Track Beauty's nose, smiling at the feel of velvet under her fingertips.

"She is a beauty...apart from the stomach." Nora tried smiling at Wesley. He didn't smile back.

"She's Mom's baby."

"Mom's other baby?" Nora teased.

Wesley shook his head. "Not even my mom sees me as a baby anymore. That's just you."

Nora exhaled heavily. "Wes...I don't see you as a baby. Or as a kid. Or as anything other than a twenty-year-old drop-dead gorgeous guy who I adore."

"You have a weird way of showing it."

"And you have a weird way of..."

"What?" Wesley asked.

"Everything." Nora ran her hands down Track Beauty's back and over her swollen stomach. She couldn't even imagine what this poor horse felt like, carrying another horse inside her body.

"What's that supposed to mean?"

"It means…you, Wesley, are weird. You had a girlfriend, right? This Bridget person? How long were you together?"

Wesley shrugged. "A few months."

"And you didn't have sex with her?"

"No. I didn't."

"Why not?"

Wesley walked around Track Beauty and started brushing her other side. Nora rose up on her tiptoes to look at him over the horse's back.

"Wesley…why didn't you sleep with your girlfriend while you were with her?"

"I didn't want to."

"Bullshit."

"What?"

Nora glared at him. "Bull…shit. You are a straight twenty-year-old guy. And I'm guessing this chick was a babe. Yes?"

Wesley paused before nodding. "She was—is—beautiful."

Nora winced internally at the simple sincerity in his voice. *Yes, she was a babe*…wouldn't have hurt. *She was beautiful….* That hurt.

"So why not?"

Wesley ran his hands over Track Beauty's long neck. The mare turned her head and rested her nose against Wesley's stomach.

"You really have to ask?"

"Guess so, since I'm asking." Nora came around and stood next to Wesley. His body seemed taut with tension. The need to touch him nearly overwhelmed her, but she feared he'd pull away from her if she tried.

"Bridget was…" He paused and took a ragged breath. "She

was something, Nora. Even you would have been all over this girl. Woman. Twenty-seven. Like old Hollywood beautiful. What are those skirts you wear to church sometimes? The tight ones that stop right about your knees?"

"Pencil skirts?"

"Yeah, those. She wore those all the time, with these classy shirts that made her look, I don't know, kind of glamorous. She turned heads like crazy when we went out. I took her to a fundraiser…everybody there worth millions of dollars and Bridget makes maybe forty thousand a year. But no woman at that party got half the stares she did. I barely got to dance with her. She had guys falling all over her. She's smart, too. Undergrad degree in equine studies, MBA from Harvard. She'll be running a farm this big someday. Probably sooner than later. For a guy like me who's going to inherit thousands of acres of horse farm? She was the perfect woman. Mom and Dad were already planning the wedding."

Nora swallowed. Every single compliment that came out of his mouth about Bridget hit her harder than Søren with a cane in his hand.

"So what was the problem?" Nora tried to ask the question calmly, without emotion. But her voice was barely louder than a whisper.

"The problem is…" Wesley met Nora's eyes for the first time that day "…she wasn't you."

For a moment Nora tried to come up with a clever response, something to make Wesley laugh, something to break the tension. But words failed her and she stayed silent.

"I couldn't sleep with her," Wesley continued, "because she wasn't you. And I have to wonder if the reason you keep turning me down is because I'm not him."

Finally, Nora understood. Completely understood. For once in her life she knew exactly what the man in front of her felt, what he needed, what he wanted. And for once in her life, she knew exactly how to give it to him.

"No. You aren't Søren. If you were, yes, I would have had sex with you last night, like I've had sex with him a million times before. But you aren't Søren, and I could get down on my knees and thank God for that right here and now but for the huge pile of horse shit that's at my feet. One Søren is enough for this world."

Now Wesley seemed incapable of speech. She decided to take advantage of the sudden silence.

"I sleep in your bed, Wesley."

"What?"

"I sleep in your bed at my house in Connecticut. I haven't slept in my own bed since the day…since the day I went back to Søren. I haven't once slept in my bedroom. I sleep in your room when I'm at the house. I sleep in your room wearing the Kentucky T-shirt you left behind in the dirty laundry. I tried sleeping in my own bed and I just…I couldn't sleep."

"You were a twenty-year-old virgin, too. You said that was when you and Søren—"

"First of all, I was never a virgin. Having an intact hymen does not a virgin make. Go to a Muslim country. Those girls take it up the ass from their boyfriends so they can still have a hymen to break on their wedding nights. Hymen doesn't equal virgin."

"Fine. But still—"

"But nothing. And butt everything. Søren started to train me for him the day I turned eighteen. No. Stop. Scratch that. He started training me for him the day we met. He taught me to sit and stand, to perform, to obey, to serve him and his every want and need and desire. He could tell me to meet him at three o'clock outside his office with just a look in his eyes. And I'm not exaggerating, Wes. By the time we spent our first night together, I was ready for him, ready to be broken. And my God, he broke me. I was shattered and every single piece of me loved him for it. But we were together. He collared me. He owned me. I was his."

"Nora, what are you saying?"

"I'm saying that the last time I had sex with a virgin he ended up in four-point restraints and had candle-wax burns. I'm saying that I might break you, too, the way Søren broke me. But you might not love me for it the next morning. And if I shatter you, I don't know how to put you back together."

"Nora...you don't get it, do you?" Wesley cupped her face and smiled at her.

"Get what?"

"That I know being with you is a big risk. And that you're worth it."

Nora's hands clenched as tightly as her heart.

"I know how to tie knots that sailors who've spent half their lives at sea have never even heard of. I can pick locks that would stump half the cat burglars in New York. I can slice a Post-It note in half with the tip of a bullwhip. I can get any kinky man in the world to drop to his knees, kiss my feet and confess his darkest sins to me just for the pleasure of having me punish him for them. But, Wesley...I do not know who to be with somebody like you. A sweet, kind, vanilla virgin has me stumped. It's been fifteen months since the last time we tried, and I still haven't figured it out."

Wesley exhaled so heavily his breath ruffled Track Beauty's mane. The horse twitched her head in mild irritation.

"You know, if you want to know how to be with me... maybe you could just ask me?"

Nora opened her mouth, paused and closed it again. "That honestly never occurred to me."

Wesley laughed and Nora laughed. And she almost cried from the sheer relief of hearing them both laugh.

"Okay, vanilla." Nora laid her hand on top of Wesley's. Track Beauty's coat bristled underneath their twined fingers. "So tell me how to be with you."

"Not that hard to explain. You know how we were together back at your house? How we hung out and watched movies and talked and ate dinner together and all that?"

"I remember. I remember it like yesterday." Her hand slipped from his wrist to his face.

"I need it just like that, except…"

"Except?"

"Except instead of us going to separate bedrooms, we go to bed together. Can you do that?"

Nora ran a hand through his long hair. "I can try."

Wesley started to lean forward, started to kiss her, before the sound of fingers snapping loudly echoed through the stall and startled them apart.

"Come on, John Wesley. We're gonna be late."

Nora saw Wesley's father glaring at her through the stall door. He gave Wesley a dark look before walking away. "Now, J.W.," he called out.

"You can come with me," Wesley said.

"Where are we going?"

"Gotta go see a man about a horse."

Nora paused on her way out of the stall. "Please tell me you mean that literally."

NORTH
The Past

Kingsley walked in the garden outside the chapel. Rose bushes alight with red blossoms surrounded him as he wandered the cobblestone path among the flowers. The garden was Father Henry's pride. To keep flowers alive in such an inhospitable clime took constant work and tending. Every free moment he had, Father Henry could be found in the garden.

"My garden *is* my Gethsemane," Father Henry joked, and Kingsley would always smile. He never understood the joke if it was, in fact, one.

Kingsley had come here to get away from the boys in his dorm room. The coming of summer heralded the end of the school year. The boisterousness had been too much even for Kingsley. The other students couldn't wait until their parents would collect them from exile and return them to the world of girls and movies and sleeping as late as they wanted. All these things would be Kingsley's as well in two days, when his grandparents came for him. But unlike the other boys at the school, he couldn't rejoice in this.

Stearns had ruined him. Ruined everything. A summer back in civilization held no appeal. Three months he'd be without Stearns, without even a glimpse of him. Kingsley already anticipated the agony of that time apart. Every ray of yellow sunlight would remind him of Stearns's hair. Every solid gray evening sky would call to mind Stearns's eyes. Every time Kingsley touched himself, he would imagine Stearns's hands on his body instead of his own. Not that Stearns had ever touched him like that, only in Kingsley's dreams. But since that day in the dorm when Stearns had held him down, things had been different between them.

They'd stopped speaking as much. But for some reason, Kingsley felt even closer to him. Whenever he found Stearns sitting alone reading or writing, he would take his own homework and sit on the floor next to Stearns's chair. Why the floor and not the sofa, the table, another chair, Kingsley didn't know. But whenever he thought of the pad of Stearns's thumb caressing the pulse point on his wrist, Kingsley wanted to sink to his knees, sit at Stearns's feet and stay there forever.

His anguish at the prospect of so much time apart from Stearns had sent Kingsley into Father Henry's garden. He wanted to try something he'd never tried before. Perhaps it was Stearns's influence…. Kingsley has seen him in the chapel just yesterday, rosary beads in hand, as he prayed in silence for a solid hour. Kingsley knew it had been a full hour, for he'd sat three pews behind him and watched him the entire time. At one hour exactly, Stearns had risen from his seat and turned around.

"What are you praying for, *mon ami?*" Kingsley had asked.

"What I've been praying for every day since I met you," Stearns said, twisting the beads around his hand.

"And what is that?"

Stearns opened his hand to display the rosary beads he'd weaved between his fingers like a spiderweb.

"Strength."

He closed his hand again and rested it against his chest, over his heart. Stearns had left the chapel, but Kingsley had remained.

Strength. That one word had told Kingsley everything. He needed no other hints, no other words. He knew the truth now. But instead of setting him free, the truth pulled Kingsley even deeper into the enigma that was Stearns.

Strength.

It meant one thing and one thing only.

Stearns wanted him.

Kingsley's fingers balled up into a fist. Stearns had prayed for strength. So should he.

Plucking the largest, most pristine of the red roses from a bush, Kingsley held it in his hand and stared into the blossom's core.

"Assistez-moi." Help me, Kingsley prayed, falling into French. He couldn't imagine God speaking any language other than his native tongue. *"Assistez-moi, s'il vous plaît, mon Dieu."*

Kingsley opened his eyes. Standing at the edge of the garden, in the shade of a tree, was Stearns, watching him pray.

In his nervousness, the rose fell from his hand.

Stearns took a step forward.

Kingsley took a step back.

Stearns stopped.

Kingsley ran.

The school sat as an oasis in a desert of trees. Nothing but dense forest surrounded the place—forest, hills, cliffs, valleys. Kingsley usually saw it as something fearsome, threatening, a labyrinth. Now he fled into it for safety.

But the trees offered little protection. As Kingsley raced

down untrodden paths, the green-leafed branches whipped at him, stinging his skin, his face. But he couldn't stop. Behind him he heard footsteps. Kingsley could only force his legs to carry on faster, despite the pain of the branches beating him, despite the fear that nearly felled him.

He entered a clearing. The sky above had turned red with the setting sun. Darkness was coming and he would be lost here in the woods. Alone…or worse. Not alone.

He jumped and spun around as the sound of a twig cracking alerted him to the presence of another. Kingsley didn't hesitate. He took off again, racing deeper into the forest. The canopy of trees closed in on him. Dropping to his hands and knees, Kingsley crawled through a small opening, crying out when the thorns of a bush cut into his forehead. His vision turned red with blood. But he pushed on, pushed through, stood up and started running again. Or tried. But a hand came out of nowhere, grasped him by his shirt and pushed him into a tree. The bark bit into his back. In the shadows, Kingsley could barely see. He groped in the darkness, felt fabric under his hands and tore. His fingers touched something cool. He pulled and it came off in his hand. The grip on him loosened a moment, long enough for Kingsley to get his footing and flee again.

Sweat and blood poured down his face. Kingsley wiped at his eyes. As his vision cleared he discovered he held a small silver cross on a thin chain. Kingsley carried it high up the side of the mountain, the footsteps still following behind him.

In another clearing, he stopped and dropped to his knees. He could run no farther.

As he gasped for air, he heard the sound of shoes sliding over a blanket of leaves. Kingsley's fingers tightened around the cross. No matter what happened to him, he wouldn't let it go.

Neither of them spoke. Kingsley put up one last fight as

Stearns stripped him naked and forced him onto his stomach. But he didn't have the strength for anything but surrender. He groaned from the pain every small movement caused him. This wasn't how he wanted it…not here on the forest floor, broken and bloodied and terrified. But he would take this pain, this humiliation. For the communion he'd prayed for, he would take it all.

Stearns caressed Kingsley from his neck to his hip. Yes, Kingsley decided, this was exactly how he wanted it.

One arm stretched out to the east. The other to the west. He kept his fingers clenched around the cross. When Stearns pushed inside him, Kingsley cried out. Stearns covered his mouth with his hand. Kingsley bit down and nodded, thankful for the fingers against his teeth.

The pain of the penetration was beyond anything he'd ever felt in his life. The knife wound to his chest had been nothing. Nothing had hurt like this, nothing outside or in, nothing in his body or soul.

In the midst of his agony he felt Stearns's mouth on the back of his shoulder. Kingsley melted into the ground. Whether or not he survived tonight ceased to be a concern. The touch of Stearns's lips on his skin was all he'd ever needed. Complete now, he could die happy, if that was his destiny.

Time passed, but Kingsley couldn't count it. After a minute, an hour, the blood began to ease Stearns's movements into him. The pain turned not to pleasure, but something more than pleasure. A kind of ecstasy that threatened to raze him, cut him down and leave nothing left of him. But it didn't matter.

Stearns was inside him.

As the red evening turned into the black night, Kingsley rejoiced in this truth. He heard Stearns's ragged breathing… or was it his own? He didn't know, didn't care. He inhaled

deeply and smelled pine in the air. A beautiful scent. He inhaled again for another lungful.

On the merciless ground, Kingsley came with a shudder
that racked his entire body.

Stearns was inside him.

His prayers had been answered. Perhaps. Or perhaps his
prayers were being punished. *Heaven* and *hell* became mean-
ingless words to Kingsley. Heaven was now, this moment
underneath Stearns. Hell had been every moment before and
would be every moment after.

Stearns was inside him.

He repeated those words in his mind until they became the
only ones he knew in any language.

It ended, finally, after an hour perhaps. Maybe two. Or
perhaps only minutes. He felt a weight lift off of him, felt his
body empty.

Slowly, Kingsley pulled his arms to his sides and rolled onto
his back. Above him the sky screamed with stars. Beneath him
the fallen leaves stroked his skin like a blanket of living silk.

He heard the rustle of fabric, of clothing righting itself. But
he would lie here under the heavens forever, naked and bleeding and unashamed. He'd died underneath Stearns. Died and
been born again.

Something touched his face. A hand? No, a pair of perfect lips. The lips moved from his forehead to his cheek and
settled onto his mouth. The kiss lasted an eternity and ended
all too soon.

"My name is Søren."

Kingsley nodded and prepared words of his own. *"Je t'aime,"*
he replied in the language God spoke.

I love you.

NORTH
The Present

Nothing had changed. Kingsley couldn't quite believe that after thirty years, absolutely nothing had changed. The road to Saint Ignatius still wound through the most desolate, dangerous countryside he'd ever encountered outside of Europe. The trees still swaddled the school like an evergreen blanket. And every last building looked like a church.

"How long has it been, *mon ami?*" Kingsley asked Søren as they exited the back of the car Kingsley had hired to drive them to their alma mater.

"Five years, perhaps." Søren stood in the middle of the quad and looked around. "I came when they buried Father Henry."

"In his garden?"

Søren smiled. "Where else?"

"Five years…a long time."

Nodding, Søren slowly turned around and gazed up into the forest that surrounded them. "I try not to come too often. It's…uncomfortable to be here now, considering."

"*Je comprende.*" Kingsley did understand. When his father

died, Søren had inherited nearly a half a billion dollars from him. The inheritance had been his father's last chance to turn Søren away from the priesthood, knowing his son couldn't keep that kind of money and still *be* a Jesuit. So Søren gave it away. Every last penny. And Saint Ignatius benefited hugely, to the tune of nearly twenty-five million dollars. "With so much wealth, you think the school would look like a palace now."

"Father Henry put most of the money into a trust to take care of the boys who were wards of the state. There have been improvements to the facilities—subtle ones. But Father Henry never wanted the school to look ostentatious. Conspicuous displays of wealth offended him."

"Interesting opinion for a Catholic."

Søren glared at him. "We're not having the Saint Peter's Basilica argument again."

"I'm getting you a pair of red leather shoes for Christmas. Why should the Pope have all the fun?"

"I miss beating you sometimes, Kingsley. I truly do."

The two of them walked toward the main building that housed the offices of the monsignor, Father Thomas, and the other priests. Kingsley kept his eyes on the door and his mind away from the past. He'd indulged far too much in memories on the plane trip here. It was in the woods surrounding this school that the boy, Kingsley Boissonneault, had died, and the man who would become Kingsley Edge had been resurrected.

And it was here that his sister, Marie-Laure, had died, never to be reborn.

"Try not to think of her, Kingsley," Søren cautioned. Kingsley would have killed him on the spot for that bit of advice but for the almost tender concern in his voice.

"It's impossible not to. She was all I had after my parents died. The day they took me from her…"

Kingsley forced the memory back and away.

"I had bruises for weeks," Kingsley said, his fingers twist-ing into fists.

"From Marie-Laure or from me?"

Kingsley looked sharply at Søren. The priest tried every-thing to avoid talking about that night they'd become lovers. And yet now, suddenly... Kingsley composed his features. "From Marie-Laure the wounds took three weeks to heal. From you..."

"From me?"

Kingsley gave him a grim grin. "I shall tell you when they do."

Søren exhaled heavily and opened his mouth to speak. But the door of the main building opened and a man in a full cas-sock came bustling out toward them.

"Father Stearns," the priest said breathlessly as he shook Søren's hand. "I had no idea you were coming."

"So nice to see you again, Father Marczak. We're only here for a short visit. This is Kingsley Edge, a friend and another former Saint Ignatius student."

"Very nice to meet you, Mister Edge."

Kingsley shook Father Marczak's hand and nodded. He was in no mood to mask his French accent today and had no pa-tience for all the questions his accent inspired. Better to keep silent. He'd learned in his days as a spy that the less he said, the more others said to him.

"What brings you both here today? Father Thomas is at a conference and I'm afraid I'm a poor substitute."

"We're here for reasons of nostalgia only. Please don't trou-ble yourself. We simply wanted to see the school again."

"Of course. We've made some improvements recently, thanks to your generosity. New plumbing. New heating units. The roofs have been replaced on all the buildings...you can't imagine how much we appreciate—"

Søren raised his hand to silence the thanks. Kingsley knew Søren would come to the school much more often if it wasn't for all the effusive gratitude he had to deal with every time he visited.

"I'm only happy that I could help the school carry on its work. This place saved my life."

"And you saved the school."

"Then we should call it even," Søren said, and Father Marczak smiled in acquiescence.

"Of course. I'll be in Father Henry—I mean, Father Thomas's office. If you require anything, don't hesitate to find me. Feel free to roam the school. The boys love having their classes interrupted by visitors."

"Thank you, Father. Speaking of visitors, have there been any of note lately?"

Father Marczak gave them each a curious look but didn't ask for clarification. "No. Not really. A few students have visited in the last few weeks. And, of course, parents of prospective students wanting to see the school."

"None of them seemed unusual at all? Suspicious? I only ask because I received an unsigned note on Saint Ignatius stationery asking about the school."

Kingsley glanced at Søren. For a priest sworn to keep the Ten Commandments, the man could lie with the best of them.

Father Marczak shrugged. "Really, no. We did have a single mother a week ago. Asked many questions about the school— more than any of the other parents combined. Many questions about the history of the school and the students who'd graduated—what they did now, what they'd accomplished."

"Did she speak with an accent?" Søren asked, and Kingsley furrowed his brow. Where had that question come from?

"No accent that I noticed," Father Marczak said. "Lovely woman, really, if you'll forgive me for saying that."

Søren glanced at Kingsley.

"Thank you, Father. We'll be sure to see you before we leave."

Father Marczak shook their hands again and returned to his office.

"We should ask him more," Kingsley said. "What she looked like, where she said she was from…"

Søren shook his head. "Too dangerous. Either the woman he spoke to is not involved in this—and likely she isn't—or she is and would have told him enough lies that his answers would be useless."

Kingsley couldn't argue with his logic. "Then what shall we look for, *mon père?* Where shall we go?"

"The photograph of us…it would have been archived in the library."

"The library it is, then."

Inside the library Kingsley discovered that much of Søren's father's money had found its way here. Their time at Saint Ignatius, the library had been a cold, sparsely furnished space. Cheap metal bookcases had been filled with decaying religious tomes. Threadbare chairs had sat on even more threadbare rugs. But when they stepped into the room now, they could have been transported to the Vatican library. The metal bookcases had been replaced with dark oak bookshelves carved with biblical scenes and symbols. Easily four times as many books filled the shelves. Elegant sitting areas were scattered about the length and width of the building. Iron chandeliers dangled from the ceiling and sent smiling light down on the boys who sat in those expensive armchairs with books and computers on their laps.

"Oh la la," Kingsley said, laughing. "A library or a palace?"

"A library should be a palace. You do read, don't you, Kingsley? I mean, something other than your own files?"

"*Bien sûr.* I read the novels your pet writes. It pleases me to read them and see how much she steals from my world to put in hers."

"It is her world, too, need I remind you?"

"It *was* her world. And she left it."

"She'll be back. I know she will."

Kingsley smiled and sighed. "Lovely to know that I'm not the only one of us who engages in wishful thinking. Yes, she'll come back to you...the day you come back to me."

Søren said nothing else to him as they headed to the archive room. Kingsley took that as a victory.

They spent an hour digging through the student archives. Christian's other photos he'd taken of the school still remained in their boxes. Kingsley took a few pictures and slid them into a portfolio.

"What are you doing?"

Kingsley grinned. "Who knows? We could get finger-prints, *peut-être?*"

"I'd rather not get your police connections involved in this."

"Very well, then. I'll call the FBI."

Søren glared at him. Again. If he didn't stop glaring at him, Kingsley was going to kiss him right there in the library in front of fifty Saint Ignatius students. And that might raise an eyebrow or two.

"I don't see that any other photos are missing. Christian numbered all fifty of them. Ours was thirty-three. This box has one through twenty-five in it. You took twenty-six and twenty-seven from the other box. Just our photograph was gone."

"How would the thief even know to look for it?"

As soon as Kingsley asked the question, he knew the answer. He tapped the top of each box and looked at Søren.

Søren exhaled and turned his eyes to the ceiling.

"Of course," he said. "It has to have been another student. One of our classmates. How else would the thief have known about the photos?"

"A student or one of the priests," Kingsley reminded him.

"We'll go to Father Marczak and ask for the names of the students who were here with us. Maybe something will come to mind. I don't recall having any unpleasant encounters with any of them."

"You wouldn't. They were terrified of you."

"You exaggerate." Søren left the library and headed toward Father Marczak's office. Kingsley followed him to the quad, then stopped and looked up into the trees.

"I was a student here for all of two weeks when Christian told me you'd killed a student at your last school. I say 'terrified,' *mon ami,* because everyone *was* terrified. I do not exaggerate. In fact, I might be understating the situation."

"I don't even know how the story of what happened in England got out. I told one of the Fathers when I came here— Father Pierre. He acted as my confessor until he died, a few months before you came."

"He told?"

"No, he wouldn't. I would trust a priest to keep my secrets as much as I would trust a corpse."

"Perhaps your father told a priest, and a student overheard."

"Possibly. He did like to brag that his son had killed a boy. Come. Let's talk to Father Marczak."

"Non," Kingsley said, still staring into the trees. "You go hunt your ghosts. I shall go find ours."

He strolled toward the tree line with more confidence than he felt. With his first footstep into the woods, a twig cracked under the sole of his boot and the memories of the night he'd run through these very trees came back to him.

Christian had told him that Søren had killed a student at his old school in England. That knowledge hadn't scared Kingsley, it had merely intrigued him, made him desire Søren more. But that night as he ran through the woods, Søren hard on his heels, he had known real terror. And yet, as hard and as fast as he ran, in his heart he had wanted to get caught. He ran so Søren would chase him. He ran because he wanted to be taken. He ran hard and ran fast, yes. But not as hard and fast as he could have.

A rustle of leaves alerted Kingsley to a presence behind him. He didn't look back at Søren, but knew the priest followed now, as he had followed him that night.

"Why did you chase me?" Kingsley asked, still not turning around.

"Because you ran."

"Do you know why I ran from you?"

"Because you wanted me to catch you."

Kingsley laughed and didn't deny it.

"Did you know you would rape me when you caught me?"

"Are we really calling it rape?" Søren asked, his voice tinged with dark amusement.

"What else shall we call it?"

"It's hardly rape when you wanted it."

"You didn't know that at the time, though, did you?" Kingsley passed through the trees that had whipped at his flesh that night and torn his clothes. Did they remember the night as well as he did?

"You stared at me constantly, followed me everywhere I went. You watched me sleep, Kingsley."

"How did you know that?"

Kingsley shivered as Søren's laugh rippled through the woods.

"I watched you watch me."

Today Kingsley managed to avoid the thorn bush that had

cut open his forehead and sent blood dripping into his eyes. When he had returned to Saint Ignatius after summer break, he had learned every inch of the woods that surrounded the school. But nowhere on the thousands of acres he'd roamed and memorized had he seen another thorn bush. Only here, guarding the clearing where he'd lain underneath Søren and let the boy he loved destroy him.

"When did you know you wanted me?" Kingsley asked as he entered the clearing where he'd died and bled and been born again. "I wanted you before I even saw you. When I heard the first notes of Ravel coming from the chapel."

"Father Henry told me a French student would be coming to Saint Ignatius. I'd never played Ravel before. I thought I should play something French so you wouldn't feel so home-sick."

Kingsley looked at Søren and said nothing. Søren merely looked back at him.

Closing his eyes, Kingsley remembered that day in the chapel, a petrified Matthew at his side trying to warn him to leave Stearns alone. Kingsley should have listened, would have listened but for one thing....

"I loved you because of the Ravel. Had you played any other piece I would have thought you merely handsome and fascinating."

Søren gazed up at the sky. "Then I'm glad I played it."

Kingsley took a step toward him and waited. Søren did nothing, said nothing to stop him.

So Kingsley didn't stop.

Another step. And then another. And after one more step he stood in front of Søren, merely a hairsbreadth apart.

"I thought you were the most beautiful creature on God's earth," Kingsley confessed. "I would have been an atheist but for you proving to me that both heaven and hell were real, even if they existed only when I was with you."

"I can't say when the moment came that I wanted you," Søren said. "Perhaps before we even met. Why else would I have chosen the Ravel? I always thought God brought Eleanor and me together."

"Then who is to blame for us? The devil?"

"I hope not." Søren sighed. "I have no intention of meeting him. Even to thank him."

Søren turned his face to Kingsley.

"You are still the most beautiful creature on God's earth," Kingsley said, meaning every word.

"I hated how you stared at me." Søren raised his hand and laid it on Kingsley's shoulder. He moved his hand up Kingsley's neck and pressed his thumb into the hollow of his throat.

"And why is that?"

"Because," Søren said, bending his regal head the four inches that separated them, "it made it impossible for me to stare back."

Their lips touched for the first time in thirty years. Even the night Søren took him fourteen years ago, they hadn't kissed. Søren had reserved his kisses for Eleanor alone. What happened that night had been mere violence, not even lust or love. But Kingsley sensed no violence in this kiss. Søren's mouth was cold and clean. Their tongues gently mingled. But the gentleness lasted only seconds, and Kingsley knew it was merely the product of their own astonishment the kiss was even happening.

Fingers on the back of his neck.

He remembered those fingers.

A hand digging into his hip with bruising force.

Kingsley remembered that hand.

Pain with every touch. Pain with every kiss. Pain with every beat of his heart.

Kingsley loved this pain.

Søren pushed him until Kingsley felt bark against his back, digging through his shirt and into his flesh. They devoured each other with kisses, bit lips, nipped tongues. Kingsley tasted blood and knew it was his own.

Or was it?

"Stop, Kingsley." Søren spoke the order against Kingsley's mouth. He didn't stop.

"You never told me your safe word," Kingsley whispered back. "I don't stop for anything but a safe word."

He laughed then and Søren's hand came out of seemingly nowhere and slapped the laugh off his lips. Then they kissed again, harder, deeper. Kingsley felt the kiss in his stomach, in his hips. The pants he wore were made by the finest tailor in the world and cost a small fortune. He wanted to drop to the ground in them, take Søren in his mouth, and afterward take the trousers to his tailor and demand he repair the tears in the knees.

"I'm stronger than her," Kingsley whispered into Søren's ear. Søren responded with so vicious a bite on Kingsley's neck that he cried out. "I can take so much more pain than she. She's gone. It doesn't matter if she's coming back or not. For now, she's gone. Let me warm your bed in her place."

"Who?" Søren pushed Kingsley even harder against the tree and thrust his thigh between Kingsley's legs.

"Eleanor."

Kingsley was free. No hands held him. No mouth kissed him. He stood against the tree, alone, untouched. Bewildered, he stared at Søren, who stood five feet away from him, panting. Søren raised his hand and wiped a drop of blood off the side of his mouth.

"Mais…" Kingsley protested.

Søren lowered his hand.

"You said my safe word."

SOUTH

He couldn't stay mad at the woman if his life depended on it. How could anyone stay mad at Nora? She had this thing about her, this force, this wildness.... Of course she hadn't slept with him last night. That's exactly what Wesley had wanted, exactly when he wanted it and exactly who he'd wanted it with. So it hadn't happened. Nothing ever happened except on Nora's terms. That's why she made him want to scream sometimes. That's why she made him love her all the time.

Wesley led Nora through the quiet stables. Dozens of horses greeted them with low, breathy whinnies. He had to physically restrain her on several occasions from reaching out to pet the horses.

"Thoroughbreds, Nor. These are Thoroughbreds, not kittens. They're geared up and ready to run. And they'll bite you if you get them in the right mood. And now, they are in the right mood."

"But they're so cute with their little socks on," she said, pulling Wesley toward another stall, where a horse named

Don't Need the Money pranced about peevishly. "Plus, I bite back."

"You know horse racing is called the sport of kings, right?" Wesley teased. Nora had a rather irreverent take on horse racing. He blamed all those clients of hers that were into pony play. She couldn't look at a saddle or a bridle without telling him about her ex-client who watched *My Friend Flicka* for the same reasons other guys watched porn.

"So what's going on here?" Nora waved her hands around at the stables.

"Prerace prep. Horses get rubbed down and dressed. Then it's off to the starting gate."

"The stands don't look that full. Do people really make money off horse racing?"

"Nora, this one race that's happening here in Charleston Park? People all over the world are betting on it."

"Damn."

"I know. The purses aren't really where the money is. You want to win races so your horse proves he can win. That way, other horse owners will pay you a fortune to breed their horses with yours."

"So they can go on to win races and not win very much money, but then sell horsey spooge to the next generation."

"Right. Disgusting, but right."

"So do the horses like running?"

"What?"

Nora turned around and leaned back against the stable wall. A horse named Good Golly Miss Molly stuck her head out of the stall window and stuck her tongue out at Wesley.

"Do they like it? Enjoy it?"

"I don't speak horse. But I think a lot of them do. They've been trained to enjoy it, trained to want to run."

"But it's dangerous."

"Being a wild horse is dangerous, too. Being an animal is dangerous. Being a human is dangerous."

"Putting bridles on them, making them do dangerous things for the pleasure of others...isn't that wrong?"

Just then Wesley noticed the wicked little twinkle in Nora's eyes. They were green today. He'd asked her once why her eyes changed colors so often. One moment they shone bright emerald-green. In a blink they could turn black as night. "I have mood eyes," she'd answered. "Green when I'm happy. Black when I'm horny."

He sort of wished they were black right now.

"You're not talking about horse racing, are you?"

Nora shook her head. "I am. But I'm not."

"Horse racing isn't like kink. Yeah, they both can be dangerous. And yeah, there's some, I don't know, non-consent involved...."

"And riding crops."

"Yeah, and riding crops. But there's a big difference between horse racing and kink."

"And what's that?" The twinkle remained in her eyes.

"It's sad when a Thoroughbred gets hurt in a race. But when Søren hurts you, I die inside."

Nora said nothing. The twinkle in her eyes faded. She pushed herself off the stable wall and came to him. Throwing her arms around his neck, she brought her mouth to his and kissed him long and deep. So shocked was he by the sudden kiss, it took Wesley a second before he could even kiss her back. But when he did, he met her passion with hunger, met her lips with his tongue, met her lust with love.

Wesley slid his hands down her back, and Nora pulled away.

"What?" he asked, searching her face for any clue as to why she'd stopped.

"Tonight," she said, panting.

"What's tonight?"

Nora laid her hands on his chest. She came up on her tip-toes and kissed him on the cheek. "What you wanted. We hang out, we watch movies, we eat dinner together, we talk. But instead of separate bedrooms…we go to bed together."

She turned around and walked away. But not before she looked back at him once and winked.

Wesley couldn't stop smiling. Her eyes had turned black as night.

He started to follow her, but heard his father calling his name.

"What?" Wesley asked, sounding more peevish than he intended. His father glared at him. "Sorry. I mean, what is it?"

"Do you want to see this horse or not?"

Wesley decided answering truthfully would not win him any points in this situation.

"Yes. Totally. Let's go." Wesley and his father walked past the paddock to another set of stables.

"Where's that woman of yours?"

"Dad, she's my girlfriend, not 'my woman.' And you know her name is Nora."

"Don't care what her name is. Just want to know where she is."

Wesley tried and failed to suppress the eye-rolling urge. Thank God he'd remembered to put his sunglasses back on. Nothing pissed his father off more than disrespect.

"She's hanging out by the stables. She'll behave herself."

"I highly doubt that."

Wesley highly doubted it, too. But with all the jockeys and trainers about, no way could Nora cause any riots. Only mild mayhem at most. Worst-case scenario was she'd offend a few jockeys with pony-play jokes. It would be a miracle if

he could get her through the day without her testing out the
riding crops on somebody.

They entered the stall where the mare his father wanted to
look at stood pawing at the ground. High-strung and well-
muscled, she would make a terrible companion horse, but
probably could outrun any gelding on the field. The veterinarian and his father talked about her stats and vitals while Wesley pretended to read her pedigree. Good genes that went all
the way back to Ruffian. If his dad knew what he was doing,
he'd put the mare and Farewell to Charms together. They'd
have one hell of a runner with that genetic cocktail, probably
a Derby winner. Maybe even the first Triple Crown winner
since Affirmed in 1978. The money would pour into The
Rails with a Triple Crown. The most famous horse farm in
the industry would become a legend throughout the world.

And Wesley couldn't care less.

"Son?"

"Huh?" Wesley looked at his father. "Oh, yeah. Could
work."

His father nodded, reading Wesley's agreement in the blank
expression on his face. A mare like this would cost money—
lots of it. Wesley had learned his poker face early on. His father had enough money to buy and sell the entire state of
Kentucky ten time times before breakfast, but he had all that
money because he never spent a cent more than necessary.

The mare settled down long enough for Wesley to give her
a pat on her flank. The horse's taut muscle twitched under
his hands. Feisty thing. She and Nora would get along well.
Nora…a year and a half hadn't changed her at all. He still
couldn't quite believe it had happened, poof, she was back in
his life again. All that time apart disappeared in one instant, in
one embrace, in one sentence she'd groaned in his ear when
she'd wrapped her arms around him.

God, you need a haircut.

Wesley still couldn't think about it without smiling. And yet he'd been so terrified at first. He still couldn't quite believe Søren was allowing Nora to be with him. But as much as Wesley hated Søren, he couldn't deny that the priest would do anything to protect the woman he considered his property, even giving her up.

Søren…who was he? For two years Nora had talked about the man, mourned his absence from her life and her bed, tried to hate him, tried to stay away from, tried to convince Wesley he wasn't the monster he thought…. But until this summer, Wesley had never met him. And as soon as he had, Wesley regretted it. Seeing that six-foot-four blond priest who looked like…looked like exactly the opposite of what he'd wanted him to look like.

Nora once tried to describe Søren to Wesley. "Think Sting plus Jeremy Irons, but taller, sexier, and scarier than both of them combined."

"You're not exaggerating a little, are you?"

"Wesley, I wouldn't exaggerate or commit hyperbole for a billion dollars in a million years."

"Nora."

And that wild light in Nora's eye had flickered and the smile faded from her face.

"He has the most beautiful mouth of any man I've ever seen…" she'd said then, talking more to herself than Wesley. "Tender…and cruel."

"Tender and cruel? You sound like one of your own books now," Wesley had teased, hoping to bring her smile back. It scared him when she got like this, when she looked past him instead of at him, and he knew she'd gone back to Søren. At least in her mind.

"Wait until you meet him," she'd said, inhaling and forcing her smile back. "Then tell me how right I am."

She'd been right.

Nora's bedroom had been the last place Wesley expected to meet the man. When Wesley and Nora lived together, the temptation to sneak off one Sunday morning and attend Mass at Sacred Heart had nearly overwhelmed him at times. But something told him that would be a dangerous mistake. He knew Nora still loved her priest, and the last thing Wesley wanted to do was give the man the satisfaction of knowing he was intimidated by him.

Especially since Søren wasn't remotely intimidated by Wesley.

But Wesley refused to be intimidated another minute more by Søren or Nora's feelings for him.

After all…just ahead of him, standing by the paddock and flirting with Jon Huntley, one of the trainers at Calumet, was the one and only Nora Sutherlin…his Nora here in Kentucky with him, with Wesley.

And he had Søren to thank for that.

Wesley still recalled his shock when he'd pushed past Søren, ready to flee Nora's house and the presence of the man who'd made a habit of turning her flawless pale skin black-and-blue.

But Søren had spoken the words that Wesley knew would change his life even before the priest had elaborated.

Wesley…I need to ask a favor of you.

Slowly, Wesley had turned around and faced the priest once again.

"A favor? What?" He heard hatred in his voice. It sounded so foreign. Wesley didn't hate anyone, or didn't think he did. Not until that moment.

"As I said, things are happening. I'm concerned that Eleanor is at risk. I'd like her to leave the area for some time. I'd hoped that Kingsley and I could remedy the situation while she was upstate this summer, but unfortunately…"

"Wait. What? You want me—"

"I know who you are, Wesley. I know what you are. I knew before I even allowed you to move in with Eleanor."

"Allowed? What do you mean, you 'allowed' me to move in with Ele—with Nora? She asked me. I said yes."

Søren smiled then and that smile had drawn a line down the center of Wesley's back with an icicle.

"Eleanor is watched."

Wesley had taken a step forward in fury.

"You unbelievable asshole. You spy on your own girl-friend?"

"It's hardly spying, Wesley. Eleanor is my property. It's my obligation to see to her safety. You lock the door to your car and never leave it on dangerous streets. Why? So it won't get stolen. I see that Eleanor is watched so she won't be harmed. It is the same principle."

"Except Nora isn't a car or a house. She's a person."

"Yes. And therefore infinitely more precious than any other chattel. Which is why the instant she took an interest in you, I had Kingsley find out who you were."

Wesley hadn't said anything at that point. He'd feared he would end up killing Søren or being killed by him with the next words he'd said. *Nora* and *chattel* used in the same sentence. Then and there Wesley decided he would do whatever it took to get Nora away from this man and keep her away from him…forever.

"The Prince of Kentucky. That's what they call you, isn't it?"

Wesley's jaw clenched. "Unfortunately."

Søren raised an eyebrow slightly.

"You never told Eleanor your family was worth roughly

one billion dollars. Why is that, young man? You aren't the deceptive sort."

"People don't look at you the same when you have money. I wanted her to see me as a person, as a man, not as…"

"Money."

As much as he hated to agree with him, Wesley had nodded.

"Back home, I can't even go to a fundraiser without it getting into the stupid gossip columns. I tried to visit some kids at a hospital and some nurse posted pics of me with those sick kids all over Facebook. I hate it. I hate that I'm John Wesley Railey, son of Jackson Railey of The Rails in Kentucky. I've got dollar signs all over me. I had a girlfriend in high school, Madison. Overheard her telling one of our friends she was only with me because it got her access to all the good parties in town. I didn't want Nora to see me like that."

"You do realize that Eleanor is as unimpressed with money as I am."

Wesley shrugged. "I didn't know that at the time. And it seemed to make her so happy to help me."

"She does love her strays, doesn't she? You were her favorite of all her puppies."

The mocking tone in Søren's voice had Wesley seeing red. And shortly after the red, he saw black. Wesley had rushed forward, intent on pushing Søren into the wall. The puppy had grown up. But with one seamless motion, Søren stepped to the side, wrapped a hand around Wesley's neck and pushed him hard into the door.

His head smacked against the wood and his vision darkened for a split second. The whole thing had happened so fast, so gracefully, that he knew he'd never be able to defeat Søren with physical force. The man was unnaturally strong and had years of practice putting people in their place. But Wesley had something Søren didn't have. And in that moment when he'd been pinned by his throat, Søren's fingers digging into his neck, Wesley's vision cleared and he knew what he would do.

"Behave yourself, young man. Eleanor's very fond of you, and I'd hate to break one of her favorites. I'll allow her to do that herself…if you're willing to take her in, take her to Kentucky with you while Kingsley and I deal with some unfinished business."

Wesley had swallowed and felt the sinews in his neck pressing against Søren's hand.

"Is this how you win fights with Nora, too?" Wesley refused to give in to the panic that threatened to overwhelm him. "Choking her? Slamming her head against the wall?"

"I'm not holding you hard enough to even lightly constrict your airway. You flinched so much that's why you hit your head. When I do this to Eleanor, she wets herself for reasons far different than the reasons you're about to."

"You're a sadist. I know you're enjoying this. I'm not going to give you the satisfaction of being scared of you."

"Enjoy this?" Søren leaned in close and put his mouth near Wesley's ear. "Forgive me, young man, but you really aren't my type."

Søren's fingers pressed into his neck tighter, and Wesley inhaled in silent terror.

"Or maybe you are…." Søren whispered. And then, as suddenly as he started, Søren let go and stepped back.

Wesley rubbed his throat and took heavy gulps of air. "If she comes with me, I'll do everything I can to make sure she doesn't come back," he vowed.

"She always comes back to me, Wesley. You know that."

"You haven't seen my world. You've got a church. I've got a castle. You've got a vow of poverty. I've got more money than God. You can't even be seen in public with her. I can stand in front of a thousand cameras with the whole world watching, and kiss her."

Taking a deep breath, Wesley turned and stared at Søren. He saw something then in his eyes.

A flash of fear.

Suddenly there. Suddenly gone. But Wesley had seen it. And it gave him the hope he needed. If Søren feared Nora would stay with him in Kentucky, then Wesley knew he had a chance.

"Fine. Yes. I'll take Nora with me to Kentucky. She can stay with me forever if she wants. I'll keep her safe, but since you won't be there, that kind of goes without saying."

"Very well. Once she returns to the city, I'll send for you."

Wesley turned to leave Nora's house...their house.

"I won't let her go back to you," Wesley said. "Fair warning."

Søren narrowed his eyes at him and smiled. "Won't let her?" he repeated. "Why, Wesley, you're starting to sound like one of us."

"Wesley?"

Shaken back to the present, Wesley spun around and found Nora standing behind him, holding a horse by the bridle.

"Nora...what are you—"

"Can I have him? He's cute."

Nora grinned at him before turning her head and kissing the horse on the snout. The animal exhaled as he shook his mane.

"His name is Spanks for Nothing. It's destiny. We belong together."

Groaning, Wesley walked over to Nora and took the horse by the bridle. "Nora...you can't go around taking horses out of their stalls. That's kind of frowned upon around here."

"He followed me."

"He did not."

"No, but I did." The voice came from behind the horse. Wesley looked over the back of Spanks for Nothing and saw a tall, handsome man of obvious Middle Eastern descent smiling at Nora.

Wesley's eyes widened. Nora giggled. The man came around the horse and stood beside her.

"Wesley, this is my friend—"

"Talel bint Nassar II," Wesley said, extending his hand.

"You've met?" Nora asked, smiling at first him and then at Talel.

"That's what I was going to ask you." Wesley saw Talel wink at Nora. Wink? One of the sons of a Middle Eastern king just winked at Nora? "You've met?"

Nora nodded with a grin. "Oh, yeah. We're old friends. Talel and I go way back."

"How is the car treating you, my dear?" Talel spoke beautiful English, more fluent in the language than a lot of Kentuckians Wesley had encountered. Not surprising, considering his Oxford degree and the years he spent in the United States. Everyone around the racing industry knew Talel.

"Still purring like a kitten, as is her owner. Wes…Talel's the friend who gave me my Aston Martin." Nora gave him a sidelong stare. Nora had once hinted that a client of hers, a member of Middle Eastern royalty, had given her the sports car as a thank-you gift after a beautiful week together. Of course it would be one of the sheiks involved in horse racing. Talel was nearly as tall and handsome as Søren, although his opposite in some very key areas—dark-skinned where Søren was pale, black hair in contrast to Søren's blond. And if he really was a client of Nora's, that meant one thing and one thing only—the man was a sexual submissive.

Wesley suddenly had a vision of Talel on the ground with

Nora standing on his back with a riding crop in her hand. The image gave him a perverse moment of pleasure.

"And how is it that you know the Prince of Kentucky, madam?" Talel asked as he took Nora's hand and kissed the back of it gallantly.

"Wes and I used to live together. I'm down here visiting him for a while. He's my—"

"Boyfriend." Wesley said the word firmly and in a tone that brooked no argument. He waited for Nora to contradict him. She probably would. He didn't even know why he said it other than Talel seemed a bit too happy to see Nora and Nora seemed way too happy to see him.

"Yes," she said as she let go of Talel's hand and reached for Wesley's. "My boyfriend. Emphasis on the 'boy.' I'm having a Mrs. Robinson moment."

"I'm not complaining." Wesley kissed Nora on the top of her head. He loved kissing her there. She was a shrimp of a thing compared to him. She might tower over him with the size of her personality, but at least he had her beat on height.

"Nor should you, young man." Talel reached out and shook Wesley's hand. "You are blessed indeed to have such a great woman in your life. We are mere princes, you and I. But she is a queen."

Nora nodded in agreement. "I can't argue with that. Well, I could, but I'm not going to. Spanks for Nothing is Talel's horse. He let me borrow him just to freak you out a little. Did it work?"

"You'll have to do better than horse theft to freak me out. You are you, after all."

"Good point." Nora kissed Spanks for Nothing once more on his nose and handed him back to Talel. "Is he racing today?"

"He is. I wouldn't bet on him if I were you, however.

You've charmed him, milady, and a besotted horse is a distracted horse."

Nora grinned ear to ear. "That's terrible. We can't have that." Stepping forward, she laid her hands on the sides of Spanks for Nothing's face and stared him in the eyes. "You have to win today. Win for me. Do you understand that?" The horse blew through his lips and Nora patted him on the head. "I'll take that as a yes."

"He would be foolish to disobey you, Mistress," Talel said, guiding Spanks for Nothing back to the stables. "As would any man."

"I like that guy," Nora said. "He has fabulous taste in women."

Wesley looked down at her. "I can't believe you know Talel bint Nassar."

"I can't believe *you* know Talel. Does everyone in horse racing know each other?"

"Yes, actually," Wesley said as they strolled past the paddock and toward the betting booths. "Does everyone in the kink world know each other?"

"Abso-fucking-lutely. At least the New York community does. I'm kind of amused at how much overlap there is. Griffin and Talel and you—"

"I'm not in the New York kink community."

"Kingsley Edge has a file on you an inch thick in his office. Whether you like it or not, you are one of us. Guilt by association," she said. "Now how do I bet on Spanks for Nothing?"

"That depends. Do you want to bet on him winning, placing or showing? You could get fancy and do a combination bet. Maybe a trifecta or superfecta."

"No idea what that means." Nora pulled out a hundred dollar bill and laid it down on the counter. "I want Spanks for Nothing to win. That is all."

The woman in the betting booth handed Nora her ticket, and Wesley escorted her to the stands. They took their seats and Wesley pulled out his binoculars. Nice firm track. Hadn't rained in at least a week. The running would be fast today. He loved introducing first-timers to horse races. They were always amazed by how quickly the race ended. On his best day, Wesley could run a mile in seven minutes. The fastest horse could do it in one hundred thirty-one seconds, barely over two minutes. It blew his mind when he thought about it— over a thousand pounds of horseflesh covering a full mile in two minutes. The horse industry, Thoroughbreds, the races… he'd grown up around them, and he'd long ago lost his interest in being a part of this world. But the horses themselves… they still amazed him.

A siren blew to alert everyone that the race would start in seconds. Nora grabbed the binoculars from him and turned her attention to the starting gate.

"Watch them burst out of the gates," Wesley said. "That's the most exciting part until the finish line. Those horses are so jacked up on adrenaline right now that it's like a bomb going off when those gates open."

"Sounds dangerous."

"It is dangerous. That's when a lot of accidents happen. Lots of horses have died right out of the gate. Broken ankles, broken legs. Lots of jockeys get hurt there, too."

"Poor little guys."

"Some jockeys are women, Nora."

"Poor little girls."

"Horse racing isn't a pretty sport," Wesley confessed. "The horses are bred for speed, not heartiness. Legs like twigs. They break easy and running that hard can make their lungs bleed. They're breakable animals."

"Breakable—just my type. Do racehorses really piss like racehorses?"

"If a horse has bleeding lungs they give it Lasix. It's a diuretic. They can pee about twenty gallons."

"Hmm…twenty gallons. Get enough chardonnay in me and I can give them a run for their money."

"We can stop by the bar later. Or you can. I'm still underage."

"Rub it in, junior. Seriously. Rub it in." Nora turned her head and smiled wickedly at him before giving the race her full attention once more. Wesley blushed. He'd been trying not to think about tonight with Nora. He wanted to be able to walk around in public without a visible erection beneath his jeans. "Spanks for Nothing is leading. How much money will I make?"

"Couple thousand dollars. Long odds on him."

"Sweet. I could use the money. Saw a riding crop in the gift shop I have to take home with me."

"Nora, how many riding crops do you need?"

"Just one more. Like always." Nora stood up and shouted "Go Spanks!" but her voice was drowned out by the roar of the crowd as the horses neared the finish. Spanks for Nothing did seem destined for a big win, by a few lengths at least.

Spanks for Nothing crossed the finish line a length and a half before the second-place horse.

Nora stood on her seat, shouted a few "fuck yeah"s that had Wesley both laughing and cringing at the same time.

"Let's go get your money." He took her by the hand and pulled her off the seat. They cashed out Nora's winning ticket and she spent half her take at the gift shop buying T-shirts.

"What are all those for?" he asked. Nora didn't wear T-shirts very often and certainly not in size large.

"One for Griffin."

"Of course."

"One for Michael."

"Who's Michael?"

"His sub."

"Why do I ask these questions?"

"One for Juliette."

"Who?"

"Kingsley's secretary. Well, she's also his sexual property. He's white and French. She's black and Haitian."

"That should be illegal."

"They're so cute together."

"Your friends terrify me."

"They're harmless. Well, as long as you don't piss them off. This one's for Talel. He should have a memento of his big win today." Nora threw the T-shirt over her shoulder and strode from the gift shop.

"He'll have about a hundred thousand dollars in purse money and a wreath of roses and a trophy. Isn't that enough of a souvenir?"

"Who would say no to a T-shirt?"

Wesley said nothing more, guessing Nora merely wanted an excuse to go talk to one of her kind again. He led her back to the stables and toward Spanks for Nothing's stall. They'd be lucky to get to Talel. With that sort of win, he'd probably be surrounded by well-wishers and sports writers and others trying to let a piece of that victory rub off on them. Spanks for Nothing had proven himself a hot property today. The price of his stud fees had probably tripled. At least.

But a scene of celebration wasn't what greeted them at they neared the stall. Wesley saw uniforms, track doctors, racing authorities.... It was a sight he'd seen before.

"Nora...let's go."

"No, I want to see Talel. What's wrong?"

"Something."

She stopped and gave him a searching look. He took her hand, but she pulled away quickly and forced herself through the crowd ahead.

"Talel?" she called out, and Wesley had no choice but to race after her.

"Nora, let's go," he said when he caught up to her, right in front of the stall. "Shit."

"Wesley…" He heard the heartbreak in her voice, the distress, and he saw the reason why.

Big, beautiful Spanks for Nothing lay on his side in his stall, quiet and unmoving. Nothing seemed to be broken. Nothing seemed to be wrong. A sleeping horse…that was all. Except horses didn't stay down for long and they certainly didn't lie like that.

Talel knelt at the horse's side, a track veterinarian whispering next to him.

"Come on, Nora. We can't help here."

Talel looked up and met Nora's eyes.

"What happened?" she whispered.

"He's dead."

NORTH
The Past

He told no one where his injuries came from. All questions he refused to answer. His grandparents came for Kingsley on the last day of school and gasped when they found him in the infirmary covered in bruises, his lip split open, his forehead stitched up, cuts on his knees, welts on his arms and one rib either strained or cracked. And those were only the wounds he let the doctor see. He knew he'd been hurt internally—torn. Definitely torn. But he kept that pain secret, as secret as he kept the little silver cross he'd ripped from Søren's neck. He clutched it in his hand all night and all day and refused to let it go.

His grandparents interrogated him as thoroughly as the priests had. Kingsley didn't even consider lying, although he could have said, "I fell in the woods," and that would be the end of it. But that night with Søren in the forest…it meant too much to him to sully it with a lie. He simply said, "I don't want to talk about it. I'm fine." He took comfort in the words. In two days he must have said them a hundred times, said them until they were the only words he knew. But even those words weren't entirely true. He did want to talk about it, but with Søren only. And he wasn't fine. Fine couldn't even begin to describe the bliss he'd experienced that night Søren had ripped him open and laid him out under the stars. Kingsley had no word for it other than perhaps *God*. He wasn't fine. He was God.

And Søren was God and Kingsley had worshipped him and did worship him. But he'd been isolated in the infirmary, not allowed to leave, not allowed to have visitors. He assumed the priests hoped the isolation would force him to open up and explain what had happened. Instead it reinforced his vow of secrecy about that night. He didn't have the words, not in English or French, to explain what had happened to him in any way that anyone would ever understand. A wall had come up between him and the rest of the world. The priest, his grandparents, the other students...they would say "rape." But Kingsley knew better. He'd run because he'd wanted to get caught. He'd let himself be stripped and violated. And when he surrendered himself to Søren, that had been the moment he became himself.

"Kingsley...please. *S'il vous plaît...*" Kingsley's grandmother laid her hand gently on the unbruised side of his face. He smiled at her attempt at French. It touched his heart that she would plead to him in his language, but still he wouldn't tell.

On the second night, his friend Christian broke into the infirmary. Kingsley woke from a light sleep to find his classmate staring at him with horrified eyes.

"It's not that bad, Christian." Kingsley smiled and yawned, and Christian only stared.

"You look...how are you even alive?"

"By the grace of God, *mon ami.*"

"Who did this to you? Tell me so I can go kill him and bring you back his heart to eat."

Christian's allegiance to him, his friendship and fury...
Kingsley wanted to pat him on the head like a loyal dog.
Good boy.

"I'm fine, Christian."

"You don't look fine."

Kingsley turned and smiled at the handsome young Christian, who now seemed like a friend he'd said goodbye to long ago.

"I have never felt more fine in my life." The words were not a lie.

The peace he'd felt lasted until he returned to his grandparents' house in Portland, and the reality of Søren's absence surrounded him. After they'd consummated whatever it was they had, Søren had walked away and left him there on the ground. Kingsley hadn't minded. It was exactly what he'd wanted, to be left alone with his wounds, with his love. He loved that Søren broke him, but he didn't want Søren to see him broken. Alone, he'd gathered his tattered clothes. Alone, he half coughed, half vomited his dinner and blood on the ground. Alone, he'd cried as he tried to stand up, and landed hard on his knees. He gave up on walking after the third try and crawled through the woods, back to the school, and collapsed on the front steps of the chapel. Father Henry found him there and, with every ounce of the old priest's strength, lifted him off the ground and carried him to the infirmary.

"Are you all right, son?" Father Henry had asked. "Son? Kingsley...are you laughing?"

But now, at home, with Søren hours away, still at school, Kingsley felt doubt begin to set in, fear. Had it really happened? Yes, and he had the healing wounds to prove it. But would it happen again when he went back? What *had* happened?

Sex. That had happened. He'd never had sex like that before, and if they were going to do it again, they really needed to find a way to do it without tearing Kingsley open. The pain he cherished, but he wanted to live to be fucked again and again. But the sex...that had been the least of what had happened.

Søren...Kingsley had started a habit of writing the name down on scraps of paper. He'd light a match then and smile as the name burned. The ritual comforted him. He'd seen Søren light little candles outside the chapel, pause and bow his head. That's what burning Søren's name felt like—prayer.

Søren... Learning the name seemed far more meaningful, more significant than even the sex had. Everyone at the school called him Stearns, apart from the priests, who called him Mr. Stearns. His first name was Marcus. Everyone knew that, although no one dared utter it. But Søren was his name. Kingsley didn't know how or know why. And he didn't care. He didn't care about anything but seeing Søren again.

The days of summer passed and Kingsley did everything in his power to prove to his grandparents that he was well, that whatever had befallen him had done him no permanent damage. He returned to his rakish ways, taking up with all his old girlfriends. During the summer he easily avoided the boyfriends and brothers who'd been the bane of his existence during his time in his Portland high school. He'd let his lovely ladies pick him up, and they'd skip the movies, skip dinner, skip everything but parking the car in the middle of nowhere and letting anything and everything happen in the backseat. But only the backseat. Susan had wanted to lay out a blanket on the ground and have sex under the stars. Kingsley refused. Such a thing he'd reserve only for Søren. He'd told Susan a lie...something about poison ivy, and the girl had surrendered to his superior wisdom and spread her legs gainfully against the leather interior of her father's Cadillac.

By the last week of July, Kingsley had nearly gone mad with longing for Søren, but he knew of no way to hasten the days or contact Søren. He feared sending him a letter. The priests sorted the mail and delivered it. Kingsley had refused to explain his injuries. No one ever spoke to Søren unless necessary. That Kingsley would be the lone student to send him a letter over the summer…no, too great a risk.

He couldn't call, couldn't write…so he waited and he prayed. And the days passed and the nights passed and his body healed completely. So completely that he finally felt comfortable taking all his clothes off again. In late July he and Jackie, the quarterback's bookish but beautiful redheaded sister, holed up in her bedroom one Wednesday night when her parents were out celebrating their anniversary. That night had been unremarkable, really. Unremarkable but for one thing, one act that had come as an answer to his unspoken prayers.

Jackie kissed her way from his hip to his neck.

"Can we do something different?" she'd whispered as she nibbled on his earlobe.

"Anything, *ma chérie*. Anything you desire…" He exaggerated his French accent with his American girls. Most boys he knew plied their girlfriends with beer to get them to open their shapely thighs. Kingsley needed only a few words of French.

"I want to do something you've never done with anyone else."

Kingsley smiled at the ceiling.

Rolling over, he pinned Jackie onto her back and pressed her legs open with his knees. He let the tip of his erection lightly caress her swollen clitoris. She gasped and laughed in the back of her throat.

Reaching out her hand, she pointed down to the floor. Kingsley raised his eyebrow in a question.

"Under the bed," she said.

He ducked his head and raised the bedskirt. From beneath her bed he pulled out a plastic tube of some kind of fluid.

"C'est quoi?"

"My father's a gynecologist. It's called K-Y. I heard him telling Mom what some people do with it."

"You know I go to a Catholic school now." Kingsley raised his eyebrow again. "Sodomy is frowned upon."

"So…?" Jackie waited.

Without another word Kingsley flipped the girl onto her stomach, pulled her to her knees, doused her with the cool liquid and pushed inside her. He groaned deeply, loudly, from the pressure around him, the tightness. Jackie squirmed underneath him and grasped his hand.

"You've done this before…" Kingsley said, noting how readily she took him inside her.

Jackie giggled. "Well…never with anyone else."

Kingsley bit the back of her shoulder to stifle a laugh. Jackie wanted to be a librarian. Of course, a librarian. It was always the quiet ones….

After they finished, Kingsley asked to keep the lubricant as a souvenir. She promised him a dozen tubes of the stuff if he would come over that weekend and do it again. The promise was readily made and easily kept.

So everything had fallen into place. He'd burned for Søren with a fire no girl or woman had ever inspired in him. And Søren had taken him on the forest floor. It would happen again. It had to happen again. Kingsley would die if it didn't happen again.

But would it happen again? Two months passed and, with his wounds completely healed, Kingsley began to fear he'd imagined everything. It had happened, he reminded himself often. Of course it had. What else would explain his grandparents' wary looks, their whispers when he entered the room?

He had one final proof that lingered even after all the bruises had faded. The cross...the small silver cross he'd ripped from Søren's neck and had clung to, had carried, during the entire night. Never did he part from the cross. He kept it always in his pocket like a talisman, like a burden, like an icon.

Two weeks before school started again, Kingsley sat on the back deck of his grandparents' house, communing with the stars. They comforted him, the stars did. These stars had been the only witnesses to that night. Did they remember it as well as he did? He started to ask them what they'd seen when he heard voices in the kitchen.

"I don't care what he says, he's not fine. He is definitely not fine." His grandmother spoke the words, and in her voice Kingsley heard the echo of his late mother. How he missed Maman. Kingsley knew his grandmother blamed his late father for the death of her daughter. She'd gone to school in Paris and fallen in love with a dashing older Frenchman. The bastard had the audacity to love her back and even marry eighteen-year-old Karen Smith and make her Madam Boissonneault. Even the two children they'd raised hadn't convinced her parents that Kingsley's father was anything more than a seducer of young girls. Like father, like son, Kingsley knew his grandparents thought. If only they knew that while he seduced girls, it was to another young man that his heart belonged.

"What do you want me to do?" his grandfather asked, his voice laced with frustration. Kingsley surmised tonight wasn't the first time they'd had this conversation.

"Father Henry called today to talk about it. He's thinking Kingsley shouldn't come back. They're worried about him, about whatever happened that he won't talk about."

Not come back? Kingsley's communion with the stars shattered at the very thought. Why would he not go back? Father

Henry hadn't said anything about him not returning. Where had that idea come from?

Søren…could it have been Søren's idea? Did he regret that night? Had Søren told Father Henry he knew something about that night?

Panic consumed Kingsley. What if this was Søren's doing? Even the priests deferred to Søren.

For days after Kingsley walked through the hours in a haze of self-doubt. He couldn't go back if Søren didn't want him there. But he had to see him again. He *had* to go back.

A week before the school year was to start, he sat at the kitchen table with his grandparents, not eating and not speaking.

"You got a letter today." His grandmother handed him a white envelope. Kingsley didn't glance at it. Another letter from Marie-Laure, surely. He'd read it later.

"School starts soon." His grandfather looked at him over the top of his reading glasses. "Your grandmother and I have decided to leave it up to you. Saint Ignatius or Portland High?"

The choice lay before him. Both options seemed untenable. He couldn't go back to Portland. Søren wouldn't be there. He couldn't go back to Saint Ignatius, not if Søren didn't want him there.

Kingsley shook his head, crossed his arms and laid his head on the table. His stomach hurt. His head ached. He needed something, anything, a sign.

The letter lay in his lap and he saw the handwriting on it didn't belong to Marie-Laure or any other woman. A man's handwriting, strong and vital.

Slowly and with trembling fingers, Kingsley opened the letter and read the only word written on the ivory sheet of paper.

Reviens.

Come back.

The letter had been signed with only a strong swirling *S* with a diagonal slash through it.

Kingsley looked up at his grandparents.

"I'm going back to Saint Ignatius."

NORTH
The Present

Kingsley stared at Søren only a moment before shaking his head in the profoundest disgust and walking off deeper into the forest. He heard the footsteps behind him and didn't turn back. Today Kingsley didn't run, but he didn't particularly want to get caught, either.

Thirty years had passed since he'd traversed this dangerous terrain with its closely packed trees that gave way to sudden cliffs. Even after so much time, his legs retained the memory of so many walks down this path. In half an hour he came to a ridge overlooking a steep canyon.

"Mon Dieu…" he breathed. After all this time…surely not. But there it was.

"It's still in use." Søren came to stand beside him. "They renovated it. It's quite nice inside."

"Our hermitage?" The old love welled in Kingsley's heart, and he forgave Søren just enough to laugh.

"Our hermitage. It was never actually ours, you know. We only claimed it for ourselves."

At the bottom of the canyon stood a tiny shack made of

stone. A hundred years ago the first Jesuits who'd come to rural Maine had built a chapel first, then their living quarters, and finally a hermitage for Father Charles, who'd taken a vow of silence.

"Quite nice…" Kingsley repeated. "Of course they would wait until after we were done with it to remodel. Always the way. My God, what a hellhole it was."

Søren laughed softly. "Indeed. But perfect for our purposes."

"*Oui,*" Kingsley agreed. "*Parfait.*"

The hermitage had been their hideout when Kingsley returned to school, when he and Søren had taken up where they'd left off.

Kingsley pulled his eyes away from the small house where he'd given up his body to Søren in a thousand ways so many years ago. A hundred yards or more from the hermitage, a huge moss-covered rock loomed large. For a full minute Kingsley stared at it. Only when he felt a hand on the back of his neck—a gentle hand, a gentle touch, entirely kind and without ulterior motive—did he blink and look away.

"It was there?" Søren dropped his hand. Kingsley missed it the second it was gone.

"*Oui.* Right there. She landed so hard.…" He stopped and swallowed. He had to blink again to wash the image of his sister's body from his eyes. "Her face…"

"*Je sais,*" Søren whispered. *I know.*

Of course he knew. Marie-Laure had been Kingsley's sister…but when she died, she'd been Søren's wife.

Marie-Laure…only twenty…a ballerina in Paris.

"We killed her, *mon père.*"

"I've absolved you of any guilt long ago, Kingsley. You must learn to absolve yourself."

"Her face was gone when they found her." He turned to Søren. "The world imagines I am handsome, you are handsome, your Eleanor is beautiful…but we are nothing compared to what Marie-Laure was. I, her brother, couldn't keep my eyes off her at times. All paled next to that face of hers. And when she died, when we killed her…"

She had no face. None. The impact of her fall had crushed her skull and sheered her face off. She'd been identified by her wedding band alone.

"She ran. She fell. You did not push her. Neither did I." Søren spoke the words in a low voice as he moved closer. How Kingsley wanted to step back and press himself into Søren. Once when they were teenagers, standing in the forest staring at the night sky, Søren had wrapped an arm around Kingsley's chest. The gesture had been simple, mindless, hardly even affectionate, only possessive. And it had saved Kingsley's soul. To feel that again with Søren…Kingsley would treble his fortune and give every last penny away.

"She loved you," Kingsley said. "And she trusted me."

And she saw them.

Together.

"Come," Søren said. "We should go back."

"You go." Kingsley smiled at him. "I want to stay a moment."

Søren raised his hand and lightly gripped Kingsley's long hair before releasing it and walking away.

"Of course."

Alone now at the top of the hill, Kingsley's eyes roamed from the rock where his sister had died, back to the hermitage. They should have been inside there, he and Søren. If they'd been in the hermitage, she would never have seen them. All Kingsley ever wanted was for Søren to want him as badly as he had that night in the forest. Søren never lost control like that again with him. Oh, Søren had hurt him, brutalized him, broken him. But he'd kept calm, controlled…he'd tamed his hunger, channeled it, restrained it. Kingsley longed for the fear he'd felt that first night. So he'd goaded Søren, challenged his authority. Finally, Søren had succumbed and dragged Kingsley into the woods. Jealously had brought about Kingsley's temper tantrum. Søren had married his sister and Marie-Laure suddenly seemed to love him more than her own brother. And as a married man, Søren slept in Marie-Laure's bed, while Kingsley once more slept alone. He had to have reassurance that Søren still desired him more than anyone. And he'd gotten it once more. Only this time the stars had not been the only witnesses.

Carefully, Kingsley made his way down the winding path that led to the hermitage. But before going to the cottage, he turned and walked to the rock.

The last time he'd gazed upon it, it had been painted red with his sister's blood. A thousand winds and a thousand rains had washed her blood away and left it gray and green once more. Kingsley laid his hand on the cool stone.

"Marie-Laure..." How good it felt simply to say her name, to acknowledge, even if only to himself, that she'd lived. She should still be alive. He'd long ago forgiven God for the death of his parents. And his grandparents...their deaths barely a splinter compared to the bullet wound in his heart that had been his parents' death.

But Marie-Laure, her death had destroyed him. It had gone off inside him like a bomb. Everything had shattered, and only the shell remained. He ate and drank death after that. Until Søren had come back and brought him to life once again.

"Ma soeur," he whispered.

"You should know, Kingsley, she's not really gone."

SOUTH

For the tenth time in one car trip, Nora shushed Wesley.

"What? Why are you shushing me?"

"I'm thinking about serious stuff. You know how hard that is for me."

Closing her eyes, she leaned her head back in the passenger seat and visualized the race...the horses surging, flanks flying and Spanks for Nothing taking the lead and refusing to give it up.

And then just an hour later...that thousand pounds of muscle in motion had lain still and dead on the floor of his stall, with no visible injuries. She'd seen the horse, gone to him, looked at him with her own eyes, before kneeling on the ground next to Talel and wrapping an arm around his shoulders. They didn't speak. She had nothing to say that would help him. She could only be there for him with a touch. Had Wesley not been there, she would have been there for Talel in other ways.

Talel...she still couldn't believe this ghost from her past had shown up in Wesley's world. Nora replayed the chain of

events in her mind. Wesley had walked off with his father and
left her alone near the stables. Out of the corner of her eye
she saw a familiar outline. Her eyes had widened, her heart
had raced. Talel? Here?

Forgetting all her promises to Wesley of maintaining de-
corum and good behavior, she'd shouted, "Talel!" and raced
toward him. He'd whipped around at the sound of her voice.
Son of Middle Eastern royalty or not, the man still obviously
worshipped at her feet. They'd embraced with laughter and
kisses. In his arms, Nora had felt a calm return to her, a calm
she hadn't felt since leaving the safety of New York.

"How is my car treating you?" he'd asked, and Nora
laughed in his face.

"*My* car. You gave me the Aston Martin. She's mine."

"And I am yours," he said, kissing her hand.

"None of that. That car has gotten me into as much trouble as you did."

"That was my plan, Mistress. I'd hoped you would get into
so much trouble only I could get you out of it." He'd whispered the words in her ear, and she'd playfully purred at him.
Talel…she'd broken a lot of rules with this man. Three years
ago Kingsley had learned that the dashing sheik who'd come to
New York ostensibly on diplomatic matters had been making
quiet inquires into where and how he could enjoy some play-
time with one of the city's legendary Dominatrixes. Kingsley
had seen nothing but dollar signs on Talel. But Nora had seen
more. Life in a strict Muslim country had left him hungry
to explore the decadences of the Western world. More than
that, however, he simply needed affection, acceptance. In his
world, his desires were taboo. His father would have exiled
him had word gotten out that Talel had a sexual submissive
streak in him as wide as the desert that bordered his country. Kingsley had one hard and fast rule about the Dominants

and submissives in his employ—no sex with the clients. With pride, Kingsley could say he was no pimp. If Nora slept with Talel, then Talel could not be a paying client.

She'd slept with him. And Kingsley had been furious. Not that Nora had cared. She'd just run off to Jordan with Talel for a week, and holed up in the grandest hotel in the country. Day after day, night after night, she'd become Talel's oasis… giving him what he'd thirsted for in his desert home, but never could find. For one beautiful week with him, she'd gloried in her Dominant side as she beat Talel, bound him, brought him to his knees again and again. He had kissed her boots, obeyed every order, lived and died between her thighs. He'd begged her for everything, for every touch, for every kiss…and only if he begged well enough did she acquiesce. At the end of the week he'd begged her for one more favor.

Stay with me…stay forever.

And for the second time in her life she'd looked into the eyes of a man she adored, a man who could give her a life of luxury, a man who wanted her more than the air in his lungs… and she'd said, "No." And she'd said it to Talel for the same reason she'd said no to another beautiful heartbroken man all those years earlier. Daniel…Talel…even Griffin…she could have had them but walked away, and all for the same reason.

Søren.

But he'd forgiven her, Talel had. And he'd loved her despite knowing she loved another. And the week after she returned to America, she'd found an inferno-red Aston Martin with a license plate that read MSTRSS sitting in her driveway.

To see him again, here at a racetrack a thousand miles from New York and a billion miles away from his home country… Nora couldn't believe her eyes, her luck. Once in Talel's arms she felt at home again. These rich Southerners with their million dollar accents and their twenty-five-million-dollar ponies, they weren't her people. Talel with his hunger for female Dominance, his willingness to submit to anything she wanted to do to him, his whispered "Yes, Mistress" in her ear—he felt like home to her.

So she grieved even more that Spanks for Nothing had been one of his horses. Such a beautiful creature with the white star on his forehead and the little red socks on his ankles. Talel had told her he'd been thinking of her when he'd named the horse. She'd slapped him on his firm bottom in reply.

"You'll get me into trouble if anyone sees us together," Talel said, grinning at her.

"Horses don't talk, right? Or do they? Mister Ed wasn't real, was he?"

"No, Mistress. Horses don't talk. Thank God. I can only imagine what this ill-tempered beast would say if he had the power of speech. Nothing a lady should ever hear."

"Good thing there are no ladies present. But he doesn't seem that ill-tempered to me. Right, Spanks?" She'd reached over the stall door and patted the beast on his velveteen nose.

"He is in a rare good mood today. Submissive even. I am certain your presence is to thank for that. But tell me about your presence here. I can't believe my eyes."

"I believe your eyes." Talel had the darkest, most soulful eyes she'd ever seen. Eyes that could keep secrets.

"My presence here… I'm with my boyfriend?" The sentence came out as a question, not a statement.

"Boyfriend?" Talel seemed as skeptical as she, and far more shocked by the word *boyfriend* than by her presence there at the race. "And your priest?"

"He knows I'm here. I'm not sure why he let me come, but I think he thought…I don't know. I never know what that man's thinking."

"But you will go back to him?"

And that question Nora had chosen not to answer.

She'd seen Wesley then, standing by the paddock looking around—for her, most likely. In the bright afternoon, the sunlight caught in his too-long hair and he'd seemed for a moment to be surrounded by a halo. The sudden sight of him silenced her words and awakened her longing. It might be the wrong decision to take Wesley's virginity and then go back to Søren again, but Wesley was old enough to face the risks.

And she had to have him.

"Wesley…" Nora opened her eyes and came back to the present moment. He had just turned into the driveway of his home. "What happened today? With Spanks, I mean?"

"I don't know. He didn't break anything. Horses are real fragile. Maybe a heart attack from running so hard? Maybe electrocution?"

"Are you kidding?"

He shrugged. "Nope. You can kill a horse with an electrical current so mild even a person wouldn't be affected by it. Bunch of horses got killed not that long ago when a wire hit some water and they were standing too close. Just an accident."

"You think it was an accident?"

"Why wouldn't it be?"

"That horse was so healthy, Wes. I petted him and kissed him. And when he ran…it was like someone turned wind into rage and turned rage into a horse…. I've never seen anything like it. It was beautiful."

"You're starting to sound like a racing fan. This isn't good. I don't need you losing every penny playing the ponies."

"You never let me have any fun."

Wesley stopped smiling. "I could say the same to you."

Nora's stomach tightened at the hurt in Wesley's voice.

"I'm trying here, Wes. With you. Figuring you out. I want

us to be together, really together. This thing with Spanks for Nothing kind of freaked me out."

"It sucks and it's sad, but it happens. It's a cool sport, but a dangerous one. You should understand that."

"I do. I really do. But people don't turn up dead all that often doing kink. The E.R. for the occasional sprained wrist or whatever? Yes. But not the morgue."

"I told you, horses are fragile and accidents happen."

"But I don't think it was an accident."

Wesley pulled up to the guesthouse and turned his car off. He looked at her and Nora steeled herself. Certain sides of her, certain parts of her past, she tried to keep from Wesley, for his own good. A sweet kid like that didn't need to know she herself had put people in the hospital, that his wasn't the only heart she'd broken, that she'd had an abortion, that she'd done the sort of things he'd never forgive anyone but her for… but she knew he needed to know this.

"Nora…what do you know that I don't know?"

She pulled a small red object from her bra. In the stall with Talel, she'd seen it, recognized it immediately and hidden it quickly where no one else would look. Now she showed it to Wesley.

"What is that?" he asked.

"It's a crocodile clip."

"Where did you find it?"

"In the stall in the hay by Spanks for Nothing's body. Wesley, you know what these are used for, right?"

"Yeah, my dentist uses them to keep the bibs on."

She gave a cold little laugh.

"Not this kind of crocodile clip. This is for carrying electrical currents."

Wesley's eyes widened in shock before narrowing with understanding. "Are you sure—"

"Yes, I am absolutely sure."

"How do you know what that is?"

"I've used them before."

His eyes narrowed further.

"For what?"

Nora swallowed before forcing the words out.

"For electrocuting people."

NORTH
The Past

Kingsley returned to Saint Ignatius in September, healed and whole and desperate to see Søren. Søren... he couldn't believe that he of all the students at the school had somehow earned the right to call Søren by his name. His friends, Christian and the others, greeted him eagerly but warily when he stepped back onto the campus, suitcase in hand, hair pulled back in a ponytail, bruises on his neck from Jackie's farewell love bites last night. But his smile and his stories of his summer exploits seemingly reassured them. No one asked him about what had happened to him two days before school let out. Had they asked, he would have simply repeated his mantra to them. He would never speak of that night to anyone but Søren.

But where was Søren?

Kingsley moved back into the dormitory and took the bed next to the one Søren had occupied last school year. Glancing there, Kingsley was troubled to see none of Søren's things—his Bible written in some Scandinavian language; his shoes, two sizes larger than Kingsley's and always polished to a perfect shine—on the floor next to his trunk. Even the large wooden trunk with the brass lock was gone.

"Your friend Stearns graduated," Christian said, noticing Kingsley's stares at Søren's bed.

"What?" Kingsley gazed aghast at him.

"Yeah. Graduated. He's moved out of the dorms and into the priests' quarters now. Thank God, right? That guy is fucking terrifying. I was always scared I'd trip in the night on the way to take a piss, and he'd kill me. The Fathers get to walk on eggshells now."

"So he is still here? He didn't leave the school." Kingsley nearly collapsed with relief.

"Teaching now. Foreign languages. None of the Fathers are fluent in much of anything but Latin, Greek and Hebrew. They've got Stearns teaching French, Spanish and German. Don't know why. You should be the one teaching French."

"Perhaps I could be his teaching assistant." Kingsley smiled at the thought, but Christian only stared at him, wide-eyed. "It was a joke, Christian."

"Better be. Jesus, can you imagine his poor students? Well, they'll learn the language at least. They'll be too scared not to."

"I don't think he's as terrifying as you think he is."

Christian slapped him playfully on the arm as he headed out of the dorm. "You're a braver man than I am, then. Or just fucking crazy."

Alone once more, Kingsley picked up his things and moved them to Søren's old bed. He didn't know if they'd ever be able to sleep together now—at least not in the same room. But Kingsley could sleep in Søren's bed. It might be enough.

That night in the dining hall, Kingsley barely ate. The need, the eagerness to see Søren superseded all other hungers. But Søren didn't show—not for dinner, not for Vespers, not for lights out.

That night Kingsley lay in bed and studied the ceiling as, one by one, the twelve other boys in the room dropped off to sleep. Their heavy, rhythmic breaths and soft snores filled the room. Kingsley turned over in bed and gazed at the light from the hallway creeping in from under the door. The light flickered as something blocked it. Something…someone.

Kingsley threw back the covers and raced as silently as he could to the door. Holding his breath, he turned the knob and opened it, praying if he moved slowly enough, it wouldn't make its usual loud squeak. His prayer was answered. Kingsley slipped into the hall, shut the door behind him and found himself immediately against the wall, his face pressed to the cool stone.

The warmth of a body burned against his back. He'd gone to bed wearing nothing but a pair of black boxer shorts that Susan had given him. So against his skin he felt buttons from an oxford shirt, the silk of a tie, the cold metal of a belt buckle. Inhaling deep, Kingsley smelled winter.

"I missed you," he whispered in French.

Søren said nothing, merely leaned in harder against him. The second he'd seen the strip of light under the door darken, Kingsley had grown aroused. He wanted to feel Søren's arousal, too, wanted it against his back, against him and inside him.

Kingsley braced himself against the wall with his hands. Søren grasped his wrists with an easy grip.

"You came back," Søren said against Kingsley's hair.

"You told me to." In those four words, Kingsley felt a kind of deep truth he'd never experienced before about himself. *You told me to.* Kingsley would do anything, absolutely anything, for Søren.

"I hurt you. Badly." Søren said the words simply, without a trace of guilt or shame.

"Oui."

TIFFANY REISZ

"You liked it." It wasn't a question.

"Oui. Mais…" Kingsley didn't know quite how to broach the subject. He stopped speaking and let his one word of objection hang in the air.

"I'll find a way to be more careful," Søren pledged. He rested his hand on the flat of Kingsley's stomach, and Kingsley inhaled sharply. The presence of Søren's hand on his skin sent pleasure spiking through him.

"I have something with me that should help," Kingsley said.

"Good." Søren kissed the back of his bare shoulder.

"Now?"

He felt Søren shaking his head.

"Not tonight. Not here. But soon."

Kingsley nodded. He would have been disappointed, but he'd hardly expected this to happen the moment he returned to school.

"Go back to bed," Søren ordered. "Go to sleep."

"Oui, monsieur," Kingsley said, grinning against the wall.

Søren's low laugh raised goose bumps that ran down the center of Kingsley's spine. Søren pushed away from him slowly and he immediately missed the heat on his cool skin.

Turning around, he faced Søren. God…he'd grown even more beautiful over the summer. His hair looked to be about an inch longer, his eyes even grayer. Søren had abandoned the school uniform for a real suit that made him look like the man he'd become.

"I'm yours," Kingsley whispered. He laid both palms on Søren's chest. "You know that."

Søren looked down at his hands.

"I know. I…" he began, and paused for a breath. "I didn't mean to hurt you as much as I did."

Kingsley smiled. "I liked that you hurt me."

"Good. I have to hurt you."

"Have to?" Kingsley met Søren's eyes. The look in them… Kingsley didn't understand it. What was it he saw there? Regret? No. Not shame. Not fear.

"I'm different." Søren turned his head and stared down the dimly lit hallway. Shadows lurked in the corners. But was Søren looking at the shadows or something in them?

"No. Not different. Better," Kingsley assured him. Søren smiled slightly and tore his gaze from the darkness at the edge of the corridor.

"I am. I can't…"

Kingsley gasped as Søren suddenly slipped his hand down Kingsley's boxers and wrapped his fingers around him.

"This," Søren whispered, putting his mouth to Kingsley's ear. "Unless I hurt you, unless I cause you pain, I can't…"

And Kingsley understood. Søren couldn't get aroused unless he inflicted pain. Everything made sense now. Søren's remoteness, the wall of self-protection he built around himself, his aloofness that kept the other boys far away from him—all done on purpose to protect anyone who would get close to him. For to get close to Søren meant walking through fire, stepping on glass, crawling through hell.

Kingsley flexed his hips, pushing himself into Søren's hand. He nearly came from that one movement alone. *"Je comprende."*

Søren slowly released Kingsley and pulled his hand back, his eyes widened slightly as if in surprise. "You understand me," he said. "But I don't understand you. You aren't afraid of this?"

Kingsley shrugged. "I told you, I'm French. Ever read the Marquis de Sade?" He grinned ear to ear and Søren's smile widened.

"Sometimes I think I am him. I've read Machiavelli, too. *The Prince.* It is better to be feared than loved."

Kingsley heard the sorrow in Søren's voice, the longing for something he thought he couldn't have.

"And…" Søren continued, "it's safer to be feared than loved. At least where I'm concerned." He smiled almost shyly and Kingsley suddenly understood it all—why Søren was so cold, so remote, why he could and did instill such fear in the hearts of everyone who came near him. He did it on purpose. He did it to keep them safe.

Reaching up, Kingsley laid his hands on Søren's chest and felt his heart beating slowly, steadily.

"I don't want to be safe," Kingsley whispered.

"You don't know what you're saying, Kingsley."

"I know exactly what I'm saying. You think you are broken. *Non,* you are perfect." He said the words in French. So much easier to speak the truth in his native tongue.

"Would you choose to be like me, if you had the choice?"

"I do choose it. You regret what you are only because you think you must keep others away from you. It will not keep me away."

"Always…" Søren glanced away again, glanced upward and sighed. "I've always wanted to believe God made me this way for a reason."

"Je suis la raison."

I am the reason.

Søren exhaled slowly. He ran a hand up Kingsley's arm to his shoulder. Cupping the side of his neck, he brought his mouth down to Kingsley's. Kingsley opened himself to the kiss and let Søren's tongue touch his. Such a gentle kiss, so intimate yet careful.

"Ma raison d'être," Søren whispered, and Kingsley shivered with need.

"You're holding back. I can feel it." Kingsley said the words into Søren's lips.

"I have to hold back. Now at least. Or I'll break you apart again."

"I want that. I want you."

Søren dropped another quick kiss on Kingsley's lips. "Soon. I'll find a way for us to be together. But I will hurt you again. I'm certain of it. You'll have to help me keep from going too far."

Kingsley gripped Søren's shirt in both hands and tried to pull him closer. Two and a half months apart had left him in an agony of need. He couldn't let Søren go. Not yet.

"I begged you to stop that night. I said 'stop' and 'please' and 'no' and you kept on. I didn't want you to stop, but I don't know what to do to make you stop if saying stop doesn't work."

"It didn't work because I knew you didn't want me to stop."

"Someday I might."

"Then say…" Søren paused and glanced around the hall-way. The cold stone walls stood unadorned but for a few pictures of various saints and popes. "…mercy."

Kingsley laughed. "Mercy? Really?"

Søren nodded. But he didn't laugh, didn't even smile.

"Mercy…" Kingsley repeated in English. "It sounds like *merci,* you know."

Mercy. In English it meant an act of pardon, compassion. *Merci* was French for "thank you."

"I know." Søren gave him a smile that nearly felled him.

"Who are you?" The question came out before Kingsley could stop it.

Søren only looked at him.

"I mean…your name, Søren. Where does it come from? They say your name is Marcus Stearns. But I know it's not."

Søren said nothing for a moment and Kingsley prayed he would tell him, that he would answer. The need for answers from Søren outweighed even his desire for sex.

"Marcus is my father's name," Søren said simply, without

emotion. "He raped my mother, and I was born. He named me after himself. But she gave me another name, her father's name. No one calls me Marcus but my father."

"Who calls you Søren? At the school, I mean."

Søren lightly touched Kingsley's lips.

"Only you."

"And why me?" That was the question that had plagued him for ten weeks, since the night of the rape on the forest floor. Of all the boys at the school…why him? Why Kingsley? Why did Søren choose him to tell his secrets to, to share his body with?

"Because…" Søren dropped his hands, to hold Kingsley by the hips. He laid his forehead on Kingsley's and took two slow breaths. "Because you aren't afraid of me."

With that, he pulled away and disappeared down the hallway. Kingsley stood outside the dorm room, swallowing huge gulps of air as he leaned back against the cold stone of the wall. With one hand over his eyes, he slipped his other hand into his boxers and stroked himself a few times, until he came with a shudder and a nearly audible gasp.

Wet with his own semen, Kingsley returned to his bed, not caring enough to even bother cleaning himself off first. Søren had given him that erection and nearly given him the orgasm. He didn't want to wash it off any more than he'd wanted to take a bath after that night in the forest. Knowing Søren had come inside him had made the entire ordeal worth all the fear and all the pain.

And soon, he'd have it again.

But how soon?

Kingsley stumbled through the next day, barely registering anything around him. He made the effort to seem aware and awake and cognizant of his surroundings. He spoke in his classes. He chatted with his classmates at lunch. During chapel he even volunteered to read one of the daily readings. But his mind existed solely for Søren. And late that afternoon, he finally caught a glimpse of him. Strolling down the second floor of the library, Kingsley heard Søren's voice. But was that Søren? It sounded like him. But not. The voice sounded happy, encouraging and drily witty. He could still safely say that, if added up, the sum total of his conversations with Søren would equal just under one hour. And each of those conversations had been fraught with tension. He stopped in the hallway and looked into a classroom. Søren stood by the chalkboard at the front, wearing brown pants, a brown patterned vest and a white shirt with elegantly turned cuffs. Before him a dozen eleven- and twelve-year-olds mumbled the Spanish conjugation of "to talk."

Yo hablo…tú hablas…él habla…nostros hablamos…

"Good. Very good," Søren said as the students finished. "Now let's try it again…but audibly this time. Talk, please. Talk? No *hablas inglés?*"

Nervous but genuine laughter rippled through the classroom. Søren smiled and nodded. This time with some measure of enunciation the students recited the conjugation again.

"Better. *Gracias.*"

In unison the class replied, *"De nada."*

Kingsley covered his mouth to stifle the laugh that wanted to explode out of him. Søren, who had scared every boy in the school when he was a student, now seemed to have the complete devotion of his students.

His students?

A realization hit Kingsley at that moment, and he dropped his hand from his mouth. He felt himself tremble as he forced himself away from the classroom scene and outside again.

The risk they were taking by being together had seemed

enormous enough when Søren was a student. But now…
Kingsley was still a student and Søren was a teacher.

A teacher…my God, he was sleeping with one of the teachers. And to think his grandparents had sent him here to keep
him away from more sexual misadventures.

Outside in the fresh air, Kingsley inhaled deeply, trying to
calm himself. His heart rate slowed and his panic passed. He
trusted Søren utterly and completely. If Søren felt they were
safe, being together, then they were.

Yes, Søren being a teacher now was bad, awkward. They'd
have to be even more careful. But it could have been so much
worse.

At least he wasn't a priest.

NORTH
The Present

Kingsley spun around and found himself face-to-face with a smiling ghost from the past.

"Mon Dieu," he breathed, recognizing the face in an instant.

"'And this is the promise He has promised us, even eternal life.' 1 John 2:25."

Kingsley stared in silent amazement.

The black cassock, the white collar and thirty years had done nothing to disguise the face that smiled at him.

"Christian?"

"Father Christian Elliot now. Remember? Or do you not read your alumni newsletter?"

Christian and Kingsley embraced like brothers. Christian had been the first boy at Saint Ignatius to befriend him and the only one of them all to try to find him after Kingsley left the school.

"I am afraid I've neglected to pass my new address on to the alumni committee." Kingsley patted Christian on the face. "It's good to see you again. You look terrible."

His old friend laughed heartily and turned around once. "What? You don't like?"

Kingsley shook his head in disgust. "You enlisted in God's army, as well. How could you? I take it very personally."

"The Fathers at Saint Ignatius make it their goal to turn one student from each class into a Jesuit. Just be glad it was me and not you."

"They would never take me alive, *mon frère*."

They looked at each other another moment and laughed again. The years between them, the very separate paths they'd taken, disappeared in an instant.

"I can't believe I'm looking at Kingsley Boissonneault. Truly, I thought I'd never see you again—not until heaven, anyway."

"Surely not even there." Kingsley flashed him the devil's own smile.

"I shouldn't be comforted that you haven't changed a bit. But I am. It's not fair. I've aged thirty years in thirty years. Why haven't you?"

"I'm French."

"Of course. I'd forgotten. I saw Stearns…Father Stearns a few years back. He's aging even better than you are." Christian smiled placidly and Kingsley knew he was baiting him with mention of Søren. Priests…they never stopped with their mind games, did they? Not that he minded. Really one of their best qualities.

"I do think he sold his soul to the devil for that face of his. You can see it today if you like. He's here with me."

Christian's eyes widened. "Really? You two are still—"

"Family. My sister died, yes. But he and I are still close. Times were…difficult for a few years."

They started walking toward the hermitage.

"You left right after…everything happened. Where did you go?"

"France," Kingsley said simply, and waited. Christian said nothing else. With a sigh, Kingsley continued. "I joined the French Foreign Legion. Distinctly not God's army."

"I've heard about *la Légion*. Doesn't surprise me in the least that's where you ended up. Interesting uniform you legionnaires wear." He gave Kingsley a once-over.

"You should see me when I'm not trying to look inconspicuous." For the trip to Saint Ignatius, Kingsley had abandoned his usual uniform of riding boots and a Victorian or Regency era suit of black or gray. He'd left the embroidered silk vests, the military jackets and his cravats in the closet. Today he wore a simple Armani suit—black and single-breasted. One of his employees had told him he looked dull and safe in the suit—exactly the look he intended. "I left *la Légion* years ago for Manhattan."

"I heard rumors you were a businessman now. Do I want to know what sort of business?"

Kingsley slapped Christian on the shoulder. *"Non."*

Laughing, Christian opened the door to the hermitage. Kingsley paused on the threshold, suddenly reluctant to enter. So many memories…all of them powerful, not all of them good.

"You can come in. It isn't really haunted. Father Henry only said that to scare the younger boys from coming out here. Dangerous terrain…oh, King. Forgive me."

Kingsley stepped into the hermitage, unwilling to let the past have any more power over him than it already did.

"Christian, it's been thirty years. I can bear a mention of her and her death. Believe me. I would have hardly stayed friends with that blond monster otherwise, would I?"

"I can't believe you two were friends in the first place."

Christian waved his hand at a chair, and Kingsley sat down in it gratefully. He missed his riding boots, their supple leather and support. These shoes…he'd have one of his assistants burn them the minute he returned to the town house. "Not to ever speak ill of another Jesuit, but he's a difficult man to get to know. Hard to imagine being friends with him at all."

Kingsley heard a note of something in Christian's voice. He couldn't place it at first because he never heard it often. The note…knowledge. Kingsley narrowed his eyes at Christian and decided to find out exactly what Christian thought he knew.

"He's not an easy man to get close to. Once you do, however, you are well rewarded," Kingsley said, subtly baiting Christian back.

Christian put the kettle on the stove. Kingsley gazed around the hermitage and saw Søren had been right about the remodel. Thirty years ago, when he and Søren had used this cottage for their assignations, there'd been nothing here but a rough wood table, one chair and rotting wood stacked by the spiderweb-infested fireplace.

"I remember this hermitage, Christian. It was a hellhole in our day. Now it appears a Fifth Avenue designer has had his way with the place. Matching furniture? Leather seating? My goodness, you're living rather luxuriously for a priest," he taunted.

Christian grinned broadly. "I'm not complaining. I gave up women for this job. At least they could give me a decent place to live."

"How long ago was the remodel?"

"Shortly after your friend Stearns donated his largesse to us. It had been abandoned again. Canadian runaways had been living in it awhile."

"Canadian runaways?"

"Or American runaways heading to Canada. We get a few

of each stripe through here every year. This valley connects the two highways."

"It's deadly out here. No one knows that better than we do."

Christian nodded. "A few have died crossing this terrain. We try to police it a bit better. They slip through. A whole family was sleeping in this cabin when we came out to start the remodel."

"I'm sure the Fathers took care of them."

"We try. Tea?"

"Oui, merci." Kingsley took the cup from Christian, who sat across from him by the fireplace.

"Ah, there's the French. You still have the accent, but I've missed the language."

"I'll never lose the accent. It pays the bills."

Christian grinned again. "You were right. I really don't want to know what sort of business you're in. I'm sure you keep that far away from your relationship with Father Stearns."

Kingsley raised an eyebrow. His lip twitched from trying not to smile.

"Bien sûr."

They sipped at their tea by the fireplace like two English gentlemen instead of what they were—one Jesuit priest and one French sinner.

"Can I ask what brought you back here?" Christian asked, studying him over the rim of his cup.

"Old ghosts." Kingsley turned his gaze to the cold fireplace and weighed his words. Christian had taken the photograph that had been sent to him and Søren. Possible he knew something. "As you're a priest now, I can trust that anything I tell will be kept between us alone." Perhaps if he gave up a little of the truth, Christian would give up even more.

"You can tell me anything. It would be an honor to hear your confession."

"Only don't absolve me, *s'il vous plaît*. I would miss my sins and they would miss me."

"You have my word. Now tell me…who is the ghost that brings you back here after all these years?"

"I wish I knew, *mon frère. Mon père*." Kingsley winked at Christian. "You remember the photographs you took of all of us?"

Christian's brow furrowed before his eyes widened with remembrance. "Yes, of course. I got that camera for Christmas. Thought I'd spend my life doing *National Geographic* covers."

"For the animals, of course. Not the native women?" Kingsley raised his eyebrow and Christian blushed slightly.

"I would go where they sent me. Yes, I remember the pictures. I tried to get a shot of everyone in the school."

"You took one of Father Stearns and me. After class. I'd been helping him grade papers for his French students."

"I don't remember the details. Were we in the library?"

"The chapel." Kingsley recalled every detail of that day. He and Søren had fought in the hermitage. Fought bitterly as they were wont to do. Young Kingsley had been tempestuous, hot-blooded, desperate for more time with Søren, more affection from the often remote young man. Søren, then as now, had been cold, calm, rational…his placidity in the face of Kingsley's fury infuriating him even more. Kingsley had goaded Søren, desperate for any sort of reaction from him. Finally, he'd gotten it. Søren had thrown him onto the cot and tied his wrists to the metal frame. For half an hour, he had fucked him in complete silence and without mercy, one hand clamped over Kingsley's mouth to silence his moans and another hand on his neck to hold him still. After the sex, Kingsley's legs had shook from the sheer overwhelming force of the orgasm Søren had wrung from his body.

They'd returned to the school and gone about business

as usual, Kingsley at peace again. In passive bliss he'd sat at Søren's feet as they quietly flipped through the stack of French homework, circling errors and making corrections. On the floor next to Søren's chair, helping him with his work, Kingsley had felt even closer to Søren then when they'd been fucking—a novel sensation he never experienced again in his life. Not until Juliette.

"The chapel. Yes. I remember now. I'd been terrified to interrupt you two. You were speaking French to each other. Not much. You seemed quiet, intent on your work. I hoped to get a picture without either of you noticing."

"We noticed. But we didn't mind."

Christian finished his cup of tea and poured another. "So my picture of you two...what about it?"

"Someone mailed it to me. The original."

"Who?"

Kingsley shook his head. "That is indeed the question."

"No idea?"

"None at all. It was sent anonymously. As a threat or a warning...or perhaps merely a taunt."

"A threat? Is it a secret you and Father Stearns were at school here together?"

Something in Christian's voice...Kingsley heard it again. He knew something. Perhaps he didn't even know what he knew. But Kingsley would find out.

"Not a secret we were at school together. *Non*."

Kingsley waited and let the silence between them fill the room like rising water.

"Your sister..." Christian began and stopped. Kingsley said nothing. He'd seen a thousand men close to breaking before and knew that look in their eyes. At this moment Christian stood poised on the edge of a cliff, a cliff like the one that had killed Marie-Laure. Nothing to do now but let him fall over. "You and Stearns…"

"What about us?"

Christian stared down at his clasped hands.

"She came to me once…in tears. She said she thought that Stearns, that her husband was in love with someone else. She said he never…"

"He never touched her."

Christian met Kingsley's eyes. "I didn't believe her. No one around but priests and us. She was the only girl within miles. And even if she wasn't, who would ever love anyone more than her?"

"He did," Kingsley said, failing to keep the note of pride from his voice. He might have lost Søren's love to his *Little One* years ago but once Kingsley had been the victor.

"He loved you." Christian said the three words as if he'd discovered the Holy Grail. "All my life, I've wondered, it's been like a wound that never healed, Marie-Laure's death. Why she died. What possessed her… You and Stearns. I thought but I never believed."

"What did you think?"

Shaking his head, Christian looked around the room as if he'd never seen the place before.

"The wedding. I watched you three. Marie-Laure couldn't stop staring at him. Of course. She was the bride. But you didn't look at her, your own sister getting married. You looked at him. And he…"

"He looked at me."

"My God…" His old friend set his cup of tea back down on the table and stared at him. He ran his fingers through what little hair he had left and rubbed at his face. His hands dropped to his sides and he stood up straight. "Before school let out…before summer break…you were carried to the infirmary. You—"

"*Non*. It isn't like that. That wasn't… It's so hard to explain."

"You had so many girlfriends."

Kingsley stood up and walked to Christian. "I still do. What is that verse? 'There is neither Jew nor Greek, there is neither slave nor free, there is neither male nor female…for you are all one in Kingsley's bed?'" He patted the side of Christian's face in a patronizing manner. His friend flinched, caught himself flinching and then laughed.

"That must be some translation of Galatians I'm not familiar with."

"It's my personal translation. Are you all right, Christian? You're looking rather pale."

"I'll recover. Maybe. I'm trying to wrap my mind around all this…. But still, certain things make sense now. Stearns, he was always so remote."

"It just happened… We were all we had—each other. No women ever stepped foot into this school except for the nurse—"

"Nurse Jan, age ninety, weight nine hundred."

"*Exactement.*"

"And your sister," Christian reminded him.

"And my sister."

"So someone sent you my photograph of you and Stearns. And you and Stearns were…"

"We were lovers, Christian," Kingsley chided. "You're a priest, not a virgin."

Christian gave him a half smile. "True. You say 'were.' It's really a thing of the past. He's a priest now. He can't—"

"Do not worry about *le prêtre*. He and I are long past. His parishioners worship him almost as much they do God. He has never betrayed their trust."

"Good…that's good. I'd never tell, of course. I can't tell any of this to anyone. But I'll sleep better knowing that your past is in your past."

"It is. Or was. Someone knows about us. Or thinks they know."

"Have there been any other threats?"

"There have been incidents. Something was stolen from my home. Father Stearns's childhood bedroom was broken into. But I can't talk about that."

"Do you think…" Christian began, and stopped. "I mean, you were at the rock where they found Marie-Laure."

"I was, yes."

"Why?"

Kingsley stared at Christian.

"*Je ne sais pas.* Paying my respects. She was all I had after my parents died. I had almost no relationship with the grandparents who took me in. They loved me because I was their grandson, and for no other reason. But Marie-Laure, she did everything she could to come to America to be with me. *Pourquoi?*"

Christian gave him a blank look.

"Why do you ask?" Kingsley repeated.

"I'm not sure. Just a thought. Do you think someone thinks her death wasn't an accident? What if someone thought…what if someone blamed you? No offense, but I remember her first day here better than I remember your first day here. Hell, better than I remember my own."

"I'm hardly offended. I have never seen her equal in beauty. You think…"

Christian stepped to the window of the hermitage and pushed back the curtain. He pointed up to the ridge, where Kingsley and Søren had been standing less than an hour earlier. "What happened that day, King?"

"She was angry with me. She ran away. She fell and hit the rock."

"Fell…or jumped?"

Kingsley couldn't meet Christian's eyes. The priest has asked him the same question Kingsley has been asking himself since the moment he'd gazed down upon his sister's shattered body.

"She jumped…I think. But I can't say for certain. She'd converted when she and Father Stearns married. She'd be denied Catholic burial if she'd committed suicide. *Mais…*"

Christian gave him a look of deep compassion. "You said you'd fought. What had you fought about?"

Kingsley groaned and squeezed the bridge of his nose. "She…Marie-Laure…" He found himself momentarily unable to go on. Talking about that time, about Marie-Laure's death, filled him with an emotion he rarely if ever felt—shame. "She caught Father Stearns and I together. She saw us."

"Good Lord." Christian raised a hand to his forehead. "It happened, you and him, after he married her?"

Kingsley nodded.

"Marie-Laure and I had nothing—not a cent to our names. We wanted to stay in America, stay together, but couldn't. She had to go back to Paris, to her ballet company. I couldn't lose her again. And Stearns, he offered the perfect solution. If he married, he would receive the trust fund his father had set up for him—millions of dollars upon his twenty-first birthday or the day he married, whichever came first."

"So she knew it was a marriage in name only."

"You've seen *le prêtre.* You remember what he looked like then—almost as handsome as he is now. She agreed to the marriage and said she understood it was only for the money. But she loved him."

"She loved him and we hated him."

"Because you didn't know him. I loved him. Anyone who

knows him at all loves him. And if they don't love him, then they do not know him."

Christian continued to stare at Kingsley. "You still love him, my friend."

Kingsley tried meeting Christian's eyes and couldn't.

"It's the one sin I'll let you absolve me of."

Christian came to him and laid a hand gently on Kingsley's forehead.

"Love isn't a sin. It's the one thing you've told me I don't want to absolve you of."

Laughing, Kingsley took Christian's hand off his forehead and pushed it into the priest's own head. Thirty years gone with one playful shove. They were men now and yet still boys.

"Does he know?" Christian asked. He sat on the kitchen table and pushed the teacups out of the way.

"*Oui.* He's always known. I loved him when we were boys and he never loved me back. Not then. Not now. Not in the same way. Or perhaps in the same way but not as much."

"He shouldn't have used you like that then."

"*Peut-être.* But even if you'd told me then he didn't love me and never would…" Kingsley found his wicked grin again "…I wouldn't have changed a thing."

"Except for Marie-Laure's death, of course." The statement came out as a question, and Kingsley was forced to answer it.

Had Marie-Laure not died, what would have happened? She and Søren would still be married. What would that have meant for them both? Søren had wanted to try to make a life with Marie-Laure. Once he realized that his young wife truly loved him, he had been determined to be a good husband to her. Their marriage had gone unconsummated for months after the wedding. Søren had been waiting for the right time to tell her about his needs that only inflicting pain would fulfill.

He'd confessed this plan to Kingsley. And then they'd

fought more bitterly than the day Christian took the photograph. Kingsley had gone mad with rage and grief at the
thought of Søren with anyone else, especially his own sister. Any other brother would have been defending his sister's honor, refusing to allow her sadist husband to tell her he
needed to beat her if they were ever to become lovers. But
Kingsley's pain had been for himself alone. If Marie-Laure
wanted pain, she had the whole world to give it to her. But
Søren's violence belonged to Kingsley.

He'd threatened Søren, threatened to tell everyone at the
school that they were lovers. A foolish, idle threat that would
have had no impact even if Kingsley had gone through with it.
Søren's trust fund had already come through. He and Marie-
Laure were rich now. Free to go wherever they pleased.
Kingsley feared that more than anything—that Søren and
Marie-Laure would go and leave him behind.

Søren had stayed calm during the worst of Kingsley's tantrum, and at the end, when he had exhausted himself with
grief and anger, Søren had taken Kingsley's face in his hands
and kissed him. And the kiss had turned into something more.
When Kingsley's shirt slid off his shoulders and landed with
a whisper on the ground, and Søren had dipped his head and
dug his teeth into Kingsley's collarbone, causing Kingsley to
groan with the pleasure and the pain and the sheer relief of it
all…that's when Marie-Laure had walked in on them. And
although her heart would beat for only a few minutes more
as she'd raced through the forest…that had been the moment
Kingsley knew she'd truly died.

"Of course," he answered now, but wasn't sure if he spoke
the truth. Had Marie-Laure lived, Søren would have become
a piano teacher and a college professor, and his calling to the
priesthood would have gone unanswered. Kingsley knew that,
without Søren, he would be a dead man. For over ten years

after he and Søren had parted company, Kingsley had lived the most dangerous life he could. He ran from death the way he'd run that night from Søren—in the hopes he'd get caught and taken. Not until they reunited had Kingsley found a purpose in his life again, a reason to live.

And Eleanor…Nora…Søren's Little One. She, too, would have had a comfortable home six feet under the earth had Søren never come into her life. Tempting, Kingsley admitted only to himself. A world without Nora Sutherlin…he'd almost like to see that.

"I mean only what happened between Father Stearns and me as teenagers. I have no regrets about that, even though now he's a priest. And a very devout one."

"But not too devout to be seen in public with you." Christian smiled.

"This is hardly public. And he's off now, likely saying Mass in the chapel with Father Aldo."

"Ah, Father Aldo is long gone. Back to South America. He's saving the soul of the Southern Hemisphere these days."

"I'm sure the students miss his cooking."

"We all do. Only Marie-Laure could make better creme brûlée. To die for."

Kingsley exhaled heavily. "Perhaps that's why she died."

Christian pursed his lips and gave him a look half amused, half disgusted.

"You're deflecting. You realize that, yes?"

"Are you a priest or a psychologist? I'm not quite sure which is worse."

"I'm both." Christian sat back on the edge of the kitchen table. "Master of Divinity and Psychology. PhD in Psychology. Priests have to be psychologists. Especially at a school for troubled boys. And it doesn't take a PhD to see that you're still deeply grieving for your sister. Every little joke you make about it is further proof."

Kingsley nearly made another joke, but stopped himself. Christian was right. Why fight the truth?

"*Bien sûr.* Of course I still grieve for her. More lately than in years. Being here doesn't help."

"It makes it much harder to forget, I'm sure."

"Talking to you helps. Admitting that I was in a large way responsible for her death."

Christian shook his head. "I'm not sure that you were. To kill oneself…that is the gravest of all sins. To kill another is to kill one person. To kill oneself is to kill all people. Seeing her husband with her brother, terrible? Yes. Absolutely terrible. But to murder the entire world for that? Perhaps there was more going on."

"More?"

Christian stood up again and started making a circuit of the small cottage. Kingsley remembered this habit of his. During study groups Christian could never sit still. He had to walk and walk if he wanted to think.

"A photograph of you and Stearns, the one I took, was sent to you anonymously. You take that as a threat."

"It is a threat. The other incidents…they, too, have been threatening. Father Stearns's childhood bed was burned to ashes. And a file was stolen from my office. The file contains private information about Stearns. Information that could ruin him. Not that he deserves that. If any man deserves to be a priest, it is he."

"So you say and I'll believe you. So all of these threats have to do with Stearns's private life. And Marie-Laure died on that rock out there. And the threats…all these threats…"

"They all involve him, *oui.* We know that."

"Who else do they involve?"

"Three people. The only three people who he has ever been with, and that is all I can say."

"Only three?" Christian smirked and Kingsley caught a glimpse of the wicked teenage boy he used to know. "Even I have him beat there."

Kingsley exhaled through his nose and stared at the bare wood by the fireplace where he and Søren had once huddled under blankets together for warmth on a bitter winter night. Kingsley had never before been so grateful for the cold.

"I simply don't know who would dare do this to him..."

"Kingsley, I'm going to tell you something and I don't want you to hate me for it."

Kingsley looked up sharply at him.

"Tell me."

"I hated Stearns. Back when we were in school. I don't use the word *hate* lightly."

"I know he was envied."

"Envied and loathed. He was better than the rest of us. And no, I'm not saying he thought he was better than us. I don't believe he did. He actually *was* better than all of us—smarter, more handsome by a mile, still more handsome by a mile than any man I've ever seen. He could learn a new language faster than I could learn a new hymn on guitar. He played piano like a god. And the priests here worshipped him. And when your sister, the most beautiful girl anyone had ever seen, came to visit, it was him she fell in love with and married. Thirty years ago, I wanted him dead."

"And now?"

Christian shook his head. "Teenage hormones and angst. Now I can only admire him. And worry a bit for his congregation."

"Do not worry. They are in the best hands. But what are you saying?"

"I'm saying that someone obviously hates Stearns. Still hates him. If they knew something about you and him, about Marie-Laure... If someone loved her even more than I did, and blamed Stearns for her death..."

Christian needed to say no more. The motive that had eluded Kingsley all summer, since he'd discovered his pack of rottweilers drugged and Eleanor's file gone...suddenly all became clear.

Søren's first lover had been his own sister Elizabeth.

His second lover had been Kingsley, a student when he'd been a teacher. Forbidden fruit in so many ways.

And his Eleanor, his true wife so much more than Marie-Laure, had been only fifteen when Søren and she had fallen in love. Fifteen and a member of his congregation.

"Christian, you might be right. Someone might have loved Marie-Laure, loved her enough to seek vengeance against Father Stearns even after all this time. You were friends with everyone at school. Who else was in love with her?"

Christian sighed heavily. He walked over to a small rolltop desk and opened the middle drawer. From it he pulled out a framed photo and carried it to Kingsley.

Kingsley took the photo from Christian and stared at it.

His breath caught in his throat and he couldn't quite swallow.

A girl barely twenty years old stared at him from inside the frame. Nothing but clichés could describe her beauty—silken russet hair, copper eyes framed by infinite lashes, a laughing smile that didn't quite meet those unearthy eyes of hers. She had a dancer's graceful neck and hands, and an olive complexion just like her brother's.

"Ma soeur…" Kingsley touched the glass with his finger-tip. He wrenched his gaze from the photograph to Christian.

"Who was in love her?" Christian repeated. "Kingsley… we all were."

SOUTH

As soon as they entered the guesthouse, Nora got on her laptop and on her phone. For some reason, Kingsley wasn't answering his private line. She tried calling his assistant and got nothing but the cryptic runaround. Kingsley—he was just the man she needed for this job.

"Nora, let it go," Wesley said as she tried Kingsley's hotline again.

"He's going to answer." Nora hit the number on her cell phone again. "It's the hotline. He always answers the hotline. I've heard that man fucking so many times, I've lost count, because no matter what he's doing or who he's doing, he always answers his hotline."

"Stop calling him. If Spanks for Nothing died from electrocution or something, the investigators will figure it out and fine whoever needs to be fined."

"But that's Talel's horse." Nora turned to Wesley, who sat on the corner of his bed, watching her where she sat on the floor. "I know Talel. He wouldn't hurt a fly, much less electrocute a horse."

Wesley got off the bed and stood in front of her.

"Look, Nora, I know he's a friend of yours and that's great. But horse racing's a rough business. It's not all silks and Millionaires' Row. It's brutal and dangerous and messy."

"But Talel..." Nora started scrolling through her cell files. Surely she had Talel's number in here somewhere. She had to talk to him about today. She knew him. Biblically, even. He wanted to be hurt—that was his kink. But to hurt another? Never. She refused to believe that.

"Talel's a millionaire horse owner and a kinky freak like the rest of your friends. He's not a saint, okay? You know how you can tell if a Thoroughbred mare has been bred?"

Nora heard the barely restrained anger in Wesley's voice.

"No. How?"

"Because the mare has scar tissue and visible stitching under her vagina. Yeah. Fact. They cut the mare open so it can take more stallion. Then she gets stitched up. Then cut again for the next breeding. Then stitched up. Then cut again. Over and over."

Nora clamped a hand over her mouth in disgust. "You've got to be—"

"Kidding? No. I've seen it myself. That's just part of the shit that goes on in this Sport of Kings. Your best buddy Spanks for Nothing could have lived thirty years or more. But either someone wanted some insurance money off him, or wanted him to have a few more wins to get those stud fees up there. You saw a horse, a pet. Talel and every other horse owner sees a dollar sign. Lots of dollar signs. Horses are just like race cars to these people. You crash the car, you call the insurance company and get a check. I don't like it, either, but that's how it is."

Nora's stomach tightened into a hard fist of guilt. "Race cars aren't alive. They can't feel pain. They..."

"Now you know why I'm not all into the family business."

"Yeah, I can see that. I'm sorry, Wes. It's just, Talel and I go way back and he's a good—"

"You slept with him, didn't you?"

Wesley asked the question without a hint of malice in his voice, and no accusation, either. Only sadness. She would rather he'd called her a whore to her face like his father had.

"Yes, I did. A few years ago. He gave me my Aston Martin."

For a moment Wesley didn't speak. Nora only stared at him as he seemed to search for words. She'd rarely seem him so somber and so silent. Back when they'd lived together, he'd joked with her constantly, teased her constantly. And she'd gloried in his young male attention. But Wesley wasn't a teenage boy with a hard-on for an older woman anymore. He'd admitted he loved her, still loved her after fifteen months apart. And he'd had his chance to have sex with his beautiful older girlfriend and hadn't taken it. No schoolboy crush this—Wesley loved her. And she'd left Søren, left her collar, for Wesley. For how long, she didn't know. But Søren had forbidden her to run from him, and the second she'd been out of his sight she'd kicked off her high heels and raced as if the world depended on her getting to Wesley in record time. She loved him, too.

Whether she wanted to or not.

"Wesley?"

"You know," he said, giving her a broken smile, "I could afford to buy you all the Aston Martins you want."

Nora tossed her cell phone aside and pushed her laptop onto the floor. Coming to her feet, she started to reach for him, but he took a step back.

"I'm gonna go feed the catfish. I'll be back."

He turned on his heel and abruptly left the room.

Looking around the empty space, Nora could only repeat, "Feed the catfish?"

She started to follow him, but her cell phone rang—Ravel's *Bolero*.

"King, thank God. I've been calling you all day. Well, for the last five minutes. Where the hell are you?"

"Maine, *ma chérie,*" Kingsley answered in his most debonair voice. "I see you called me many times. How much do you miss me?"

"Not a damn bit. But I have missed your connections. Guess who I ran into today?"

"Talel."

Nora held out her hand and stared at the phone a moment before putting it back to her ear. "I hate when you do that, know more about my life than I do."

"I pay attention, *ma chérie.* You, on the other hand, are a writer."

"Point taken. Anyway, his horse died. And it might have been electrocuted. I don't think—"

"*Chérie…*" Kingsley exhaled heavily and Nora heard something in his voice she rarely if ever heard—frustration. "I'm afraid the death of a horse is the least of my worries right now. Your priest and I have much graver concerns."

"But—"

"It's for your own good, *Maîtresse.* Let it go. It's only a horse. They make an excellent entrée."

"But—"

"Nora?"

"What?"

"You're on your own."

And with those truly unhelpful words, Kingsley hung up.

Nora stared at the phone for a few seconds before tossing it onto the floor and racing after Wesley.

Feed the catfish? Did that mean he was actually going to… feed the catfish?

Outside the guesthouse, Nora paused and looked around. Where the hell had Wesley gone? She found a cobblestone path at the back of the house and decided to follow it. A low stone fence bordered the path. As she walked, Nora thought about the past couple of days with Wesley. Everything had been perfect and a wreck at the same time.

Their first hours together they'd done nothing but talk non-stop about the past fifteen months, everything that had happened while they'd been apart. Fifteen months had separated them when they'd embraced each other in the White Room at The 8th Circle. But as the hours passed and they told story after story, that gap between them closed. Nora told Wesley about reuniting with Søren, how weird it had been those first few weeks as his property again. The night they'd shown up at The 8th Circle with her in her collar again, the entire club had stared, aghast. She'd been so nervous, so uncomfortable— she'd been a Mistress, and now she'd become Søren's submissive once more. How the mighty had fallen. But then she'd seen it—money changing hands. High-fives. Fingers pointing. And lots of told-you-so's and I-knew-it's. People had been making bets about when she'd go back to Søren. It had never been a question of if she'd surrender to him. Merely when.

And Wesley, he'd told her about what had happened in his world during those fifteen months after he moved out of their house and back to Kentucky. Nothing...nothing had happened, according to him. He'd finished out the school year in a daze, packed his things, gave away his beat-up yellow VW and flew back to Kentucky. A couple days a week he worked at a local hospital as an orderly, just to keep his head on straight about all the money and privilege in his world, and all the poverty and suffering everywhere else. The rest of the time he helped out on the farm. The Rails consisted of several thousand acres littered with million-dollar Thoroughbreds. The farm had not one but two equine hospitals on the premises, dozens of barns that were as palatial as mansions, even swimming pools…for the horses. Wesley admitted he felt more comfortable, more at home, in his room at Nora's little Tudor cottage in Connecticut than he ever did on his parents' farm. That's why he hadn't told her about the money, the farm, the fame that he wore like an ill-fitting suit in racing circles. That's why he'd bought a used Bug to drive in Connecticut, and hadn't brought his Shelby Mustang with him to school. That's why he'd left his Gucci at home in Kentucky and had worn clothes from the GAP and Old Navy while at Yorke. And when Nora had decided to become a Dominatrix again, and Wesley had offered her every penny he had, that's why she should have taken it.

Nora had fallen asleep in the middle of Wesley's chest their first night back together. They hadn't kissed, hadn't made love…only talked. But their words had brought them back together that night. And words, being the powerful force they were, had tonight pulled them apart.

As she neared the end of the cobblestone path, Nora inhaled the scent of warm stagnant water and algae. Ahead of her she saw a high spotlight shining onto a wooden dock that overlooked a large pond. And at the end of the dock stood an ornate gazebo, as well-appointed as her own house back in Connecticut, with wild ivy twisting up its sides and half a dozen burning citronella candles keeping the mosquitoes away. Wesley stood at the edge of the dock, the gazebo behind him, staring out across the black water. A thousand stars shimmered across the still surface.

"So…" Nora came out onto the dock and stood at his side. "Feeding the catfish?"

He didn't look at her when he nodded. "Yup. Watch this."

He picked up a metal scoop of what looked like dog food and tossed it across the pond.

"Good arm," Nora said. The dog food had arced high in the air and now floated on the surface thirty feet out from the dock.

"That's not the cool part. This is."

"What is—oh, my God, what was that?" Nora heard a loud splash and saw the water start to churn.

"The catfish." Wesley smiled. "Damn city girl."

She stuck her tongue out at him. "That's so...holy crap, there's millions of them."

The water began to writhe with what seemed like hundreds of long brown bodies flipping and flopping and turning in the water.

"Only about a hundred, I think." Wesley threw another scoop of food across the water. "Can't remember how many they counted last time. They sleep on the bottom all day, come up at night. Especially if you feed them. We've got a couple albino ones in there. You see a gray one anywhere?"

"No mini Moby Dicks." Nora dropped to her hands and knees at the edge of the dock and studied the water. Long scaly whiskers peeked out of it, far cuter and less intimidating than shark fins. "Wes, they're so cool. Can I have one?"

She reached out and touched the back of one of the writhing catfish. It felt warm and clammy against her finger. Squealing as it splashed her, Nora jumped back up to her feet.

"You can have them all."

"Thank you. I'll just keep them in the pond for now."

"Good plan."

Wesley sat the metal scoop back down, crossed his arms over his chest and looked up into the night. Nora followed his gaze. They didn't seem to be staring at the moon or even the stars, but the few dark places in between.

The fish ate their fill and the water went still once more. Nora found herself holding her breath and not quite knowing why.

Wesley inhaled and exhaled deeply and slowly.

"Nora…I should hate you. You know that, right?"

She glanced at him and nodded. Turning her eyes up to the sky, she found one bright star and studied it. "Yes. I know."

"You electrocuted people. I'm trying to wrap my mind around that."

"Don't try. There's no need to. It's just part of the job. Some people like being flogged. Other people like being whipped. Some people like having electrical currents run through their bodies. Everybody has their kinks."

"I don't."

"Not being kinky is a kink in itself."

"Thanks for not telling me again how vanilla I am."

"Wesley…why am I here?"

"We're feeding the catfish. That's why you're here."

"You know what I mean."

He shook his head. "If you don't know why you're here, then I certainly can't tell you."

Nora laughed awkwardly. She never knew how to handle Wesley when he got like this—so distant that two feet between them seemed like two miles.

"It's nice here. Beautiful. I like the gazebo."

"My parents got married in there." Wesley turned and looked at it. "Right under that arch. All the guests lined up on the dock like some kind of honor guard. Wedding of the year, they said. They said I'd get married out here, too."

Wesley walked to the arched entryway of the white gazebo and stared down the long dock. "I used to come out here to get away from everything. It was a nice safe place to think about you. Or try not to think about you, really."

"I thought about you every day we were apart," Nora confessed. "Every single day."

"Me, too. No matter how hard I tried not to. I'd come here and stand and look at the stars. And when I turned around I'd see you walking down the deck toward me."

"I did that tonight."

"Not the way I dreamed of." He smiled shyly. "In my dreams...you were in a wedding dress."

Nora flinched, but only on the inside. "I think I'd look a little silly in a big white wedding dress."

"Not in my dreams. In my dreams...you looked beautiful."

She took a step closer to him, wanting to touch him, but suddenly afraid to.

"Wes, you shouldn't love me this much. I'm a lot of things, but good for you is not one of them. I don't know why I'm here other than I can't be anywhere else right now. I couldn't leave if I tried."

"Not yet, anyway. But you will leave again, won't you?"

Nora exhaled heavily. "Someday you'll learn not to ask questions you don't want the answer to."

"No reason not to ask the questions. You can't hurt me anymore, Nora. Not more than you already have. You broke me."

"I never meant to hurt you. I was trying to save you."

"Save me? From what?"

"Me. My life. My world."

"I didn't need saving. I just needed you. I needed our life together in our house. That was our house, you know. You bought it—I know that. But it was ours."

A lump swelled in Nora's throat and she had to swallow twice to get rid of it.

"I could have bought your house from you with the money I had in my checking account," Wesley continued. "That's pocket change in the Railey family. You don't know this, you probably didn't even notice, but every now and then, when you'd send in your mortgage payment to the bank...I'd take the check and tear it up. And I'd make the payment myself, just because I could. So yeah, it was our house."

Nora didn't try to speak again. She wasn't actually sure if she could.

"And you kicked me out. For Søren. You made me leave after living with you for a year and a half. After doing your dishes and cooking your meals and cleaning up your office and carrying you to bed after you passed out from either too much wine or too much writing...or both...I was gone. As if all that meant nothing to you."

Finally, Nora found her voice. "It meant everything to me. I just...Wesley..." She closed her eyes to obliterate the stars. "You were eighteen years old the day I met you."

"Seventeen."

"What?"

"I was seventeen. Birthday's in September, remember? I turned eighteen during the second week of classes."

Nora pressed her hand to her stomach. "Seventeen...not even old enough to vote. Seventeen the day I met you, the first day of class. Kingsley called me that morning. I was hungover and on top of Griffin Fiske when the phone rang. One of Kingsley's best clients was the academic dean of your old school."

Wesley laughed coldly. "I didn't want or need to know that."

"You need to know this. Kingsley called me and ordered me to Yorke, to your school. The guy who was supposed to teach that freshman creative-writing class had a heart attack. They need a sub...I mean, a substitute. I was the one writer they could get on such short notice. God, that was a fucking awful morning. Fighting with Kingsley about the job, fighting with Griffin about how I'd never let him top me, half-sick from a few too many shots the night before…and then my old editor at Libretto sent me seventeen pages of changes on my book. Seventeen fucking pages. I told her she had me confused with Nora Roberts—I wrote smut. I got my six hard fucks in the book. Take it or leave it.

"Bad day. Very bad day. All I wanted that day…all I desperately fucking wanted, was Søren. I ached for him. He would have made all the bad stuff go away. Had I been his that morning, he would have put the fear of God in Griffin, told Kingsley to find someone else, told me to shut up and do whatever my editor told me to do, and then he would have stripped me naked, put me into bed, pressed his beautiful naked body to mine and held me until I fell asleep and woke up human again."

"I don't want to hear this. I don't—"

"Wesley, just listen. The day I met you started out horrible. So horrible all I wanted was to give up on the life I'd made for myself, and go back to Søren and live at his feet. You think he's terrifying and dangerous. The truth is I was never safer than I was when I was with him. And when I left him…things got scary and they got ugly and they got hard. Some days I loved working for Kingsley. Some days I would nearly puke in my car after a session with a client who paid me to do things no one should have ever done, not for love or money. I was ready to do it, to go back to Søren. I was going to call him…that day. I'd go to your school and check out this stupid class, raise some hell in the hopes that they'd show me the door, and then I was going to call him and ask if I could meet him at the rectory. And once there, I'd give him my collar, get down on my knees and beg him to take me back. That was the plan. And it would have happened. No doubt in my mind. Except for one thing."

Wesley tore his eyes from the night sky and looked at her. "What?" he whispered.

Nora smiled.

"I saw you."

Finally, Nora silenced Wesley.

"I saw you, my Wesley. And I just…forgot. I forgot I was going to go back to him. Totally slipped my mind. And for the rest of that day, after that first class, you were all I could think of. Those big brown eyes of yours and that smile and the way you looked at me like…like—"

"Like I'd never seen anything like you before and didn't think I ever would again, so I better not take my eyes off you for one second."

"Yeah." Nora sighed. "Just like that. And I didn't even remember to go back to Søren the next day. Or the next. I had you. Remember all those lunches we had in the cafeteria at Yorke? All those looks we got?"

"They couldn't believe I was having lunch with my hot writing teacher and bringing my Bible with me."

"Those were some good debates we had. I'm still sad, though, that I never converted you to liberation theology."

"Too Methodist. Sorry."

Nora laughed. Then the laugh faded and died. "You said you thought you'd have to leave Yorke. Scared the hell outta me. That's why I asked you to move in."

"I only said that hoping you'd say something about missing me. Winter break was coming up. I just wanted your phone number."

"Well, you got that and then some."

"More than I ever dreamed I'd get."

"But still not enough?" Nora met his eyes and tried to smile.

Wesley rested his forehead against hers for the barest second. "That might be one of those questions you shouldn't ask."

"Wes, I…" And nothing. Nothing else came out. No words could heal the hole she'd bored in his heart.

"I'm going to bed," Wesley said as he stepped back and away from her. "It's late. I'm sorry I brought you down here. We should have stayed up north somewhere. I just wanted you to see my world. But it's not as pretty as I thought it was."

"You're here. And that makes this beautiful country."

Wesley said nothing, only looked back up at the night sky.

Nora reached out a hand to touch his arm and stopped without making contact. Funny…during those fifteen months apart she'd felt closer to him than she felt right now, only a foot away.

She took a step back. And another. Tomorrow…tomorrow would be better. Tonight they'd sleep and clear their heads if they could.

Three days in and Nora had to admit that things between them would never be like they used to be.

"Nora?"

She spun back around. Wesley turned the full force of his gaze onto her face. His eyes burned as bright as the candles in the gazebo.

"What is it, Wes?"

"I should hate you…but I don't."

Nora recognized the look in his eyes. She'd seen it in the eyes of dozens of men—the heat, the hunger, the need…. But never had it shone so sweet, so bright and so beautiful.

No, things would never be the same between them again. But they might be better.

For three years Wesley had loved her and wanted her. He'd even saved himself for her.

Three years…she wouldn't make him wait another day longer.

NORTH
The Past

One day passed. Two days. By day three Kingsley thought he would die if Søren didn't make some kind of move on him again. He'd never been in this position before. Always he'd been the pursuer, the seducer. He chose a girl and made the right moves on her, and when he invited her to his bedroom and told her to open her legs, she did as she was told. Always. Without fail. Then he let her go and left her to wait by the phone for his next summons.

Now he waited and watched and told himself, "Today…it will be today." But it wasn't today. Or the next.

Kingsley had never been more grateful that the bathrooms in the older boys' dorm had doors that locked. He'd been spending more time than usual there, and not for reasons of hygiene or gastrointestinal distress. This torture, this horrible waiting for Søren to strike, kept Kingsley in a constant state of nervous arousal. He'd come and in mere minutes would be feeling the familiar tightness in his stomach, the ache in his back, the strain in his thighs…. Nothing could and would alleviate the need but a night with Søren. A night that never seemed to come.

After one week back at school, Kingsley decided that Søren had been fucking with him. That night in the forest had been violence and nothing more. Not lust, not love...mere violence. It had meant everything to Kingsley and nothing to Søren. At least that's what he told himself, or tried to. Had he still been Stearns and not Søren, Kingsley might have believed that night had meant nothing. But he knew Søren's name now and he felt the power of that. So he continued to walk around with his testicles as heavy as lead, his stomach sore, his heart in agony.

On Friday night sleep was impossible for Kingsley. The physical discomfort paled before the mental anguish of wanting Søren and waiting for Søren and getting absolutely nothing from Søren.

At some point Kingsley nodded off, because he dreamed of a house and a bed on fire, and woke up just as the flames began to lick at his legs. His eyes shot open and he sat up in bed, panting. Raising a hand to his forehead, he felt his sweat-soaked skin. He ran his fingers through his long, wet hair.

A cup of cold water came to his lips and Kingsley gulped it eagerly.

Wait. Water?

Kingsley nearly choked on the water, but a hand covered his mouth and silenced his cough.

"Are you sick?"

Kingsley felt the whisper more than heard it.

He shook his head and the hand slowly came away from his mouth.

"Merci," he said. "Not sick. Just a bad dream."

The bed shifted slightly and Kingsley's eyes quickly adjusted to the dark. Søren sat on the edge of his bed, holding the now-empty glass of water.

Kingsley blinked, not quite certain he was awake. Søren on his bed in the middle of the night. He'd dreamed of this. Daydreams, but still dreams.

He'd never seen Søren so casually dressed before. He had on only pants and his white oxford shirt unbuttoned at the collar. No tie. No vest. No jacket. No shoes, even.

No shoes? Kingsley looked at Søren's bare feet. Silence. He wore no shoes so he could move in the corridors in silence. Good thinking. Kingsley would remember that.

"What are you doing here?" he asked in French. If one of the other boys woke up and overheard them talking, at least he wouldn't understand what they were saying.

Søren didn't answer at first. But no words were necessary, not with the look in his eyes. For days now Kingsley had lived on the edge of panic at the mere thought of another night with Søren—or worse, that he'd never have another night with him. But now that Søren sat on his bed, ready to take him, Kingsley went utterly calm. His racing heart stilled. His breathing settled.

Anywhere…he'd follow Søren anywhere. And anything… he would do anything Søren asked of him.

Søren stood up and walked to the door. Reaching under his bed, Kingsley grabbed his T-shirt and a small overnight bag.

As they left the room, Kingsley glanced around to make sure all his dorm mates still slept. As clever as he was with lies, he couldn't think of any probable explanation for why he and Søren were skulking about in the middle of the night together.

In silence they slipped through the dormitory, the tile of the floor cool and slick beneath Kingsley's bare feet. He walked behind Søren, not beside him. Søren hadn't told him to in words, but the imperious nature of his posture demanded Kingsley walk behind, and something inside Kingsley gloried in taking the lesser role.

He tensed when they reached the door to the grounds. Søren opened it for them and Kingsley bowed his head in thanks as he walked past. The door shut behind them. They were alone outside under God and all the stars.

"Where are we going?" Kingsley asked as they tread carefully across the cool, dewy grass. Luckily, September in Maine was still warm enough that only their toes would get cold tonight. Kingsley breathed in the night air and tried to memorize the scents on the breeze. Pine...so much pine. Hard to smell anything other than pine. But he could detect a trace of the not-too-distant ocean on the air, and the faraway smoke from someone's fire. Beautiful, this perfume the night wore—he would remember it always. He told himself that as he followed Søren to the edge of the forest and down a well-trodden path.

"There's a place I go and read sometimes. You'll be safe there."

"You're concerned about my safety?" Kingsley almost laughed.

Søren paused and turned around. "Of course I am," he said, and started walking again. "That night...I won't apologize."

"I don't want you to."

"I want...it's hard to explain what I want."

"Can you try?"

Søren exhaled and Kingsley winced. He didn't really care why Søren wanted what he did or why, as long as Kingsley was somewhere in the wanting. But he was curious.

"I need to cause you pain. For years now pain has been the only pleasure for me. Or at least the only way into pleasure. I think what happened when I was younger made it impossible for me to be...normal."

"Good," Kingsley said, and meant it. "I spend too much time with normal. I like that you aren't normal. I like that you want to hurt me. I've had so many girls. You can't believe how many girls I've had. Fifty, maybe? Not all girls. Women, too. A teacher once, even. Now, I suppose, two teachers."

Kingsley grinned as Søren laughed softly.

"I suppose you've never been with a girl. Doesn't matter. You haven't missed much, really. She lays there and giggles and sighs while you stick it in her. I can do better most nights with my own hand. Only…sometimes, if she's a little scared of me, or a virgin and very scared of me…then I enjoy it more. That fear—I could drink it."

"I feel the same," Søren agreed as he veered off the main track and down a narrower path dense with trees. "But with pain. The thought of doing what you just described with anyone…it leaves me dead inside, cold. I don't believe I could ever be with anyone like that. Not without hurting them first. But you should know something. I have been with another person."

"Who was he?" Kingsley winced as he stepped on a sharp rock. Søren glanced over his shoulder with a smile and kept walking. This was it, part of the plan—Kingsley without shoes on a path he'd never walked before. His feet would be bloody by the time they made it to the end. And he knew Søren would grow more and more aroused with every wince and gasp of pain he heard fall from Kingsley's lips.

Kingsley stopped watching where he stepped and let the forest floor eat his feet.

"It wasn't a he."

"A girl? I thought you lived here for years?"

"I've been here since I was eleven."

"Eleven? The only girl I talked to when I was eleven was my own sister."

Søren paused and turned around. He said nothing, but he didn't have to.

"Mon Dieu…" Kingsley whispered. "You…and your sister?"

Søren turned back around and resumed walking. "Stop wasting time."

Despite his rabid curiosity, Kingsley closed his mouth and kept going, wincing with each stick or rock his foot landed on. If they didn't get there soon, Søren would have to carry him back to the damn school.

The path opened up onto a clearing. A huge flat rock jutted out from the hilly forest, overlooking a steep drop into a valley below. Kingsley set his overnight bag by a spindly tree and stepped onto the stone plateau. The sky exploded with stars all around them. Kingsley walked to the very edge of the cliff until he stood with his toes overhanging the abyss. Stretching out his arms to the left and right as far as he could reach, he gave up, surrendered, let go of himself and let the night have him.

His peaceful surrender lasted as long as it took for Søren to wrap an arm around his chest, drag him back from the edge of the cliff and throw him hard onto the ground. The force of the fall knocked the wind out of his lungs. As Søren stripped him naked, Kingsley could only lie there gasping painfully for breath, like a fish washed up on a sandy beach.

Air. He needed air. The stone beneath his torso felt like an iron lung. He knew tomorrow his back would be a mass of bruises from how forcefully Søren had thrust him to the ground. Tomorrow he'd barely be able to move…if he survived tonight.

"Breathe," Søren whispered in his ear. Kingsley nodded, still unable to speak.

Søren dipped his head to the center of Kingsley's chest and kissed him over his racing heart. The touch of Søren's lips to his bare skin was all he needed. Once more he went calm and slack in Søren's arms.

"Good. Relax for me." Søren spoke quietly, almost gently,

but Kingsley knew these were orders, not requests, and he sensed the punishment for disobedience would be as severe as the reward for compliance.

Kingsley relaxed as Søren commanded, letting his body go limp against the stone. Søren slipped a hand between his legs and pushed a finger inside him. Kingsley arched hard and grasped at Søren's shoulder.

Søren took Kingsley's hand and pushed his arm back towards the ground.

"Don't fight me."

Kingsley shook his head. He didn't want to fight Søren, only touch him. But Søren seemed intent on doing all the touching tonight. He remained fully clothed—pants on, shirt on—while Kingsley lay naked underneath him. Søren brought his mouth to Kingsley's and kissed him with brutal force. Biting, tugging, skin-breaking…Kingsley had never kissed a girl with half the passion with which Søren kissed him. The finger inside him found a spot Kingsley didn't know he had, and when Søren pushed into it, Kingsley cried out from the sheer shock of pleasure.

But the pleasure was short-lived. Søren pulled out of Kingsley and left him on the ground as he stood up and walked to the edge of the forest. He picked up the bag Kingsley had brought, but also pulled a whip-thin branch from a tree.

"Hands and knees," Søren said as he dropped the bag back onto the ground and stood at Kingsley's side.

"What?"

Søren put his foot on Kingsley's chest and pushed him hard, rolling him onto his stomach.

"Hands…and…knees," he repeated, and Kingsley dragged himself painfully up as ordered.

Søren brought the branch down onto his back. Once. A

second time. A third. After five Kingsley stopped counting. After five minutes, Kingsley stopped breathing.

He collapsed onto his chest and was only vaguely aware of Søren tossing the branch aside, and then the zipper to the bag opening and something cold and wet filling him. But when Søren started to push inside him, Kingsley came back to himself.

"Yes…" He exhaled the word as Søren went deep into him. It hurt. No denying it hurt. But it healed him, too. The welts on him, the cuts and bruises, had been the price he'd paid for such a prize as this moment.

Kingsley dug the heels of his hands into the stone to steady himself as Søren drove into him over and over again. He pushed back when Søren pushed forward. In that moment of total penetration, Kingsley ceased to be a person, a human being, and became nothing but property, chattel, an object to be owned and used for the pleasure of another. That other was Søren, whom Kingsley loved. To be owned by him was an honor higher than any he could imagine. Had the world offered him castles and thrones, the chance to reign as a prince or a king, and all the riches that he could imagine, in exchange for giving this up, Kingsley would have said no, and he would have not regretted his choice. Not then. Not ever.

Kingsley's body started to open up for Søren. The pain lessened. The pleasure increased, while Søren moved in him with methodical thrusts and in utter silence. Kingsley ached for something, anything from him—a touch, a word, some kind of comfort or reassurance. But he also relished that Søren deemed him unworthy of all the niceties of sex among the civilized.

Søren dug his hand into the back of Kingsley's hair to hold him still as he pushed into him even harder. More than uncivilized, this was savagery, and Kingsley loved every primal second of it.

He wanted to say something to Søren, wanted to tell him how he felt about what was happening to him, but he didn't know the words—not in French, not in English, not in any of the languages Søren knew but Kingsley didn't. He had to tell him something. What he felt…he felt used, owned, like property, like a slave, treasured, wanted, needed, like an object of infinite value so coveted Søren had lowered himself to theft to make Kingsley his own. Underneath Søren, Kingsley came more alive than he ever felt on top of any girl. He loved his girls, had loved them all. But this was more than love. He couldn't think of the word for it—not *l'amour,* not *la passion….* *la vie.* It was the closest word to what he felt that he could find.

La vie.

Life.

Søren's fingers moved from Kingsley's hair, over his shoulders, down his back, until they held Kingsley by the hollow of his hips. He needed to come, had to come, but somehow instinctively knew he shouldn't. Not yet. Not until given permission. Søren didn't even touch him or stroke him, and yet Kingsley felt he could explode at any moment. Breathing deeply to contain his need, he stared at the ground, the stone almost black in the night. Kingsley wasn't sure what time it was, but he hoped dawn approached. He wanted to greet the morning with Søren. This morning and every morning after.

But the stars stayed in the sky and the sun lurked beneath the horizon. It seemed an hour passed, though the more rational part of Kingsley's brain knew it only felt that long. The pain stopped time in a way more powerful than even boredom could. Ecstasy passed in seconds. Agony lasted forever. And on the cold rocky cliff, with Søren bruising him with every touch, Kingsley had both.

"Please…" The word came out of Kingsley before he even thought it. He said it again. And one more time.

"Tell me," Søren ordered, pushing him flat on his stomach. Kingsley turned his head to cushion his face from the rock. But Søren stopped him with a touch. Crooking his arm, he rested it on the ground. Gratefully, Kingsley lay his cheek against Søren's forearm. The gesture, so simple but so protective, nearly undid him. He would have cried from the joy of it had he not already been crying from the pain.

"I don't know…." And he didn't. He didn't know why he'd said "please," didn't know what he asked for. But he needed something from Søren.

Somehow Søren instinctively seemed to understand what Kingsley needed even better than he did. With a final thrust, he pushed into him and came in utter silence, his teeth leaving a bruise on the back of Kingsley's neck.

Kingsley bit Søren's forearm to stifle his groan of pain as Søren slowly pulled out. He grasped Kingsley by the shoulders and pushed him onto his back. By the light of the moon and stars, Kingsley watched as Søren unbuttoned his shirt and pulled it off. He folded it neatly, lifted Kingsley's neck and placed the shirt under his head. Kingsley relaxed into the makeshift pillow and averted his eyes as Søren gazed down at him. Instinctively, Kingsley also knew he shouldn't meet Søren's eyes—not without permission. Right now he was less than human and didn't deserve the same privileges as other people. Or perhaps Søren was more than human right now and therefore had the right to act like a god among men. *Act?* At this moment, with the moon on his shoulder and the entire world beneath his knees, Søren *was* God.

And God kissed him.

The kiss startled him at first with its utter gentleness. Kingsley's lips parted and he breathed Søren's air. Søren pushed

Kingsley's mouth open farther. Their tongues touched and intermingled. Søren didn't just smell of winter, he tasted of it, too. Although warm, Søren's mouth tasted like ice. It soothed Kingsley's dry and burning lips. He wanted Søren to melt into his mouth so he could drink him.

When Søren moved his mouth away, Kingsley moaned in distress. The kiss…he could have lived in that kiss forever. But he sighed with newfound bliss when Søren pressed his lips into the panting hollow of his throat. And from his throat, Søren's lips moved to Kingsley's shoulder. The left one, then the right. Over his heart, Søren kissed him again. Then down his chest and over the hard, flat surface of Kingsley's stomach. Had they been in a bed, Kingsley would have dug his fingers deep inside the mattress to hold himself steady. But he had nothing but rock below him. He scratched at it and found nothing to hold on to.

Søren seemed to sense his need. He took Kingsley's hands in his and locked their fingers together. The intimacy of the act filled a space inside Kingsley's heart that he hadn't even realized had been empty. He wanted everything to stop right then and there so he could talk to Søren about it. What they were doing now, Kingsley knew, was as powerful as the millions of years of sun and wind and rain that had carved this plateau out of the side of the mountain. Every kiss eroded something of the old Kingsley and carved a new shape into him.

But Søren's kisses moved lower and he took Kingsley into his mouth. And then Kingsley didn't want anything to stop. This could go on forever. Dozens of girls had done this to him in the past and he always loved it, whether or not they knew what they were doing. The sight of those innocent girl-ish faces between his legs, with his cock between their soft, angelic lips—the lips they kissed their grandmothers with… the deviancy of it alone was enough to get him off with spectacular success every time. But now that Søren did it to him, the entire meaning of the act changed. He felt unworthy of having Søren's mouth on him. Before, with his girls, a blow job had been his right. He asked for it and received it. With Søren it felt like a gift he didn't deserve. The pleasure was beyond anything he'd felt in his entire life. Nothing compared to it. Nothing ever.

Kingsley arched as wave after wave of sensation washed over him. His hips rose off the ground and his fingers clenched Søren's viciously. He closed his eyes tight as Søren brought him to the very edge. Then, suddenly, his body felt a rush of cold air as Søren pulled away from him. Without warning Kingsley was forced over and up onto his hands and knees again. He couldn't stop the orgasm, so when he came it wasn't into Søren's mouth, but onto the cold stone ground beneath him.

The sudden change in Søren's demeanor shamed him. His semen on the ground shamed him. Søren holding him immobile as Kingsley caught his breath shamed him. The last shudder of his orgasm passed through him and the pleasure he took in the shame shamed him.

Kingsley rolled onto his back and winced from the pain. What would it be like tomorrow? He already ached to see the welts and the bruises. They were gifts to him, gifts from Søren. Kingsley would treasure every moment he bore them, and when they faded he'd beg for more.

Absurd, wasn't it? Treasuring bruises as if they were gold? Madness. And yet, so true.

Something welled up inside Kingsley. Something he couldn't keep in. He opened his arms wide again as if to give himself over to the sky. And without knowing why, he began to laugh. The laugh filled him up and poured out of him. It rose into the air and expanded, slipping into the forest and echoing throughout the valley below.

And Kingsley heard something else. Another laugh. Søren's laugh. Had he even heard Søren laughing before? No. Of course not. He would have remembered such a sound. So unlike him—so light and alive, but so weighty and real. If God laughed it would sound just like that.

Søren reached for Kingsley and dragged him close. Kingsley lay across Søren's legs and relaxed into the heat of his body. Søren draped an arm over Kingsley's back, and in silence they both stared out at the night. They remained quiet for five full minutes at least, until Søren spoke again.

"Are you cold?" he asked.

"No. I'm fine."

"You did well." Søren ran two fingers down the center of Kingsley's back, and his spine sang at the touch.

"Merci," Kingsley sighed. He'd been aching to hear three words from Søren, the same three words Kingsley had said to him after their first night on the forest floor. But for whatever reason, "You did well" seemed a bigger thing, a better thing than simply "I love you."

"It's late. You need to sleep. Get dressed. I'll take you back to bed."

"Yes, sir." Kingsley rolled up off of Søren's lap and slowly stood. Everything hurt. Not like the first time. The first time, he'd been torn open and apart. Tonight he'd only been broken. This was good. Give him a week and he'd be ready for another night like this.

"Sir?" Søren repeated. Kingsley laughed again as he pulled on his clothes. "You're a teacher now, but not one of the priests. I heard your students calling you 'sir.' Seemed to suit you. I could call you 'monsieur.'"

Søren cupped the side of Kingsley's face and he immediately stopped laughing.

"I like 'sir.'"

He traced Kingsley's bottom lip with his thumb. Kingsley said nothing, only nodded.

Søren dropped his hand and stepped to the edge of the cliff. Dressed now, Kingsley came and stood at his side.

"It's Maine," Kingsley said.

"Is it really? I hadn't noticed."

Kingsley suppressed the urge to roll his eyes. "I mean...it will get cold soon. Too cold at night to meet like this."

Søren's face remained implacable. "You assume this is an ongoing arrangement?"

Kingsley's heart dropped to the bottom of the valley. Or started to, until he noticed the smile lurking at the corner of Søren's lips.

"You blond monster," Kingsley said, shoving him.

Søren laughed and shoved back with twice the grace and ten times the force. Kingsley ended up on his back again, with Søren straddling his thighs.

"Say it," Søren ordered. "Apologize."

He pinned Kingsley down hard to the ground.

"I'm sorry, sir."

"Good boy."

Kingsley groaned as Søren dragged his aching body off the ground.

"We'll find somewhere," Søren said. "If I have to build a house with my own hands...we'll find somewhere to be together."

Together... That one word healed every wound inside Kingsley. The bruises remained on his body, the welts and the cuts. But the pain evaporated. He became whole again.

"What about there?" The first rays of dawn light started to peek over the tops of the hills. At the base of the valley stood a tiny cobblestone cottage nearly swallowed up by ivy and weeds.

"That's the old hermitage. It hasn't been used since Father Leopold in 1954."

"It has four walls, a chimney...." What else did they need? Nothing but shelter from the elements when winter came.

"It's a hellhole. I've seen it."

Kingsley stared down at the tiny cottage.

"Hell is fine. Surely God wants nothing to do with us, anyway."

NORTH
The Present

Kingsley found Søren in the chapel, sitting at the piano and playing before a spellbound audience of twenty teenage boys. In this day and age, Kingsley could hardly imagine teenagers being so enthralled by classical music. Baroque music, he corrected, as he recognized the piece—Vivaldi's "Winter," the Allegro for Piano. Søren did have a fondness for Vivaldi, the Red Priest, as he was known in his day. Kingsley lingered at the back of the chapel, closed his eyes and let the music wash over him.

Antonio Vivaldi… Kingsley had written a paper on the composer thirty years ago for Father Henry's music appreciation seminar. Søren had suggested that composer. Kingsley remembered little about the man. He did recall Vivaldi suffered from asthma so severely he couldn't say Mass. In lieu of parish life, he'd been sent to an orphanage, where he taught music to the illegitimate daughters of courtesans. When Kingsley read that in Vivaldi's biography, he'd understood why Søren had thought Vivaldi and he would get along so well.

The piece ended, and Søren stood up and gave a self-

deprecating bow to the herd of boys who'd gathered to listen. A few came up to him and chatted as he tried to work
his way to the back of the chapel. They'd probably never met
a priest like Søren before—one who could so obviously have
had any woman or man he wanted, could have had a career
in any field he desired, but instead had taken a vow of celibacy and poverty and given his time and his talents to God.
Or at least, most of his talents he'd given to God. A few he'd
reserved for his Eleanor. Lucky bitch.

Søren came to him and Kingsley said nothing, only nodded, indicating his readiness to leave. Søren waved a polite
farewell to the boys, shook hands with a few priests as they
departed. Once safely inside the car, with the glass up between
them and the driver, Kingsley finally felt safe to speak freely.

"You know something," Søren said before Kingsley could
even open his mouth.

"I know nothing," he replied as he watched Saint Ignatius
disappear behind them. "But I have a theory, at least."

"Tell me."

"I saw Christian. He's a priest now. Did you know that?"

"Of course," Søren said. "I attended his ordination. Is he
in the hermitage now?"

"*Oui*. We talked at length."

"About?"

Søren sat across from Kingsley, who couldn't resist stretching out his legs and resting them on the seat next to Søren's
thigh.

"Your wife."

Søren narrowed his eyes at him and Kingsley grinned.

"Your sister?"

"The very same. Christian thinks it's possible someone
knew about you and me while we were at Saint Ignatius, and
assumed that Marie-Laure committed suicide because of it."

"You believe she did commit suicide."

"I always have. You married her, but you didn't know her. She was incapable of love—only obsession. She nearly ripped my arm off the day they separated us. She was obsessed with you, and when she saw us together..." Kingsley stopped and said no more.

"She ran off in tears and fell to her death. Perhaps it was suicide but that was *her* choice. You bring too much guilt upon yourself."

"Do you want to know this theory or do you want to save my soul?"

"Both. But your soul will take a little more time. Tell me the theory."

"Christian thinks that this someone was in love with Marie-Laure and is now threatening us in revenge."

"Revenge..." Søren sighed heavily as he leaned his regal head back in the seat. "Such melodrama this all is. The photograph, the burning bed... I have a lover, Kingsley, and half the Underground knows it. I fell in love with her when she was fifteen years old. And on that day I determined I would have her. On that day I started training her for my bed. This is not a secret. I am one phone call to the bishop away from being excommunicated. If someone wants to ruin my career as a priest, they hardly need to go to such lengths."

"You have a lover, yes, and all the Underground knows she and I would destroy anyone who tried to destroy you. And yes, you fell in love with her when she was fifteen, but you didn't take her until she was twenty, a feat of Herculean proportions, considering how she spent those years attempting to seduce you. Even if your congregation caught you with your hand around her throat and eight inches inside her on the altar of the very church where they worship, they love you too much to tell a soul about you. You might very well be the safest man on earth."

"So what is this, then?"

"It may be more than ruination they are after, *mon père*. This, pardon my French, is a mindfuck. Which, as everyone in the underground knows, is your specialty. Someone is doing unto you what you do unto others."

"And you believe it's someone we went to school with?"

"It would have to be. Who else would know about us? About that photograph of us Christian took?"

"Eleanor has a copy."

"Do you think Eleanor is behind all this?"

"Of course not."

"Then who?"

Søren exhaled through his nose, shook his head in obvious frustration and turned his head to stare out the window. Although he knew he was in as much danger as Søren from whatever the thief had in mind for them, Kingsley couldn't help but take perverse pleasure in Søren's impotence in this situation. No matter what happened in their world, Søren always had it under control. In any situation that arose, he always had the knowledge, the answers and the fortitude to deal with it. When a sadist at The 8th Circle got out of hand, Søren put him in his place. When a young submissive stopped being able to tell the reality of the outside world from the fantasy of the scene, Søren talked sense into her. No matter what drama befell their world, Søren handled it. He handled the drama, he handled the Underground and he even handled Nora Sutherlin, the one woman Kingsley or any other man on earth couldn't handle.

But Søren seemingly couldn't handle this.

"Kingsley…" he began, and met his eyes. "Who do you think it is?"

Kingsley could only shrug. "*Je ne sais pas.* I can't imagine. But I think Christian has a point. We were so wrapped up in each other at the time, we barely noticed that we were the only two at school who weren't in love with my sister."

"She was a beautiful girl."

"And the only girl within fifty miles of the place. They never allowed women on naval ships or pirate ships for just that reason. A lone woman among men means disaster."

"Disaster would be an understatement." Søren raised a hand to his forehead and rested his elbow on the window ledge. "It was a catastrophe. All of it."

Kingsley bristled at the implication.

"All of it? I think that's something of an exaggeration. What you and I had before it was ruined…"

"What you and I had was something God wanted nothing to do with."

Søren's words came at Kingsley like bullets.

"I refuse to believe you mean that." Kingsley leveled a stare at him.

"Those, Kingsley, were your words after our second night together. That is what you said as we stood on the cliff over the hermitage. You were the one who said, and I quote, 'Surely God wants nothing to do with us, anyway.' You, not I."

Kingsley heard the edge of old anger in Søren's voice, the tinge of bitterness, the hurt. The hurt?

Thirty years ago he'd made an offhand remark after being beaten and fucked halfway to unconsciousness…and three decades later Søren remembered it word for word. Remembered the words and remembered the pain.

"*Mon Dieu*…I never thought the day would come. Finally and for once, I have hurt you."

Kingsley did laugh then—loudly and decadently. And Søren only glared at him until he, too, laughed.

"God, Kingsley, we were children then. Foolish children playing dangerous games after dark."

"Games? Is that what it was to you? My blood on your body, that was a game?"

Søren sighed heavily. He clasped his hands almost as if in prayer and gazed at Kingsley over the steeple of his fingers.

"No. Not a game. Not at all. In a way, what you and I had… it was my salvation. I thought of it as such back then. Prayed that's what it was, prayed that God had sent you to me. When you said God wanted nothing to do with us…yes, it hurt."

Kingsley kept his face composed and tried to pretend Søren's words didn't fill up his heart like water poured into a cupped hand.

"I saved your soul by shedding my blood for you. How Christian of me."

Søren gave him a wry smile. "God saved my soul. You, however, saved my sanity. Before you, I thought…"

Søren's voice trailed off and Kingsley found himself leaning far forward in his seat. He wanted to touch Søren—his knee, his hands, his face—but dared not lest the moment shatter. Søren did confess to him on rare occasions. Late at night at the town house, at the rectory, when they'd both had too much wine and too little sleep…Søren would sometimes bare his heart a little to Kingsley, just enough for him to remember that Søren did have one.

"What did you think?"

"Horrible thoughts, *mon ami*." Søren smiled. "After what happened that summer with Elizabeth. I thought I had to stay apart from everyone, far away from them lest they be contaminated with whatever it was that had turned me into this. Even before Elizabeth I knew there was something different about me. With her I discovered what it was."

"You inherited your father's sadism like I inherited my father's eyes. But I am no more my father than you are yours. You have a conscience. He didn't."

"I know that now. As a child…I didn't understand, couldn't understand. I thought I'd been born broken."

"Broken?" Kingsley could hardly believe his ears. "When I saw you the first time, I felt…healed. If you are broken, then I only pray someday I break, too."

Søren lowered his clasped hands and held them between his knees. Once that had been Kingsley's home. He loved sitting at Søren's feet between his knees. At the hermitage, after they'd spent their lust and brutality on each other, they would turn from beasts back into students. Søren would read and grade papers while Kingsley rested his back against Søren's shins and work on his own studies. Such civility after such violence…neither one of them ever noted the strange irony of it. It felt right to them in the moment. It would feel even more right…right now.

Kingsley slid out of his seat and knelt on the floorboard at Søren's feet. He slid his jacket off and tossed it aside. He kicked off his shoes, his socks, took off the tie and unbuttoned his collar. It had been so long since he'd done this, let his submissive side take over, that he'd almost forgotten how to sit. But as he sank into the floor it came back to him. Respectfully, he lowered his eyes to the floor. He didn't speak. He relaxed his ramrod straight posture and surrendered to his fate.

"Kingsley…" Søren sighed his name, and Kingsley rested his forehead against Søren's knee.

"I know you need this, sir," Kingsley whispered. "It's dangerous for you to deny yourself. We both know that."

"I'm fine." Søren's voice had a hard edge to it, but Kingsley heard the crack in his resolve. "She's only been gone a few days."

"Even when she is here…you hold back with her. I've seen

it. You worry about breaking her. You know I can take ten times the pain your Little One can. You remember, don't you? How much I can take?"

Kingsley stopped talking and let the silence speak for him. Pain…so much pain. The things Søren had done to him when they were teenagers—it was a miracle Kingsley lived to be eighteen. Even on the hottest days, when the other boys stripped out of their uniforms to play baseball on the lawn, Kingsley kept his clothes on to hide the bruises, the welts, the cuts, sometimes even the burns. He drank pain in those days, drank it like water, got drunk on it like wine. For years now, his tongue had been dry with the thirst to drink it again. Eleanor Schreiber…Kingsley had taken Søren's submissive and turned her into Nora Sutherlin, the most celebrated Dominatrix in the world. But he hadn't created her for the world. He'd made her for himself. And after he'd trained her, he became her first client. He paid through the nose for sessions with her, and she earned every penny. But no matter how vicious and brutal she was with him, it never compared to the pain Søren caused him. Nora could hurt his body in beautiful ways. But only Søren could tear open his soul.

"This can't happen again…." Søren laid his hand on top of Kingsley's head as if to bless him.

"Pourquoi pas?" Why not?

"Theresa of Avila…she wrote once that she didn't love God and didn't want to love God, but she wanted to want to love God. I understand that."

Kingsley hid his smile. "You don't want to want me," he said, turning his eyes up to Søren. "But you do."

Søren's slid his hand from the top of Kingsley's head to the side of his face.

"Yes."

Kingsley waited. It would come. Søren would raise his

hand and bring it down onto his face with a slap, a slap that would hurt worse than the many punches he'd taken in his day. And then Søren would grip him by the throat and force him onto his stomach or his back. With Kingsley's own belt, Søren would beat him, perhaps even choke him. There was no end to the possibilities. Some sadists took years learning to master the art of inflicting pain without causing harm. But Søren was a natural. He was fluent in nineteen modern languages, five ancient languages and the one true universal language—pain.

"I am yours." Kingsley slipped into French, the language they always spoke to each other during their most private moments. French was Kingsley's first language, and he fell into it when tired, when weak, when at his most vulnerable. With others he used it as a weapon to disarm or a shield to deflect. With Søren, he spoke French in his moments of surrender. French was what he had spoken as a small child. With Søren, he became that defenseless yet again.

Je suis le vôtre. J'étais toujours le vôtre, monsieur.

I am yours. I have always been yours, sir.

"*Oui. Tu es le mien.*"

Yes, you are mine.

Kingsley froze, not able, not willing to move. For the first time in thirty years, Søren had called Kingsley *his.* He'd waited decades for this moment.

Slowly, Søren traced Kingsley's lips with the tip of his finger. Kingsley remembered that first night on the forest floor... Søren pushing Kingsley's broken body onto his back, and those perfect pianist's fingers on his mouth. The fingers then replaced by lips. The kiss had seemed less personal than the touch. He'd kissed his mother, his sister, his father, his friends. All the French kissed all the time. A kiss was nothing. But to touch fingertips to another's lips...so erotic, so possessive, so intimate. By now, Kingsley had easily kissed a thousand women, half a thousand men. But he could count only three people who he'd ever allowed the liberty of touching his face with their hands—Nora, Juliette and Søren.

"I still love you as I did that night you broke me." Kingsley spoke the confession aloud, his lips moving against the back of Søren's hand. "You can break me again."

"I can't break you." Søren shook his head. "I never could. Your body, yes. But there is a core inside you that I could never touch, never reach, never break. It's the part of you that was never afraid of me."

"Is that why you loved her and not me?"

"She has that core, too. And it's why of all the people in the world, it's only you and her I've ever loved."

Kingsley's heart rose. Hope buoyed it. That Søren would even put him in the same sentence as his Little One meant more than the touch of his hands against Kingsley's lips.

"I have nothing in me that you cannot break. I would let you destroy me, and then I would resurrect myself from my own ashes for the honor of being destroyed by you again."

"Your sister died because of what you and I were to each other. I can't risk losing Eleanor the way we lost Marie-Laure."

"Marie-Laure loved me madly. I was her brother. And she loved you even more madly. You were her husband. We are neither to your Eleanor. And she has left us both. Close your eyes, monsieur. Do you see her now? She's in his bed right now, opening her legs for him. She's beneath him. He's inside her. She walked away from us. No…she didn't walk. She ran."

Søren dropped his hand from Kingsley's lips. Leaning back into the seat, he closed his eyes.

"You might be the devil, Kingsley."

With a rueful laugh, Kingsley kissed Søren's knee before sliding back up to his seat. He became the notorious French

Dominant again, his feet on the leather seat, one ankle crossed over the other.

"The devil is the Prince of Lies, remember?" He returned to his English. "And you and I both know I speak only the truth."

The brutal truth hung between them the rest of the journey back to New York. Kingsley pushed no further. If it would happen, it would happen at the time of Søren's choosing, not his. That was always the way. Their underground world had taken the wildness of relationships like theirs and tamed them, domesticated them. They used labels like Dominant and submissive, and bandied about slogans like Safe, Sane and Consensual. They all had safe words. Even the most violent and perverse among them played by the rules lest they be ejected from their underworld Eden. But Kingsley knew it was all artifice, window dressing, self-deception. He and Søren, they were more than a Dominant and submissive, and the rules didn't apply to them. This was no game. When Kingsley said "I am yours" he meant it. If Søren had desired to burn him, maim him, sell him, break him—he could, and Kingsley knew he would not and could not stop him. His love for Søren had sold him into slavery, and all the riches of all the kingdoms left in the world couldn't buy him out of it.

By midnight they finally returned to Kingsley's town house. Although Søren hadn't touched him with anything other than a finger to his lips, Kingsley felt he'd been flogged. Seeing the rock on which his sister had died...sitting in the hermitage where Søren had nearly killed him so many times... being back at the school that had been the home to his greatest heartbreaks...

Kingsley trudged up the stairs. He knew only one thing could help him right now. But it was the one thing denied to him. So he planned on drinking himself into a stupor instead.

Kingsley and Søren walked to his grand bedroom at the end of the hallway on the second floor.

"I'm thinking Amontillado tonight," Kingsley said as he opened the door to his bedroom. "I have a vintage as old as Poe. It would make him proud to see us drink it."

Søren stood at the end of Kingsley's bed, his shoulder against the bedpost, his arms crossed. "Poe married his thirteen-year-old cousin when he was twenty-seven. Should we really endeavor to make him proud?"

Kingsley peeled out of his jacket and tossed it on the floor. He couldn't wait to get back into his normal clothes—his dark gray suit and embroidered vest. His riding boots. His cravat. This Armani nonsense felt like a costume to him. In it he could blend into a crowd of well-heeled businessmen and disappear. Anonymity did not suit him.

"I don't think either of us has the right to judge Poe. Or anyone. Your Eleanor was only fifteen, remember? And me... we both know my crimes."

Søren said nothing, merely looked away as Kingsley started to strip off his clothes. He did that always. Even as teenagers. Even when Søren had been inside Kingsley's body only moments earlier, out of something—discretion, respect, denial, perhaps—Søren always turned away when Kingsley dressed and undressed in his presence. Kingsley had to wonder if he did the same with Eleanor or if he watched her, devouring every second of her naked curves. Kingsley knew he held a privileged position in Søren's life. Technically, they were related, or had been, by marriage. Søren and Kingsley could spend all the time alone together they desired and no one from outside their world could judge them.

Kingsley pulled his riding boots on, but left his shirt off for a few minutes longer. A childish trick to pull on Søren, but he couldn't help himself sometimes. Not when the priest stood with his jaw tight and his eyes looking anywhere but at Kingsley.

"Are you staying?" Kingsley asked as he moved to stand directly in front of Søren, trousers and riding boots on and nothing else. Usually he appreciated when the many men and women who visited his bedroom didn't stare at his chest. His body was riddled with old scars and bullet wounds from his days working for the French government under the auspices of a captainship in the French Foreign Legion. Lovers always stared at his chest right before beginning the interrogation process.

How did you get the bullet wounds?

I was shot.

Who shot you?

All the husbands. Yours isn't armed, is he?

Kingsley always deflected the questions with his wit, and his lovers loved him even more for it. Only Søren knew the truth of his wounds. Kingsley never converted to Catholicism at Saint Ignatius as Søren had. But he did tell the priest all his secrets. How did he get the bullet wounds? The people he was paid to shoot sometimes shot back. How did he get the pale scars on his back? He'd been held hostage for one month by a foreign terror cell and tortured. How did he get the poorly healed cuts on his wrists? He'd nearly ripped his own hands off trying to get free from the manacles that they'd shackled him with.

Of course, those scars meant nothing to him. He had them; they'd healed. His scars gave him an air of mystery and danger in the Underground. The wounds that mattered to him were the ones Søren had left. Kingsley's one regret about his year as Søren's lover was that no matter how brutally Søren beat him and tortured him, he had no scars at all from their time together.

At least none anyone could see.

"I should go," Søren said. "It's late. I'm hearing confession tomorrow morning. And I want to pray about your theory, Father Christian's theory."

"Pray all you want. I'm certain there's something to it. To even know about that photograph of us…you know it must have been a student there. Or one of the priests."

"So you say, and you may be right. Sleep well." Søren met his eyes for only a moment. "Lock the doors."

"I never lock the doors," Kingsley reminded him as Søren started to leave.

"I know, and that's why Eleanor's file is missing from your office."

"I never lock my doors for a reason. If it appears that I'm afraid of this city, then I will have to start being afraid of this city. Everyone knows I don't lock my doors, and that scares them more than any security force in the world could."

Søren leveled a stern stare at him. "This isn't about your image, Kingsley. It's about your safety. Do as I say."

Kingsley strode toward Søren. "I don't answer to you anymore. I'd sell what's left of my soul for one more night with you. But until you decide to take off that damn collar of yours and take ownership of me and what you've done to me again…" Kingsley paused and drew a breath, hoping to tamp down some of his anger. Only Søren ever dared to tell him what to do. Not even his Juliette took such a liberty. "I will not obey your orders until you've earned the right to give them to me again. Now you should go. And I'll be certain to leave the doors unlocked behind you."

"How you've lived this long without getting murdered is beyond my powers of imagination."

"Your powers of imagination disappeared when your writer

disappeared. Perhaps you should go fetch her from her new rich young lover."

"I have an excellent imagination." Søren stood face-to-face with Kingsley, who knew he did so simply to emphasize the four-inch difference in their heights. The man was an ass—an utterly, insufferably arrogant ass. "I'm currently imagining a few creative ways of causing you extraordinary amounts of pain."

Kingsley raised his chin. Mere inches separated their faces.

"Stop flirting. You know we don't have time for that."

"I wasn't flirting. The pain I'd inflict on your right now… only one of us would enjoy it."

"Only one of us ever did."

"Don't make me laugh. You begged for it. Night after night, you begged for it."

"Of course I did. Pain is the only way you know how to show love."

"It's not the only way I know how to show love. It's the only way I chose to with you. You showed up at Saint Ignatius and decided to become king of the school. Someone had to turn you into the little prince you actually were."

"Not so little. I think we're rather well-matched in one certain area."

"Your arrogance, Kingsley, was beyond and is beyond anything I'd ever seen in my life."

"Anything you've ever seen outside your own reflection, you mean."

"You're trying to pick a fight with me. It won't work."

"It already has. You've already threatened to cause me bodily harm. I'm already hard. I think it's safe to call this one of our typical arguments."

"I'm leaving now."

"Good night, sir."

Søren opened the door to Kingsley's bedroom and stood on the threshold. Kingsley watched and waited. His hands trembled for reasons he didn't understand, so he shoved them in the back pockets of his trousers, raised his chin and stared at Søren.

"Forgetting something?"

With his hand on the doorknob, Søren turned to him. "Did you mean it…back then…that God wanted nothing to do with us?"

Kingsley laughed softly. "A foolish offhand remark. Had I known it would hurt you so much…I would still have said it."

Now Søren laughed and shook his head. "I needed to believe then that God brought us together."

Kingsley exhaled heavily. "He did, perhaps. It did have the scent of destiny on it—you and I. God did bring us together. Only when we were together…like that, I think He tried not to watch."

Søren nodded.

"I can't blame Him for that."

Smiling, Kingsley took his hands out of his back pockets and walked to Søren. He took Søren by the wrist and opened his hand. In his palm he laid a tiny cross on a broken silver chain.

Søren stared at the cross in his hand, the cross Kingsley had torn from his neck the night they'd first made love. Time stopped. The world ended. No one noticed except Kingsley.

Reaching up to his neck, Søren pulled off his Roman collar. He stepped back into Kingsley's bedroom and locked the door behind him.

God closed His eyes.

SOUTH

Wesley took one deep breath and in that one deep breath let himself freak out that the moment he'd been waiting for and praying for and lusting for and dreaming of was happening.

Right now.

He released both the breath and his fears. A deep and abiding calm settled into his being. This was Nora, his Nora. The woman he loved, yes. But more than that, she was his best friend. He trusted her even though he couldn't say why. And no one in the world made him feel more comfortable with himself. He'd waited long enough. They both had.

Wesley dropped his mouth to hers, and she lifted her lips to his. Warm…her mouth was so warm…. He loved the heat of her body. Once, she'd claimed to be a medical anomaly. Her natural body temperature even when healthy was ninety-nine-point-five, not the typical ninety-eight-point-six. She'd said this was proof she was hotter than other women—literally. But it was no joke. Her skin burned to the touch. And tonight, he wanted to be consumed by the fire of her.

Her tongue pushed into his mouth, but Wesley pushed back, not wanting to rush the moment. He'd loved Nora for three years now, lived for her. And now he was going to lose his virginity to her. No, not lose…give.

"Are you sure?" she whispered into his ear as he backed her into the table at the center of the gazebo, candles still burning all around them.

"More sure than I've ever been in my life."

Nora wrapped her arms around his back and held him close. Yes, that's what he needed more than anything. The reassurance of her arms.

"Good. I'm here, Wes. I'm not going anywhere."

He nodded, bereft of the words he needed to tell her how her words made him feel. He wished he had her talent for words. When he'd have papers due in class, he'd always go to her for help. "I want to say this but don't know how…" he'd say to her, and she'd take his fumbling attempts at coherence and spin them into beautiful sentences, brief and powerful. Right now he needed her to help him tell her how much he wanted her, but not just in a sexual way. And how he loved her, but not just in some stupid greeting-card way. And he wanted to tell her he didn't ever want to hurt her—not the way Søren did. Not the way anyone did.

"It's okay, Wes. Don't be afraid." Nora ran her hands up his arms. "Just talk to me and keep talking."

"Tell me what to do," he said as Nora started to unbutton his shirt.

"Anything you want." She smiled up at him. A dozen spotlights ringed the dock and gazebo, and cast soft white light onto the pond. And in that light Wesley could see the happiness shining in Nora's eyes. Happiness…not guilt, not fear, not shame and not Søren.

"I need a little more than that. I'm…"

"Nervous?"

"Oh, hell yes," he said, and laughed. God, she felt so good in his arms. So soft and warm and real. Real and solid. Her breasts pressed against his chest. Her fingers dug into his shirt. Her fingernails bit lightly into the sensitive skin of his upper arm where he shot himself with his insulin on occasion. She must have noticed the slight wince because she immediately moved her hands to his shoulders.

"Okay. We can do this. No nervousness necessary. You sure you want to do this here?" She glanced around the gazebo. They were exposed. Anyone who walked down to the pond could see them.

"Yeah. No way would I make it back to the house. And everyone's in bed by now. Mom and Dad at least. We're okay." He tried to sound more confident than he felt.

"Good. Relief." Nora laughed and he heard the slightest hint of nervousness in her voice. Instead of worrying him, it gave him comfort to know the one and only Nora Sutherlin got nervous around him. "Let's see...first time. We better keep it simple. Table?"

"Table." Wesley slid his hands down her back and wrapped both palms around the back of her soft thighs. She clung to his shoulders as he lifted her up and set her on the edge. Already he burned to bury himself inside her. "Do we need—"

"Nope." She shook her head. "I've been tested. Totally clean. Good on the birth control. And you're a virgin. Right?"

Wesley grinned. "Not for long...I hope."

"No. Not for long." She started in on his shirt again, reaching the bottom and attempting to yank the fabric from his pants. A button got stuck on his waistband and Nora groaned with frustration.

"This never happens in my books," she said, tugging more gently on Wesley's shirt to free it. "Nobody's shirt ever gets stuck in their pants. And nobody has to worry about their damn parents walking in on them. And you never have the guy raising up his head and saying, 'Um, I think you're getting a yeast infection.'"

Wesley almost collapsed with a mix of disgust and laughter.

"What? You're telling me romance novels and erotica novels aren't one hundred percent realistic with the sex scenes? I'm shocked."

He rested his head on her shoulder and she dug her fingers into his hair.

"Afraid not, kid. Nobody ever has morning breath. No one ever gets a cramp. The guys can always go forever. There's never any ED scenes."

"ED?"

"Erectile dysfunction."

"Well, I can't imagine you've dealt with much of that in real life. Except maybe morning breath," he teased. He'd lived with Nora for a year and a half. He'd seen her at her absolute worst—straight out of bed, hair gone crazy, morning breath, the works. She looked even more gorgeous just crawling out of bed than most women looked after two hours primping.

"Oh, I've had it all. Had a charley horse once during sex with Kingsley. Screamed so loud his secretary called an ambulance."

"ED?"

"Not much of that. Unless you count Søren."

Wesley watched Nora's smile fall from her face.

"Søren?"

Biting her bottom lip, she nodded. "Unless he hurts me… or someone, he can't…perform."

"Can't or won't?"

"Can't. He. Can. Not." Nora gave a wan smile. "He doesn't hurt me just for fun, you know. It's foreplay. I told you that."

Wesley remembered that conversation. He hadn't even moved in with Nora yet. Barely eighteen years old and a freshman at Yorke…December…almost Christmas break. And he couldn't bear the thought of life without Nora at his school next semester. But she'd been brought in to teach only that one class. Spring semester would come and she'd be gone.

He'd fibbed a little and said his parents might take him out of the very expensive liberal arts college. Nora hadn't missed a beat. Immediately, she told him he could move in with her, as room and board were at least half of what students paid at Yorke. But, she warned him, she wasn't just a writer. She worked as a Dominatrix, as well. The look she took as shock had been merely confusion. He'd never heard of a "Dominatrix" in his life.

Then she'd told him about Søren, her complicated relationship with him, how he was both in her past and yet…and yet… And Wesley recalled the surge of testosterone he'd felt at the very idea of a man raising his hand to Nora, the woman he loved with a passion so furious he could barely breathe when around her.

"Just don't let him around me," he'd said, almost puffing his chest out. Even now he couldn't think about that moment without blushing. He'd been so cocky, such a teenager. And he'd had no idea how truly intimidating Søren could be.

"What? You think you can take on Søren?" And then Nora had laughed. Laughed. It would have hurt his feelings less had she patted him on top of his head. "Wesley…never fuck with a sadist. For Søren, torture's just foreplay."

And Nora's eyes had gone black as a starless night then, and something burned in them and turned in them and scared the shit out of him. That's when he realized he no more knew Nora Sutherlin than he knew the number of stars in the sky.

"Why did you stay with him?" He'd asked the question in a whisper, as a whisper was all he could manage.

Nora had smiled, a smile that took over her face and her eyes, and all he could do was stare into that smile like he sometimes stared into the crescent moon.

"I like foreplay."

"You said you liked it, when he hit you," Wesley said now, running his hands up and down her legs. With every pass his fingers inched higher.

"I did like it. I do. But sometimes it's exhausting. Pain hurts, and to have sex with Søren means submitting to pain. Sometimes I had to wonder what it would be like to have sex and not have to be subjected to ten kinds of agony first."

Wesley didn't say anything. He only cupped Nora's face with both his hands and rubbed the arch of her cheekbones. She wrinkled her nose and he laughed.

"What's that face for?"

"Your hands smell like catfish food."

Wesley pulled his hands away from Nora's face and, more importantly, from her nose.

"Sorry. Maybe you're right. We should do this back at the house. I can take a shower first."

"No, no, no. We're doing this. Absolutely. Just catfish food hands…yet another thing that doesn't happen during sex scenes in romance novels." Nora reached out and dug her fingers into his belt loops to pull him closer. "Or this. Goddammit."

"What?"

Nora raised her hand up into the light. "Just chipped the hell out of my manicure. This is hopeless. We're hopeless, Wes."

Laughing, she leaned her head against the center of his chest and exhaled. Wesley sighed and rested his chin on top of it.

"I have hope for us," he whispered. "We might get the sex wrong, but I think we get everything else right. In romance novels, the woman is flawlessly beautiful, right? You've got that part down."

Nora turned her exquisite face up to him and smiled in the moonlight. A lightning bug flashed its light by her eyes and Wesley's stomach clenched.

"Definitely got that," he repeated.

Nora reached up and pushed his shirt open and started to slowly slide it off his shoulders.

"Men in romance novels always have perfect bodies. Big broad shoulders with sexy definition, flat, hard stomach, those good veins in the forearms…." As she dragged his shirt off him, she touched every inch of his chest—his shoulders, his stomach, his forearms. "You've got the perfect male body down. Definitely. We're almost there."

"What are we missing?" Wesley gently pulled the clip out of Nora's hair, freeing the black waves to fall down her back. She raised her arms and he pulled her shirt off, leaving her in only her black bra and skirt.

"We have to make love now. Not fucking. Not sex. Making love. They never call it fucking in romance novels. Oh, unless it's between the villain and his mistress. They're allowed to fuck. The hero has to make love to the heroine. Gently at first, until the passion overcomes him and he's lost in the blah-blah…all that garbage."

"Make love to you. I can do that. I think."

Nora grinned. "None of that. Can't have any honest self-doubt. Gotta be kind of an asshole if you're going to be a romance-novel hero. Only Alphas, no Betas. Sorry." She wagged her finger at him before laying her hand on his stomach and tracing the line of his hips with her fingertips.

"Then I don't want to be a romance-novel hero. I just want to be me with you. And I've got nothing but self-doubt right now. Nora…what the hell do I do?"

She slid both hands up to his chest and rested them right under his collarbone.

"It's me. You can do anything you want."

Wesley nodded and took one more deep breath. He held her by the nape of the neck and brought his lips to her mouth in a kiss more ferocious than he ever dreamed he'd be capable of. Nora moaned softly in the back of her throat as she leaned into the kiss.

He ran his hands all over her skin—her soft smooth arms, up and down her back, over the exposed tops of her breasts. Her breasts…no woman in the world had breasts like Nora. Wesley reached behind her back and unclasped her bra.

"Holy…I got it this time."

"Good job, kid." Nora shrugged her shoulders as he slid the straps of her bra down her arms. "Practice makes perfect."

"We didn't need the bolt cutters this time."

"No. We just needed you." Nora rolled back on the table and Wesley could only gaze at her breasts. He laid his hand on her stomach, which contracted under his touch. His nervousness gave way to pure desire. He took her breasts in his hands and held them, kneading them gently.

"Is this okay?" he asked, wanting Nora to feel as good as she made him feel.

"Very okay. But don't forget the nipples. That's where the magic happens."

"I would never forget the nipples." He took her nipples between his index fingers and thumbs and lightly pinched. Nora gasped, her back coming an inch off the table. Wesley froze. "Good gasp or bad?"

"Good. Really really good gasp."

"Good. Great." He returned to her nipples with renewed confidence as Nora lay beneath his hands, panting with his every touch. Soon touching wasn't enough for him. He pulled her closer to him, slid an arm under her back and brought his lips down onto her breast. Gently he drew her nipple into his mouth. Nora's soft panting turned into loud moaning. She dug her hands into his hair again as he kissed his way from one nipple to the other.

"I'm starting to like the longer hair. It's…useful."

She grabbed a fistful of his hair and playfully tugged at it.

"Does that mean you'll stop bugging me to cut it off?"

"Nope. Keep kissing."

"Yes, ma'am."

With relish Wesley returned to Nora's breasts, kissing her nipples, sucking them, turning them between his fingers. He wanted more, but also never wanted to stop. The way she breathed and murmured small sounds of pleasure in the back of her throat intoxicated him. He couldn't get enough of it, enough of her. The first time they'd tried this they'd been on Nora's bed back at her house. Everything had been perfect then—the sunlight filling the room, the evening light that crept in under the door, the silk camisole he'd pulled off Nora before putting her onto her back…and now they were out on the damn dock where anyone could find them. Moths and mosquitoes danced around them. He was dirty. She was definitely going to get splinters in her back. And he couldn't care less. The doubt had gone. The fear. Everything but the desire and the sense that even if he screwed this up somehow, it would still be right.

"Wesley…" His name escaped Nora's lips on a breath.

"I'm here," he said, kissing the center of her chest.

She raised her head and rested a hand on the side of his face. "You're killing me."

Wesley's eyes went wide. "Wait…what? I'm killing you?"

"There's foreplay and there's torture. Torture's what you-know-who does."

"I thought…I thought you liked it."

Nora propped herself up on her elbows.

"I fucking love it. And if you don't get inside me in the next five seconds, I'll love it so much I'll die."

Blood rushed to Wesley's face. And from his face rushed straight to his groin.

"I can do that. I think."

"You can. You will. Or we'll die trying."

Wesley pushed Nora's skirt up to her hips and started to yank her panties down her legs.

"Tear them if you have to. Hell, tear them if you don't."

"I'm trying to stay calm here, Nor. This isn't helping."

"I'm beyond calm now. Underwear off yet?"

"Now it is." Wesley tossed her black silk panties on the ground. Now more than ever he wished they had some decent light. He'd dreamed of seeing Nora naked, of her spreading her legs for him and letting him see every part of her…. But even in the low light he could make out her thighs parting for him, her folds opening, and the tiny silver stud shining at the entrance of her body. "God…"

"Clit hood piercing. Does it freak you out?"

Wesley placed his hands on her inner thighs and pushed them open a little wider.

"Opposite of freaked out right now. God, Nora, you're so beautiful."

He gently brought two fingers to her and pushed her open.

"You never saw your girlfriend—"

He shook his head. "Never got that far with her. Kind of a point-of-no-return place." He couldn't believe how soft Nora felt, how silky…like flower petals.

"No going back now. Just forward. And in."

She reached down between her legs and touched herself.

"I haven't had sex in a week, Wes. Just a warning."

"Oh, no. A whole week."

"That's like a year in vanilla time. We might need some extra lubrication to get you in. I haven't forgotten what you're packing."

"Lubrication? I don't have—"

Nora rolled up and wrapped her arms around his shoulders and pressed her bare breasts to his chest. Her mouth came to his and she pushed her tongue between his lips.

She bit down on his tongue and whispered, "Lubrication."

And then he understood.

Nora stretched out on the table again. Wesley pushed her legs back open as he licked his lips in nervous anticipation.

"Lip licking is good. But mine. Not yours."

"Right. Okay. Definitely." He separated Nora's folds with his fingertips once more. "I have no idea what I'm doing."

"Just kiss me. Only down there. Think of it as a kiss."

"Just a kiss..." he repeated, and brought his mouth down onto her.

He'd dreamed of doing this to Nora. One of his Yorke friends complained that he had to go down on his girlfriend for half an hour to get her to orgasm. Nothing else would do it. Wesley remembered hearing that and thinking that spending thirty minutes with his head between Nora's thighs sounded like the best thirty minutes of his life. And now he could taste the tartness of her on his tongue, smell her scent that was so womanly and erotic, feel the ball of her piercing, her swollen clitoris and the folds of her labia with his mouth.

Nora lifted her hips and he pushed his tongue into her vagina.

"Wesley...please," she moaned, and he didn't have to ask what she meant this time.

He pulled away from her long enough to open his pants and free himself from his jeans and boxers. Nora reached down between them and took him in her hand. When she stroked him it became Wesley's turn to moan.

Nora let him go as she raised her knees close to her chest, and Wesley waited.

"Nora?"

She took his hands in hers and twined their fingers together.

"I love you, Wes." She said the words simply and Wesley could reply in only one way.

He pushed inside her.

For years he'd dreamed of this moment, dreamed of joining his body with hers. And now she surrounded him, enveloped him in her warm, wet heat. So complete…he felt so complete inside her. Inside Nora…Wesley was inside Nora. I am *inside Nora*…. The words echoed through his mind, the idea as potent as the reality.

He thrust deep into her, not able to stop himself from burrowing in as far as he could and wrapping as much of her around him as possible. Nora arched on the table, her back lifting off the white wood.

Stunned by the shock of sensation, Wesley nearly forgot he was supposed to move. But the intense undulations of Nora's hips urged him on, and he began to thrust—slowly at first, and when she moved—no, writhed under him—he began to push harder into her.

"God…Nora," was all he could gasp. He had no other words. God and Nora. They became the same person at that moment. He worshipped at the altar of her body and for a moment he felt the power of their union as a communion.

Nora wrapped her legs around his back, bringing him even closer into her, even deeper. Trapped in the circle of her legs, Wesley could only make short, sharp thrusts that brought him to the edge. But he was no kid—*twenty years old,* he scolded himself. He would make this last longer than five minutes if it killed him. And it just might kill him.

Deliberately, he slowed his breathing, looked past her breasts, her body, and out onto the rolling acres, black and silent under the shroud of night. He studied the fireflies as they illuminated that darkness like tiny earthbound stars. He breathed in and inhaled the pungent scent of the pond in August. Calmer now, he brought his gaze back to Nora—to the smile that swept across her face, through her eyes—and down to where their bodies joined together. He had to look, had to watch himself moving in and out of her. But only for a second or two. If he watched any longer, he'd…

With his eyes shut tight and a desperate, near-silent gasp, Wesley came inside Nora.

He nearly collapsed on top of her from the force of the orgasm her body had wrenched from him.

"Father of Mercy," Nora said, raising her head and wrapping her arms around him. She held him close to her and ran her hands through his hair. Her touch felt almost motherly then—the way she cradled him to her chest so he could hear her heart beating so wildly under his ear. Wildly…his Nora did have a wild heart. And he knew this one act with her hadn't tamed it. Nothing would ever tame it, and for that he loved her even more.

"Are you praying? Is that a Catholic thing?" Wesley grinned against her skin as Nora stroked his hair and ran her fingernails lightly over his shoulders. He'd never felt anything like this before…this simple peace. Nothing felt wrong about this moment, nothing dirty or sinful, even as he lay on her with his body still embedded deep inside hers. "Praying after sex? I mean, making love?"

"Catholics tend to use the Lord's name in vain whenever

appropriate. Having a virgin come inside you so hard you feel it qualifies as an appropriate moment."

Her words sounded hoarse and breathy, as if she'd been running or something equally absurd. He loved that he'd done that to her voice, changed the whole tenor of it. Already he wanted to do it again.

"You felt it?"

She bit her bottom lip and nodded slowly. "And that takes some doing, kid. So congrats. That was borderline hurricane-force ejaculation."

Wesley slapped a hand over his face and groaned. He slowly pulled out of her. If he could, he would have stayed inside her all night.

"I don't think the heroines in the romance novels are supposed to say 'hurricane-force ejaculation.' Not that I've read a lot of them."

Nora kissed the top of his head as she pried his hand off his face.

"Let me tell you a little secret...." She held him by the chin and turned his eyes up to her. "I'm no romance-novel heroine. I might even be the villain."

"Good. The villains are more interesting than the heroes, anyway. And I don't want to be anybody's hero."

She smiled at him and he saw something strange in her eyes, something that didn't belong there—sadness.

"Talel's horse got murdered today, and I have the evidence. And neither of us is doing a goddamn thing about it. Safe to say neither of us is the hero here."

Nora kissed the top of his head and lay back down on the table. Wesley caressed her face, her lips, stroked the line of her body from neck to waist and back again. He grew hard simply from touching her, from watching the little smile on her face broaden even as she kept her eyes closed. Gathering her to him, Wesley pushed into her again. Nora wrapped her arms around his back and buried her head against his chest. There. Right there. That was where she belonged, safe in his arms. And he was where he belonged…inside her. Their lips met as he pushed slowly deeper and deeper.

Her words stung—neither one of them heroes. He had to be a hero for her. He wished the world still had dragons so he had something to slay for her. He ached to prove himself to her, to prove his worth. And if the death of Talel's horse had hurt her, he would make it right. For her. For them.

Against his chest, Nora released a raspy breath. He'd waited three years to hear that sound, the sound of her shivering with the pleasure his body gave hers. Three years. Twenty years. It had been worth the wait.

"Tomorrow," he whispered in her ear as she brought her mouth to his again.

"What's tomorrow?" She gazed up at him through eyes hooded with desire.

"We'll start acting like heroes."

NORTH
The Past

He never thought he'd live to see this day—and Søren, Stearns, or whoever he was, doing manual labor. At age seventeen, watching Søren scrubbing the floor of the hermitage with soap and water and steel wool, with his bare hands and on his knees, Kingsley knew he could die at this moment and safely say he'd seen everything.

"You're supposed to be helping, Kingsley." Søren rinsed the steel wool in the water and tackled a stain with renewed vigor.

"So sorry. I'm in shock. Haven't recovered yet, *mon ami*."

A smile played at the corner of Søren's lips.

"Our Lord was a carpenter or possibly a stonemason. The apostle Paul was a tentmaker. They worked with their hands—grueling, backbreaking work. If it wasn't beneath them to get their hands dirty, it should not be beneath me."

"I want to be beneath you."

"You are beneath me, Kingsley, in every way but literally. And if you want to be beneath me—literally—before morning, I would suggest helping me. I told you the hermitage was a hellhole."

With a heavy sigh, Kingsley grabbed a sponge and dropped to his knees.

"You did not exaggerate." Kingsley glanced around and took in once more the spiderwebs, the ashes ground into the dirt-covered floor, the droppings from the mice and birds that had made a home of the hermitage after Father Leopold had gone to meet his maker. "We should find somewhere else."

"There is nowhere else. Not for miles."

"It's disgusting."

"This is Maine. Winter is coming and it's coming fast. We have two weeks of warm nights left, perhaps."

"It's beyond disgusting."

"Once clean, it'll be perfect for us."

"Perfect for you to beat me and fuck me?"

"Exactly," Søren said, not even cracking a smile. No smile necessary, Kingsley realized, as Søren wasn't joking. Good. "The students never come out here."

"Pourquoi?" Kingsley put his back into his scrubbing. It appeared a mouse had died in this spot and the grease of its bones and marrow had left a permanent mark on the wood. A lovely place to give his body to the man he worshipped.

"Someone started a rumor that Father Leopold's ghost haunts the hermitage since he died out here. They didn't find his body for a week, as a blizzard trapped everyone inside the school."

"Just the ghost of a priest. Nothing to be afraid of."

"The story claims that Father Leopold's ghost takes sexual liberties with anyone who comes within his reach. In death he feasts on what he denied himself in life. Do you believe that?"

Kingsley looked at Søren with wide eyes. "No...but I very much want to."

Søren laughed and threw his steel wool at him. Kingsley caught it against his chest and attacked the mouse-grease stain with determination. It took two entire hours to clean the floor. Another hour to sweep away the spiderwebs and kill the inhabitants. He crushed a wolf spider with gusto. Too much gusto for Søren's taste.

"Can't you catch them and set them outside, Kingsley? Killing them seems excessive."

Kingsley leveled a cold, hard glare at Søren.

"Catch the spiders and release them outside? Did I ever tell you I passed blood for three days after our first night together? *Pardonez moi* for saying your Catholic respect for the sanctity of life would be more convincing were you not a sadist."

Søren rose to his feet and straightened. He strode over to Kingsley. "I have no desire to hurt spiders like I want to hurt you. There's a difference."

"Really? How so?"

"First of all, I don't find spiders attractive."

Søren raised his eyebrow. Kingsley couldn't stop the laugh inside him from bursting out. But Søren's lips on his silenced him.

The kiss lasted for but a moment before Søren pulled back.

"Back to work," he ordered.

Kingsley dropped to his knees in front of Søren and gazed up at him.

"Yes, sir."

Søren stared down at him and Kingsley easily discerned the hunger in his eyes.

"Back...to...work..." Søren ordered. It sounded as if he was telling himself as much as Kingsley.

Kingsley frowned. "Yes, sir."

Sighing, he grabbed the sponge and started in on the one and only chair they were able to salvage from the rotted furniture left in the hermitage. He halfheartedly scrubbed at it until he heard Søren mutter with disgust, "Kingsley, have you never cleaned in your life?"

"*Non*. I have a sister."

Søren narrowed his eyes at him. Kingsley laughed.

"It's true. I have an older sister—Marie-Laure. She and Maman did all the cleaning. Papa worked. And I…I did whatever I wanted."

"Why am I not surprised? There are orphans at this school who spent half their childhood on the streets and are more disciplined than you."

"I imagine it would take a great discipline to survive on the streets. I rather enjoyed being spoiled. The only son in a French family is an enviable position. And you? I can't imagine you did much cleaning in your house."

Søren's eyes darkened at the question, but his face remained composed. "My father's house had a large staff to take care of it. My sister Elizabeth and I were required to keep our rooms neat. Other than that, we had little in the way of chores. Other than surviving under that roof."

"That bad, was it?" Kingsley asked, hoping to draw more secrets out of Søren about what had happened between him and his sister.

Søren nodded as he kept working. His hands never stopped. He seemed like a being of pure determination as he ran the soapy rag over the table.

"Being the only son in a family controlled by a child-raping madman is an unenviable position."

Kingsley dropped the sponge. "You said…you'd said he raped your mother. She was—"

"Eighteen," Søren stated, still cleaning. "But my sister was eight. Only eight."

"*Mon Dieu.*"

"*Non. Pas du tout.* God has much more to do with us than

he had to do with that. The monster who calls himself my father raped her. I was away at school in England while this all was happening, otherwise I would have two lives on my conscience instead of one. But I'd rather not talk of that. Tell me about your sister."

Kingsley swallowed. He wanted nothing more than to hear about Søren's childhood. As wretched as it sounded, it was still him, his life, his past. Kingsley drank up every precious revelation like wine. No one at school knew anything about Søren—not even his real name. They heard rumors, told stories, but no one knew him, the real him. The intimacy of the secrets was almost as potent as Kingsley's and his two nights together.

Almost.

"Marie-Laure…" Kingsley pulled his eyes away from Søren, who seemed to be deeply engrossed in cleaning the stones of the hearth. "She's beautiful. I'm her brother, and even I will admit she's the most beautiful girl in the world. She dances."

"Dances?"

"Yes. She's a ballerina. In the chorus of the Paris ballet. But she's good. Very good. She'll be a prima ballerina someday."

"Do you miss her?"

"Very much. She's all I have left now, really. My father's parents have been dead for years. My mother's parents—they don't even speak French. And they never liked Papa. It's hard to be close to them. Marie-Laure feels like my only family. She sends me letters every week. Horrible letters. I can barely read them for all the smears."

"Smears?"

"She cries when she writes me. Cries about Maman and Papa. Cries about us being apart. I thought she would kill me at the funeral…"

"Convenient place for a murder."

"Very." Kingsley grinned even as the memory of that horrible day came back to him. The two urns side by side on the altar. The seemingly endless parade of mourners, most of whom Kingsley had never met before. His father's business associates. His mother's friends. All of them had hands that needed shaking, cheeks that had to be kissed. And all he wanted to do was collapse onto the floor and sob for days and weeks and months and years until he died and could be with his parents again.

After, his mother's parents came for him. Their solemn 'It's time to go now, dear,' were the six most painful words spoken to him since those other five terrible words Marie-Laure had whispered three days earlier: "Maman and Papa, they're gone."

Kingsley had let them lead him away, his mind in a daze. But his dazed state shattered when he felt ten sharp fingernails digging into his arm.

"Non. Non…" Marie-Laure had cried, clinging to him as if her own life hung in the balance. Her beautiful face twisted in agony and her vocabulary was reduced to a single word— *non*. For ten minutes she'd held fast to her little brother, weeping on his shoulder, stroking his hair…. And Kingsley had finally cried then, too.

Their parents had gone away on a second honeymoon, to Tuscany. That had been the plan. They'd never even made it out of Paris. And now he and Marie-Laure had only each other. And he would be taken from her, to live in America.

"Marie-Laure…she went mad after the funeral. I'd never seen her like that. Both my arms were streaming blood by the time our grandparents finally pulled her away from me."

Kingsley worried about his sister. She loved too much. Far too much. Him. Their parents. Anyone she turned her attention to. He wished she could come be with him in America.

It would calm her down, settle her nerves. Perhaps she would start to heal here, as he had.

"Sometimes inflicting pain is the only way to show love."

Kingsley looked up sharply at Søren. "Is that why you hurt me?"

Søren's face didn't betray anything. He showed no expression at all when he answered simply, "I certainly don't hurt you out of hate. But go on. What of Marie-Laure?"

"She's not doing well. She worries about me. When I got hurt at school, she started selling Maman's jewelry so she could afford to come visit me. She has no money. Papa had debts. They left us very little when they died."

"You sound equally worried about her."

Kingsley focused his attention on the table. "I am. She's emotional. Not weak. She's very strong, really. Strong passions. Everyone she loves she loves as if she'll die without them. It's not…it's not good to care that much about people."

"And why not?"

"Because they die. Or will die…someday. Even you. We're doomed from birth. Might as well just have all the fun we want, *oui?* Doesn't matter, anyway."

"You Satanic Huguenot. I can't believe I'm sullying myself with a Calvinist."

"Neither can I," Kingsley said, trying to keep a straight face. He refused to let Søren see how much he enjoyed sullying himself with this Catholic pianist who scared everyone at the school but him. "What were you thinking?"

"Clearly, I wasn't." Søren came over to Kingsley and took the rag from his hand. "Clearly I'm not."

Raising his hand to Kingsley's neck, Søren began to unbutton his shirt. Soon Kingsley had been stripped naked and lay facedown across the table. The edge of the rough wood tabletop cut into his hips. Søren had removed his leather belt and now used it to show him just how little he thought of Kingsley's theology.

And after the extended whipping, when the back of Kingsley's entire body was raw with fiery welts, Søren showed him how little their differences in theology mattered to him. Two hours of pain and pleasure passed in a red haze. They both ended up on the now spotless oak floor of the hermitage—Kingsley naked and Søren still clothed; Kingsley smiling and Søren trying not to.

On the floor they lay next to each other, staring up at the ceiling. Kingsley reached between them and sought out Søren's hand. He found it next to his hip and let his fingers rest against Søren's. And although Søren had been inside him only a minute earlier, it seemed too much of a liberty to hold his hand.

"I think I'll like it here," Kingsley declared. "Hellhole... *peut-être*. But it's our hellhole."

Søren finally smiled.

"It is. And it'll be better when we're finished. We can bring out a clean cot and mattress from the school. There are dozens in storage."

"The floor works."

Søren shook his head.

"I might hurt you on the floor. I want you to be comfortable. And we may have to sleep out here some nights."

Kingsley's eyebrow twitched. "Have to? Or want to?"

Søren turned and faced him. "Either. Both."

Kingsley decided that *both* was his new favorite word. A minute earlier he'd been too shy to take Søren's hand. But now he rose up, leaned over Søren's chest and kissed him. Søren did nothing at first, didn't even respond.

"You Satanic Catholic—kiss me back," Kingsley said against his lips. Søren laughed, but then gave in and returned the kiss, lazily at first, but then with renewed passion. In seconds he had Kingsley on his back once more. The rough wood bit into Kingsley's skin, but he relished the discomfort, gloried in the pain. This was life. Pain, sex, fear, sin…he thought he'd died the day his parents' bodies were cremated and their ashes put into jars. But with Søren he discovered a new life, a life that wouldn't have been his had his parents not died.

"Please…" Kingsley begged. *"S'il vous plaît.* I want you…." He fell into French and out again as they kissed. He hungered for Søren's body and the moment of union they always shared after the beating ended.

Søren pulled away and gazed down at him. He touched Kingsley's lips.

"I can't."

With a sigh, Søren rolled onto his back. Side by side once more, they stared up at the ceiling—Søren utterly silent and Kingsley panting from frustrated need.

"You meant it. You can't…" Kingsley let the words trail off. He thought he'd believed Søren that night he'd confessed that he couldn't become aroused without inflicting pain first. But that kiss, that incredible kiss…no man could kiss like that without his body responding.

"No. Something broke in me a long time ago. I won't ever heal. Can you forgive me?"

"Non. I mean, no, you aren't broken. You're different. I must be different, too, that I don't mind, that I like the pain."

"You are different."

"Vive la différence, oui?"

"Oui," Søren said, laughing softly. *"Vive la différence."*

"Do you think…maybe…somewhere there are others like us? Or is it just in the books by de Sade?"

Søren exhaled. "I think there would have to be others out there like us."

"Terrifying thought." Kingsley smiled at the ceiling.

"Truly." Søren seemed to relish the idea. Kingsley certainly did.

"I'll find them someday," Kingsley decided then and there. "And I'll give them to you. You can have a thousand people at your feet whenever you want them."

"I wouldn't need a thousand."

"Just one, then. We should have a girl, you and I. If only for variety."

"A girl would be nice."

"Mary or Mary Magdalene?" Kingsley asked with a devilish grin.

"Mary Magdalene, of course. I've always found her the more interesting of the Marys."

"And what will our Mary Magdalene look like?"

"She can't be blonde," Søren said. "And she can't look like you, either."

"Somewhere in between us? She'll be pale like you but with dark hair like me."

"We don't ask for much, do we?"

"It's a dream. We can make her however we want. Let's give her green eyes."

"I prefer black."

"Both then," Kingsley said gamely. "Black hair and green eyes. Or perhaps green hair with black eyes."

"She sounds lovely. What is she like?"

"Wild." It was the first word that sprang to Kingsley's mind. Søren seemed to be so controlled, so cold and restrained. He should have someone warm and wild to balance that out.

"Wild...yes. Untamed," Søren suggested.

"But not untamable. Otherwise she'll run away."

Søren shook his head. "She will run away, I'm sure. She wouldn't be truly wild if she didn't."

"But she'll come back?"

"Yes...she'll come back. She wants us to tame her."

"At least we'll tell ourselves that," Kingsley said, rolling onto his side and caressing Søren's neck and collarbone.

"She'll be wilder and more dangerous than both of us together."

"I adore her already. But I promise I'll share her with you," Kingsley pledged.

"You're giving her to me, remember? I'm the one who will share her with you."

"Of course. Forgive me. She'll be yours and you'll share her with me, because no one man will ever be enough for such a girl as her. And the three of us shall be a new unholy trinity."

"God help us all."

"He'll have to, with such a girl as this."

"She sounds perfect."

"She'll be as perfect as we are."

"Poor girl. What should I get you in return for such a gift?" Søren asked as he took Kingsley's hand from his neck and laid it on his stomach.

"*Rien*...nothing. I have all I want."

"That's not true. You were saying earlier how much you missed your sister."

Kingsley sat up and looked down at Søren.

"*Oui. Mais*...she can't afford a visit. Both of us...neither of us...we have no money."

Søren raised his eyebrows and gave Kingsley an arrogant half smile that sent his stomach dropping into his groin.

"I do."

NORTH
The Present

Kingsley stood for a solid hour in his shower, letting the hot water and the steam soothe his aching body. They weren't quite doing enough for him. He'd either have to give in and soak in the bathtub or ingest a Vicodin and vodka cocktail. Or both.

Both.

He'd wanted this pain, prayed for this pain, he reminded himself. For thirty years he'd craved this pain like a starving man craves food. And he'd been fed pain tonight—a feast of pain so bountiful he'd nearly choked to death on it.

Looking down at his feet, Kingsley saw the water turning from red to pink and then clear again. Søren had been particularly thorough with him tonight. His poor Eleanor—she really had no idea the level of violence her beloved was capable of. Søren kept himself in check with her. He had to. Only five foot three and one hundred twenty pounds at the most, she earned her pet name "Little One." At the height of her career as a Dominatrix, she'd been deceptively strong. He'd made her strong. A little girl like her had to be strong if she wanted to compete with the other, more physically intimidating Dominatrixes on the market. What she'd lacked in height and weight, she'd made up for in strength and uncommon viciousness. Others of her kind balked at the dark fantasies their clients laid at their feet. If Nora balked she never let on. She only grinned and said, "I'll do it…if you're a good boy." And they were all good boys if they paid enough.

But no amount of personal training could change the fact that Nora Sutherlin was a woman and fragile. At least compared to him. And when Søren gave in finally and beat Kingsley, he held nothing back.

Kingsley turned off the water and grabbed his plushest, softest towel. Even it felt like salted sandpaper against his raw, bleeding, welt-covered back. Maybe he would simply go to bed wet and sleep on his stomach. But lying on his stomach would be something of an issue, as well. Kingsley looked down the front of his body.

"Good God," he breathed as he saw the mass of bruises his abdomen and thighs had become. God, even his…

A wave of vertigo struck Kingsley as he studied his ravaged body. Welts and bite marks were the least of the damage. He'd seen an intruder attacked by his rottweilers who'd ended up less brutalized than he appeared right now. It would take weeks for the worst of the bruises to heal. They covered his body in deep black whorls, marbling his skin from neck to knee. He feared sleeping. Tomorrow morning he knew he'd barely be able to move. Søren had destroyed him more completely than the night he first took his Little One to bed. Kingsley had tended to twenty-year-old Nora for a week after that night—icing her bruises, rubbing ointment into her welts, picking the shards of glass from her feet and bandaging her bloody skin. She hadn't cried. Not once. Not even when she'd woken up bleeding onto the sheets. More than not crying, the damn girl had even smiled. Smiled like only a woman in love could. Kingsley hated her for that, for not shedding a single tear no matter how much she suffered. Søren had broken her body the night she'd lost her virginity to him, but he hadn't broken her spirit. And Kingsley had to respect her for that no matter how much he envied her Søren's wounds.

But now the wounds were his.

Kingsley nearly stumbled on his way to bed. Rarely did he ever sleep alone. His town house was never without a beautiful boy or girl more than willing to act both as his company and as his pillow at night. Now he wanted nothing in the world more than to be alone. He would lie in bed and get as comfortable as he could. And he would bring to mind over and over again the memory of what Søren had done to him only hours earlier. Even now images flashed across his mind's eye.

Hands on his face…his neck…his back against the wall…the sound of fabric ripping…the touch of teeth on his sternum…fingers digging into his throat…the leather on his back, his thighs…hitting the floor with his knees…salt on his tongue…sweat on his stomach…his arms aching from the cuffs that held him immobile on the bed…and the penetration, so necessary and brutal…. He'd closed his eyes at one point and wasn't sure he'd ever open them again.

Kingsley grasped the bedpost with his left hand. With his right hand he grasped himself. He came hard onto the bed, wincing with the agony of the orgasm. Søren had left no part of him undamaged. Kingsley Edge, the King of the Underground, a man who hadn't gone a day without sex in twenty years, would have to remain celibate for at least a week while he healed enough to be inside someone again. And it would be at least a week before Søren could be inside him. At least. Sadist. They left their notches not on their lovers' bedposts but on the very bodies of those who braved their beds. Kingsley could count all night and still not reach the end of the number of lashes Søren had inflicted on those he loved. He could count until dawn and still not find the grand total.

Of course, Søren's Little One had an even higher butcher's bill to pay.

Carefully Kingsley started to climb naked into bed. Usually he adored his massive bed, draped in its red-and-black sheets. Bigger than a king-size, he joked that it was Kingsley-size, and all of the Underground spoke of it with respect. But now he hated its height. Every inch he had to move felt like a mile of agony.

Damn you, mon père. Kingsley sighed with a smile. *Damn you to hell.*

As soon as his head hit the pillow, a knock sounded on his door.

"Arrête!" he called out tiredly. He had no strength for orders longer than one word.

"Monsieur? *S'il vous plaît…*" The voice of Sophia came through the door. Or was it Cassandra? They all blurred together now. No woman mattered to him but Juliette, and he'd sent her off to Haiti for her own safety, for reasons he refused to think about right now. "What is it?" he called out as he pulled a sheet over his body. Even lifting the light silk fabric hurt. Tomorrow…tomorrow he would take painkillers, many of them. Tonight he would accept the pain, revel in it. Søren had given it to him, this pain, and he would cherish the gift.

"Les chiens, monsieur."

Kingsley's eyes flew open. The dogs? The last time someone had come to him about his dogs was the night the thief had broken into the town house, drugged his infamous pack of rottweilers and stolen Nora's file. If someone had drugged the dogs again…

Despite the pain, Kingsley rolled out of bed in an instant, pulled on his pants and a shirt, and headed for the door.

He opened it and found little redheaded Sophia, his night secretary, standing there, her face white as the moon.

"Quoi?"

She didn't answer him.

"Mon Dieu…" he breathed, and followed her down the hallway. She raced down the stairs and Kingsley kept up as best he could. The last thing he needed was for his staff to see him weak, in pain. He swallowed the agony and kept moving.

At the bottom of the steps he saw Brutus, Dominic and Max pacing and whining. He reached for Max and touched his warm nose.

"Sadie?" he called out. Sophia turned to him with a tearstained face. She pointed.

In the darkness at the corner of the room, Kingsley saw a black shadow. As he approached it, the shadow took the form of a dog.

Sadie…his little girl lay unmoving on the white tile, blood seeping from a wound in her chest. He reached out and touched the blood. She'd been stabbed in the heart.

"Oh, ma fille…" he whispered, stroking her coat. On the wall behind her he saw five words scrawled in blood. Only five. And none of those five words was a name. Yet as soon as he read them he knew who'd killed his dog, who'd stolen Nora's file, who'd sent the photograph and burned Søren's bed.

"Sophia?"

"Oui, monseiur?"

"Call Griffin Fiske. And if he tries to tell you that he's still on his honeymoon with his new true love, tell him he'll be persona non grata in the Underground if he isn't in my bedroom by noon tomorrow."

"Oui. Bien sûr."

Sophia raced off and left him alone with three rottweilers mourning their only sister. Kingsley knew how they felt.

He stared at the writing on the wall. Christian had been right...about everything.

All Søren wanted was for Kingsley to find out who was after them. And now Kingsley knew.

He knew and he would never tell.

SOUTH

Nora woke up on the pillow across from Wesley's. Only a few inches of sheets and fourteen years separated them. But in the early morning light, Wesley seemed a stranger to her. Where had her boy gone? The boy that had followed her around her house in Connecticut like a puppy, ticking off everything she needed to do that week lest she be arrested for tax evasion, evicted for not paying her mortgage or hospitalized for not eating...where had he gone? Her Wes...her Brown Eyes...the kid she teased and tormented. Hell, she'd even called him Purity Ring half the time they were living together, until Wesley begged her on his hands and knees to stop.

As she watched him sleep she couldn't help but think of all those nights she'd stood in the doorway to his bedroom and listened to the slow, rhythmic breathing that signaled he'd fallen into deepest sleep. She didn't know quite why it comforted her so much, hearing Wesley breathe in his sleep, but she couldn't get enough of it. After leaving Søren, she didn't make much of a habit of sleeping with others. She'd get in, get what she wanted and get out. An 11:00 a.m. breakfast on her own worked just fine for her. Then, suddenly, she had this kid in her house who got up at 7:30 a.m…even on the damn weekends. And he cooked breakfast for her. And balanced her checkbook. And made sure the bills got paid on time. During that one summer they'd lived together, he'd even mowed the lawn once a week.

Living with Wesley had given her the most horrible thoughts. One night she'd sat on the edge of his bed and read the first chapter of her new novel to him. Later, in her own bed, she'd wondered if being a mother would be that much fun—reading books by Dr. Seuss or Lewis Carroll to her own son. Then, a week later, Wesley would have to unclog her bathroom drain—too much of her damn hair had gotten caught in the U-bend again. And she'd watch him under the sink and think that maybe being married to a semi-normal guy wouldn't be the soul-sucking nightmare she'd always imagined it would be. And when she'd written at her desk for too long, and every square inch of her body ached like it had been beaten in the not-fun way, and Wesley dragged her to her room, put her into bed and rubbed her back with his big, strong hands that knew how to make the pain go away inside and out, she'd think that not only might it be okay to be married to semi-normal guy, but she might even kind of like it.

Maybe more than just kind of.

Nora reached out and touched Wesley's dark blond hair. Maybe she could get used to it being this long. Maybe. As long as it didn't cover his eyes. Wesley stirred in his sleep and pushed closer to her. He settled back down again quickly and Nora smiled when he grunted softly and buried his face in the pillow. Gently, so as not to wake him, she lifted the sheets for a second. Naked. They were both completely naked and in Wesley's bed together. After they'd made love on the dock, they'd straightened their clothes and returned to the guest-house. Nora had assumed she and Wesley would get into bed and sleep, but sleep had been the last thing on his mind. As soon as they'd entered the house, the clothes had come flying off. They'd had sex twice before they'd even hit the bed—once in the entryway the minute they'd gotten in the door and once in the hallway only feet from the bedroom. Both times Nora had ended up on her back with her legs wide-open and Wesley on top and inside her. So strange…she never had sex like this, in basic missionary position. No pain, no bond-age, no nothing but their two bodies joined together. Never had she imagined she could enjoy sex that simple. Wesley had been on top both times, but he certainly hadn't been domi-nating her. With every initial penetration, he asked if it was okay, if he needed to do something different to make her feel better. She whispered words of instruction in his ear, words of encouragement. She'd never done anything like that with Søren. Sex with Søren was one of the rare times Nora shut up. He needed no instructions, required no encouragement. Had she tried either with him he would have gagged her in seconds and not let her speak again until he was done with her. And when inside her, he was always on top, while Nora ended up on her stomach or her hands and knees. They did have sex in missionary position on occasion. The last time, he'd sliced her open with a razor blade first.

All she ever said to Søren while he was inside her was, "yes, sir" or "no, sir" or more often simply, "I love you, sir."

Once in Wesley's bed, Nora put the boy on his back and climbed on top of him. Wesley seemed immediately uncom-fortable with the position.

"What's wrong?" she'd asked him as she came down onto her hands and let her nipples brush his chest.

"I…it feels weird."

"Weird? How?"

"I don't know. Just weird. My…it's sort of a weird angle. Good view, though." He caressed her breasts and Nora sighed.

"Okay, but I've got to get you into something other than missionary. Vanilla is bad enough," she'd teased as she rolled off him and onto her side. Wesley spooned into her and she felt his erection pressing against her lower back. Moving up, she tossed her top leg over his, took him in her hand and slid him inside her. Wesley gasped as he moved deeper into her. "Better?"

Wesley covered her neck and shoulder with kisses.

"Definitely. This…good. Very." The words were lost in a mumble of more kisses all over her shoulders and back.

"Missionary and spooning," she said as Wesley nuzzled her hair. "The Underground must never hear of this."

Wesley had stopped moving then.

"Is this bad? Do you not like it?"

"Don't stop. Don't stop…." Nora reached behind her and grabbed his hip.

Laughing, Wesley resumed moving as ordered.

"I will never stop again."

Nora pulled a pillow to her chest and rested her head on it as he continued his slow, sensual thrusts.

"No…I like it. I do. It's just different for me. I'm either really dominant in bed—on top, him under me, usually tied down. Or…"

"Or?"

"I'm really submissive. Like with—"

"Yeah, I know." Wesley lightly touched the tips of her nipples. "So what's so different about it? Just the positions?"

He pushed in a little harder and deeper and Nora's vagina clenched around him. After a few seconds she'd caught her breath enough to speak again.

"Um…no. It's hard to explain. When I'm being the Domme or the sub, I fall into this role…. This other part of me takes over and I become *the* Nora Sutherlin if I'm on top. Or if I'm with Søren, I turn into his Little One."

"Little One?"

Nora nodded. "That's what he always calls me. It's his pet name for me. He's huge, you know."

"We've met."

Nora grinned at the disgust mixed with envy in Wesley's voice.

"He's six foot four. And I'm…not."

"I can't believe he calls you Little One. It's so…"

"What?"

"Fatherly."

Fatherly…Nora couldn't really argue with that assessment. He was Father Stearns, after all. To the world, anyway. Within five minutes of meeting him, he'd told her his real name—Søren—and said she could and should call him that when no one else was around. Calling him Father Stearns had always seemed like an inside joke to her. Even after twenty years, she could hardly say it with a straight face.

And yet…he'd practically raised her. As soon as they'd met, her reliance on her parents, minimal to start with, had become nonexistent. She'd answered to him and him only. Even now…being here with Wesley had been Søren's idea, Søren's gift to her. But for the life of her, she couldn't figure out why.

"Why…" she whispered across the sheets as Wesley stirred and opened his eyes.

"Why what?" he mumbled, pulling her close to him. For a minute he and Nora wrestled with arm placement. With Søren in the mornings, she'd simply drape herself across his broad chest—no arm wrestling necessary. She wasn't used to this side-by-side, face-to-face, can't-figure-out-where-every-one's-arm-goes thing.

"What are you doing?" Wesley asked as Nora wriggled against him, trying to find a comfortable position.

"I think I'll need to cut my arm off if we're going to lie like this. Or you'll have to cut yours off."

"Nora, have you never cuddled before?"

"Not like this. Here. You lay on your back. I'll lay on you."

"Fine. Fine…" Wesley rolled onto his back and Nora collapsed onto his chest. He let out a puff of air as she scrambled into position. "Are you made of lead?"

"I'm solid muscle and evil. Stop bitching and cuddle me."

Laughing, he wrapped his arms around her. "Yes, ma'am."

Closing her eyes, Nora nestled against Wesley's chest—not quite as broad as Søren's, but warmer, closer. And Wesley's young heart beat faster than Søren's. Was that his natural rate or just a side effect of having a naked woman on his body?

"How are you this morning?" Nora asked, turning her eyes up to his.

"Good." Wesley nodded after he'd paused to think about his answer. "Really good. I feel like I could do anything I wanted today."

"Welcome to afterglow. It's nice, right?"

"Very. They should sell this stuff on the black market."

"They do. It's called pot."

"Kentucky's unofficial number-one cash crop."

Nora's eyes widened. "I like this state more and more every day."

Groaning, Wesley sat up and sent Nora sliding onto her back. He slapped her lightly on the bottom and she yelped much louder than necessary. Wesley stared at her with shock.

"Sorry," she said. "Force of habit. What?"

"Let's go. Clothes on."

"Both of those are horrible ideas. Why and where?"

"We've gotta figure out what happened to Spanks for Nothing."

"Really? We are?" Nora crawled off the bed and started throwing clothes on.

"Yeah. You said Talel's a good guy and wouldn't kill his own horse. If you believe in him, so do I. After all, no horse owner in his right mind would kill their own moneymaker. Not unless they were completely desperate for quick money."

"And Talel has money, so that can't be it. Any theories?" Nora pulled on her jeans and T-shirt. She probably should have taken a shower, but she didn't want to waste the time and she sort of enjoyed smelling like sex with Wesley. Maybe more than sort of.

"Nope. Let's just go over there and talk."

"Good plan. You talk. I'll...not talk."

"Deal."

In ten minutes time they were in Nora's Aston Martin, heading down the parkway.

"Where are we going?" Nora asked as they took an exit. She'd let Wesley drive, since he knew the way and she planned to imbibe extraordinary amounts of coffee.

"Paris."

Nora choked on her coffee.

"Paris? That's a little more than a day trip, Wes."

"Paris, Kentucky. That's where Talel's farm is. Well, one of them."

"How many damn farms does he have?"

"Two less than we do." Wesley glanced at her and winked.

Nora rolled her eyes. "So much for my semi-normal guy fantasy."

"What? Who's a semi-normal guy?"

"You are. Or were. When we lived together, I would catch

myself thinking about how nice it was to be with a semi-normal guy. I mean, semi in that you're way hotter than actual normal guys. And smarter. And a virgin. Well, you were back then. But now you're not. You've got more money than God. Or at least more than Talel."

"Well, it's my parents', really. But I'll inherit it all someday, I guess. Ten thousand acres at last count, including the satellite farms in Maryland and Tennessee. Two hundred horses in training. Five or six hundred broodmares and yearlings."

Nora turned away from him to stare out the car window. She'd never seen so many miles of green in her life.

"What will you do with this empire of yours?"

Wesley shook his head. "I don't know. The amount of work my father does every day—it's insane. He's gotten up at 4:30 a.m. every day for as long as I can remember. He looks strong and healthy, but he's been fighting ulcers since I was ten."

"Sell it."

"What?"

"Sell it. Sell it all. Get rid of it if you don't want it. You went to college in Connecticut, never told me one word about your life here. We went horseback riding, but only for fun. You want to be a doctor, not run an empire, right?"

"Right."

"Then sell it. Griffin sold off his grandfather's horses. Never looked back."

"This farm is a legend. And it's been in my family for generations. It's my father's obsession. It's my father's legacy."

"Stealing cars, chopping them up and getting whacked by the mob is my father's legacy, Wes. Just because our parents care about something doesn't mean we have to."

Wesley shook his head. "Can't do it. I'd never forgive myself for selling The Rails."

"Then what's the other option?"

"I don't know. Mom and I talked about it. She said I should marry a woman into horses and let her run the farm, while I did whatever I wanted. Mom's allergic to horses. She has to take shots every week just to breathe through her nose."

Nora laughed. "I like your mom. Good thinking. We'll have to find you a wife who's really into this shit so you can go play doctor."

"I'd rather have a wife who's into me."

"That's crazy talk."

Nora and Wesley crazy talked all the way to Paris. When they drove up to Unstableside Farms, Nora couldn't help but gasp aloud again.

"What?" Wesley demanded.

"Wesley, this is insane. Why does everyone in Kentucky live in a fucking palace?"

"Clearly, I need to take to you to eastern Kentucky. You're getting a very skewed perception of this state."

"Eastern Kentucky? What's there?"

"Ever seen *Deliverance?*"

Nora pushed her sunglasses on and scoffed. "Seen it, Wes? I've lived it."

Wesley rolled his eyes as he parked the car in the circular driveway in front of the massive colonial manor that comprised the main house at Unstableside.

"Unstable? Adorable," Nora said. "Talel has a little too much fun with his English."

"He gives his horses the most fun names. Mom names all our horses and she's real conservative. No BDSM references."

"I want to name a horse."

"If you stay here, you can name all the horses from now on."

Nora's heart tightened at the smile on Wesley's face. She was so used to Søren loving her that it hardly registered anymore. Søren's love was like the sky—huge and ubiquitous, always there without fail. She no more expected his love to go away than she would ever imagine walking outside at night and seeing a void where the stars should be. But Wesley's love...it seemed so strange to her, so novel. Where had it come from? And why? She would understand the origin of the stars before she ever got why this beautiful boy, so sweet and pure, would love a woman like her.

Wesley rang the bell at Talel's front door and took her hand as they waited.

"So we can just drive up here and ring the bell?" Nora asked, shocked by the lack of security.

"Nope. We can't. But I can." He grinned at her again and Nora stuck her tongue out.

"Fine. I get it. You own Kentucky. When we go back to New York, I'm going to take you places only I can get us into."

"Do we have to?"

"Have to what? Go into places only I can get us into?"

"No..." Wesley's smile left his face. "Go back to New York."

Nora sighed heavily as she squeezed his hand. "This is your world, kid. Not mine. You know I don't belong here."

"You told me once you loved it down south."

"I was talking about anal sex."

"Of course you were."

The door opened and Wesley started to introduce himself to the young woman who'd answered. She ushered them in before Wesley could even get his name out.

When the woman turned her back, Nora stuck her tongue out at Wesley.

"Big shot," she mouthed.

"Big money," he replied, not sounding terribly impressed with himself. Nora could sympathize. Wesley didn't really care about horse racing. During the year and a half they'd lived to-

gether, he'd talked at length about his med-school dreams...
becoming a pediatrician, treating kids like himself, with type
1 diabetes and other diseases. Helping people, helping children. He cared as much about his family money as Søren
cared about his. Søren had given away every cent he'd inherited. His trust fund had gone to Kingsley, and had financed
the Underground empire. The bulk of his inheritance he'd
given to his two sisters. As a Catholic parish priest he made
about thirty thousand dollars a year. Of course, with Kingsley around, Søren had access to anything and everything he
needed. And Nora kept him well supplied with grand pianos
and high-thread-count Egyptian cotton sheets. Even when
he told her not to.

Nora squeezed Wesley's hand as Talel—wearing jeans and
a black shirt and looking as exotically handsome as usual—
came down the stairs toward them with a smile on his face.

"It's always a good day when the Prince of Kentucky and
the Queen of the Underground come calling." Talel shook
Wesley's hand and kissed Nora on the cheek.

"Ex-Queen of the Underground," she told him. "I've retired."

"I heard the rumors. I didn't believe them, then. I don't
believe them now. Let me take you to the stables and hand
you a riding crop. We'll see how long it takes before you start
swatting someone with it."

Nora released a wistful sigh. "I do miss all my riding crops.
I kept the red one, of course."

"You'd be Arthur without Excalibur had you given it up.
Now, to what do I owe the pleasure of this visit?" Talel asked
as he ushered them into the front room.

Nora's eyes widened at all the silver cups and trophies that
littered the massive living room. They sat on the fireplace
mantel, the windowsills, on shelves and tables and podiums.

Ribbons spilled out of the cups. Sashes draped across the trophies.

"Damn." She nodded in approval.

"If you're impressed by my winnings," Talel said as he beamed his smile around the room, "it's only because you haven't seen the trophy room at The Rails."

"No, I haven't. Why is that, Wes?"

"Because Dad won't let you in the house," Wesley reminded her.

"Right. Forgot. Anyway, Talel…we just came by about Spanks for Nothing. What the hell happened?"

Talel sighed heavily and shook his head. "We're trying to find that out. He was on some medication for some slight congestion. Possibly the dose was off. I can't say for certain. It's a tragedy. Amazing horse. Impressive speed and stamina. Could run on any track. Headed for the Derby."

"And he was cute, too," Nora said, frowning.

"And he was cute." Talel gave her hand a quick squeeze.

"Who's investigating?" Wesley asked, not even glancing at the trophies around the room. Nora saw him staring directly at Talel. Surely Wesley didn't suspect him of any foul play.

"The usual—the track veterinarian, the insurance company. Spanks for Nothing was insured for forty." He shrugged as he straightened a blue ribbon.

Nora felt her eyes nearly explode from her face.

"Forty million?"

"We were being conservative. Such a waste…" Talel sighed. "I'm trying not to think about it too much until they've finished the investigation. I don't want heads to roll. I'm sure whatever happened was simply an accident. I'd just like my horse back."

"I know how you feel," Wesley said. "We lost Aphorism to colic last year. Dad acted like he'd lost his best friend."

"Aphorism was a fine animal. Impressive specimen. As was Spanks. But we've a few fine specimens left."

"Do you mind if we tour the stables?" Wesley asked. "Dad told Nora she's not allowed near our horses. She's been in the mood to play with the ponies."

Talel paused a moment before answering. "Of course. I'd love to accompany you, but I've nothing but meetings today, about the incident. Should I get my manager for you?"

Wesley waved his hand. "We'll find our way around."

"Forgive me, but please, visit the stallion barn only. Our other barns are going through some renovations right now. For your safety. The stallions are in the main stable."

"Definitely," Wesley said. "Nora just wants to see some horses."

Nora kept her face composed. Mr. Railey hadn't banned her from the stables. He'd probably thought about it, but he hadn't outright said she couldn't be around the horses.

"Mistress, a pleasure as always." Talel kissed her on both cheeks, and she patted him on top of his head, as patronizingly as she could.

"For old times' sake."

She and Wesley left the house and paused on the porch.

"What?" she asked as Wesley exhaled loudly through his nose.

"Something's smelly."

"That's all the horseshit. I think I got some on my shoe." Nora lifted her foot.

"Not literally smelly. I don't know. Something's weird about Spanks for Nothing. Talel should be more upset about it. That horse was a money machine. And forty million's about what he'd make in one year on stud fees."

"And?"

"Some horses live for twenty years or more. That horse

could have brought in one or two hundred million dollars over the next five to ten years."

"But Talel's richer than God. That's pocket change to him."

"Nora, a hundred million dollars isn't pocket change to anybody. Come on."

She followed Wesley to the car, and in silence they drove half a mile to where half a dozen stables stood in a ring at the end of the drive. They left the car and walked to the nearest one. Nora whistled when they stepped inside.

"Wesley, this is ridiculous," she said, glancing around. "I know Connecticut insurance execs whose houses aren't as well decorated as these damn stables."

"Tell me about it. The Rails has swimming pools for the horses, heated stalls, spas…. Our top horses get massages, have homeopaths doing acupressure on them…. It's crazy how spoiled these damn animals are."

They walked up and down the center corridor of the stable. Horses poked their heads out and whinnied peevishly at them. Nora reached out to pet one and Wesley pulled her hand back.

"I know, I know. These are Thoroughbreds, not kittens. They bite."

"Exactly. And they bite hard."

"So do I," Nora said, baring her teeth at him. A big brown horse chomped at her and Nora growled in reply. He gave her a shocked look before retreating into his stall. "What, pray tell, are we—shit—!"

Nora grabbed the back of Wesley's shirt as she tripped on something and nearly fell.

"Nora? You okay?"

"What the fuck? I kicked something. Sorry." She bent down and dug through the straw, pulling up a piece of rotted wood with a rusted silver hinge attached to the end.

Wesley took the board from her hands and examined it.

"Weird."

"Weird, what?" she asked.

Wesley didn't answer. Turning around, he walked down the corridor again, pausing at each stall.

"Wes…what is going on?"

He shook his head. "I don't know. Come on. Let's go see the mares."

With the rotted board in one hand, he grabbed her with the other and nearly dragged her from the stallion stable.

"Talel asked us to stay in the stallion barn."

"I know. That's why we're not staying here. The stallions are the big money. They're the ones everyone cares about. Those are the prizewinners in there. I want to see how the other half lives."

Wesley seemed on high alert as they left the stallion stable and headed down a path toward a white barn with green trim. It looked just as elegant and well-maintained, but when he reached the door and saw a big silver padlock hanging off the door handle, he swore.

"Dammit. Locked." He stared at it with such intensity Nora thought he was trying to open it with sheer mental power.

"Why would anyone lock up the mares, but not lock up the prizewinning stallions?"

"That's my question."

"Well, better find out the answer, then."

Nora pushed past Wesley, opened her bag and pulled out her lock-pick set. "Cover me."

"Nora, what are you doing?"

"Stop freaking out. I'm just picking the lock. Give me a second."

"How do you know how to pick locks? And why do you have a lock-pick set in your purse?"

"Wesley, my boy, I got arrested at age fifteen. That was arrest number one. There have been twelve since. You get arrested as many times as I have, and you start planning for all contingencies."

"Nora…"

She popped the padlock and it fell off the handle. They slipped inside the barn and closed the door behind them.

"Fine." She turned her face up to Wesley. "Søren's really into bondage. Huge shocker, right?"

"I'm stunned beyond words."

Nora rolled her eyes. "I learned how to pick locks to piss him off. I wanted him to know that anything he put me into, I could get out of. Even if I didn't try."

"Why? I thought you loved him."

"I do love him. Love and having an escape plan are not mutually exclusive. They are, in fact, both highly recommended." Nora found a light switch and flicked it on. "Now this is weird."

"Yeah, tell me about it."

In silence they studied the stable. It was empty. Completely empty. No horses. No horse tack. No staff. No jockeys. No nothing. Just old straw on the floor rotting away in the sweltering darkness.

"Looks like it's been empty for a long time." Wesley peeked his head into every stall.

"Feels like it, too. Weird putting a lock on an empty stable and not on the one full of moneymaking horses."

"Let's check out the others."

"I've got my picks."

Nora followed Wesley from the second stable to the third. Again they found it padlocked. Again they found it empty. The fourth and fifth stables were also empty. No horses. No nothing.

"What the hell is going on?" Wesley stood in the final stable and stared at the nothingness it contained.

"You tell me. You're the horse expert."

"I don't know. Unless Talel's moved all his horses to another farm… Makes no sense. A farm this size should have hundreds of horses—yearlings, stallions, broodmares. Even if he'd moved all his horses to another farm, he should at least have some mares here that he's boarding for others. We're boarding about a hundred horses that aren't ours."

"I should go ask him. He'll tell me anything."

"Don't ask him. Not yet. I want to ask some of my own questions first."

"Like what?"

Wesley held up the board from the stallion stable. "Fresh paint over rotting wood, Nora? My first question is going to be why can't a billionaire afford to fix his broken stall doors?"

Nora looked at the wood and then looked up at Wesley. He saw something in her eyes, something like understanding. He waited, but she didn't seem willing to enlighten him. Heavily, she exhaled, as the light in her eyes went out again.

"Damn good question."

NORTH

The Past

Kingsley groaned in the back of his throat, a groan Søren swallowed with his mouth. He pulled on the rope that bound him to the cold metal at the head of the cot, but couldn't free his hands.

Now this was pure torture. Kingsley lay with his hands and feet tied to the ends of the bed, while Søren slowly, gently kissed him. His mouth…his neck…his collarbone and chest received nearly five full minutes of attention….

"Please…*s'il vous plaît…*" Kingsley pleaded, and didn't even know why he begged and what he begged for. Søren never heeded his pleas—neither for mercy nor for consummation. Everything happened in Søren's time, by his will and his will alone. But Kingsley couldn't stop himself from begging, from pleading. No girl had ever kissed him like this. He felt like an object and nothing more. When Søren kissed him, Kingsley knew it was for Søren's sake alone. The pain was for Søren. The pleasure was for Søren. Kingsley existed for Søren and he knew it. A month ago he'd bragged to Søren about the privileged position he held, being the only son in a French family. His mother had worshipped him and asked nothing from him. His father had spoiled him. His sister did the work he was never expected to do. A little prince...that's what he'd been, growing up. And every night, his mother read to him from *Le Petit Prince,* his favorite story. But underneath Søren, Kingsley ceased to be a prince or a king.

He was nothing but a slave, a servant, a body to be used by Søren and for Søren.

Nothing pleased Kingsley more than to disappear to the hermitage at night and find Søren waiting for him. The crown his parents had placed on his head, even naming him Kingsley, although a less French name had never existed...he'd take off that crown and lay it at Søren's feet. And the prince would become a servant and the king a commoner all night long.

Søren slid his hand down the center of Kingsley's chest, over his stomach, creeping ever lower. Kingsley moaned in near pain from the need, the incredible ache. He had to be touched...soon. But Søren's hands and mouth roamed over every inch of him...except for the inches he most needed kissed, most desperately desired touched.

"You hate me," Kingsley whispered, and Søren laughed into his skin.

"I don't care about you enough to hate you." Søren brought his mouth to Kingsley's ear and kissed him from the nape of his neck to the tip of his shoulder. "You're nothing to me."

"Is that why you're trying to kill me?" Kingsley raised his hips, seeking some sort of satisfaction and feeling nothing but renewed pressure in his stomach. He'd come if he wasn't careful. And he knew better than that. Søren would beat him nearly bloody if he ever came without asking permission first. He had the week-old welt on his lower back to prove it.

"I would never kill you," Søren said, sliding his hands over Kingsley's inner thighs, massaging them, running his fingers to the very edge of Kingsley's painfully straining erection before pulling away again. Only another man would ever understand the absolute agony of this kind of teasing. Only a sadist like Søren would ever inflict it. "It would be a waste of my valuable time, killing you."

"You would have to find someone else to torture like this if you killed me," Kingsley said, laughing even though his eyes held unshed tears of frustration.

"Exactly...a waste..." Søren kissed his rib cage. "Of..." Søren kissed his hip. "My time..." Søren kissed his stomach, only an inch away from where Kingsley so desperately wanted him to.

"I'll die anyway if you don't let me come."

"Your penchant for exaggeration is embarrassing. You should be ashamed of yourself."

"I am. Or would be if I had any shame...which I do not."

"No shame? One would think someone with no sense of shame would beg more than you have been...."

Kingsley heard the hint in Søren's voice and nearly laughed out loud with joy. Søren did that sometimes...guided him toward the desired response. At these times Kingsley most felt like a servant, a child, like property. Søren wanted Kingsley to perform for him—to beg when begging was desired, to cry when crying was desired, and always, always to submit to him, for submission was what Søren most desired.

Submission... Kingsley had never understood it until he'd spent his first full night with Søren. That first night in the forest had simply broken his body. The second night had broken his will. But when they spent their first night together in the hermitage, and hadn't given up until dawn, Kingsley learned that submission didn't mean surrendering to an enemy, but to an ally. Although Søren never confessed love for Kingsley or even affection, he felt it in every "we" uttered during that long night.

"We should stay here tonight," Søren had said.

"We should sleep…at least for a while," Søren had whispered.

"We shouldn't go back together. Someone might see," he'd decided in the morning.

During their first night together in the hermitage, Søren had beaten Kingsley before tying him facedown on the cot and penetrating him again and again. And with every thrust, Kingsley had whispered *"Je t'aime"* into the sheets. A thousand times that night he must have said it. A thousand times he'd meant it. He'd awoken the next morning with his head on Søren's stomach and those perfect pianist's fingers twined in his long hair. The pain had rendered him nearly immobile, but he couldn't stop smiling.

One of the priests in chapel that week had given a homily about Jacob grappling with an angel until he'd wrested a blessing from the angel—an angel who turned out to be God Himself. Jacob received His blessing that night, and along with it a limp that never healed. The message was that no one walked away from God entirely whole. Kingsley would limp away from Søren that morning and every morning after a night with him. He would limp away and know he did so not because he'd been cursed, but because he'd been blessed.

So if Søren wanted him to beg, then Kingsley would beg. And beg he did.

"Please…" He sighed. "Monsieur. I will do anything you ask of me. Anything at all. Only let me come…please…." and on and on. Kingsley debased himself as Søren continued his sensual assault. Assault—it felt like an assault. The more gently Søren touched him, the more gingerly, the more Kingsley ached for more. Even violence would hurt less than this kind of tenderness. Only Søren could make pleasure so brutally painful. His light caresses set every last nerve in Kingsley's body on edge. After an hour of Søren's hands on him, of his mouth, every touch felt like sandpaper rubbing an open wound.

"More," Søren ordered as he pressed a kiss into the hollow of Kingsley's throat and worked his way slowly over his chest and stomach yet again.

"Give me relief and you will own me for eternity," Kingsley pledged. "My body, my heart, my soul…take it all if you'll only let me…"

"I already own you." Søren's tongue flicked lightly over the sensitive skin of Kingsley's side—the one part of him slightly ticklish. Tears slid from his eyes and into his hair. He willed himself to come but couldn't. He had to be touched. "All of you, for what it's worth, which isn't much. I own your body…." Søren slid both hands up Kingsley's bound arms. "I own your heart…" He pressed his mouth to Kingsley's chest. "As you're French and not a Catholic, I'm not even sure you have a soul…."

"I do have one. I keep it in my cock. Feel free to suck it out," Kingsley said, now desperate enough to taunt Søren.

Søren rewarded his insolence with a quick, hard slap to the face.

"That is not the way to get what you want."

"Then tell me what is…please." Kingsley's voice broke and his throat tightened. "There's nothing I won't submit to if you let me come. Nothing."

"Nothing?" Søren straddled him at the thighs. Kingsley had been stripped naked the moment he'd stepped into the hermitage, but Søren still wore his trousers, shirt, vest and tie. The need to feel Søren's skin on his was nearly as great as his need to come. "Will you submit to being sodomized again?"

"God, yes." Kingsley swallowed the knot in his throat. After the first beating tonight, Søren had bent him over a chair and sodomized him. Søren had ordered him not to come, and had touched nothing but his shoulders while inside him.

"Will you submit to being cut open?"

Kingsley paused and then nodded.

"*Oui*. Anything." Søren had cut him only once before, and the sight of the razor blade had both terrified and aroused him beyond comprehension. He'd never seen Søren's eyes turn so black with desire as they had at the sight of Kingsley's red blood on his olive skin. To see that look again, Kingsley would let Søren cut his tongue out, if that's what he wanted.

Søren slid his hands from Kingsley's wrists to his shoulders… across his chest and down his stomach, then up again, pausing at last when they wrapped firmly around Kingsley's throat.

"Would you let me kill you?" Søren stared down at Kingsley with his steel-gray eyes so empty of compassion.

Kingsley swallowed again and felt his Adam's apple press against Søren's hands.

He whispered, "Yes."

"Good." Søren's fingers tightened around his throat, and for one beautiful, terrible moment, Kingsley saw the white light of the World to Come and God standing before him. But the hands around his neck disappeared and he felt incredible heat on him. Søren pushed a finger inside him, and when he touched that spot that sent him into paroxysms of pleasure, Kingsley flinched. And with one guttural cry, came inside Søren's mouth.

The orgasm lasted forever, so long Kingsley not only felt it would never end, but feared it would never end. On and on, waves of release washed over and through him. Later he realized it had lasted only seconds, but the sheer relief of *finally,* after an hour of torture, *finally…at last…*being allowed to come had stripped him of his senses, of any comprehension of time. Søren had that power. Not only did Kingsley bend to Søren's will, time itself did.

A day or a year or a few minutes later, Kingsley started to come out of the haze. Opening his eyes, he found Søren untying his ankles from the bars of the cot.

"*Merci…*" Kingsley breathed, a smile leisurely spreading across his face.

"*De rien.*" Søren wrapped up the rope ties neatly. Kingsley loved watching Søren with rope—he had such a natural grace about him. Everything he did to Kingsley seemed so controlled, so ritualistic. Even the beatings had a strange beauty to them. "You did well."

"I try to please you." Kingsley spoke the words before he even thought them. He said them in a tone of pessimism, feeling, as always, that nothing he did would ever be worthy of Søren.

Søren freed his wrists and Kingsley extended his arms as blood rushed through his cool fingers. He flinched when he felt Søren's hand on his face again—this time not a slap, but a light touch.

"You do," he said, tapping Kingsley under the chin before leaving the bed.

Kingsley rolled up into a sitting position and pulled a blanket over him. During the hour of torture, he'd been nearly sweating from desire. Now he felt cool, almost cold, and so calm he knew that if left alone and undisturbed, he could sleep for the next ten hours.

"I do?"

"Don't sound so surprised. Why would you think you don't please me?" Søren had brought a small trunk from storage, and they used it to conceal their makeshift bonds and the belts he used to beat Kingsley.

Kingsley shrugged.

"*Je ne sais pas. Mais*...you ask so much of me. I can't believe I'm giving you what you want."

"Kingsley, you put your life in my hands. There's nothing you haven't let me do to you that I've wanted to. You please me more than I can say."

Heat warmed Kingsley's face as he flushed from the compliment. While they were in the moment, Søren said the most awful things to Kingsley—that he was nothing, a slave, a servant, mere property to be used for Søren's pleasure. Did he not really mean those things? Or did he mean them at the time and not after? Or perhaps...perhaps he did mean them, and it pleased Søren that Kingsley didn't argue?

"I'm..." Kingsley nodded as he pulled the blanket tighter around him. "I'm glad I please you. It's the most important thing."

Søren came back over to the bed and touched a strand of Kingsley's hair. Kingsley willed himself not to move. He wanted to turn his face and kiss the palm of Søren's open hand, but he stayed strong. He'd debased himself enough tonight.

"It should be." Søren smiled at him before lightly flicking Kingsley's swollen lips with his fingertips. Kingsley winced and Søren laughed as he walked back to the trunk.

"Asshole," Kingsley said, employing his favorite American curse.

"Just for that, you'll get an extra beating next time we come here."

Kingsley rolled onto his side and nestled down deep into the blankets.

"When will that be? Soon?" He always asked that, and prayed the answer would be yes.

"*Ça dépende.*" Søren came back to the bed and stood at the head. Kingsley rolled his eyes dramatically as he sat back up and started to unbutton Søren's vest. Of all the tasks Søren imposed on him, this one—undressing him for bed—was Kingsley's favorite. The last thing he wanted was for Søren to know how much he loved tending to Søren's clothes—carefully removing them piece by piece, folding them and setting them neatly aside even as Kingsley's own clothes lay in heaps on the floor. Søren never missed an opportunity to step on Kingsley's clothes when he walked through the hermitage.

"On what?" Kingsley slid the vest off Søren's shoulders and rebuttoned it before folding it in half and laying it on the bed. Søren had taken off his tie earlier to use as a gag. Kingsley opened Søren's pants and pulled his shirt free. With every button he unfastened, he placed a kiss onto Søren's bare chest. Søren never commented when Kingsley did this, never sighed with pleasure or elicited any disdain. He ignored it. Simply ignored it. "Is something happening at the school? I know it's almost midterms. I'm sure you'll be too busy for me."

"I am always too busy for you," Søren said as Kingsley removed his shirt. He said this often—that he had no time for Kingsley. But they came back to the hermitage again and again. Once, when Kingsley had been brave enough to ask why Søren made time for him, he had responded, "I don't make time for you, Kingsley. I make it for myself."

"So it is midterms?"

Søren smiled slightly to himself as Kingsley drew his pants down. Søren stepped out of them and stood naked before him. Kingsley sat on the edge of the bed and rested his head on Søren's stomach. He didn't dare take any more liberties. If he was good, Søren would let him sleep all night in the cot with him. If he displeased him in any way, he'd be sent with one blanket to sleep on the floor in front of the fireplace.

"No. The school will have a visitor soon. I'm afraid we will have less time together because of her."

"Her? Who is it? Another sister?" Two weeks ago, a Benedictine nun had visited the school for three days. Sister Scholastica had come as a special guest lecturer in Father Patrick's theology class. She'd been sixty and swathed in her habit from head to toe. But the very presence of a woman at Saint Ignatius had caused even placid Father Henry to blush and stammer.

"Yes," Søren said, placing a hand on Kingsley's chin and turning his face up. "Yours."

NORTH
The Present

Kingsley stood at his bedroom window and stared out onto the city. Ever since coming to Manhattan and laying siege to the Underground, making it his own playground, he'd felt a sense of responsibility for his adopted home. France had spit him out onto the shores of Manhattan, and he'd crawled into the borough and decided to buy it. These people in his world—they were freaks. Damaged, broken, discarded, disdained…they had money, most of them, but they lacked pride, lacked dignity. The world had told them they didn't belong, and they had believed the lie. Or perhaps it wasn't a lie. Perhaps people like him—the men who felt that rush of power when bringing a woman to the edge of terror…or who, also like him, felt that rush of bliss when brought to their knees—really didn't belong in the world. Not the daylight world, anyway, the downstairs world, the world that made itself presentable for company. He and his kind belonged in darkness, in the night, in the upstairs rooms where no one was allowed to go. A woman like Nora Sutherlin… what would the world do with her? Too strong and smart to surrender to domesticity, she was doomed to spinsterhood in the world's eyes. She'd have a thousand lovers and no husband. And Søren, *le prêtre,* only half of him belonged in the world. The world saw a good priest and the world was right. But the other side of Søren few saw and few could speak of.

Kingsley wanted to guard the people who came to life only in the shadowy corners of the world. But who could guard them all? So he guarded the shadows instead. And someone had breached the boundaries of his shadows and shed blood in Kingsley's house. Shed blood in the one manner Kingsley never allowed under his roof—without consent.

"You're late, Griffin." Kingsley turned around and saw the handsome, if exhausted looking young man standing in the doorway to his bedroom.

"I came as fast as I could, King." Griffin dropped his suitcase on the threshold as he came toward him. "What the hell is going on? Mick's freaked out. So am I. Not that I told him that."

Sighing, Kingsley picked up his sherry and twirled the contents to coat the sides of the glass. He set it down without drinking.

"How is your new pet?" Kingsley looked Griffin up and down. Love had been kind to Griffin Fiske. As tired as he must be, he still looked ready and able to break anyone in half with his bare hands. Good. It might come to that. "Adjusting to life in his collar?"

Griffin grinned as he crossed his arms over his chest and leaned against the bedpost.

"Seems to be. Mick…he and I, we're good. Really fucking good."

Kingsley raised an eyebrow in amused approval. So much said in so few words. But Kingsley didn't need the words. The glint in Griffin's dark eyes told him everything he needed to know. Griffin Fiske, age twenty-nine, with the intimidating physique of a rough-and-ready bodybuilder, had found his match in the guise of a scared, nearly silent seventeen-year-old. The whole Underground still buzzed with the news that their wealthy, bisexual Lord of the Bacchanal had been brought back to earth by love. Everyone had scoffed in derision...until they'd seen Michael, that is, and those silver eyes that shone like the moon on a starless night. Kingsley had seen a little of himself in Michael—the young boy who worshipped the man who owned him, who needed fear and pain as much as he needed trust and gentleness. But Michael was only one-half of Kingsley. The boy hadn't a dominant bone in his body, as Nora had explained to Kingsley. Kingsley had first served, and it had whetted his appetite for more. Not for more servitude, but to become a master himself.

"I'm pleased to hear all is well with you and your pet. Sadly, not all is well with me and my pets."

Griffin's eyes widened slightly.

"What happened?"

"Sadie...she was killed."

"How?" Griffin dropped his arms and came to Kingsley, staring him in the face. Kingsley glanced away, not wanting him to see how deeply Sadie's death had touched him.

"Stabbed. In the heart."

"Holy shit. Who has that much of a death wish?"

Who indeed? Kingsley knew Griffin's question was merely rhetorical. He wasn't asking who had actually killed Sadie, but who on earth in their right mind would dare harm one of Kingsley Edge's precious rottweilers? *No one* was the implied answer. No one at all. Only someone, as Griffin said, with a death wish. Or worse, someone already dead.

Kingsley gave a shrug as his only answer. He knew who had done it, but he would never tell, could never tell. But he could not allow anything to go further. He needed time. Time to think and plan and... He raised a hand to his face and rubbed his forehead.

"King...I'm so sorry." Griffin touched him on the shoulder, and Kingsley nodded. No doubt Griffin mistook Kingsley's moment of frustration as grief for his dead dog. Let him think what he wanted. The truth could never come out, anyway.

"As am I." Kingsley faced Griffin with a smile. "But there's nothing for it. She's gone and we must do what we must to protect us all. Someone, whoever it is doesn't matter, wants to harm us. I can't allow that."

"No. Of course not. What can I do?"

Kingsley exhaled. What could Griffin do? Nothing now. Not really. Kingsley trusted so few people in the Underground that simply having Griffin back in the city calmed him. He needed his closest companions with him now, those he could rely on. The Mistress had abandoned them. His Juliette he'd sent away.

"*La Maîtresse*...she is away. And I believe the person who killed Sadie also has designs on her."

"On Nora? Why?"

Kingsley heard the fury lurking underneath Griffin's question, and knew that's why instinctively he'd sent for him. Griffin had loved Nora once...or tried to. And he still loved her, although not with passion and hunger anymore, but with loyalty and devotion. Nora had brought Griffin and his young lover together, and for that reason alone, Kingsley knew Griffin would walk on hot coals to protect her. And if things continued as they were, he might have to.

"Why? I cannot say, *mais*...I believe the person who killed Sadie is also responsible for the theft of a file from my private office. The file of *La Maîtresse*."

"Shit. Someone's breaking into your office…killing your dog. Kingsley, what the hell is going on?"

"I wish I could say, *mon ami*. As you can imagine, I would prefer if this does not get far. Rumors that my home is unsecure…" Kingsley let his voice trail off. He didn't need to tell Griffin how bad it would be if the world knew that Kingsley's home had been breached. Fear kept the city in line. Fear of Kingsley and his reach. In the archives in Kingsley's office were thousands of hours of footage of the upper eche- lons of society engaging in every decadent, tawdry, immoral, indecent and criminal act known to man. And a few acts that had surprised even Kingsley. Rich and powerful alike had been caught on tape engaging in bondage and sadomasoch- ism, participating in drug deals and arms deals. And in shad- ier deals that had lead to the deaths of more than one wealthy benefactor who'd made the fatal mistake of having a far too generous last will and testament. All this footage Kingsley had saved and cataloged after, of course, letting the police chief or the judge or the senator or the mayor or the socialite see the video. Kingsley would never use their crimes against them, he'd promised. He wanted neither their money nor their fa- vors. He merely asked that if the time came, they would do him the kindness of taking his call and giving him five min- utes of their precious time. He never had to explain the threat more than once. If they wanted to save themselves, they'd merely have to promise to help him whenever called upon.

"God knows I don't want anyone getting into your office," Griffin said, shaking his head.

"I burned your tapes long ago," Kingsley lied. Griffin ex- haled with obvious relief. He'd been a good boy for the past few years, but he was no saint when Kingsley brought him into the Underground. His drug addictions had nearly lost him his trust fund. In one particular high-definition photograph in Kingsley's possession, one could even make out the wings on the butterfly tattoo on the back of the stripper underneath the pile of cocaine…and, of course, the face of Griffin Fiske with a hundred-dollar bill rolled up to his nostril.

"Thank you. So what? I'll do anything for Nora. Hell, I left my honeymoon for you," Griffin said with a roguish wink.

"The honeymoon can continue. Take your pet to *La Maîtresse's*. Stay there. Watch the house. She keeps too much there that could harm her. I don't want the house unattended."

"Where did Nora go?"

"*La Maîtresse* is in Kentucky."

Griffin's eyes widened before he quickly composed himself. "That's…news. How is Søren taking that?"

Kingsley paused before answering. He did trust Griffin. The boy had earned his regard and his confidence long ago. And without Juliette here to confide in…

Carefully, so as not to betray how much pain he suffered with each movement, Kingsley unbuttoned his shirt and held it open.

"Oh, fuck. Jesus, Kingsley…" Griffin flinched as he took in the mass of bruises and welts that comprised Kingsley's chest. He looked and then glanced away before looking back again in horror.

"I believe you have your answer. That is how Søren is taking it."

Kingsley buttoned his shirt up to his collarbone. He'd need a tie if he went out. His neck bore the unmistakable imprint of fingers.

"Did you…was that…"

"It was consensual, I assure you. Consensual if not entirely comfortable."

Griffin shook his head. "I didn't know you were…I didn't know. Kingsley…you're a switch?"

Sighing, Kingsley ran his hands through his hair. So hard to explain.

"I suppose. If we need a name for it, a label, that would do. I trust this is also nothing you will share with any others, not even your pet."

"No. Of course not. Although he'd probably feel better knowing the most intimidating man in the city played sub sometimes. He's still trying to get comfortable with what he is."

"And he will still be trying when he is my age."

"Does Nora know?"

"*Oui. Bien sûr.* What the priest knows she knows. And she… she's almost as good at it as he is."

The implication of Kingsley's words took a moment to sink in. Then Griffin's handsome face lit up with a combination of mirth and shock.

"Oh, shit. Nora's kicked your ass? God, I would have paid through the nose to see that."

"Not for all the money in the world, young man."

"Damn. Well, I did ask her once who her first client was when she became a Dominatrix, and she wouldn't tell me."

"And now you know."

"Now I know. Damn," he repeated, laughing softly. Kingsley couldn't help but smile. Perhaps this was the real reason he'd summoned Griffin—to force him to smile for the first time in what felt like ages. "Okay, I'll take Mick to Nora's house, as ordered. Fucking Mick in Nora's bed will be a dream come true. Or would be if she was there, too. But we'll make do."

"See Sophia. She'll have a set of keys for you. The house is alarmed. She'll give you the codes, as well."

"We'll stay there until you give us the all clear."

"*Bon. Merci.*"

"Of course. Anything. You know you just have to ask."

Griffin headed for the door. But he paused before leaving and turned around.

"He is good. Søren, I mean," Griffin said. "Couple of weeks ago, I had to let him top…I did it for Mick."

"I know. Anything that happens at The 8th Circle, I know about it."

"He didn't even lay a hand on me. He didn't have to. Broke me in half with words."

"He knows how to break you and yet leave you feeling more whole than you ever had before."

"Don't tell him I kind of liked it," Griffin said with a wink.

"Your secrets, as always, are safe with me." Kingsley gave a slight bow and Griffin laughed on his way out the door.

Kingsley straightened up, wincing as he did so. Alone now, he didn't have to hide his pain. He considered sitting down and then thought better of it. He could still barely move, much less sit or lie down. The adrenaline from his night with Søren had faded, leaving him in agony. Everything ached, everything throbbed. Søren had nearly killed him last night. Kingsley could only hope that he still healed as quickly as he used to.

The only thing that would truly heal him would be another night with Søren.

Summoning Sophia, he ordered a muscle relaxant and something sturdier to drink than sherry. She brought them quickly and Kingsley discarded the pills and the drink before imbibing either. All the Underground knew of his penchant to overindulge. Kingsley cultivated with care the reputation of being a lush. Few people realized how little he actually drank, how rarely he ingested any illicit substances at all. He wanted everyone to think he had more weaknesses than he did. And now more than ever he needed the shield of the debonair drunk to protect him.

For the rest of the afternoon, Kingsley worked in his office. Or pretended to. In reality he merely stared at reports from the managers of his various clubs and enterprises, while his mind lingered thirty years in the past.

How…how had it happened? Had he known? Thirty years…how could anyone… It made no sense, yet it made perfect sense. He refused to believe it, but it was the only explanation. He wanted to rejoice, knowing the truth now. But what was the truth?

Christian. He should go talk to Christian again. That priest knew more than he'd said. He'd tried…tried to tell Kingsley, but couldn't.

"Sophia," Kingsley barked into the phone. "I need to return to Maine. Make the calls."

"Oui, monsieur? When?"

"Now."

He hung up before the girl could say another word. Now was no time for conversation or questioning of his orders. He considered calling Søren, but decided against it. Søren had an uncanny gift for reading people. It served him well as a priest and a Dominant, but made it nearly impossible to keep any secrets from him. One look and he would know that Kingsley knew…knew who their stalker was, who the thief was, and the motive behind the threats.

Threats. Only threats, Kingsley reminded himself as he returned to his bedroom and pulled on his jacket. No one had been hurt yet. Just a dog. And no one would get hurt. Not if he could help it.

He headed down the stairs and toward the front door of his town house. He had to get back to Saint Ignatius, get more information out of Father Christian. And he would, if he had to string the priest up by his ankles and flog him.

"Monsieur?" Sophia called out as his butler raced to open the door for him.

"No time, Sophia. Take a message."

"It's Master Griffin, sir. He's at Mistress Nora's home."

"Lovely news." The door opened. He saw his Rolls-Royce idling out front on the street.

"But, sir...he needs to talk to you."

Finally, the panic in his secretary's voice penetrated Kingsley's fog of concentration. He whirled around and faced the girl, who stood pale and shaking, a black phone in her hand.

"About what?" Kingsley asked, not wanting to talk to Griffin, already fearing the worst.

"He says he got to the house as fast as he could but..."

"But?"

Sophia swallowed, her pale skin now white.

"Someone got there first."

SOUTH

This was what heaven felt like. Had to be. All his life he'd heard about heaven from pastors and preachers and teachers. He'd read it about it in the Bible, learned about it in Sunday school…. Heaven was paradise where everything became complete, where man saw God and rejoiced in the knowledge that this place of ethereal beauty and utter peace would last forever and ever.

Wesley looked down and smiled at the sight of Nora's hair draped across his stomach, her mouth around him, taking him between her lips, caressing him with her tongue. A knot tightened in the pit of his stomach as she moved from the base to the tip, over and over again.

"Nora…I'm going to come if you keep doing that."

Nora paused long enough to give him a look of amused annoyance. "That is sort of the point."

"But—"

"No butt," Nora declared as she stroked him with her hand. "We'll do that later. Blow job now. I've wanted to blow your bugle for years. Shut up and let me."

Wesley laughed as she put her lips to the bugle tattoo on his hip and gave him a noisy raspberry.

"I'm in much less danger of coming now."

"I can fix that." Nora moved to take him in her mouth again, but Wesley caught her off guard by rolling her onto her back and sliding down her body. Without a word of protest, she opened her legs wide and Wesley pushed easily into her wet heat.

"Sorry..." he whispered into her ear. "I just needed this."

"It's okay." She wrapped her legs around his back and drew him even deeper into her. "I need it, too."

He did need. Inside Nora he felt...he couldn't even think of the right word for it.

Complete, maybe...that's what Wesley felt when inside Nora. He lacked for nothing as she lay beneath him, her thighs wide and open, her breasts rising with every gasp of pleasure, her dark eyes glowing like the aura that surrounded the moon. Her skin...so soft...he'd dreamed so long of touching her. But the parts that he'd fantasized about—her breasts, her thighs—while as spectacular as he'd hoped, paled before the parts of her that had never before entered his imagination. If he kissed her spine a few inches under her neck, her shoulders would raise and she'd laugh like a child. Lower...if he touched the small of her back with his fingertips, she'd moan like she did when he'd penetrated her the first time. He'd never felt anything softer than the skin at the back of her knee or underneath the bone of her ankle. This was the second time he'd made love to her that night. At one point during the first time, she'd put her legs on his shoulders and he'd turned his head to kiss the inside of her calves. She had a tiny birthmark by her left ankle. How had he never noticed that before?

"You're so quiet," she whispered as she arched beneath him. He loved the way she moved when he slowed down his thrusts. She'd stretch out like a cat in the sun and sigh luxu-riously. "Something wrong?"

Wesley kissed her cheek, her neck, her mouth.

"I'm inside you. There's nothing wrong. Anywhere. Ever."

Nora laughed and he gasped a little as her inner muscles tightened around him. He'd never known that...never known the vagina tightened when a woman laughed. What else didn't he know about Nora? If he had to he'd spend the rest of his life discovering the secrets of her body. He'd spend the rest of his life discovering the secrets of her body even if he didn't have to.

"Nothing wrong anywhere? Spoken like a man getting laid." Another thing about Nora during sex...her voice dropped about an octave and everything she said came out all husky and breathy. He'd never heard anything quite like it. He felt her words as much as heard them. They rubbed against his skin like velvet.

Wesley dipped his head and kissed her shoulder, moved lower and sucked on her right nipple. Slowly he moved his mouth from her breast to her chest. She loved having her chest kissed; she said the thin skin there made every touch tickle.

"I'm not getting laid. That's not what this is." He closed his eyes as a wave of pleasure passed through him from knee to neck. Having sex made him aware of his own body like never before. He'd never known that the slightest shift of his hips could take him from comfortable enjoyment to the very edge of orgasm in seconds. Before his first time with Nora, his arms had existed merely to hold things and move things. Now the muscles in his arms were there to hold him up and over Nora, keeping his full weight off her so she could writhe beneath him. He'd never given his shoulders much thought until Nora had bitten them, never considered his back until she'd scratched it during a particularly heated kiss, never given a moment's notice to his rib cage until Nora had lain across his chest after sex and ran her fingers over every line of it.

"Then what is it, Wes?" She looked up at him as he pushed deeper into her. "Are you making love to me?"

He buried his face in her hair and whispered a "yes" in her ear. "Only because I love you."

She whimpered in the back of her throat, and Wesley immediately stopped moving.

"Did I hurt you?" He still hadn't gotten quite used to how intense sex could be. Sometimes he'd push too deep and Nora would flinch or gasp. She never complained, never told him to stop, but he always panicked at the very thought of hurting her in bed.

"No." She raised her hand and caressed the side of his face. "Not in the bad way, anyway."

Wesley smiled as he slowly relaxed down on top of her. Sometimes he'd let his full weight rest on her body. She seemed to like it, although he couldn't imagine why.

"I should have been doing this for years," he said into her ear. "Or at least doing it since the first time you offered."

"Back in the pool?" she asked, pressing her hips up into his. The first time they'd had sex tonight had been quick and hard. Now, with one orgasm out of the way, he could move slowly and leisurely in her. At the moment he felt he could last all night. But if she kept doing that thing with her hips, he'd come whether he wanted to or not.

"Back then. Maybe not in the pool. But right after getting out of the pool."

Wesley remembered that night near the end of his first semester at Yorke. Nora had called him out of the blue and practically dared him to meet her at the natatorium. He'd gone alone and found his creative-writing teacher in her racerback swimsuit standing on a starting block. A few days before that he'd complained to her that his only gripe about Yorke was their lack of a swim team. He had a killer freestyle that was going to waste, and Nora mentioned she'd been on her swim team at New York University. So she'd surprised him by challenging him to a race. He'd won, of course. Male versus female. Age eighteen versus age thirty-two. Six feet tall versus five-three. Of course he'd won. But just barely. He couldn't believe how close behind him she'd stayed. That night in the pool he'd seen as much muscle on her petite body as he'd seen curves. He'd mentioned his surprise at the tautness of her arms and shoulders, and she'd said that she had to be tough to beat up on all her little bad boys and girls. He'd thought it was a joke. And then she'd asked if he wanted to have sex with her. But that, he knew, hadn't been a joke.

"Why did you tell me no back then?" she asked as she pressed her breasts into his chest and lightly scratched his back from hip to shoulder.

"You could have gotten any guy on the planet." Wesley kissed her forehead as he pulled out of her until only the tip remained, before sliding all the way back in again. "I mean, you're Nora Sutherlin…and you write those wild books and you're so beautiful and sexy. I just didn't want to be another guy to do. Another, I don't know…"

"Notch on the bedpost?"

He nodded. "Something like that."

"You would never have been a conquest to me. I adored you, Wes. Even then."

"So it wasn't just about sex?"

Nora shook her head. "I wanted to be with someone like you, someone sweet and gentle…maybe just out of curiosity, since I'd never had that before. But it wouldn't have been just about the sex. You were never about the sex. Except now. Right now is just about the sex."

Wesley got the hint and began moving harder and faster inside her. He loved the wetness of her, the warmth that surrounded him. She felt like flower petals on the inside...so soft, but slightly textured. Next, he might simply lie between her open legs and explore her with his fingers for an hour or twelve. He wanted the rest of his life to get to know her body, but with Nora...who knew? He might have only tonight.

He grabbed her legs and moved them over his thighs. He loved her so open like this, so spread out and relaxed underneath him. He dipped his head and wrapped his lips around a nipple, sucking gently as she moaned and dug her fingers into his shoulders.

"Nora..." he panted, and she kissed his cheek.

"It's okay. Don't wait for me."

He nodded as he buried his head against her chest and came, after another thrust. He pulled out and felt the rush of wetness as his semen poured from her onto the sheets.

"I'm sorry," he said, laughing as he lay on his side. "I'm new at this."

"Sex is a skill, Wes. You're just starting to learn how to do it. Don't feel bad."

He rubbed his face as Nora rolled onto her side.

"It's just..." He paused for courage. The whole thing was so embarrassing. "Can I ask you a question?"

"You can ask me anything. You know I have no shame."

"You also have no orgasms. At least...not with me, right? You haven't yet?"

Nora winced. "I'd kind of hoped you hadn't noticed that."

"You thought I wouldn't notice that in the ten times we've had sex, I've come ten times and you've come...zero?"

"A lot of men don't notice those sorts of things."

Wesley sat up and looked down on her. So beautiful, his Nora. After sex, with her hair all wild and her skin flushed and her eyes glowing, she looked more lovely than she would in a five-thousand-dollar dress with ten layers of makeup on.

"I did notice. What am I doing wrong?"

Nora sat up and scooted back against the headboard. Tucking the sheets up to her neck, she tamed her hair and gave him a smile so kind and so pitying that he almost hated her for it.

"Wes, haven't we discussed how you shouldn't ask questions you don't want the answer to?"

"But I want to know. For your sake."

"You're barely twenty. And you were a virgin until a couple days ago. You have no idea what you're doing in bed. You don't know how to touch me, don't know how to fuck me. You're so terrified to hurt me that I barely feel anything. You get me very revved up and then…nothing. Which is fine. I'm certainly adept at giving myself orgasms."

Wesley felt himself shrinking with each sentence. "You mean, you give them to yourself? When?"

Nora shrugged. "After you fall asleep."

"You do that when I'm asleep? Why?"

"Don't want to get blue balls, right? Or blue…uterus, if that's a thing."

"But…I want to do that for you."

Nora exhaled through her lips, blowing out the air like the horses did. It got a laugh out of him. A very small laugh.

"I want that, too. I can show you some things that'll work. You put one finger inside me. I need three. I need my clitoris touched, a lot and for a long period of time, if you want to get me off. Harder thrusting is good. Different positions. I can't get much clitoral stimulation in missionary position."

"I think I should write all this down. Anything else? What works for you?"

"Oral helps. Going down on me."

"I love doing that, but you know…if I've already come in you it's…" Wesley winced.

"You don't like tasting your own semen?" Nora batted her eyelashes at him.

"No. Does any guy?"

"Do you want the list in alphabetical order by first name or last name?"

Wesley scrubbed his hands through his hair in amused frustration.

"I am so bad at this. Do I want to know what else works for you or should I quit while I'm behind?"

"Kink works."

He glared at her.

"You asked, Wes. You can skip a lot of foreplay with me if there's good kink going on. That works better than anything. Not saying we have to do it. Not now, not ever. You asked what works for me. That's the answer."

"I can't do that."

"I'm not asking you to."

"Then what—"

"Just come here and pay attention. I'll show you where the clit is. It's lesson three. Or C, more accurately."

Wesley rolled his eyes but did as he was told. He hated that he didn't know how to make Nora feel as good as she made him feel.

He spooned up next to her and Nora threw her leg over his hip. Taking his right hand in hers, she guided it between her legs.

"The clit is like the eye," she began.

"That's the grossest analogy I've ever heard in my life."

"That's not what I mean, twerp." She gave him a quick kiss. "I mean, you don't touch the eye directly. If you need to touch it, you touch the eyelid. So you don't touch the clit directly.

You touch around it and over the clit hood. It's very easy to find on me, as I have a shiny piece of metal in it."

"How handy. Literally."

"Exactly."

Nora pressed two of his fingers around her piercing and started to move his hand in gentle circles.

"Right there is a lovely place to hang out and linger for a while."

"I'm definitely not complaining," Wesley said, feeling something starting to swell under his fingertips. "I could live here."

"You might have to. I don't orgasm super easily. Takes a bit of doing."

"Did it take a long time for Søren to figure out how to… you know…make you come?"

Nora turned her face up to the ceiling.

"Why do you ask?" Her response was casual, annoyingly casual.

"I don't know. He was—is—a priest. You told me that before you and him…well, you said he hadn't had sex in a long time."

"He hadn't. He beat people—consensually—but no sex. He was celibate from age eighteen to thirty-four."

"I guess he was as bad at this as I am, right?"

Nora didn't say anything. Her silence said it all.

"Damn," Wesley breathed. "Didn't think I could hate that guy any more than I already do."

"Wes, you don't want me to talk about this."

"No, I do. Tell me. He was celibate for sixteen years and he could make you orgasm? Even at the beginning?"

Nora nodded slowly. "Even then. The first time. The first night together…" Her voice trailed off and her eyes turned black, and he knew he'd lost her to Søren again.

"I haven't made you come once in ten times. How many

times did he the first night?" Wesley pulled his hand away from her, suddenly not wanting to touch her, not with Søren between them.

"I don't remember."

"Nora, don't lie to me, please. You have the best memory of anybody I know. Just tell me."

"You sure you're not a masochist, kid? I told you, I don't remember how many." Nora sat up again and grabbed her shirt and panties off the floor.

"That's not true and you know it. You—"

"It is true. I don't remember how many orgasms Søren gave me the first night he fucked me. I don't remember because after the fourth orgasm, I lost count."

I lost count.

Three little words that hit him harder than a riding crop on the flank of a racehorse.

"That's why I don't remember," Nora continued, yanking her clothes on. "And that's why you should finally learn not to ask questions you don't want the answer to."

Nora left the bedroom, and Wesley threw on his jeans and followed her. Damn, the girl could walk fast when she was in a mood. She'd already disappeared from the hallway. Wesley checked the guest bedrooms. No Nora. The bathroom door was open. No Nora there, either. She tended to be an emotional eater. Kitchen. Of course.

In the guesthouse kitchen, he found Nora sitting on the edge of the table in front of the stone fireplace. Without a word he came to her, threw a couple logs in the fire and set them alight.

"Wes, it's August."

"It's cold in here and you don't have much on."

Nora laughed tiredly and shook her head. "Goddammit,

Wes Railey, will you stop being sweet to me for just one second?"

Wesley stood in front of her and she rested the top of her head on his chest.

"Nope."

She pulled back and looked up at him.

"This is a good look for you, by the way. Shirtless and wearing only jeans? You'll pull it off better than any man on the planet."

"Finally, I've got something up on Søren."

Slowly, Nora ran her hands up and down Wesley's chest and sides. He shivered, but not from the cool night air.

"You remember that night in the kitchen at our house? That day you got so mad at me for flirting with Zach?"

"That was not flirting. That was seducing. Which I know you're really good at. I just never had to watch it in our own house before."

The smile left Nora's face and she nodded.

"I never thought about it like that. I didn't know you were in love with me then. Seriously. No clue. Otherwise I would never have done that to you. You have to believe that."

"I do. At least I want to."

Nora sighed. "I was so pissed at you that night. The thoughts I had about you, Wesley Railey, would have made Søren blush. The fantasies, the desires…the things I wanted to do to you… I even had this mantra about you I'd repeat to myself when my hormones started to run away with my better judgment."

"You had a mantra?"

"Look but don't touch."

"Nice."

"So that night you were all mad at me for flirting with Zach…I don't know. I just wanted payback. You never even hit on me, barely flirted, and yet the second I had another man in my life you acted like I'd punched your puppy."

"Don't punch my puppy."

Nora giggled as she took his hands in hers. The entire kitchen brightened with the sound of her laughter and the low fire in the hearth.

"That's why I hit on you so hard that night. I wanted to get a reaction from you. That's all. Just for my sake. Just to prove to myself I wasn't the only one walking around dreaming of you tied to my headboard while I gave you the sort of blow job most men have to hire out for."

A blush suffused Wesley from chest to head. "Well, I was the one who had to deal with wall-sex fantasies every time you wore a skirt or dress around the house."

"Wall sex? You're into wall sex?"

"I was very into it in my mind." Wesley's heart started to beat harder as his whole body remembered his favorite fantasy about Nora. "I thought it would be so hot holding you up with your skirt around your waist and your legs around mine and...damn."

Wesley had gotten hard just talking about it, and Nora clearly noticed.

"Damn..." she repeated as she pressed her hand flat against his erection. "Too bad I don't have a skirt on."

"Who cares?"

At that Wesley brought his mouth down on hers so hard it surprised him. Nora's arms wrapped around his shoulders as his hands raked down her back and wrenched her panties down her legs. He pushed her back on the table and shoved her legs wide open.

He penetrated her with three fingers liked she'd told him to do, and was rewarded with a gasp of pure pleasure. With his thumb he stroked her clitoris, and Nora arched so high her entire back came off the table.

Never had he heard her pant so hard before. Never had he felt her inner muscles so tight around his hand before. And never ever had he needed to be inside her more in his life.

"Nora..."

"Fuck me, Wes. Right now."

"Definitely."

He pulled his hand out of her and opened his jeans. It took a few seconds longer than necessary as the need consumed him, enough to make him clumsy. Nora rolled up and Wesley dragged her to the very edge of the table. He took himself in his hand and pushed into her. As soon as he'd gone as deep as he could go, he wrapped her legs around his back.

"Wes, I'm heavier than I look, remember?"

"Yeah, but I'm stronger than I look." And with that he lifted her off the table and pushed her into the stone wall by the fireplace.

Nora winced.

"Stone wall—bad idea." Wesley tried to cradle her closer to him.

"Amazing idea. I like it. Don't stop."

Wesley didn't think he could stop if someone put a gun to his head. He thrust hard into her, harder than he thought he could, and a sound escaped Nora's lips that was so potently erotic he wished he'd recorded it. He thrust again just as hard and the sound came again. Nora bent her head and bit her teeth into his shoulder. The pain didn't bother him. It merely made him think he might be doing something right for once.

His mind shut down and his body took over. Wesley ran, he swam, lifted weights and rode big, dangerous horses, and all the strength and power he'd acquired from those activities he used on Nora now, lifting her high, pounding into her harder. Every muscle in his body had gone taut as a high wire. Sounds came out of him, too, grunts and breaths so guttural anyone hearing would think he was in pain. And it was pain…his arms strained to hold Nora up; his back tensed to keep him from letting go and coming too soon. But the pain meant nothing to him. How could it, with Nora wrapped full-body around him, and him so deep inside her he couldn't go any deeper if he tried?

He kissed her neck, her mouth and ears. She dug her fingernails into his back. With each of Wes's thrusts up and into her, Nora pushed her hips against his in some kind of primal desperation. He'd never felt so wanted, so needed. Especially as her cries grew throatier, more strained. Her breath came in short puffs through her teeth. He could feel her tighten even more around him….

The cry in his ear rang out sweeter than any melody he'd ever heard. Nora's climax shook her whole body. She flinched as if in pain, even as he kept driving into her with bruising force. Pounding…he heard the pounding as much as he felt it in his stomach and thighs.

"Wes…" Nora breathed. But he heard nothing else as his own orgasm exploded out of him and into her. The release shook him to his core. And even Nora saying his name over and over again couldn't mute the pleasure and the power and the surrender to the moment.

Slowly, Nora slid down him and put a tentative foot on the floor as Wesley pulled out of her. Breathing hard, he leaned against the wall, his forehead against the stone.

"What…what's wrong?" he said as Nora started throwing her clothes on, fast and furious.

"The door. Somebody's pounding on the door."

Reluctantly, Wesley opened his eyes and looked at her. He

glanced at the clock over the hearth as he started to pull himself together. He looked down at himself.

"Dammit."

"Yeah, they never put the copious amounts of girl-boy fluids in the romance novels, either. Here." She tossed him a kitchen towel, and Wesley used it to wipe himself off before zipping up his jeans.

"I'm starting to think those things aren't very realistic."

"Don't ever tell anyone that," she said as she grabbed one of Wesley's jackets off the back of the kitchen door and wrapped it around herself like a bathrobe.

With each of them half-dressed, Wesley raced down the hall to the front door of the guesthouse. Middle-of-the-night knocks usually meant only one thing.

He threw the door open and found his father standing outside.

"Who is it?" Wesley asked as Nora came to stand behind him, her hands on his hips.

His father gave her only the most cursory of disgusted glances before looking back at Wesley. "I guess I'm interrupting. Never mind. I'll take care of it myself."

"You're not interrupting, Dad. Who is it?"

"Track Beauty. Coming?"

"What's going on?" Nora asked from behind him.

Wesley laid his hand on top of hers. "Track Beauty is about to give birth. Can get complicated. One of us always tries to be there."

"Let's go, then." Nora squeezed his hand and started down the hall. "I'll be right with you."

As soon as she disappeared, Wesley heard his father sighing.

"Dad, drop it. Nora and I are a fact of life. Get used to it."

"I'm used to it the way I'm used to my herniated disc. It's also a fact of life—doesn't mean I've got to like it."

Wesley kept his retorts to himself. After all, he'd just made Nora come so hard his ears would probably ring for the next two hours. Nothing his dad said or did about her could make a dent in his impenetrable wall of happiness right now.

"Ready," Nora said as she returned, wearing pants and carrying a T-shirt for Wesley. "I've never seen a horse give birth before."

"It's nasty and disgusting," Wesley's father said as the three of them headed to the waiting pickup truck. "So much placenta sometimes you have to yank the little one out of it. Momma often eats the afterbirth."

"Fantastic." Nora grinned from ear to ear. If his dad was trying to scare her off, he had no idea what kind of woman he was dealing with. "I'll film it for YouTube."

"Don't you dare put a Rails horse on the internet," Wesley's father said, his voice unnecessarily cold and stern.

"Dad, she was kidding."

Nora held up her empty hands. "No camera. Promise." She smiled broadly. Orders delivered in a cold and stern voice tended to have the opposite effect on her than his father had intended.

They arrived at the mare stable in under two minutes. Wesley's father hopped out of the truck before he'd barely turned it off, and ran straight to the door.

"What's the hurry?" Nora asked as she trotted next to Wesley, who moved almost as fast. "Doesn't this take hours?"

"It can. She's probably been at it for a while, though. But we have to be there in case something goes wrong—you've only got minutes to save mare and foal sometimes."

They entered the barn to the sound of low panting and soft moans.

"That sounds familiar," Nora said, and Wesley smacked her lightly on the bottom.

At the door to the stall they stopped and looked in. Track Beauty lay on her side in the hay, her long legs wobbling from exertion. Even on the ground, with a distended belly and sweat on her flanks, she lived up to her name.

Wesley entered the stall and found his father and Dr. Fischer, the resident veterinarian, taking the mare's vitals and conferring.

"What's wrong?" Wesley asked, kneeling down and gently stroking Track Beauty's sweat-stained nose. Horses were intelligent animals, although Thoroughbreds tended toward instinct over reason. But usually some awareness shone in Track Beauty's dark eyes. Now she seemed merely a dumb animal, however. Pain and fear had taken all the perception from her gaze.

"She's been down there a long time," Dr. Fischer said. "We need to pull."

"Poor thing," Wesley said to the laboring horse. "Can't imagine how much this is gonna hurt." Track Beauty's stomach undulated as the unborn foal struggled inside her.

"What is it, Wes?" Nora asked, her voice soft as a whisper. She might not know anything about horses, but was smart enough to know trouble when she smelled it.

"She's in some distress. We're going to pull the foal out."

"Who's we?" Nora asked as Wesley disinfected his hands and arms. "Wes?"

"We is me," he said, deciding in that moment he'd be the one to do it. His father had a bad back and Dr. Fischer was in his sixties. Any minute now every last person who worked on the farm would start to gather outside the stable to await news. Wes wanted to make sure the news they received was good. "Come hold her head, Nora. Beauty's more comfortable around women than men."

"Son, I don't know—"

"It's fine, Dad. Just back off so Beauty will calm down."

Dr. Fischer stayed in the stall, but way in the corner where the horse couldn't see him. Wesley watched Nora tiptoe into the stall and kneel by Track Beauty's head.

"You know you've got options," Nora whispered to the horse as she stroked Track Beauty's tangled mane. "IUD… the pill…do they make NuvaRing for horses? Or would that be hula-hoop size? Maybe just abstinence. It's the only one hundred percent way."

Wesley laughed softly as he reached down and pushed Track Beauty's flopping tail to the side and saw the placenta bubbling out.

"No commentary, Nora. Please," he said as he pushed an arm inside the mare.

"I won't say a single word," she pledged as she took the horse's head in her lap. "Except that this reminds me of my last date with Griffin."

Wesley reached in deep and found what he sought—a bone-thin ankle. He found another right next to it.

"Keep her still as you can," he said, glancing at Nora. "I'm going to pull hard and steady, and this is going to get messy."

Nora nodded as she ran her hand down Track Beauty's neck in a soothing massage. Wesley came up on the balls of his feet and started to pull firmly and slowly. At first the foal didn't want to budge, and he feared breaking one of the fragile legs in utero.

"Come on, gorgeous," Nora said to the mare. "Let him go. Can you push a little for me?" She blew straight on the horse's face and Track Beauty twitched. The twitch caused just enough of a push that Wesley could finally pull the two ankles out of her. He tore off the placenta and wrapped a towel around the foal's legs.

Wesley inhaled deeply and started to walk backward, slowly

dragging the baby horse with him. It took all his strength not
to let go of the slippery legs, and all his gentleness not to grip
them so hard they cracked in his hands. After one last tug,
the foal's head came out, along with several gallons of fluid
and afterbirth.

Dr. Fischer and his father swooped in quickly with needles
and towels. They hovered around the foal while Wesley saw
to Nora and Track Beauty.

"That wasn't so bad, was it?" Nora asked as Wesley tow-
eled his arms off.

"A little gross but not terrible."

"Gross? Don't listen to him, gorgeous. You have a lovely
vagina, and I'm sure if you do your Kegels, you'll get your
post-baby muscle tone back."

Wesley couldn't resist leaning forward and kissing Nora
even as his father watched in disapproval. But the disapproval
disappeared off his father's face when the foal started squirm-
ing in his first attempt to stand.

"Wow. They walk fast." Nora giggled as the foal stood up
and went down again immediately. Giggled? Nora Sutherlin giggled? Wesley couldn't believe it. He'd heard her laugh
a thousand times, but never had he heard her giggle so girl-
ishly and with such childlike delight. But the foal's attempts
to stand were hilarious and pitiful at the same time.

"That's a boy there," Wesley's father said as the foal finally
made it to all four feet and stayed there. He stood by the newborn and ran his hand up and down his coat, checking him
for imperfections. With Track Beauty as the broodmare and
Farewell to Charms as the sire, there would be no imperfections to be found. "Wonder what to name this guy…"

"Nora should name him, since she was here for it. All Rails
horses are named by women. It's good luck."

"Well, I've named a lot of characters," she said. "And that guy looks like a character."

Wesley and Nora watched as the foal took his first tentative steps. Forward two…back one…and back one more…

Wesley's father released a slight oath and a grunt of pain as the foal stepped right onto his toe.

"Wonderful. He steps on feet." The older man laughed and patted the baby on his tiny head.

"Well, we know what to name him, then," Nora said, grinning at Wesley. That smile took him back to the first day they'd gone horseback riding together. Wesley had picked a big sorrel stallion named Bastinado. Wesley had thought nothing of the exotic name until Nora had asked if the horse had a habit of stepping on feet. The stable girl replied that he did, and Nora had explained that Bastinado was a fancy term for foot torture.

"Bastinado it is," Wesley said. "Pretty damn sure that's not in the registry."

Nora crawled over to the foal and stroked his face. Wesley hadn't seen a chestnut foal that cute and small in a long time. Farewell to Charms had been a little guy, too, and then had sprouted up into the longest-legged monster horse he'd ever seen.

"I love him. I'm going to keep him." Nora kissed the horse on his nose. "In my house. It's a big bed. He can fit."

"Madam, that horse is worth—" Wesley's father began.

"Dad. Joking. Nora is joking."

"She jokes an awful lot. She ever say anything she means?"

"No," Nora said, winking at Wesley. "And I really mean that."

"I don't find you particularly amusing, young lady." Wesley's dad glared at her.

"I don't care if you love me or hate me. You called me 'young lady' and that makes you my new favorite person."

Wesley watched his father's face tighten with anger before he exhaled and shook his head. "How's our girl doing, Fisch?"

Nora scooted over to Bastinado and continued rubbing him down as Dr. Fischer and his father gave the mare a once-over followed by a twice-over. Wes and Nora kept their attention on little Bastinado as he sorted out how his legs worked. Nora even found a riding crop somewhere and teased Bastinado with it as if he were a kitten and not a million-dollar Thoroughbred.

They watched for several hours, laughing at his progress, wincing at his falls, encouraging him to stand back up again when he went down into the hay.

"Poor little guy…" Nora cooed as she peeled hay off his coat. "I know it's hard. You get enough wine in me and I can't walk very well, either."

Bastinado pushed his nose into her hand and Wesley could only watch them. He'd seen Nora with children on a few occasions. She was so good with them, teasing them and talking to them like adults, giving them her full attention as if no one else in the world existed but them. She was just as good with Bastinado. Something in Wesley ached at the soft, motherly tone of her voice, the radiant smile on her face.

He couldn't help but let his mind wander into dangerous territory. Nora would look so beautiful pregnant. She'd bitch and moan the entire time about her swollen ankles and sore breasts, and yet he knew no woman in the world would make a better mother. How endlessly patient she'd been with him as a teacher, how loving and protective she'd been as a roommate. How she managed to find him in the hospital after his diabetic ketoacidosis scare still baffled him. With a child of her own, of their own, he knew she'd be ten times as diligent, as protective, as concerned. And God, to see her hold a baby in her arms? He'd sell the whole Railey empire on eBay if he had to for that. He might even sell his soul.

"You tired, Wes?" Nora asked as she reached out and squeezed his hand. "It's almost dawn, I think."

"A little."

"You're so quiet."

"Just thinking. How's your back?" he asked in a whisper. He still couldn't believe he'd had sex that rough with Nora, still couldn't believe he'd loved it so much.

"I'll have a couple bruises. Good job," she said, and gave him a wicked grin.

"Not bad for a vanilla twerp, right?"

"Not bad?" She whistled softly under her breath. "That might have hit my top ten."

Wesley beamed with male pride.

"Next time I'll shoot for top five."

Nora started to say something in reply, but then closed her mouth and looked at his father.

"What's wrong?" she asked, and Wesley, too, noticed the concern on his face.

"Track's been down too long. It's been almost four hours. Let's get her on her feet."

Wesley stood up and helped his father coax the mare to stand. Track Beauty whinnied in protest but made it to her feet, and Wesley exhaled a breath he hadn't realized he'd been holding.

"Good girl." Wesley's father patted her on the nose and started to walk away. The second he turned his back, however, Track Beauty's knees buckled and she went down again.

"Dammit." Wesley ran his hands over her as his father and Dr. Fischer listened to her heart and lungs once more.

"We've gotta get her back up," his dad said.

"What's wrong?" Nora asked, her arm around Bastinado, holding him across her lap like a dog. "She's tired. She just gave birth to a baby the size of a horse. Because it *was* a damn horse."

"She has to get up," Wesley explained. "She's been down too long now. Horses can't stay down. It's deadly for them."

Nora's eyes widened. "That's not good. What's the problem?"

"Stubborn. Worn-out. Who knows? Her lungs are clear." Wesley's father stared down at Track Beauty as if willing her to stand. Wesley joined him and started to pull on the mare's halter. She gave a halfhearted effort before dropping her head back to the ground.

"Shit." Wesley rubbed his forehead. Track Beauty wasn't just the best broodmare on the farm, she was his mother's favorite horse. He had to get her up.

"Come on. Try again," Wesley's father said, giving the mare a few encouraging scratches and rubs. His voice remained calm, but Wesley could see the lines of tension in his face. Track Beauty had been insured for nearly twenty million dollars—but that was nothing compared to his mother's happiness.

All three men put their collective muscle into the attempt to pull Track Beauty to her feet. All three of them failed. Wesley had seen this before—horses growing weary and listless, unwilling to get back on their feet for no apparent reason. Giving birth had exhausted Track Beauty beyond reason or instinct.

"We'll have to get a sling, pull her up. Nothing for it," Dr. Fischer said. "I'll call for backup. We'll have to get her in the ambulance."

"Wes?" Nora's voice came from behind him.

Wesley ignored it. "Is that her only option? You know she won't stand for that," he stated.

"Wesley?" Nora's voice came again.

"Just a second, Nora."

"Are mother horses really protective of their young?" she asked.

"Of course they are," he said, and knelt by Track Beauty's head. Her eyes had emptied out—he couldn't find the will to live in them. Not even the ambulance, the hospital, putting her up in the sling could bring that back. "Why?"

The sound of a whimper, heartrending and tiny, sliced through the tense silence in the stall. Wesley stood and spun around. Nora had the riding crop in her hand and the miserable whimper had come not from her but from Bastinado. She lifted the crop and struck the tiny horse on the back once more. And once more the foal released the smallest, most pitiful cry of pain Wesley had ever heard in his life. The foal flinched and tried to scurry away, but his newborn legs wobbled underneath him. Once more Nora hit Bastinado with shocking force, force he hadn't known Nora possessed. Once more Bastinado whimpered and balked, his eyes wild and dark with terror. And from behind Wesley he heard the cry answered.

Wesley had to run for it as two thousand pounds of furious mother horse hoisted herself to her feet and surged forward.

"Nora!" Wesley started toward her, but his father beat him to her. He yanked Nora out of the way of Track Beauty's fury and pulled her from the stall. Wesley didn't even bother going through the door; he threw himself over it. All four humans stood outside the stall, watching as Track Beauty nuzzled Bastinado's nose. The fragile newborn had three parallel welts on his back, but Wesley saw no blood. He might have scars. But he also had his mother alive and on her feet.

"Nora?" Wesley looked at Nora and found her panting, wide-eyed and silent, clutching the riding crop in her white-knuckled hand. "Are you okay?"

She shook her head.

"I'm fine," she said, although he wasn't sure he believed it.

"He'll be fine, too." Wesley gently took the riding crop from her hand and hung it on the wall with the other horse tack. Wrapping his arm around her waist, he pulled her close. She didn't melt into his body like usual. She only stood there, breathing and staring.

Wesley tensed as his father came up to her, a new look in his eyes.

"That was the damnedest thing I ever saw in my life," he said, glancing between Nora and Bastinado.

"I hope he'll be okay." Nora slowly met the older man's eyes.

"I suppose I should say thank-you." Wesley's father held out his hand to shake. Nora only looked at it before giving him a slight and dangerous smile.

"At least now you know that when I have to...I can be very serious."

NORTH
The Past

Kingsley wouldn't believe it until he saw her. Over a year had passed since he'd seen his sister, since their grandparents had wrenched him from Marie-Laure's grasp at their parents' funeral. How had Søren done it…arranged for her to come all this way to see him? Søren claimed to have money, and from what Kingsley had heard, that claim was something of an understatement. Søren's father had married money, then taken the family fortune and with ruthless business acumen trebled it in twenty years.

Money was the least of Søren's allure for Kingsley. Had he been poor as a church mouse, Kingsley still would have slept at his feet, kissed his hands and crawled on command across burning coals if Søren asked that of him.

It wasn't the cost of bringing Marie-Laure to visit him that engendered such disbelief in Kingsley. During their nights together, when Kingsley knelt at Søren's feet or lay beneath him or submitted to his discipline, Søren always told him how little he mattered, how little he was worth. Kingsley knew he was nothing but a body to Søren, a body to be used and abused and discarded when he'd had his fill. So why...why would Søren do this kindness for him?

It made no sense.

And yet...

A black car wove its careful way down the one road that led from the narrow highway to the school. Kingsley stood alone in the bitter December air, waiting for its arrival. Søren had played a thousand terrible mind games with him since their first night together at the hermitage. Some days Søren would refuse to acknowledge his existence. Kingsley would speak to him and Søren would carry on with whatever he was doing as if Kingsley were some kind of ghost trying and failing to connect with the living. Other days Søren would watch his every move, watch and criticize. Kingsley's shoes would have to be retied, his homework rewritten in a neater hand, his clothes changed for no reason other than Søren ordered it of him. Once, at the hermitage, Søren had told Kingsley that he no longer wished to continue this game together, that he'd tired of it, tired of him. Kingsley had dropped to his knees in dismay and pleaded with Søren to give him another night, another chance. Tears lined the corner of Kingsley's eyes until he'd noticed the subtlest of smiles playing at the corner of Søren's lips. In fury, he had come to his feet and thrown a punch at Søren. Søren had caught it with shocking strength and deftness.

"Temper, Kingsley," he had whispered as Kingsley had struggled to wrest himself from that iron grip.

"I hate you." Kingsley said the words in English. They were too ugly for French.

"I know. I know you hate me. But I don't hate you. *Hate* is far too strong a word to describe what I feel for you."

"Why...why do you do this to me?"

At that Søren had released his hand. Kingsley rushed at him

again and Søren had kicked him hard in the thigh and sent him sprawling across the floor. He'd started to stand, unwilling to give up the fight even though he knew how useless the struggle was. But Søren straddled him at the knees and pushed him back to the floor. Digging his hands into Kingsley's hair, Søren held him immobile against the cold hardwood.

"I do it for one reason and one reason only…" Søren hissed into his ear. Kingsley's body tensed with fury and the far more unwelcome rush of desire that he could never defeat when Søren touched him. "I enjoy it as much as you do."

And that night, as Søren beat him and fucked him over and over again, he had done so in complete silence, even as Kingsley begged for the grace of a single word. Only at dawn had Søren spoken to him again, and then only one word.

Goodbye.

So it wouldn't have surprised Kingsley at all if the promise of a visit from his sister had been nothing but an elaborate ruse on Søren's behalf. Somewhere in one of the buildings, Søren stood at a window watching the scene unfold, Kingsley was certain. The car would pull up in front of Kingsley and stop, and someone—a priest, a nun, a rabbi for all Kingsley knew—would get out and look at him in surprise. And no Marie-Laure. Why he even bothered going through with the charade was beyond him. But Søren had arranged this joke and Kingsley would do anything for Søren—even debase himself by standing in the freezing cold and waiting an hour for his sister, who would never come.

The car drew nearer and nearer. Kingsley dug his hands deeper in his pockets. Glancing around, he saw faces at the windows of the classroom building, the offices, the library… his classmates, all waiting in the warmth and comfort indoors, watching him. He tried to prepare himself for the humiliation he'd feel when Marie-Laure's visit was revealed to be nothing more than a mind game of Søren's. Søren… Kingsley saw the face of the pianist he'd come to hate as much as love waiting in the uppermost room of the classroom building. Kingsley exhaled and wrenched his eyes from Søren's perfect face and back to the car. It had slowed almost to a stop. But it hadn't stopped. Not yet. And still the passenger door started to open and two small feet in black shoes with ribbons that laced around the ankles appeared.

"Kingsley!" called a voice he hadn't heard in over a year. His eyes could barely take in the scene, his heart could barely contain his happiness, his legs could scarcely keep him standing as his sister raced to him and enveloped him in her arms.

"Marie-Laure…" Kingsley breathed her name into her dark hair. She'd let it grow long and loose in their year apart. She'd been the most beautiful girl in Paris when he'd last seen her. Now, he noted with brotherly pride, she'd become the most beautiful girl in the world. "I can't believe you're here."

She wrapped her graceful ballerina arms around him. In perfect Parisian French she whispered to him how much she'd missed him, how she thought she'd die if she didn't see him soon, how awful it was without him, how she would never let anyone pull them apart again. With his chin on her shoulder and her mouth at his ear, Kingsley looked up and saw Søren still at the window, still watching.

Kingsley mouthed a single word at Søren.

Merci.

And Søren merely nodded in return, before disappearing from the window. Kingsley turned his attention back to Marie-Laure.

"How…? I can't—"

"I'm here," she said. "A plane ticket came to my apartment. And an invitation to visit you. I couldn't believe it." Marie-

Laure took his face in her gloved hands and kissed him on each cheek.

"I didn't believe it, either…until I saw you. I'm not sure I even believe it now."

"How…" She shook her head and tendrils of hair blew across her face. "Was it *Grandmère* and *Grandpère?* Did you…?"

Kingsley rolled his eyes. In her presence, he fell instantly back into his old French habits.

"It is a long story. I will tell it to you…but not yet."

"I don't care. All that matters is that I'm here and so are you." She took him into her arms again and Kingsley embraced her. Out of the corner of his eye he noticed that he and Marie-Laure were no longer alone in the cold. Several of the other boys had come outside, no doubt to get a better look at Marie-Laure. They hadn't seen a woman in months—at least not a young woman who hadn't taken a vow of chastity.

"This must be the sister." Father Henry's jovial voice came from behind them. "Bonjour, mademoiselle," he said, shaking Marie-Laure's hand.

Kingsley took his sister's arm as the priest ushered them into his office. Kingsley barely heard a word as Father Henry welcomed Marie-Laure to the school and apologized in advance for any of the flirting the boys would subject her to.

"We don't usually allow female visitors," Father Henry said, stammering slightly. "Not unmarried women, at least. Or women who aren't in an order. But Mr. Stearns explained the situation to me, that you two had been separated since your parents' death. We're happy to have you here for the duration of your visit. Kingsley will have to attend classes and keep up his schoolwork. But you're welcome to join us in the dining hall for all our meals. We have private guest quarters on the top floor of this building. I'll have one of the boys carry your things up."

"Merci, mon père," Marie-Laure said, beaming a wide smile at Father Henry. Kingsley nearly laughed out loud at the blush that utterly enveloped Father Henry from his collar to the top of his bald head. Marie-Laure had the same effect on men as Kingsley knew he had on women. All either of them had to do was smile.

Kingsley and Marie-Laure went directly to her room on the top floor of the office building. She wandered around, laughing at all the icons on the walls—the crosses, the pictures of saints, the Virgin Mary statuettes strewn about.

"Catholic school?" she teased. "Papa is turning in his grave."

Kingsley laughed and shrugged. "I know. It wasn't my idea. The boys at my old school hated me."

"For seducing all their girlfriends and sisters, no doubt." Marie-Laure wagged a finger at him.

"Well…of course. But stabbing me was an overreaction."

Her eyes widened. "Stabbed? You said it was a scratch."

"A big scratch."

"I don't know if Papa would be proud of you or if he would try to kill you himself."

"Both," Kingsley said, and they laughed. "What about you? Are you still breaking every heart in Paris?"

"Of course." She sat next to him on the sofa and crossed her muscular, graceful legs. "I have to break their hearts before they break mine."

"You should find a rich old man and marry him. He would die soon and leave you all his money. Then you could stay in America with me."

"Stay in America? Why would I do that? If I married a rich man, I'd pull you out of this awful place and take you back to Paris with me."

Kingsley leaned back on the couch and crossed his ankle over his knee.

"I don't know. I think I might like it here. America…it's not so bad."

"What is this? My brother…monsieur *Paris is the Only City in the World*…wants to stay in America? What's her name?"

Kingsley's eyes widened.

"Don't look so innocent," Marie-Laure said, poking him in the chest. "What is her name? You must be in love to want to stay in this country."

With a groan to cover his awkwardness, Kingsley turned his face to Marie-Laure.

"I promise you…I'm not in love with any girl in this entire country. Not even Canada, which is half a meter that way." He pointed north. "I like America. Paris is decadent, luxurious…but America…there's something untamed about this place, something wild."

Marie-Laure sighed. "If you love it here, then I would love it here. For now, all that matters is that you are here."

"Me and fifty boys who haven't seen a pretty girl in months?"

She raised her eyebrows. "I won't complain about that part. Now perhaps you should show me around this place, if I'm going to be living here for the next month."

Kingsley stood up and took her hand, pulling her to her feet.

"A month?"

"It's all I can stay. I had to lie to the director of my company and tell him I had a sprain that had to heal for a month. If I'm gone any longer than that, I'll lose my place in the chorus."

"You shouldn't be in the chorus. You are the prima ballerina."

"I will be. Someday. But we all must pay our dues. And besides, Laurent can't make me prima yet. Everyone would be suspicious."

"Another conquest?"

Marie-Laure batted her eyelashes. "Male dancers…they have such powerful legs."

Kingsley waved his hand as they put on their coats and headed out the door again.

"I don't want any details of your conquests. You might be beautiful, but you are still my sister."

"Well, I want to know all the details about your love life. Oh, wait, you're at an all-boys school. You don't have one."

She slapped him lightly on the cheek to tease him as she skipped ahead into the cold.

Ah, Marie-Laure… Kingsley sighed to himself. If she only knew.

Arm in arm, they wandered the grounds of the school. He showed her the dining hall and introduced her to Father Aldo. Marie-Laure and the priest conferred for several minutes about that evening's menu. He'd planned a soufflé. She suggested quiche. Kingsley feigned falling asleep and Marie-Laure pinched him in the arm, as she always did when they were children.

Kingsley flinched at the pinch, hard enough that Marie-Laure started.

"When did you get so sensitive?" she asked as they left the dining hall. "I only pinched you."

"It's fine. You just pinched me where I already have a bruise. I'll survive."

"I'll find a part of you that isn't bruises, and that's what I'll pinch next time. *Oui?*"

"*Oui.*" He smiled, but he knew it would take a great deal of searching to find a part of him that didn't carry a bruise or a welt. Last night, Søren had been absolutely merciless with him. The beating had seemed interminable. The sex even more so. Upon reflection, Kingsley realized the intensity of their night was because Marie-Laure's presence would make meeting much more complicated. But they would find a way. They had to be together, Søren and Kingsley. They belonged together.

"What's that?" Marie-Laure paused outside the chapel.

Kingsley cocked his head to the side and smiled. From within he heard the sound of a piano playing the haunting rhythms of...

"Bolero," Kingsley said. "Ravel."

"Ravel..." Marie-Laure sighed and looked at Kingsley with a mix of sadness and longing in her eyes. He knew she had lost herself in the same memory he had—Papa and his records. Of their father lying on the floor of their apartment in a patch of sunlight, eyes closed, and humming along with the music...

"I miss him," Kingsley whispered as he took her hand and squeezed it.

"So do I. But I've missed you more. So much...so much I thought I'd die."

Kingsley shook his head. "Don't die. We're together now."

The music swelled and Marie-Laure turned her face toward the chapel.

"Can we go listen?"

Kingsley started to lead her there, but as soon as they crossed the threshold into the church, something deep within him warned that he should stop, go back.... The music grew louder as they neared the source of it. Kingsley shook off his sudden strange fear. Marie-Laure followed the music, her eyes as wide and mesmerized as a child of Hamlin.

At the door to the sanctuary they stopped and looked inside toward the nave. Søren sat at the ancient and battered grand piano, his jacket off, his sleeves rolled up to his elbows, revealing his muscular forearms. He played the piece with such stunning virtuosity and passion that once more Kingsley felt

the music come alive around him. Closing his eyes, he let
the notes touch him, dance about him, tickle his face, brush
through his hair, whisper secrets in his ear.

God, how he loved Søren. Loved him. Loved him like
a father, like a brother, like a friend and a lover...and loved
him like the enemy that forced him to be stronger, smarter,
wiser, braver. Søren had become everything to him.... Kingsley opened his eyes and saw not Søren, but God at the piano,
and knew he'd chosen the right man to worship. Even now
he would fall on his knees before him.

Kingsley felt Marie-Laure's hand begin to shake in his grasp.
It brought him out of his communion and back to the world.
He looked at his sister and smiled. He understood everything
now...Søren had brought her here for him, for Kingsley. Søren
had done it out of kindness. He'd done it as a grace, as a mercy.
Like all of God's gifts, it was given out of love.

Søren loved him. Kingsley knew that now in his heart.
And those mind games he played were just that—mere games.
Søren punished him with silence even as he gave him his un-
divided attention. He insulted him before bestowing the most
passionate of kisses. He said Kingsley meant nothing to him
before spending half the night inside him. *Søren loved him. Søren
loved him. Søren loved him.* The refrain in his heart matched
the insistent beat of the music. No one could or would understand the love they had for each other or how they showed
it. Only Søren, Kingsley and the music knew, and the music
would never tell.

"Mon Dieu..." Marie-Laure breathed the words, her eyes
trained on Søren with a blank, unblinking stare. Once more
the fear returned to Kingsley's heart.

No...not her, too. Anyone but his sister...

She pulled her hand from his and raised it in front of her.

Kingsley's eyes widened in fear as he saw the subtle tremor that had overtaken it.

"Mon Dieu," she had whispered. My God.

Kingsley took her hand again and pulled it tight to his chest. He would hold her close and keep her safe from the love that he knew would enter her soul like a demon.

"Don't be afraid." Kingsley kissed the back of her hand and smiled at her—a false smile meant to break the spell of the music and the blond god who played it. "He does that to everyone."

NORTH
The Present

Kingsley left the Rolls-Royce idling in front of his town house. Everyone knew of Kingsley Edge and his silver Rolls, which ferried him all over Manhattan. He needed anonymity today. So instead he returned to his house, changed into black jeans, a gray T-shirt and leather jacket, pulled on sunglasses and hid his long hair in a low ponytail. At the back of the town house was a garage that most of Manhattan assumed held only the Rolls-Royce and its twin brother. But at the back under a suede car cover sat a sleek black Jaguar with unregistered plates. Only in emergencies did Kingsley ever leave his home incognito. And this certainly qualified as an emergency.

He started the car and left the town house by the back streets, cursing Nora the entire way to Connecticut. Stupid girl. Foolish girl. Why did she have to live so far away? She could afford Manhattan or anywhere in the city. Why she had to buy a Tudor cottage in a bourgeois and pedestrian suburb was something he would never understand. Only a year into her career as a Dominatrix she'd saved up enough money to afford the down payment on her home. She'd paid it in cash, and moved out of his town house the first chance she could. In five years, Kingsley had been to her home only once. He'd nearly died of boredom just from the drive there alone. Standing in her living room, full of comfortable but unremarkable furniture, and bookcases stuffed with novels, he'd turned to her and asked only one question.

"Why?"

And she'd smiled and shrugged and sighed and laughed and shook her head and done everything she could to avoid answering him in words.

But he'd stared at her until the smile died and the laugh left her eyes. Those eyes of hers…if he had to guess, he would have said she'd stolen them from the devil himself.

"I like it here, King. I feel…human here. Normal."

Kingsley had walked across the beige carpet toward her and taken her by the chin.

"You are the most famous Dominatrix in all the world, *chérie*. I made you a monster and a monster is what you are. Live here if you must, but remember that inside these walls you are Eleanor Schreiber. Nora Sutherlin does not live here."

Her only response had been to return his stare with one as hard as his own, and that's when Kingsley had realized the terrible truth—he hadn't created Nora Sutherlin at all…he'd only unmasked her.

An hour passed and he finally reached Westport. Another fifteen minutes took him to Nora's neighborhood. In front of her house sat a red Porsche—Griffin was still here. Griffin and no one else. Good. The boy hadn't been so foolish as to call the police.

Kingsley didn't knock, merely entered through the front door, and found the house as he remembered it—tame, safe, suburban, bourgeois.

"In the bedroom, King," he heard Griffin call to him. Kingsley found the stairs and raced up them two at a time. At the end of the hallway he found Nora's bedroom…

Or what was left of it.

"Shit…" Kingsley breathed, too shocked even for French.

"Yeah, that's what I said." Griffin stood at the edge of the room, staring at the carnage before them.

"Where is Michael?" Kingsley asked, pronouncing the name in the French manner, as *Michelle,* a habit he tried to break for the sake of Griffin and his boy.

"I got him out of here fast. Sent him to his mom's house to stay the night. He almost puked when he saw the place."

"I can sympathize."

Kingsley swallowed hard as he studied the damage.

In the center of the room were the charred remains of what had once been the most fantasized about bed in the world. On top of the blackened ashes lay what appeared to be Nora's entire wardrobe of Dominatrix clothing—every last piece slashed and desecrated.

Across the walls was splattered blood—animal blood, Kingsley guessed. Guessed and hoped. Bloody words, bloody handprints. Blood on bloodred walls. The pale carpet below their feet also carried bloodstains, bloody footprints. And bloody words.

"What does it mean, Kingsley?" Griffin asked, staring at the writing. "It's French, right? My French is shit these days."

"*Oui,* it's French." Kingsley read the words and his stomach tightened as he recognized the same ones that had been written on the wall above the body of his dead Sadie.

Griffin squinted at the messages, clearly making no sense of them. "I told you…." He shook his head and sighed. "What does it say?"

Kingsley exhaled heavily, not sure he wanted to tell Griffin or anyone about the writing. But even if he told him, Griffin wouldn't know what it meant.

"It says, 'I will kill the bitch.'"

"I will kill the bitch? Nora? Who is he talking to?" Griffin rubbed his face and turned even paler. "King…does someone want to kill Nora?"

Kingsley saw something on the walls he hadn't seen at first. Holes. No, not holes, stab wounds. Someone had taken a knife and repeatedly plunged the blade into the drywall, leaving one-inch slices everywhere he looked. He went to the bed and picked up one of Nora's bloodied corsets. The slash marks had been concentrated in one spot. The stomach. Had Nora been wearing this while it was stabbed, she would have been dead in seconds.

"*Oui*. Someone very much wants to kill our Nora."

"But…" Griffin turned wide and horrified eyes to Kingsley. "Why? Nora's never hurt anybody. I mean, not without their consent."

"I fear this person feels Nora has taken something that doesn't belong to her."

"Nora's never stolen anything in her life, either. Well, other than all those cars when she was a kid. But nobody would kill over a car."

"No. Not the cars. That is not it."

"Then what the fuck is it? What did Nora steal? Whoever this fucked-up freak is, I'll pay him off."

"No amount of money could buy what they want, I'm afraid."

"I'll be the judge of that," Griffin said, in the tone of a man who'd been raised to believe he could buy anything or anyone he wanted—including another's life. "What does he want?"

Kingsley reached into the pile of Nora's clothing and found what he knew he would find. He pulled out a string of rosary beads—bloodred and worn smooth with a thousand prayers that would have made the Magdalene herself blush. He knew Nora kept the key to the box that held her collar behind the crucifix of her rosary beads. He found the beads...the crucifix...and no key.

Kingsley wrapped the beads around his hand and held them out toward Griffin by way of explanation.

"Søren?" Griffin asked, fear replacing the determination on his face. "This freak wants Søren?"

Kingsley nodded. *"Oui,"* was all he said.

Griffin pressed his hands into his stomach. Now it seemed he was on the verge of illness.

"Kingsley...this is crazy. No one comes after any of us. Your money and power...my money and power...and Søren? Who would ever go after Søren?"

"Someone who cares nothing for money and power. And I fear such people do exist."

"What does it mean...all of this?" Griffin looked again at the bloody words on the floor, the pile of shredded clothes and the bed itself—charred and bloodied. To anyone but Kingsley, the scene would be incomprehensible. What *did* it mean?

Kingsley knew exactly what it meant. After running away from Saint Ignatius he'd joined the French Foreign Legion. First his facility with English had caught the notice of higher-ups, that if he concentrated he could speak it without any trace of a French accent. Then his other skills came to light—his intelligence, his way of charming anyone into telling him anything he wanted to know, his natural gift of marksmanship... and his utter disregard for his own personal safety, for his own life, even. They'd made him a spy first and then so much more after. He'd seen the deaths of thousands begin with a single act that took place behind closed doors in a bedroom like this. Oh, yes, he knew exactly what the scene before them meant.

"It's a declaration, Griffin."

Kingsley pulled the keys out of the pocket of his leather jacket. He had to go now and find Søren. The time for secrets had come to an end.

"Of what? Insanity?"

"No, *mon ami*. Of war."

SOUTH

Nora stayed calm and collected for the entire trip back to Wesley's house. She barely blinked and didn't cry. No emotion showed on her face or in her hands. Long ago she'd learned how to control herself under the most difficult of circumstances. She'd had to for her job. Lesson number two from the great Kingsley Edge, King of the Underground—you are the Dominant. Act like it.

Those seven words had kept her face straight and her hands still even as one submissive after another had come to her with the most desperate and dangerous of fantasies. One Wall Street trader had wanted to drink her urine from a wineglass. The deputy mayor of New York confessed to the most graphic of rape fantasies involving him as the victim. A Texas cattle billionaire had begged her on his hands and knees to brand his back with his own branding iron. No matter how disturbed she'd been by their fantasies, their fetishes, she always had to stay calm and in control, even as they begged her, pleaded with her to hurt them as they dreamed. "No," she often told them. "You haven't earned it." That was her line, her cover for when she knew no amount of love or money could convince her to do such a thing. And then they would beg harder, up their offer and she'd acquiesce.

"Now you've earned it," she would say, which was code for, "now you found my price."

I am the Dominant, she'd told herself over and over again, even as she wanted to run or crumble. *I will act like it.*

And now, as Wesley's father watched her in silence out of the corner of his eyes, as he drove her and Wesley back to the guesthouse, Nora told herself the same thing. Hitting a newborn foal with a riding crop should have earned her at least a year in prison for cruelty to animals. Even now she wanted to roll up into a ball, and cry or puke, or both. But her guts had told her all it would take for Track Beauty to find the will to stand up and live was to see her baby in pain. It had worked. Not only had the mare gotten to her feet again, but it had seemingly earned Nora the respect of Wesley's father...or at least his fear. And in her world, they were one and the same.

The older man pulled up to the guesthouse and Wesley got out first. Extending his hand, he waited, and Nora took it with the grace of an English duchess descending from her carriage.

"Thank you, sir," she said as her feet touched the ground. "And good night, Mr. Railey."

Nora turned her head just enough to smile at Wesley's father over her shoulder. Kingsley had taught her that little move, as well—no one flirted quite like that Frenchman.

"Good night, son. And you, madam."

She walked to the house without waiting for Wesley. She could hear him whispering back and forth with his father. Usually she would have been rabid to know what they were saying about her, but now she didn't care. All she cared about was getting into the house and finding the bathroom.

Five minutes, she prayed. *Just stay out of the house for five more minutes, Wesley.*

Nora made it to the bathroom, shut the door behind her and threw up everything she'd eaten since lunch. It came up and out hard and fast, so hard her eyes watered and her stomach ached as if she'd taken a punch to the abdomen. She flushed her vomit away and crawled into the shower. The hot water blasted down even as Nora struggled to remove her sodden clothes.

When she heard the door open, she quickly composed her face.

"I'm in the shower, Wes. I'm covered in horse placenta."

"Yeah, me, too. Make room."

Nora gave a mirthless laugh as Wesley shoved in next to her, also fully dressed.

"Good idea," he said as he raised his hand and started to unbutton her wet shirt. "It's a shower and laundry all at once."

"I've got nothing but good ideas."

"I'm starting to think that's true." He grunted in frustration when Nora's shirt remained stuck to her soaking body. With a roll of his eyes he simply tore it and sent three small buttons to the floor. "Oops."

Nora shrugged. "It was your shirt, anyway."

"Damn." Wesley laughed and brought his mouth down to hers, but Nora pulled her head away before he could kiss her. "What's wrong?"

"Nothing," she said. "I have horse placenta breath. Let me brush my teeth before you kiss me."

"That might be the grossest thing I've ever heard in my life."

"What? Placenta's a good source of protein, right?" she asked, and laughed again.

"Nora…are you okay?"

"Yeah, sure. Of course I'm okay. Why not? I mean, why?"

Wesley looked down at her and Nora could barely meet his brown eyes, which bored into her with the fiery love of a guardian angel. God probably had eyes like Wesley's...anyone who looked into them wanted to immediately apologize for any and all sins ever committed.

"You're standing under hundred-degree water and shaking, for one thing." He cupped her face in his hands. "Every time you laugh, I worry the mirrors are gonna shatter. Talk to me."

He caressed her cheek, kissed her forehead and brought her head briefly to his chest. Goddamn tall men...she hated them. All of them. They made her feel so small and so weak by virtue of their size alone. And she hated feeling small and she hated feeling weak and hated Wesley for reminding her how much she hated that.

"I hit a baby," she whispered into his chest.

Wesley sighed and pulled her even closer.

"You hit a horse, Nora. Not a baby. And he'll be fine. Which he might not have been had his momma died on that stall floor or in a hospital room. Horses don't mend well. They're not like dogs and cats. They get sick, you just put them down. Track Beauty might not have survived a week even if the vet had got her in a sling. And—"

"You can stop talking now, Wes."

"Yes, ma'am."

Underneath the steaming shower spray, Nora stood in Wesley's arms and cried, letting the water wash the tears away before they could even drip down her face. Ten minutes passed, maybe fifteen, while the pain and the shame she'd felt every time she'd brought the crop down with vicious strength on the little horse's back eased out of her. Finally, she'd cried out all the tears she had, and found herself laughing against Wesley's chest.

"Now that sounds like a Nora laugh. What are you laughing at?"

"Us," she said, rubbing her face on his shirt to wipe her runny nose. "How come we always end up in the bathroom with me having a nervous breakdown and you keeping me together?"

"I dunno. The bathroom seems to be your favorite place to go have a breakdown."

"It's good for reading, too."

"You're so disgusting."

"What? I read in the bathtub. What were you referring to?"

Wesley laughed and rested his chin on top of her head. "Nothing. Nothing at all."

He sighed so heavily Nora felt his chest heave against hers.

"Now what's your problem, kid?" Pulling back, she looked up at Wesley and started to peel off the rest of her clothes.

"You. You're my problem. I'm crazy about you and you're going to leave me. Aren't you?"

"Wes, I just got here a few days ago. And now it seems like your dad doesn't hate the very sight of me. So that's progress."

"That's not an answer to my question."

"Ask it again."

Wesley met her eyes as Nora removed her underwear and stood before him wet and naked.

"Are you going to leave me...again?"

Nora's stomach clenched even worse than it had back in the stable when she'd realized what she had to do.

"I didn't leave you the first time, Wes. I went back to Søren. And I made you leave me. I couldn't have left you. That's why I kicked you out. I wasn't strong enough to leave you. I was only strong enough to order you to go away."

"Will you order me to go away again?"

"No. I thought it would kill me the first time I did it. I

could barely speak for a week after you were gone. I cried constantly."

"Søren must have loved that."

"He loved me. And forgave me every tear. And not once did he tell me not to miss you, not to talk about you, not to love you."

"I hate when you tell me nice things he's done. Makes it harder to hate him."

"Don't ever hate Søren." Nora unzipped Wesley's jeans and started to tug the wet denim down over his hips as he finally pulled off his wet and snot-covered shirt. "Hate me, but never hate him."

"I have to hate him."

"Why? Hate does not become you, my Wesley."

"Nora…he put you in the hospital. I was there, remember? I drove you to the hospital after he——"

"He didn't," she said in a hollow voice and hated herself the second the words came out. She'd promised herself she'd never tell Wesley about that night.

"Didn't what?"

"He didn't put me in the hospital that night I went back to him. That's not what happened."

Wesley's eyes widened. Nora turned off the shower, stepped out and grabbed a towel. Naked but for a towel, Nora sunk down on the floor. Still dripping wet, Wesley sat opposite from her, his back to the bathtub.

"The night I went back to Søren, it was rough. We played rough. He started with a hard slap. A good one. My favorite kind."

"I should have broken his face for that."

"Wesley—Søren slaps because I like slapping. I do it to clients all the time. It's part of my kink. He knows that. He slapped me."

"I don't want to hear this."

"I can't let you hate him. I thought I could but only because I thought it would make you hate me, too. I have to tell you the truth. You have to know what you're asking me to do every time you ask me to stay." Nora stared deep into his dark brown eyes.

"Nora..."

She heard the plea in Wesley's voice, a plea she couldn't heed.

"One slap and then he flogged me. A good thorough back flogging. I'd had one like that a thousand times before. Loved it. Then we were both so turned on and desperate for each other, he took me upstairs and we—"

"I know. You fucked, right?"

She shook her head.

"No. He made love to me. As gently as you have. He couldn't stop telling me how much he loved me."

"I saw you the next day, Nora. I know what he did to you."

Nora narrowed her eyes at him and let him see that side of her she so often had to hide. "You don't know anything about what he did to me. After we made love, I begged for more. He laughed and called me insatiable. He tied me to the bedpost and flogged me again, a bit harder this time. Then a little caning action. Just enough to leave some bruises. And I waited. Waited for my chance."

"Chance for what?"

Nora's mind went back to that night, the night she'd gone back to Søren after five years apart. She knew she had to do something, something ugly, something that scared even her. She had to do it so Wesley would want to leave her.

"Søren untied my hands and stepped away to get something—cuffs, another flogger, I don't even know. As soon as he turned his back on me, I fell."

"You fell? Like fainted?"

"No. I fell on purpose. Hard against the hardwood. I landed on the side of my face and on my ribs. It was like cutting down a tree. Timber..." she said, and with her hands feigned the falling of a heavy tree to the ground. "I hit the floor full body with my whole weight behind it. That's how I bruised my ribs. That's how I busted my lip... He didn't do it. I did it to myself."

She knew Wesley believed her when all he could ask was, "Why?"

"Why?" she repeated. "For you. I thought if you thought Søren had really beat the shit out of me in a really ugly way, then you'd think I was...I don't know...a hopeless cause. I thought it would scare you enough you'd want to leave. If I made you think he was a monster and you knew I loved him, then you would think..."

"I would think you were a monster."

The deep sorrow in Wesley's voice shamed her. She'd tricked Wesley into thinking Søren was an abusive brute. She'd terrified Søren by falling during that night. She didn't deserve either of them—Søren or Wesley.

"I scared the shit out of Søren, too, you know."

"Nora...please don't make me not hate him. I need to hate him."

"I hit the floor so hard he thought I'd passed out or something. I knew I'd scared him bad. It was the one time he'd ever called me 'Nora.'"

"I have to hate him. Please..."

Nora ignored the "please." She couldn't stop now. He needed to know it all.

"He said, 'Nora!' and he knelt on the floor and ran his hands over me. And he looked at me, looked in my eyes. And he knew. He knew why I'd fallen on purpose. And he didn't say a word. He knew I was going to lie to you about how I got so banged up, and he was going to let me lie. He knows not to ask questions he doesn't want the answer to."

Wesley bowed his head; he dug his hands into his wet hair.

"He picked me up off the floor and carried me to bed. He held me close and he…he told me to pick a number between one and one hundred."

"Nora, I don't want to hear any more."

Nora felt something wet running down her face. Water from the shower? Or something else?

"It's a game we play. Pick a number, but you don't know what you're picking. Are you picking one lash or one hundred lashes? Are you picking one kiss or one hundred kisses? I picked one hundred."

Wesley went silent. Nora kept talking.

"He started to count…" Nora paused as she remembered the pain in her side, the blood on her tongue. Søren had gotten a cold wet washcloth and he gently dabbed her mouth. "He started to count the one hundred different things he loved about me."

"Nora…don't."

Never had she heard such hurt in someone's voice.

"Number one—he loves the way I laugh…all the time. And number seven—he loves the way I never answer my office phone like a normal person. And number fifty-eight—he loves the way my hair looks when I wear it pinned up."

"You're a sadist. You know that, right?" Wesley tried and failed to laugh. Nora did laugh, but it was a hard laugh and it hurt coming out.

"Are you just figuring that out, kid? I laughed at sixty-six. He loves the way my voice catches when I say his name while he's inside me."

"What was reason one hundred?" Wesley asked as water rolled down his cheek and dripped onto his clasped hands.

"One hundred. He loves that when he's especially lonely for me, all he has to do is read one of my books. And he can hear my voice in the words I've written, hear it so clearly it's as if I'm in the same room with him. I think if you asked me...I could tell you all one hundred reasons."

"Please let me hate him," Wesley begged, finally meeting her eyes again.

"Why do you have to hate him? He doesn't hate you. I'm here now and he doesn't hate you."

"Because you'll go back to him. And I'll be alone again. And if I don't have my hate, what will I have?"

She smiled at him and hated herself for that smile.

"You'll have your parents. A huge farm. Millions of dollars."

"So that's your answer?" Wesley's eyes hardened and Nora knew she'd hurt him far worse than she'd hurt Bastinado.

"I don't know what else to say...I belong to him. He owns—"

"He doesn't own you, Nora." Wesley stood up and started to strip out of his wet clothes. You and your stupid kinky bullshit rules. No one owns anybody. People aren't property anymore. Søren doesn't own you. "You don't belong to him. You can leave him and stay with me if that's what you want."

"It's not kinky bullshit rules." Nora took a towel of her own and followed Wesley back to the bedroom. "That's not what I'm talking about. I'm not talking about collars and leashes and leads. When you love somebody, they own you whether you're kinky or not. Surely you can understand that."

"I understand love because I love you." He turned around in the center of his bedroom. "And you love me, right?"

"God, yes, I love you. You know that."

"Stay with me. Please."

"Wes…"

"Please," he said again. Please was all he had.

Nora only leaned against him and sighed. She made the only pledge to him that she could.

"I'll try."

At dawn the next morning, Nora awoke and gently extricated herself from the tangle of sheets and legs and arms that imprisoned her. Looking down on Wesley's sleeping face, she quietly dressed and prayed he'd still be asleep when she returned. Last night, after he'd pulled out of her for the last time, rolled onto his side and gathered her into his arms, she'd made a decision.

She left the house and got into her car. Without consulting anything but her keen memory for directions, she drove the forty-five minutes to Talel's horse farm. Once there, she opened the trunk of her car and found the riding crop she'd brought with her from her house in Connecticut. She loved this crop. Short and red and vicious, it had earned her the nickname Little Red Riding Crop early in her career as a Dominatrix. Stories had been written about this crop. It had become the stuff of legend. But it was very real, very painful, and she was about to use it on someone, without any remorse.

She knocked on the door and waited. A bleary-eyed servant answered the door and let her inside. But when he tried to bar her from going upstairs, Nora had to remind herself of Kingsley's rule number two.

You are the Dominant.

Act like it.

She acted like it. The five-foot-ten, two-hundred-pound butler ended up on the floor with his arm behind his back.

"I'm just here to talk to Talel, who is an old, dear friend of mine. That Aston Martin out there? He bought it for me. I know he's still in bed. That's where you should be. Go now or everyone in this state will find out that a five-foot-three woman put you flat on your face. Say 'yes, Mistress' if you understand."

"Yes, Mistress."

"Good boy. Scoot." Nora let him up and raced for the stairs. She had no idea where Talel's bedroom was, but it didn't take long to find it, or Talel, wide-awake and waiting for her by the window.

"I heard you coming, Mistress. I'd know that engine anywhere."

"You should. It was your engine before it was mine. Need it back?"

Talel turned around and smiled sheepishly at her, not meeting her eyes.

"I wouldn't say no."

"I would have given it back had I known you needed the money enough to kill a horse over it. How much do you owe?"

"Mistress...I didn't—"

Nora stormed up to Talel and slapped him viciously across the cheek. He flinched and stared at her in shock that turned quickly to desire.

"How much do you owe?" she asked again.

"I don't—"

Nora twirled the riding crop in her fingers. That had been her signature trick—the twirl. Playing with the crop like a baton before catching it by the handle and bringing it down hard.

Talel watched the spinning crop with fearful eyes. Nora let it slide through her fingers until she grabbed the grip and hit the back of Talel's knees. He crumpled to the floor.

"Don't lie to me. I defended you to Wesley. I saw the stables—the empty stables. How much do you owe?"

Talel didn't answer, but that didn't surprise her. He loved being broken, loved having his pride stripped of him. He'd give her the answers she wanted, but she'd have to work for them. She could do that.

"Take your clothes off," she ordered. In seconds and without any sort of fight, Talel stripped naked. She wasn't at all surprised to see him hard. The more vicious she'd been with him, the more he'd wanted her. "On your back."

Nora straddled Talel's stomach and sat on his erection. He winced in discomfort. Jeans plus force against naked skin couldn't have felt good. She didn't it want it to feel good. Holding the riding crop at both ends, Nora pressed it against his neck.

"Your cock just twitched under me, Talel. You always liked being choked. I haven't forgotten that."

He swallowed hard and didn't speak.

"I also haven't forgotten how much you love submitting to a woman who'll beat the shit out of you before fucking you for her own pleasure. You liked that, didn't you? Being used? Answer me."

"Yes, Mistress. I loved it."

"I know. You didn't have to tell me." Nora sighed. "I'm really very unhappy here, Talel. I liked you. Genuinely liked you. It impressed me that you're royalty in your own country, but you stay in the States so you can be treated like a normal person. Kingsley told me I shouldn't fuck you, that I should see you as a paycheck and not a person. But I adored you. Stupid me."

Nora stood up and put her foot on the center of Talel's chest.

"Kiss it." She let her dirty, horse-shit-covered shoe hover by his face. Talel lifted his head and obediently kissed the toe.

THE PRINCE

"Good boy," she said, before bringing her foot down to rest on his throat. All she had to do was drop her full weight onto her foot and Talel's next breath would his last breath. "Now... how much do you owe?"

"Thirty million dollars." The words were barely audible.

"That should be nothing for you."

Talel shook his head. Nora lifted her foot a millimeter.

"My father found out...about me."

Nora swallowed the pang of pity that threatened her resolve.

"He disinherited you?"

"I don't know. I'm cut off for now, at least. The farm, the banks, the creditors...thirty million is an amount no one will forgive."

"And Spanks for Nothing was insured for forty. Convenient. A miracle and spare change. You're saved." She glared at him with a mix of fury and pity.

"Not entirely. The investigators...they could discover it wasn't an accident. We were careful but..."

Talel's voice trailed off and the implications of that "but" hung in the air between them. Nora pulled the red clip out of her pocket and showed it to him.

"Not that careful."

He said nothing, only stared at the evidence that could keep him from his miracle.

"Your creditors...are we talking banks? Or deep pockets?"

"Both."

"Shit." Nora's jaw clenched. Deep pockets...that meant the mob. "Horse Mafia, huh?"

"Anywhere there is money there is the Mafia...as you know, Mistress."

She nodded. Talel hadn't merely been her lover, he'd been her friend. And she'd told him the truth about her background—her father with his Mafia ties, growing up in a chop shop, the car thefts that had gotten her sentenced to community service supervised by her priest. She better than anyone knew the reach and the power and the money of the mob. And if Talel got on their bad side and stayed there…it would be only a matter of time before the Underground had one less male submissive.

"Your friends…the Raileys," Talel began and Nora pressed her foot harder on his throat again.

"Careful…" she warned. "You have no idea how much I care about Wes Railey."

"You're here and not with the priest. I think I know."

"What about the Raileys?"

"They wield more influence than any investigators."

"Wes said his uncle is the governor of Kentucky."

"And his grandfather is the distinguished gentleman from Georgia."

Nora rolled her eyes. "Grandpa's a senator? Lovely. Wesley left that part out."

"He's a humble young man. And kind. Too humble and too kind for this ugly business. Too kind for us."

"Too kind for me, you mean. Tell me something I don't know."

Talel lay on the floor in silence. She wanted to kick him in the face and bust it open, but she stayed her wrath. Søren had taught her the lessons of sadism, but he'd taught her the lessons of mercy even better.

"What do you need from me?" she asked, cutting through the conversational niceties. Wesley was an early riser and she'd rather not explain where she'd disappeared to today.

"Can you convince Railey Sr. to make a phone call on my behalf? One call from him would put an end to the investigation."

"I'll try. Can't promise he'll do it. I'm not his favorite person, but at least I'm not his least favorite person anymore."

"I'm sure he'll bend to your will. We all do."

"I said I'd try. But you killed a horse, Talel. For money. It's murder...insurance fraud...."

"I've easily paid forty million dollars in insurance. It's my own money they'd give back to me. And it's hardly fair for a woman with more leather in her closet than I have in my stables to call the death of one animal 'murder.'"

Nora said nothing as the unpleasant truth of Talel's words sank in. When it came to issues of morality, she had long ago surrendered the moral high ground. She left that lofty plateau to Søren and his unusual code of right and wrong. Right now she wished Søren was here to tell her exactly what to do. Even during their years apart, she found herself going to him for advice and counsel and guidance, while she ran from his love and power and control.

"Nora," Talel said, his voice soft and desperate, "they'll kill me."

Nora closed her eyes. He was right. When the mob caught up with her father, they'd torn him up with so many bullets cremation had been the only option for his burial. One man...one horse.

"I'll talk to Mr. Railey," Nora said, knowing exactly what Mr. Railey would say to her request. She knew what he would say and she knew what she would do. And she knew Wesley would be devastated. Just last night he'd asked her if she'd stay with him or leave. If she did this for Talel, she'd have no choice but to go.

"Thank you, Mistress. Thank you...."

Nora removed her foot from Talel's neck. He came to his knees and knelt at her feet. Starting at the tip of her toes, he kissed his way up to her ankles, to her calves and up her thighs.

Sighing, Nora let him worship her in his favorite manner. She had missed this, missed the foot worship, missed men at her feet. But she couldn't deny the simple truth that as much as she missed the Underground, she would miss Wesley more.

"But there is a price to be paid for me talking to Mr. Railey for you."

"I'll pay it. Anything." Talel gazed up at her from the floor. Nora tried to not let the sight of his exquisitely burnished flesh and his erotic obedience affect her. She had Wesley waiting at home in bed. She didn't need Talel underneath her. Wanted… perhaps. But needed, no.

"The price is this." Nora stepped to the window and left Talel kneeling on the floor. "You're going to sell every horse you have left. You can keep the money, but you're out of the horse-racing business. Forever. And you're banned from the Underground. If I were you, I wouldn't even set foot in New York."

Talel stared at her with his mouth agape.

"It's done, Talel. Don't bother begging. That shit doesn't work on me anymore."

He closed his mouth and visibly swallowed. Standing up, he bowed his head.

"Yes…Nora."

"Good. You know how much Kingsley loves those dogs of his. You'd be lucky to make it out of Manhattan with your own hide still on." She hoped the bluff would work. Kingsley couldn't care less about a dead horse in Kentucky. "You should sell the farm, too, and get out of the state. You don't deserve to be in the same county as my Wesley. He'd cut off his own hand before he'd hurt anything on earth, for love or money."

"Then what is he doing with you?"

Only Nora's training as a Dominatrix kept her from flinching visibly at Talel's words. But Talel hadn't been the first man to wound her to the core of her being. That had been Søren. Had Søren said something like that to her, she would have responded with fury or tears. But Talel didn't merit such a reaction. So instead she merely smiled.

"I ask myself that same question every day, Talel. I've decided not to answer it."

Nora walked back to him and stood in front of his kneeling form. For that comment, for making a liar out of her to Wesley, and most importantly, for killing Spanks for Nothing, she gave him one very special farewell.

"Kingsley was right. I should have kept you as just a paycheck."

With a well-placed swat of her riding crop, she hit Talel squarely in the testicles with brute force. He lay on the floor in the fetal position, writhing. He'd be down there for the next hour or two.

Good.

All the way back to The Rails, Nora's conscience gnawed at her—a strange sensation, as up to that point she hadn't been entirely certain she had a conscience. What else could she have done? she asked herself over and over again. Turn in Talel? He'd be fined for killing his horse and perhaps banned from Thoroughbred racing. Proving intent to commit fraud would be a case no one would bother making, especially since admitting to electrocuting Spanks for Nothing would mean the insurance claim was null and void, anyway. A slap on the wrist...no more. What she'd done to him had been a far more severe punishment than any racing commission could impose on him. Kingsley Edge had a far reach. Banning Talel from the Underground meant no legitimate establishment of kink would ever let him through their doors again. For a man like Talel who couldn't be himself in his world, cutting him out of hers was akin to a death sentence—a spiritual one, at least. She'd felt something like it during her year in hiding after leaving Søren. For those like her and Talel, their sexuality was almost a sixth sense. Being cast out from their dark paradise would be like losing one's sight or hearing. Without Søren, without the Underground, Nora had felt blind for a year. Her eyes hadn't worked. As deeply as she grieved, she hadn't been able to cry.

Nora returned to The Rails. Instead of driving straight to the guesthouse, she went to the main house, knocked politely on the door and waited. Wesley's father himself opened the door.

"Weird," Nora said the second she saw him.

"Good morning to you, too, young lady," Mr. Railey said with confusion, but not his usual animosity.

"I'm sorry. Just thought you'd have a housekeeper or secretary or something to answer the door."

"Don't need one. Learned how to open a door a long time ago. Never forgot how."

Nora laughed. "It's just like riding a bike, I guess. Never learned that, though."

"You don't know how to ride a bike?"

"Do motorcycles count?"

"No, they do not."

Nora sighed. "Damn. Can I talk to you for a minute?"

Mr. Railey stared at her before taking a step back and ushering her into the house.

"Ohh...beautiful. Nice chandelier."

"Thank you. It's from Versailles," he said as she followed him upstairs.

"I thought it was pronounced *Ver-sayles?*"

He glanced over his shoulder at her and raised his eyebrow.

"Oh," Nora said, wincing. "The real Versailles."

"That's a fact. Now what can I do for you?" Mr. Railey

asked as they entered what had to be his personal office. He waved at a chair as he sat behind his desk.

"Nice house," she said, making the understatement of the century.

"We try to keep it up."

"So far so good." Nora glanced around the office and took in the various photographs of horses draped in blankets of roses. So many of the pictures included Wesley. In four feet of wall he aged from eight to eighteen. He got taller, got broader, but those eyes of his never changed—sweet and innocent in every last photo.

"I suppose asking you for a favor is a bit presumptuous of me," she began without further preamble. "But I promised I would do it. And keeping promises is, for me, incredibly uncomfortable. I treat them like Band-Aids and let them rip."

"A good philosophy, I suppose." He leaned back in his chair and studied her. "Go on."

"Talel killed his horse. He admitted it to me. Wasn't an accident. He's getting out of racing for good and selling all his horses. Getting him in trouble with the racing commission won't do any good and would just cause a lot of trouble where none needs to be. Would you be willing to make a phone call or two to get the investigation called off?"

"Why would we call the investigation off? And why would you want them to?"

"Talel is an old, dear friend of mine. And he's in some trouble. Serious, dangerous trouble that could get him killed. And that trouble will go away if we all pretend Spanks for Nothing died by accident and no other reason. Horses die pretty easily, right?"

"On occasion. They're fragile animals."

"I've noticed."

"Sons are fragile, as well."

"I've noticed that, too."

Nora stopped talking. She had a feeling saying another word would work against her cause. Instead of speaking, she merely braced herself for the inevitable.

"I don't like you, Miss Sutherlin." Mr. Railey looked her dead in the eyes as he said the words. Nora kept silent, neither questioning nor complimenting his taste in women. "But I don't hate you."

"I appreciate that, sir," she said, and closed her mouth again.

"You did something last night I'd never seen before. That took nerves of steel and an iron will to get our Track Beauty back on her feet again. I've registered Bastinado's name already. And I haven't said a word to my wife about how close we came to losing her four-legged baby."

"I'm glad everything turned out okay." Nora clenched her jaw. This not saying everything she wanted to say was more painful than getting flogged. Would this be life at The Rails? Behaving herself? Not talking back? Not making waves or causing trouble? Perhaps it really was for the best that Mr. Railey would trade doing this favor for her in exchange for her promise to leave Wesley once and for all.

"So am I, young lady."

Mr. Railey said nothing more and Nora waited, biting her tongue.

He smiled, sighed and shook his head.

"'Four things greater than all things are...women and horses and power and war.'"

Nora stared at him.

"That's Rudyard Kipling," Mr. Railey explained. "One of my favorite sayings. Women and horses and power and war... story of my life."

Nora smiled. "Mine too these days. Apparently."

"Did you need anything else?" Mr. Railey asked, tapping his desk with obvious impatience.

"No…that was it. Just…"

"Go on back to bed. It looks like you could use a few more hours sleep. I'll make your phone call. But your friend better never step foot onto a race track ever again."

"He won't."

"Good. Go on now. I've got work to do."

Nora opened her mouth and closed it again just as quickly.

"Thank you, Mr. Railey." She bobbed a curtsy for no reason she could explain, other than the moment seemed to demand it. Mr. Railey laughed as he shooed her from the room.

At the bottom of the stairs, Nora peeked into the drawing room. Wesley's mother sat at a petite desk with a fountain pen and a stack of cards, white with red trim, in front of her. With Mrs. Railey engrossed in her writing, Nora took a moment to look at her. Lovely lady really, with eyes as big and brown as her son's.

She glanced up and smiled at Nora.

"I didn't mean to interrupt," Nora apologized before Mrs. Railey could speak.

"You can interrupt the thank-you-note writing anytime you wish."

Nora whistled at the stack of thank-you cards in front of Mrs. Railey. It looked like she'd written a hundred notes and still had another hundred to go.

"Writing that many thank-you notes is my definition of hell."

"Mine, too," Mrs. Railey admitted, capping her pen. "But we had two hundred people donating exorbitant sums to The Rails Foundation. Have to say 'thank you.'"

"I'd tell them to keep the money."

Mrs. Railey nodded. "I've wanted to a time or two. Have a seat if you like."

"I won't stay and bug you. This is just the first time your husband let me in the house."

Mrs. Railey's smile broadened. "My husband is as stubborn as a mule. He's a good man. Only...difficult."

"I'm well-versed in good, stubborn and difficult men."

"Never considered my son to be difficult. He was, still is, the sweetest child you could ever hope to have. He gets that from me," she said with a wink.

"I can see that. It's the sweetness that makes him so difficult."

With a sigh, Mrs. Railey sat back in her chair and gave Nora a long searching look. "You're not planning on staying around these parts, are you?"

"I..." Nora shrugged. "I don't really plan much."

"I can see that about you. You look like a woman who never completely unpacks her suitcase."

Nora opened her mouth to protest and then shut it again. Ruefully, she laughed her agreement.

"Someone called me a pirate once," she said, not wanting to say Søren's name to Wesley's mother for some reason. "A born marauder destined for the high seas."

"Even a pirate needs a safe harbor."

"But is that harbor still safe when the pirates dock their ship?" Nora would have smiled as she asked the question but for the sudden lump in her throat.

The look Mrs. Railey gave Nora would have impressed even Søren. "I just don't want to see my boy hurt again."

"Then we're in agreement there."

"He loves you."

"And I love him."

"But?"

"Takes more than love for a ride off into the sunset to-gether."

"That's true. It also takes hoses."

Nora glanced out the window. Right on the east lawn she saw dozens of horses dotting a sea of green.

"I thought Wes was the brainiac in the family."

"He also gets that from me."

Nora nodded. "You have good genes. I'll let you get back to your thank-you note slash prison sentence. I'll get back to…"

"My son?" Mrs. Railey asked with a twinkle in her eyes.

"That guy." Nora found her grin again. The pirate in her took hold of her tongue as she headed for the door. "He's horny as hell in the mornings. He'll notice if I'm not there."

Mrs. Railey didn't even bat an eyelash. She uncapped her pen again and picked up another blank note.

"He gets *that* from his father."

All the way back to guesthouse, Nora tried to figure out what had happened. Mr. Railey had agreed to help Talel at her request…and he'd asked nothing in return. She would have bet her own life that he would have demanded she leave in exchange for his help. But he hadn't. And he hadn't threatened to, either. He'd said "yes" and sent her on her way.

She'd been almost counting on Mr. Railey trading her departure for saving Talel. And now that he hadn't…

Nora started stripping out of her clothes the second she got into the guesthouse. She found Wesley only half-asleep in bed. Glancing at the clock, Nora couldn't believe it was barely 8:00 a.m.

"Where were you?" he asked as she scooted in next to him. He pulled her close and she melted into him, her back to his chest.

"Just ran an errand. Go back to sleep. I'm about to."

"Good idea," he said, pushing his hips into hers. Nora laughed softly. Kid had been having sex for all of one week and he'd already turned into a typical horny-in-the-morning male. And she loved him for it.

And she loved him for everything else, too.

And she didn't have to leave him.

And since she didn't have to leave him, that meant eventually she'd have to answer Wesley's question.

Would she stay with Wesley? Or would she leave him… again?

NORTH

The Past

The fear that at the time seemed irrational, the fear that had nearly kept Kingsley from stepping into the chapel, had proved itself justified beyond all belief. One month from the day Marie-Laure arrived at Saint Ignatius and glimpsed Søren for the first time, she and Kingsley returned to the chapel, hand in hand again. Midnight on December 21...the time chosen by Marie-Laure. His birthday, she'd said, smiling. And the longest night of the year, Kingsley had said, staring at his sister until she blushed. Blushed... His sister who had taken half of Paris to her bed had actually blushed.

"Can you think of a better choice for a wedding night?" she'd finally said, and Kingsley's stomach had churned.

And now he waited in the narthex of the chapel. Checking his watch, he mourned the time—one minute until midnight.

She looked beautiful; he couldn't deny that. More beautiful than he'd ever seen her. A blizzard had kept the entire school trapped in their valley. There had been no opportunity for shopping for wedding dresses. Instead, she'd taken one of her own dresses and some of the old lace altar cloths and sewn a train and a veil by hand. She wore no makeup, as she'd run out a week ago and could not go anywhere to procure more. Her naked face had never shone so brightly, nor had she ever looked so innocent. Innocent...almost virginal. Her hands twisted together. Nerves? His sister who had worn next to nothing to dance on a stage before tens of thousands during her two years in the Paris Ballet Company? She was nervous?

Kingsley took her hand in his and held it. Her fingers felt like ice against his skin.

"Are you scared?" he asked, trying to feign support, affection, while anger lurked under his calm exterior.

"*Oui*...so much." She took a breath in and let it out. A white cloud surrounded her face like a halo. The chapel was nearly impossible to keep warm in the winter, but she'd insisted they be married in the church. Kingsley prayed for a short ceremony or they all would die of hypothermia before dawn.

"Then why are you marrying him?" He asked the question with more honest emotion in his voice than he'd meant to betray. But Marie-Laure, lost in her own thoughts and fears, seemed not to notice.

"I've never met anyone like him. I've never... I love him." She turned her face to Kingsley's and the intensity of her smile brought light and warmth to the cold, candlelit chapel.

"You've known him one month."

"It doesn't matter. I loved him the moment I saw him. And I told him that."

"Did he say he loved you, too?" Kingsley asked, fearing the answer. Søren had never even said those words to him, although they escaped Kingsley's lips every time Søren entered him. He'd said "I love you" almost as often as he'd said "I hate you" to Søren. It never mattered which one he said— love or hate—as they meant the same to Kingsley. They meant "I am yours no matter what." But he knew Søren loved him.

He never needed the words—only the bruises and the welts and the memories of their bodies joined in the deepest hours of the night, when even God had given up and gone to sleep. And Marie-Laure…with his own money Søren had brought Marie-Laure to Kingsley. That had been love. And for once, Kingsley wished Søren had loved him a little less.

She shook her head. "No. Not in so many words. But he said something better than 'I love you.' He said, 'We can be married.' He didn't hesitate, not a moment. It was as if he'd been waiting for me to tell him I loved him so he could ask."

"What do you mean—"

"Shh…" Marie-Laure raised a finger to her lips. A light appeared at the altar; a single candle had been lit. "It's time."

She held out her arm and Kingsley took it. And in utter silence but for Marie-Laure's shallow breaths, Kingsley escorted his sister to where Søren waited next to Father Henry. Father Henry, as usual, wore a smile. So did Marie-Laure. But Søren and Kingsley didn't smile as their eyes met. Kingsley looked for something in Søren's eyes—an apology, a hint of explanation, a purpose or a plan…something to explain this madness. But he saw nothing in Søren's eyes at all.

Marie-Laure's smile only broadened as Father Henry began to speak. Kingsley heard his voice, but his mind could comprehend none of the words. Another silence descended and Kingsley realized that he'd just been asked a question.

"I do," he answered, remembering that he had one line in this farce—Father Henry had asked him who gives this woman to be married to this man. *I do*—two words. All Kingsley had to say. Seeing his parents' bodies become ash to be stored in silver urns hurt less than those two words had. He knew he was to stand at Marie-Laure's side now—as the only woman at Saint Ignatius, Marie-Laure had no one to ask to serve as an attendant. But Kingsley couldn't do it, couldn't stand with his own sister. He went to Søren's side instead. Marie-Laure didn't even notice his defection.

The service proceeded. There would be no communion. Only last evening had Marie-Laure been baptized. For Søren she had converted and become Catholic, so theirs could be a union blessed by the Church. What would Kingsley's father say had he been alive to see this? Monsieur Auguste Boisson-neault, proud descendant of the Huguenots...he would have died in the chapel at the sight of his daughter becoming Cath-olic to marry a Catholic. Kingsley counted his father's death a blessing now. Better to be dead than to live through this. He, too, wished for death. If only he and Søren could have had one last night together...Kingsley would have begged for Søren to kill him. And he knew in his love and power and mercy, Søren would have granted that request.

Kingsley came back to the moment as Father Henry beamed his smile at Søren and Marie-Laure.

"May almighty God, with his word of blessing, unite your hearts in the never-ending bond of pure love."

The assembled students and priests, the only guests, intoned in unison a solemn "Amen."

Amen...so be it.

Only Kingsley and Søren did not speak the amen.

Father Henry nodded at Søren, who took Marie-Laure by the arm. And together they left the chapel. For once that hell-ish day, Kingsley felt the touch of God's mercy. For whatever reason—propriety or by request of the groom—there had been no kiss.

Kingsley walked on leaden feet behind Father Henry up the aisle and to the narthex. Søren and Marie-Laure waited in the shadows by the door. Søren had taken off the jacket of his suit and given it to Marie-Laure. Had he given her the keys to a kingdom, she could not have smiled with more love and gratitude. It sickened Kingsley to see it.

"Father Henry, will you take her to her room?" Søren asked as Kingsley waited by the shrine of the Virgin Mary.

Distress crossed Marie-Laure's wide amber eyes. Søren soothed her fears with a smile.

"I'll be there soon," he pledged. Her smile returned and Father Henry threw another robe about her and bustled her out into the cold.

For nearly a minute, Søren and Kingsley stood not speaking to each other as the students and other priests filed out of the chapel and into the cold. None of them congratulated Søren. None of them even glanced their way. Jealousy...all of them ached with jealousy. One perfect girl had come into their midst and all of them adored her. Yet she had chosen the one they all feared. The last to leave, Kingsley's friend Christian, turned back and glanced at him on the way out the door.

"Are you all right?" Christian mouthed to Kingsley, not even granting Søren the courtesy of eye contact.

Kingsley nodded. The nod had been a lie.

"You aren't." Søren finally spoke once they stood alone in the chapel.

"No. I'm not."

"I did this for us, Kingsley," Søren said.

"I wish you hadn't."

"This will help you both."

Kingsley exhaled and the air that came out of him turned opaque in the cold. He looked like he'd been breathing fire.

"She's not ours. Remember our dream? The girl wilder than both of us together. Green hair and black eyes."

"Black hair and green eyes," Søren corrected. "Untamed."

"But not untamable." Kingsley remembered every word of their dream. "We were going to share her."

"Because no one man would be enough for her."

"The unholy trinity." As the final student left the chapel, Kingsley reached out and took Søren's hand in his own.

"You know I come from a wealthy family. And try as he might, my father can't seem to sire another son. At age twenty-one I would have inherited my trust fund. But if I married, I'd inherit it immediately."

"You married my sister so you could have your money?"

"No." Søren turned and gazed down into Kingsley's eyes. "I married her so we could have it. You and I. And her, too, of course. I know how much you love her, how much you missed her. Now all of us can be together."

"She thinks you love her."

"She'll understand. If she has half your intelligence and in-sight, she'll see the wisdom of this arrangement."

Kingsley's eyes widened. Intelligence and insight? Had those words come from Søren's lips? How many times had Søren held him down and with disdain whispered how worthless Kingsley was, how useless? Did Søren not actually believe that?

"She's my sister."

"I know. And I know how you care for her. I have no intention…" Søren stopped, and the words he didn't speak said everything Kingsley needed to hear.

"You won't?"

"I can't…. You know that better than anyone." A slight smile, the first Kingsley had seen on Søren's face in days, ap-peared at the corner of his lips.

"You could…." He could if he hurt Marie-Laure. If he treated her the way he treated Kingsley—with violence and scorn, beating her and humiliating her and subjecting her to every type of sexual degradation…then they could be lovers. But only then.

"I wouldn't. I have no interest in her like that. Only you."

Hope filled Kingsley's heart. "Only me? Why?"

The slight smile on Søren's lips spread to his entire face. Kingsley could scarcely breathe from the sight of it. Not even Marie-Laure, flush with love and in her bridal glory, had looked more beautiful than that one smile.

Søren cradled the left side of Kingsley's face and Kingsley closed his eyes, relishing the touch of Søren's skin on his. How long would it be before he felt it again?

"Do you even have to ask?" Søren whispered.

"Yes."

Søren spoke no more, but Kingsley felt the touch of lips on his. And he understood the truth then. Søren hadn't married Marie-Laure because he loved her. Søren had married Marie-Laure because he loved *him*.

Kingsley sensed Søren's reluctance when he pulled away. Such a kiss as that had always been a precursor to a night of passion. Passion…Kingsley never understood passion until he'd come to a Catholic school and learned of Christ's passion. Passion…before Søren it had been merely a synonym for lust, for sexual hunger and pleasure. Now it took on new meaning, true meaning. Now passion meant what he felt for Søren. And passion meant what Søren did to him.

"I have to go," Søren said as Kingsley opened his eyes.

"I understand."

"I knew you would. And she will, too…eventually."

"Will you tell her what you are?" Kingsley asked.

"She is your sister. What do you think? Tell her? Or no?"

Marie-Laure would be devastated to learn what kind of man she'd married, but more devastated if he didn't touch her with no explanation why.

A choice lay before Kingsley. And he knew the right answer.

"Don't tell her," he said. "Not yet."

"If you think that's what is best."

"I do," he lied without meeting Søren's eyes.

He looked up and found Søren staring at the door to the chapel, staring at it like an enemy that must be defeated.

"You don't want to go to her."

"No," Søren said. "I want to stay with you."

"Then stay with me. Stay forever."

Søren found his mouth again and kissed him...a deep kiss, a slow kiss, a kiss of utter ownership. He ended the kiss and stood tall and straight. Kingsley had never seen him look more handsome or more miserable.

"That's why I married her, Kingsley. So I could."

The kiss still burned on Kingsley's lips, the moment still hovered in the air like the final note of a piano sonata.

Søren looked away and took one step, but paused, turned around and shoved Kingsley hard into the wall of the chapel. This first kiss had been an apology of sorts from Søren, the second kiss an explanation. But this kiss, the third and final, it was an attack. Kingsley let Søren bite his lips, his tongue, dig his fingers into his throat....

"Mercy..." Kingsley whispered against Søren's teeth.

Søren stopped immediately.

"Mercy? Or *merci?*" he asked.

Kingsley raised his hand and wiped the blood from his mouth.

"Does it matter?"

Søren shook his head.

"No."

Søren wrenched himself away from Kingsley and stepped out into the longest night of the year. Of course, Marie-Laure would understand eventually, even if Søren didn't tell her what he was. It was for the best for all of them. The money meant freedom—freedom for them all to do whatever they desired. For Kingsley and Søren it meant they could be together always

without fearing what anyone thought. For Marie-Laure...
Kingsley didn't know what it would mean for Marie-Laure,
but surely between something as tenuous as love and as tan-
gible as money, she would choose the latter.

Yes...of course she would understand....

Bien sûr.

But she didn't understand.

Kingsley stood with Marie-Laure in the tiny kitchen of the
guest quarters she now occupied with Søren. The Fathers at
Saint Ignatius had promised she could stay for the rest of the
school year, while Søren finished his first year of teaching.
As much as the students feared Søren, the priests loved him.
Kingsley knew Father Henry would have done anything to
keep Søren at Saint Ignatius, even adopting him as a son if
it came to that. And Marie-Laure had made herself useful.
She tutored the younger boys in French, helped Father Aldo
cook for them all. She worked every day in the school library,
reshelving the books and encouraging the boys to keep working, keep studying, keep reading. In short, she became the
perfect teacher's wife. And yet...

"I don't understand. I thought he loved me," Marie-Laure
said to Kingsley as she put the teacups carefully away in the
cabinet.

Kingsley heard the distress in her voice, the sorrow.

"What is it? Did you two fight?" He kept his voice light
and curious. He hated himself for being relieved at her pain.
But the thought of Marie-Laure sleeping in the same bed as
Søren every night sent Kingsley into paroxysms of jealousy.
It should be him in bed with Søren, not her. He ached for
their nights at the hermitage, and falling asleep and waking
up with Søren's body next to his.

"*Non,* we don't fight. I fight. He listens. I could claw his eyes out, and he would simply sit there and listen." She shook her head as tears started to flow from her eyes. Kingsley stood up and put a hand on her shoulder. He said nothing, only waited. "Kingsley...he doesn't touch me. Ever. Not once. Not on our wedding night...not before, not after. Never."

Kingsley could have cried from relief. He had feared that Søren, like every other man who'd met Marie-Laure, would succumb to her beauty.

"He's complicated." Kingsley's conscience gnawed at him. "Ask him to explain why it is he won't be with you...maybe then you'll understand."

"I don't want to understand." She set the teacup down so hard it shattered on the counter. "I want my husband to touch me."

Marie-Laure crumpled to the floor as her slight body shuddered with the wave of grief that overtook it. Kingsley knelt next to her and gathered her in his arms.

"I'm sorry...." He didn't know what else to say. What could he say? As much as he loved Søren, he still hated to see his sister this unhappy. They would have to tell her...or show her...something.

"What is it?" Marie-Laure whispered. "What's wrong with me?"

"Nothing. Nothing at all." Kingsley turned her tearstained face up and smiled at her. "There's nothing wrong with you. It's him. I promise you it's him."

"Is there..." She paused to swallow a sob. "Is there someone else?"

Kingsley stiffened slightly. What could he say to that? He had to tell her about Søren. But he couldn't. Søren had said he would explain in time. As much as Kingsley loved his sister, his loyalties had become Søren's that night in the forest.

"Kingsley..." Marie-Laure put her hands on either side

of his face and stared at him with more darkness and determination than he'd ever dreamed his slight sister possessed. Somehow she'd felt his tremor of fear pass through him, the fear that he would tell her even against Søren's wishes. "He is your friend. Tell me what you know. Is there someone else?"

"There might be."

She wrested herself from his arms and stood up.

"Marie-Laure...what is it? What—"

Her spine went ramrod straight. Her face hardened like the granite that filled the hills around them. Her eyes blazed. *There might be....* Those words ignited a fire in Marie-Laure's eyes. It burned so bright that Kingsley feared for his own safety. Such fury could burn the world down and leave nothing but ashes.

"If that is true...if there is someone else...then I will walk the world if I must..."

She stopped to breathe. Her tears had ceased. She gazed down at Kingsley and looked not at him but through him.

"Marie-Laure?" Kingsley could barely recognize her.

"And I will kill the bitch."

NORTH
The Present

A forty-minute drive separated Nora's home from Søren's rectory. Once more Kingsley cursed the madness that kept the most important people in his life so far from the city, where he wanted them. A priest of Søren's upstanding reputation, education and erudition should have been in New York preaching to the educated masses or teaching at the Jesuit University…not wasting his talents in a domesticated small town with only the most bourgeois of sinners about him, committing sins so banal they weren't even worth the bother to absolve. Kingsley wondered at times if Nora and Søren lived outside of New York because he lived in it.

"Merde." Kingsley swore bitterly as a wedding procession at the edge of Wakefield halted his progress. A horse and carriage carrying a blushing bride and her plain-faced groom trotted slowly through an intersection, a hundred smiling, laughing guests following on foot.

If only Marie-Laure and Søren had had such a wedding—a daylight wedding with guests who greeted their marriage with joy and not bitter jealousy. If only the love had been mutual and not one-sided. If only...

At last the wedding procession passed by, and Kingsley sped all the way to the rectory. Once there he barely turned off his engine before racing into Søren's home without knocking. His body still ached with every step. Even as teenagers Søren had never brutalized Kingsley so thoroughly as he had last night. Kingsley wanted to believe it was proof of love, but he wasn't the fool he'd been as a teenager. Now he knew the difference between lust and love. Back then they were one and the same.

Kingsley didn't find Søren in the rectory, but he didn't despair. He'd seen the black vintage Ducati parked just outside—Søren's one mode of transportation. He couldn't have gone far. For the first time in years, Kingsley entered Sacred Heart, feeling the weight of guilt pressing down on him as he took in the candles, the shrines, the tiny chapel of perpetual adoration. His was not Catholic guilt. It went far deeper than religion, deeper than faith. It went as deep as his own blood, the blood that ran in the veins of his sister, the blood he'd betrayed the day he'd goaded her young husband into kissing him, knowing full well she would see them together.

Søren wasn't in the sanctuary. He wasn't in the chapel. Finally, Kingsley found him in his secretary's office. At her desk Søren sat with a printout of what appeared to be a newspaper article in front of him.

"*Mon père...*" Kingsley said, and Søren looked up at him.

Søren held out the piece of paper and Kingsley took it. He scanned the date—January 1980. He read the headline, Canadian Runaway Missing for Three Weeks—Feared Dead. He stared at the picture of the missing girl. She had long brown hair, a lithe figure...a dancer's body. Had they removed the missing girl's face, she would have been interchangeable with his sister.... Christian's words came back to him. That valley where the hermitage stood…it had been an underground railroad for runaways. And suddenly he knew how it had happened. Marie-Laure had found the runaway and seen her chance. Seen her chance and taken it.

"It's Marie-Laure," Kingsley said, without preamble. "She's alive."

Søren stood up and looked him in the eyes.

"I know. Your sister is alive. Which means—"

Kingsley's knees nearly buckled with the realization. It hadn't even occurred to him until that very moment, as he stood inside Sacred Heart with Søren before him in his Roman collar and clerics and his vows of obedience and poverty and chastity perfuming the air like incense…

"Your wife is alive."

SOUTH

Wesley had a plan. A stupid plan. A terrible plan. The worst plan. But it was the only plan he had. And he could only hope that Nora, who was the queen of stupid terrible plans, would go along with it. It started with a horse.

"I'm not getting on that thing." Nora stood at the white fence while Wesley walked his horse past her.

"You don't have to get on this thing. This thing, which is actually a saddlebred stallion, is my thing. Your thing is still in the stables."

"Is my thing much shorter than your thing?"

"Much shorter and much tamer."

"Good. Then let's get this dog and pony show on the road. Where's the dog?"

"We don't have a dog. It's just a pony show."

"I can live with that."

Wesley dismounted from Bob for Short, the most trustworthy and sure-footed of the two dozen saddlebreds his parents kept on the farm, and tied him to the fence while he took Nora into the stable. He saddled up a mare named Purse Nickity and handed Nora the reins.

"I can't believe you're making me do this," Nora said as they walked the horse out in the sunshine.

"Making you do what? Go horseback riding with me?"

"Yes. After this morning? And last night? And yesterday afternoon?"

Wesley stared at her blankly. Nora rolled her eyes as she came to stand directly in front of him.

"Young man, you have fucked me raw." She poked him in his chest. "I am saddlesore and I haven't even been on a saddle."

Wesley winced in sympathy. "Ow. I'm sorry. I didn't know…I'm sorry."

A huge grin spread across Nora's face.

"I'm not. Let's do this."

She put her foot in the stirrup and swung up into the saddle, not even flinching as she adjusted her seat.

"Come on, Wes. If I'm not sore after sex, I assume someone did something wrong."

Wesley laughed, hopped in the saddle, grabbed his reins, trotted Bob up to Nora.

"Well, I'm glad you're just sore and not in actual pain. I know that's kind of your thing, but I'm afraid it won't ever be mine."

"It's okay," she said as Wesley led them out of the pasture and onto a well-worn trail that wound through a few acres of hardwoods. "I don't miss the pain as much as you'd think. It's been kind of nice not feeling like I have to pay for the pleasure with a day off my life. Not that I'm complaining or anything. Kinky sex is intense, to say the least. But being with you…" She turned and smiled at him. "It's been good, Wes. Better than I ever would have dreamed. Better than I wanted to dream. What about you? You doing okay being with a woman old enough to have given birth to you had she gotten knocked up at age fourteen?"

Wesley gripped the reins and pulled Bob around so he'd be looking Nora straight in the eye when he answered. "More than okay. It's been the best thing ever."

"Ever?" she asked, her face flushing. Wesley prayed the color on her cheeks was inspired by his compliment and not simply the exertion of riding in the last summer heat up the side of a sloping hill. He could have picked an easier trail, but he had something to show Nora and the only way to get to it was up. "Ever's a long time. Almost as long as forever. And definitely longer than for-fucking-ever."

"I kind of like the thought of forever," Wesley said as they passed under a canopy of bowed tree limbs and came out on the other side into the early morning sunlight. "Don't you?"

Nora shrugged. "Depends on the forever we're talking about. Forever waiting for something you want is another definition of hell in my book. Forever with someone you love? That's the other definition of heaven."

"Want to know my definition of heaven?" Wesley asked as they reached the top of the hill.

"Does it involve a swimming pool full of mud, me in fishnets, a hunting horn and seven-layer chocolate cake?"

"No."

"Then yes, tell me."

"Here. I'll take Zach's advice and show you instead of tell you." They paused at the edge of the clearing and looked down. "Just look out there."

"My God…" Nora breathed, and a smile as wide as Kentucky spread across her face. "Damn."

"Exactly."

Damn indeed. Wesley had seen this land, this valley a million times, but until he saw Nora's face light up when she looked on it, he knew he'd never seen it until now. He was happy that his first time really looking at it was with her. He wanted all his first times to be with her. And his last. And everything in between.

From the summit of the hill, they could see for miles into the valley below them. Winding stone walls carved S-shapes in the lush blue-green grass. A thousand horses pranced and danced behind gleaming, pure white fences. The pond glimmered like a diamond in the sunlight.

A diamond glimmered in Wesley outstretched hand.

Nora's eyes widened at the sight of it.

"Wesley?"

"Everything you see down there is mine. Or will be. I hate being called the Prince of Kentucky, but only because it's kind of true. I have a kingdom and that's it. And there's nothing in the world more beautiful...except you."

"Wes...you..."

"Stay with me, Nora. Stay here. Forever. Everything you see...I can give it to you. And you can love it and keep it, or hate it and burn it to the ground. I don't care, as long as you're here with me and you never go back to him. I know he can give you things I can't—loneliness and pain and shame and humiliation. But I can give you a few things *he* can't. Marriage. Kids if you want them. No kids if you don't. A life together out here in the sun, where everyone can see us. You'd never have to hide if you were with me, or pretend. You'd have the whole world. You'd never have to work again. You wouldn't have to even write another book if you didn't want to. Or you can write until your hands fall off, and I'd hire the best doctor in the world to sew them back on. You can name all our horses, like you name your characters. You can drive my parents crazy by making riding crop and pony jokes every single day of your life. You can…" Wesley's voice faltered. Bob grew restive underneath him. Drawing a breath, Wesley took Nora's hand in his and held it tight, the diamond ring pressed into her palm. "You can be safe and no one will ever hurt you again. I won't hurt you and I won't ever let anyone else do so. Not now. Not ever. Not even if you go crazy and decide you want them to. I'll make you happy. I'll keep you safe. Just please say yes or no before these damn horses bolt and kill us both."

Nora stammered and shook her head. "—I don't know, Wes. I mean, are you asking what I think—"

"Dammit, Nora. You always have to make things harder than they are. Will you marry me? That's what I'm asking. Yes? No? Maybe?"

Nora pulled her hand away from his, but took the ring. He waited, praying she'd put it on her finger. Instead, she only stared at it.

"It was my great-great-grandmother's on my mom's side. It would have been my sister's had I had one. Lucky me— only child."

"It's beautiful."

"They said my great-great-grandmother was the most beautiful woman in all of Georgia in her day. She had men fighting duels over her. I thought that was the craziest thing—two guys killing each other over a girl. Then I met you and I swear the thought of seeing Søren's body being dragged through the streets behind Farewell to Charms made me smile like nothing else."

"I've had the same thought a few times," she said with a nervous laugh. "But, Wesley—"

"No buts. You don't have to answer. You can think about it if you need to. I hope you don't need to, but if you do…then you do. Actually, don't answer. Don't say anything about it.

Just think about it. You can tell me yes, no or maybe when we get back to the barn. Okay?"

Nora took a shallow breath as she studied the ring in her palm. Wesley didn't know much about it other than his mom had once said something about ten carats and two million dollars.

"Okay…" Nora wrapped her hand tightly around the ring and held it close to her chest.

"We'll head back. We shouldn't talk on the way down, anyway. It's pretty steep."

"Lips are sealed."

Wesley watched as Nora slipped the ring onto her thumb—close enough to her ring finger to give him hope—before taking up her reins again. They started back down the hill, the only words spoken between them the occasional "watch out there—big rock" and an "I see it."

A half hour later they made it back to the stables. The return trip had been torturous with waiting, and yet Wesley loved Nora enough not to panic her or push her.

He forced himself to go slow with the horses, to take his time. He unsaddled them carefully and brushed them both down—actions that calmed his racing, waiting heart. He wanted to rush, to get it over with and find out Nora's answer. But he feared the answer as much as he wanted it, and so went as slowly as he could, delaying what he feared was the inevitable.

"Good girl," Wesley said to Nickity as he put her back in her stall and offered her a fistful of oats.

"Nice to have such a pretty girl eating out of the palm of your hand, isn't it?" Nora asked as he ran his hand down the horse's long nose.

"She's really not the girl I've got my heart set on."

"Too bad. I hear she's kinky."

"Let me guess—she likes riding crops and pony play?"

"Who doesn't?"

"Nora…"

Nora sighed and raised her hand to Wesley's face.

"Goddammit, I missed you while we were apart. I wish you knew how much."

"I know how much I missed you, and never want to feel that way again. And I know we never have to. Just say yes. You know he can't give you the life I can. You know he can't…Nora?"

Nora's eyes had left his face and now looked over his shoulder. Wesley glanced back and saw nothing but shadows in the corner of the stable.

"Nora?"

She said nothing, but Wesley saw fear in her eyes. Fear? Of who? Of what? They were alone apart from the horses. Did the thought of marrying him scare her that much?

"Nora, please. What—"

"Yes." She looked up at him as she wrenched the diamond off her thumb and shoved it onto her ring finger. "Yes, I love you. I'll marry you. Let's go tell your parents so they can start the freaking out immediately."

Wesley nearly collapsed into the straw. His relief trumped even his happiness.

"Thank God." He started to drag her into his arms, but Nora pulled away.

"Now. Let's go tell the fam. Come on." She grabbed his hand and started to yank him forward.

"I don't even get to kiss you—"

And the world went black and stayed black for a long time. A few minutes, a few hours, he didn't know and couldn't tell. When he woke up, all he knew was pain.

Pain, such pain…he'd never known pain like this before.

Wesley slowly forced his eyes open and found himself face-down in the straw, still in the stall. Everything hurt…maybe. His head ached so violently he couldn't even be certain the rest of his body still existed.

"Nora?" Her name came out with the force of a cough. Wesley heard no answer. Pulling himself to his hands and knees, he looked around and found the usually flat, trampled down straw a mess, as though someone had wrestled in it.

He called Nora's name again as he lifted his hand to the back of his head. His fingers came away red and sticky with blood.

"Oh, shit…" Wesley nearly vomited at the sight of his own blood. Someone…someone had hit him in the head. But where was Nora?

Two parallel lines in the straw led from Nickity's stall to the stable door. Someone had been dragged, the heels of their boots cutting through the bedding.

Dragged…blood…the fear in Nora's eyes…

Wesley half ran, half stumbled toward the door. He had to get out, get his parents, call the police….

He had to find Nora.

But he stopped before he touched the door. In the wood someone had carved five words—the five most terrible words Wesley had ever read, even though he couldn't read them. And he knew he couldn't tell his parents, couldn't call the police, could do nothing but pull his cell phone out of his pocket and dial a number he wished he didn't know. His instincts, however, told him this was the only number he should call.

The phone answered on the first ring.

"Søren…it's Wesley." He choked on the words. He'd throw up any minute now. But he had to get it out. He stared at the words carved on the stall door.

"Wesley? What is it? Where's Eleanor?"

"*Je vais tuer la salope.* What does that mean?"

"It's French," Søren said, sounding both furious and deadly. "It means 'I will kill the bitch.' Wesley...where is Eleanor?"

"I don't know. Someone has her."

"What do you mean, someone has Eleanor?"

As a small child Wesley had heard the phrase "the wrath of God" in church, and sat and wondered what that meant, what that sounded like.

Now he knew.

"Søren...she's gone."

* * * * *

ACKNOWLEDGMENTS

I keep forgetting that I'm allowed to put acknowledgments in my books. It's only after I send off the final that I remember, "Oh, shit, I forgot to thank all those people who helped me." So forgive me for putting three books' worth of acknowledgments into one short page. My brain is so often lost in my fictional world I forget the real world is full of people even more wonderful.

First, thank you to my parents for being so surprisingly supportive of your unrepentant smut-peddler of a daughter. Thank you to my sister Alisha for being my biggest cheerleader.

Thank you to Patricia Correll, Robin Brecht and Jeff Hoagland for being my first ever beta readers and whipping, nay flogging, *The Siren* into shape.

Thank you to Karen Stivali for being the most eagle-eyed of all my beta readers.

Thank you to Team Awesome and my fearless editorial assistant Alli Sanders, otherwise known as ED.

Thank you to Sharon Biggs Waller, brilliant writer and

horse expert, who told me everything I got wrong and how I could make it right. I love horses, and I have nothing but respect for the Sport of Kings. I only wish the racing drama in *The Prince* was a work of pure fiction and not based on actual tragedies and crimes that the few bad apples in the racing industry have committed (sadly, it is). If I get stuff right about horses in this book, it's thanks to Sharon. If I get it wrong, I take the blame.

Bless you, Sara Megibow, my visionary agent, who three years ago saw the potential in my weird, twisty world and, against the advice of experienced others, took me on as a client. Boss—L'Chaim!

Most profound thanks to my editor, Susan Swinwood, who saw the magic of Mistress Nora three years ago and somehow knew the world would be needing the services of a young, smart, fearless kinky woman. Susan lets me get away with murder in my books. Okay, maybe not murder but everything else (and I do mean everything). I had a vision for my Original Sinners series, and I prayed at night I'd find someone who would trust my vision, would trust my judgment and let me put my guts on paper. I found the answer to every writer's prayer in my editor. Thank you.

And thank you to Andrew Shaffer for coming into my life just when I need you even though I didn't realize it at the time. Thank you for bring my editor, my other agent, my manager, my graphic designer, my best friend, my other half, my reason for coming to bed at night, my reason for not wanting to get out of bed the next morning and for being the most important thing of all—my Sir. I love you, Sir.

If you missed the first book in THE ORIGINAL SINNERS *series,*
check out the following excerpt from
THE SIREN.

N|umbing.
   As an editor Zach often forced his writers to dig deep, cast aside the obvious and find the perfect word for every sentence. And the perfect word to describe this book release party he'd been forced to attend? *Numbing.*

Zach stalked through the party saying little more than the occasional hello to various colleagues. He'd only come because once again J.P. had twisted his arm, and Rose Evely—the guest of honor—had been a Royal House writer for thirty years now. What a ludicrous party anyway—someone dimmed the lights to create a nightclub sort of atmosphere but no amount of ambience could turn the banal hotel banquet hall into anything other than a beige box. He wandered toward a spiral staircase in the corner of the room to surreptitiously check his watch. If he could survive two hours at this party, maybe it would be long enough to placate his social butterfly of a boss.

Scanning the crowd, he saw his twenty-eight-year-old assistant, Mary, trying to talk her new husband into dancing with her. His first week at Royal, he'd been pleasantly surprised to find out his spitfire of an assistant was, like him, Jewish. He'd teased her he'd never known a Jew named Mary before and started calling her his pseudoshiksa. Mary, for all her endearing brusqueness, only ever called him "Boss." J.P. stood with Rose Evely. Both J.P. and Evely had been happily married to their respective spouses for decades but nothing stopped J.P. from chivalrously flirting with any woman who had the patience to listen to his literary rambles. Everyone seemed to be enjoying themselves at this miserable party. Why wasn't he?

Once more he glanced down at his watch.

"I can save you, if you want," came a voice from above him.

Zach spun around and looked up. Smiling down at him from over the top of the staircase was Nora Sutherlin.

"Save me?" He narrowed his eyes at her.

"From this party." She crooked her index finger at him.

Zach's better judgment warned him that climbing that staircase could be a very bad idea indeed. Yet his feet overruled his reason, and he mounted the steps and joined her on the platform at the top. He raised his eyebrow as he cast a disapproving gaze over her clothes. That morning at her house, she'd worn shapeless pajamas that concealed every part of her but her abundant personality. Now he saw on full display what his mind had before only imagined.

She wore red, of course. Scarlet red and not much of it. The dress stopped at the top of her thighs and started at the edge of her breasts. She had miraculous curves that the dramatic floor-length red jacket she wore over her dress did nothing to hide. Even worse, she wore black leather boots that laced all the way above her knees. Pirate boots and a roguish grin on a beautiful black-haired woman...for the first time in a long time Zach felt something other than numb.

"How do you know I want to be saved from this party, Miss Sutherlin?" Zach leaned back against the railing and crossed his arms.

"I've been watching you from my little crow's nest here since the second you walked in. You've said maybe five words to four people, you've checked your watch three times in as many minutes, and you whispered something to J.P., which, guessing from the look on his face, was a death threat. You're here against your will. I can get you out."

Zach cocked a self-deprecating smile at her.

"Unfortunately, you're right. I am here against my will. I have to wonder, however, why you're here at all. Didn't I give you homework?" he asked, remembering his rash decision this morning to give her one chance to impress him.

"You did. And I was a good girl and finished it. See?"

He tried and failed to look away as she reached into the bodice of her dress and pulled out a folded piece of paper and handed it to him. The paper was still warm from her skin.

"This is it?" he asked, seeing only three paragraphs on the page.

"Don't judge a book by its mother. Just read."

Zach glanced at her once more and wished he hadn't. Every time he looked at her, he found something else to attract him. Her jacket had slipped down her arm and her pale sculpted shoulder peeked out. Sculpted? His petite little writer had some muscle to go along with her impressive curves. Tougher than she looked.

Remembering himself, Zach turned from her, tilted the page into a patch of light and read.

First she noticed his hips. The eyes might be the windows to the soul, but a man's hips were his seat of power. She doubted he'd cho-

sen those perfectly fitted jeans and that black T-shirt that belied the tautness of his stomach for the purpose of flattering his lower body, but he had and now she lost herself in the thought of caressing with her lips that exquisite hollow that lay between smooth skin and elegantly jutting hip bone.

She had to meet his eyes eventually. With reluctance she dragged her gaze to his face, as dignified and angular as the rest of him. Pale skin and dark Brutus-cut hair contrasted with eyes the color of ice. Glacial, she decided his eyes were—they spoke of hidden depths. A stark beauty, he was a man made to be admired by intelligent women.

Lean and tall but with the substantial mass of an athlete, he was utterly masculine. The world had fallen away in his presence and now that he was gone, she was left in the equally potent presence of his absence.

Zach read the words one more time trying all the while to ignore the annoyingly pleasant image of Nora Sutherlin caressing his naked hips with her mouth.

"I've noticed you usually shy away from long descriptive passages in your book," he said.

"I know people think erotica is just a romance novel with rougher sex. It's not. If it's a subgenre of anything, it's horror."

"Horror? Really?"

"Romance is sex plus love. Erotica is sex plus fear. You're terrified of me, aren't you?"

"Slightly," he admitted, rubbing the back of his neck.

"A smart horror writer will never put too much detail in about the monster. The readers' imaginations can conjure their own demons. In erotica you never want your main characters to be too physically specific. That way your readers can insert their own fantasies, their own fears. Erotica is a joint effort between writer and reader."

"How so?" Zach asked, intrigued that Nora Sutherlin would have her own literary theories.

"Writing erotica is like fucking someone for the first time. You aren't sure exactly what he wants yet so you try to give him everything he could possibly want. Everything and anything…" She enunciated the words like a cat stretching in sunlight. "You hit every nerve and eventually you'll hit the nerve. Have I hit any nerves yet?"

Zach clenched his jaw. "Not any of them you were aiming for."

"You don't know what I was aiming for. So what do you think of the writing?"

"Could be better." He refolded the page. "You use 'was' too much."

"Rough draft," she said unapologetically. She stared at him with dark, waiting eyes.

"The last line's the strongest—'*the equally potent presence of his absence.*'" Zach knew he should give the page back to her but for some reason he stuck it in his pocket. "It's good."

She gave him a slow, dangerous smile.

"It's you."

Zach only stared at her a moment before pulling the folded page back out.

"This is me?" he asked, his skin flushing.

"It is. Every last long, lean inch of you. I wrote it right after you left this morning. I was, needless to say, inspired by your visit."

Swallowing hard, Zach unfolded the sheet again. *Brutus-cut black hair…ice-colored eyes…jeans, black shirt…* It *was* him.

"Excuse me," Zach began, trying to regain control of this conversation, "but didn't I repeatedly insult you this morning?"

"Your kvetching was very fetching. I like men who are mean to me. I trust them more."

She tilted her head to the side and her unruly black hair fell over her forehead, veiling her green-black eyes.

"Forgive me. I might be speechless right now."

"Your orders," she said. "You told me to stop writing what I knew and start writing what I wanted to know. I want to know…you."

She took a step closer and Zach's heart dropped a few feet and landed somewhere in the vicinity of his groin.

"Who are you, Ms. Sutherlin?" he asked, not quite knowing what he meant by that question.

"I'm just a writer. A writer named Nora. And you can call me that, Zach."

"Nora then. I'm sorry. I'm not used to being hit on by my writers. Especially after verbally abusing them."

Nora's eyes flashed with amusement.

"Verbal abuse? Zach, where I come from 'slut' is a term of endearment. Want to see where I come from?"

"No."

"Pity," she said, sounding not at all surprised or disappointed. "Where should we go then? I promised to save you from this party, didn't I?"

"I really shouldn't leave," Zach said, terrified what would happen the second he found himself alone with Nora.

"Come on, Zach. This party sucks and not in the good way. I've had pap smears more fun than this."

Zach covered a laugh with a cough.

"I must admit you do have a way with words."

"So you'll edit me then? Please?" She batted her eyelashes at him in mock innocence. "You won't regret it."

Zach glanced up at the ceiling as if it could give him some hint of what the hell he was getting himself into. Nora Sutherlin…he had only six weeks left in New York until he left for L.A. Why was he even considering getting involved with

Nora Sutherlin and her book? He knew why. He had nothing else in his life right now. He liked Mary and enjoyed working for J.P. But he'd made no friends in New York, no connections of any kind. He hadn't allowed himself to even consider dating. One day he'd taken off his wedding ring in a fit of anger and couldn't find a reason to put it back on. He wouldn't consider inflicting himself on any woman right now. At least working with Nora Sutherlin might give him a much-needed distraction from his misery. She seemed like the type of woman who'd help you forget about your headache by setting your bed on fire.

Won't regret it? He already did.

"You do realize that working with you could be bad for my career," Zach said. "I do literary fiction, not—"

"Literary friction?"

"I can't believe I'm doing this." Zach shook his head.

Nora leaned in close to him. He was suddenly and uncomfortably aware of the long, bare curve of her neck. She smelled of hothouse flowers in bloom.

"I can." She breathed the words into his ear.

Zach exhaled slowly and pulled, reluctantly, away from her. "I'm a brutal editor."

"I like brutal."

"I'll make you rewrite the whole book."

"Now you're trying to turn me on, aren't you? Shall we?"

"Fine," he finally said. "Save me then."

"Let's do it," she said. "If J.P. gives you shit about leaving the party with me, tell him it was my idea for us to go work on my book. J.P. won't spank me."

"I'm not certain of that," Zach said.

"I knew I liked that man for a reason."

"I need to say a few goodbyes if we're leaving." J.P. for

one. Then Mary. And he hadn't met her husband yet. And Rose Evely, too.

"Nope. Can't do that," Nora said. "Never say goodbye when you leave a party. That way you leave a mystery in your place. They'll have so much more fun talking about us than they ever would talking to us. Can't you already hear them? *Zach Easton just left with Nora Sutherlin. Are they...surely not... of course they are—*"

"We aren't," Zach said with finality.

"I know that. You know that. They don't know that."

Zach looked around the room. Everywhere he looked he saw eyes glancing furtively in their direction. The most intense gazing came from Thomas Finley, his least favorite co-worker. Zach noted that Finley didn't so much stare at him as he did at Nora. And the look in his eyes wasn't particularly friendly.

"I prefer not being a topic of gossip," Zach said.

"Too late. At least with me, it'll be really good gossip." She strode down the staircase with an audacious kick of her heels on each step.

Zach followed in her wake. The crowd parted for her as she cut a bloodred swath through the center of the room.

Finally free of the suffocating party, Zach threw on his coat and breathed in the bracing winter evening air.

A cab stopped within seconds for Nora and she slipped gracefully inside. He took a sharp breath as her black-booted legs disappeared into the cab. One more time he asked himself what the hell he was doing before sliding in next to her.

Nora said nothing as he joined her, only turned her head and gazed out at the night. She seemed to be trying to stare down the city. He had a feeling the city would blink first.

Nervously, he rubbed the empty spot where he'd once worn his wedding band. Nora reached out and wrapped her hand around his ring finger. Facing him now, she raised her eyebrow in a question.

"Grace," he answered.

Nora nodded. "You married a princess."

Princess Grace—her mother called her that.

"She hates being called 'Princess.'" Zach heard the anguish in his voice.

Nora lifted his hand and brought it to her neck. She pressed his fingers into her throat. Her pulse throbbed through her warm, soft skin.

"Søren," she said and met his eyes. In those dark, dangerous depths he saw a glimmer of something human—not merely sympathy but empathy. And he felt something inhuman in response—not passion but pure animal need. For a brief moment he imagined his hands digging into her thighs and the bite of her leather boots on his back. He tore his gaze away before her uncanny ability to read him saw that image in his hungry gaze.

She released his hand just as the cab pulled up in front of Zach's apartment building. He opened the door and got out. He wanted to ask her up, wanted to spend a few hours forgetting his pain and all the reasons for it. But he couldn't, could he? Because of Grace, not that she would care anymore. Zach opened his mouth but before he could ask Nora up, she reached out to shut the door.

"See, Zach? I told you I'd save you."

She wanted him…
More deeply, more strongly than
she'd wanted anyone

Nora Sutherlin is hiding. On paper, she's following
her master's orders—and her flesh is willing.

But her mind is wandering to a man from her past,
whose hold on her heart is less bruising, but whose
absence is no less painful. Instead of letting him
make love to her, she'd let him go.

Dazzling, devastating and sinfully erotic
—Miranda Baker

The Original Sinners

The Siren • The Angel • The Prince

www.millsandboon.co.uk

The anonymous note wasn't for me

Don't get me wrong, I'm not in the habit of reading other people's mail, but it was just a piece of paper with a few lines scrawled on it. It looked so innocent... It was not.

Before the notes, if a man had told me what to do, I'd have told him where to go. But there's something freeing about doing someone's bidding. In fact, the more I surrender, the more powerful I feel. It's time to switch the roles...

We're playing by *my* rules now.

www.millsandboon.co.uk

You want him. You're married.
What would you do?

The first time I saw my husband's best friend, I
didn't like him. Didn't like how his penetrating
eyes followed me everywhere. But that didn't
stop me from wanting him.

It was meant to be fun. Something the three of us
shared through those hot summer weeks Alex stayed
with us. Nobody was supposed to fall in or out of
love. After all, we had a perfect life. And I loved
my husband.

But I wasn't the only one.

www.millsandboon.co.uk

1112/MB403

Regency society already believes she's a scarlet woman.

Why not become one?

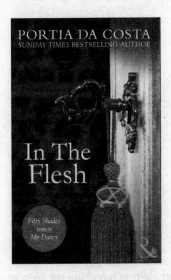

Beatrice Weatherly's reputation is in tatters. With scandalous pictures of her being scrutinised by the *ton* and her brother running them into debt, Beatrice's only hope—a respectable marriage—is dashed. Then powerful, wealthy Edmund Ellsworth Ritchie offers an indecent proposal: for one month of hedonistic servitude, he'll pay off her brother's debts.

www.millsandboon.co.uk

I longed for a whole new life...
but nothing prepared me
for what I found

Shy writer Bettina has clung for years to her safe,
suburban world, until she receives a mysterious
invitation to an infamous writers' retreat. Her
urge to leap into the unknown is at once
terrifying and irresistible.

Swept up in a maelstrom of lust, obsession and
jealousy, Bettina finds herself torn between her need
for two very different people in a love triangle where
she will either be cherished...or consumed.

www.millsandboon.co.uk

1112/MB404